"Bali was the most immora
nation where the majority o

mastermind of the Bali Bombs

The district of Kuta, Bali, is a postcard, a destination, a sunset, a ten-foot wave. Someone once described the resort as 'a cesspit of multi-national companies, local hawkers, surfers and honeymooners intermingling in an endless riot of greed.' Another called it 'a paradise frontier where East meets West.' They both knew the place well.

On Friday, 12 October 2002 tourists and locals crammed into Paddy's Bar on Kuta's main strip. At 23:00 a man slipped into the bar lugging an oversized backpack. At 23:05 the man detonated the backpack, killing himself and eight others. People piled out onto the street where, only a few metres away, a car exploded outside the Sari nightclub. Witnesses described a deafening roar, a bright red ball, a mushroom of white smoke. The electricity died. Screams filled the endless dark.

The next day a haze hung over Kuta Beach. Roads closed. Shops shut. Buildings destroyed. At the blast point there was a police barrier and a crater. No club, no music, no hope, nothing. Just nothing.

Survivors hurried to the airport, going home to lives changed forever. The people of Kuta, with no such escape, started to re-build their home.

Two hundred and two people died. Hundreds more were injured.

After a prolonged investigation the Indonesian police arrested members of the Islamic group, Jemaah Islamiyah. On 9 November 2008, a firing squad executed three of those convicted of carrying out the attack, Imam Samudra ("Heri"), Amrozi bin Nurhasyim ("Amrozi") and Huda bin Abdul Haq ("Mukhlas"). They all hailed from the neighbouring island of Java.

The authorities have since detained or killed numerous other major and minor figures in Jemaah Islamiyah.

Many believe that all the plotters have yet to be brought to justice.

BOOK 1:
THE BIG DURIAN

Two months before... 10 August 2002

Leon could tell from the faint outline of the sun that he was travelling east. He ran his hand through his hair, closed his eyes and thought about the next two months. A dream of Indonesia: a vision of a temple; the image of a volcano; *kretek* cigarettes in the blue shade.

His hand trembled as he wound down the taxi window. Mouth agape, he sucked in his elation and released a whoop. Perhaps touched by the surge of adrenaline, the driver accelerated, 'Welcome to my country,' he said, a smile of gums and crooked teeth captivating his face.

They raced along the airport toll road and climbed an overpass. Below, corrugated iron shacks clung to the bank of a mud-brown river. On the horizon, swirls of mist enveloped the distant skyscrapers. And on the taxi forged, jolting into pockets of space, a blast of the horn accompanying each acceleration, brake and muttered curse.

Leon lifted the guidebook from his lap, flicked

through its contents and stopped at the section marked Jakarta. A map showed a grid of unusual names and unknown paths. He tapped his travelling companion, Josh, on the arm. 'Look, we're here,' he said, placing his finger on the map. 'Man, I can't wait to get out there.'

'I'm not sure I want to,' Josh said.

Leon followed his gaze out the window to a street ablaze with commerce: mobile food stalls sold meatball soup and chicken *satay*; a man strode through the traffic, a bundle of newspapers under his arm; a conductor hung out a bus, yelling its destination.

'Of course you do. It looks amazing,' Leon said, refocusing on the map.

The taxi steered this way and that. It slowed, sped up and slowed again. A blast of whistle. The driver grumbling. A sharp turn left.

'Right,' Leon said, lifting his eyes and looking out the window. 'We should only be a couple of minutes away. Hang on...'

'What?'

'Is that Merdeka square? It is... that massive white tower thing is the National Monument. He's taking us the long way.'

'He's not. He couldn't go right becau–'

'Oi, chief,' Leon said, rapping the driver's shoulder. 'Jalan Jaksa. Understand?'

'Jaksa. Yes. Soon. Very soon.'

They drove for half a mile, Leon's brow becoming heavier with each passing yard. The driver turned right. Leon's finger shot right on the map. He turned right again. Leon's finger followed the movement. He gripped his lower lip with his teeth. Breath hissed through his nose.

'Why the little cheating bast... I knew it. He's driven us round in a circle.'

'Will you calm down and listen?' Josh said. 'When you weren't looking a policeman whistled at him and made him turn left.'

'What about every turning since?'

'We've probably lost about thirty pence.'

'It's the principle,' Leon said, slapping the guidebook shut. He cast it aside and watched the car enter a familiar scene: a street littered with traveller cafés and guest houses.

'Jalan Jaksa,' the driver said, bringing them to a halt at the side of the road. He sprung out, rounded the vehicle, opened the boot and lifted their backpacks onto the street.

Leon got out on the pavement side and watched Josh climb out after him. Sloping shoulders and translucent skin. Face impassive – as always. He approached his rucksack, hoisted it onto his back, looked up to Leon and lifted his eyebrows like he was waiting for him to do the same.

He didn't care about what had just happened. He actually didn't.

Leon shook his head, stepped towards the driver and rested his hand on the back of his neck. 'How much you cheating cocksucker?'

'*Argo, argo*,' the driver said, pointing at the meter in the taxi. It said 80,000 RP in red lighting. The driver held up eight fingers.

'Yes, I understand,' said Leon. He opened his wallet and took out close to 1,000,000 rupiah. The driver's eyes widened. Leon withdrew four 20,000 rupiah notes. The driver's hand moved towards the money. His fingers started to close. Leon released his grip. The driver watched the money blow along the pavement and looked back to Leon in bemusement. With an anguished cry, the taxi driver set off in pursuit, trying to trap the money with his sandaled feet.

*

Cinta sat in the back office of Jaksa Travel staring at a box of receipts that were festering on her desk. Before 5pm, she had to account for and file the contents. She dipped her hand inside, drew out a ball of paper, opened it and flattened it with the palm of her hand. The departure airport was Jakarta. The date, time, price and destination of the flight were indecipherable. She pressed the palms of her hands against her ears to block out the chatter of her colleagues and re-examined the receipt. The voices and laughter grew louder. In the main shop a gaggle of her co-workers loitered next to the front desk. As usual they all spoke at once. Each sentence started and ended with an interruption. Everything was given: nothing taken away.

A click of the handle. The jangle of the front door. The entrance of two customers. The girls fell silent. A moment passed. A maelstrom of Indonesian femininity descended upon a middle-aged white couple.

Cinta pushed her chair back, got up and strode to the door. She'd seen the rest before. Even the weariest traveller couldn't resist the relentless energy. They enchanted customers and then devoured them. Women searching for bus tickets to Surabaya left with cruises to Singapore. Men seeking directions to the National Monument bought flights to Kalimantan. Sucked in, chewed up, swallowed and digested, the customers didn't notice the condition of the office: the discarded tickets and loose papers scattered amongst the lip gloss, Diet Coke cans and chewing gum wrappers.

The white couple were already seated. Brochures filled their hands: charm their ears. Cinta shut the office door. A bit too hard.

Muffled voices accompanied her back to her desk. The door crashed back open filling the room with sound. Her cousin, Elok, strutted inside, her hip movement exaggerated, her breasts thrust against her low-cut blouse. She reached Cinta's desk and perched on the arm of her chair. 'What's wrong with you?'

'It's just difficult to concentrate on my work.'

'It's only admin. No big deal.'

Cinta's eyes dropped to the surface of her desk. The pad of paper next to the phone. Her pens and pencils inside their holder. Her filing tray empty save for that one outstanding task. Her entire job was 'only admin.'

'Are you still coming out for a drink after work?' Elok said.

The girls from the travel agency often went out for drinks together but it was the first time they'd asked Cinta. She'd been looking forward to it all week. 'I can come if I finish this work.'

'Does your father know you are coming?' Elok said.

'I said that I was working late.'

'You actually lied to him?'

'I had to. Imagine if I told him I was going to a bar on this street?'

Elok released a sharp laugh, 'Don't look ashamed. I'm proud of you.'

'Is your boyfriend coming?'

Elok tilted her head and flicked those long, fake lashes. 'I have no boyfriend.'

'I saw you sharing a car this morning,' Cinta's voice reduced to a whisper, 'with a white man... a *bule*.'

'Oh him... he's not my boyfriend.' A smile formed around the edges of Elok's lips. Her stare intensified. 'I met him in the bar we are going to tonight. Maybe you could meet one as well.'

Cinta looked down at her desk and picked up one of the receipts to distract from the blood that trapped in her face.

'Don't be shy,' Elok said. 'I've seen the way you look at the foreign customers and those pictures you pull out of the magazines and –'

'I'm not sure it's a good idea,' Cinta said. That wasn't true. She was certain it wasn't a good idea. But it was a bad idea that she thought about every day. A bad idea that even someone as self-involved as Elok had noticed. 'Anyway, I'm not sure I'll be able to make it. This job I'm doing is impossible.'

'You can finish it tomorrow.'

'Jusuf does not like things done tomorrow.'

'I'll talk to him.'

'Will he listen?'

'Yes.'

Cinta perceived a flicker in Elok's dark eyes. Her question had been stupid. Of course, their boss, Jusuf, would listen to Elok: every man listened to Elok.

A roar of hilarity came from the shop. Cinta trailed Elok to the doorway to discover the source - feeling relief when she realised that, for once, it wasn't her. A taxi driver scuttled past the window snatching at the ground. Seconds later, he returned clutching some banknotes, yelling and gesticulating back down the street. The girls revelled in his misfortune, mimicking his gestures and waving at him through the shop's facade.

*

Josh collapsed on the bed and buried his face into one of the few unstained sections of the mattress. The stench of dried sweat was actually a relief from the room's general reek of rotting plaster.

He'd followed Leon around six identical hostels negotiating over the equivalent saving of one pound a night. Leon had bartered hard, wagged his finger at the owners, flounced out when they refused to meet his price. After the incident with the taxi driver he was on a mission not to be 'ripped off by everyone in this entire country.'

Flip-flopped feet approached. 'What's up with you?'

Josh rolled over onto his back. 'Why do you have to argue with everyone all the time?'

'It's called bartering. I must have saved you thousands of pounds on this trip.'

'And cost me thousands of hours.'

'I bet you almost all of the time I get it as cheap, if not cheaper, than the locals.'

'And is it worth it?'

'What do you mean?'

Josh motioned his head towards the bathroom. A rusted door hung off its hinges. Inside, the toilet was a crouch-down hole in the ground with cracked, porcelain footrests on each side. A large bucket of water sat in the corner. A smaller bucket floated in the yellow liquid: the flush.

'It's got a shower and hot water and...' Leon paced across the room, head circling, desperately searching for a further redeeming feature. 'A powerful fan.' He stood beneath it pointing upwards, his clothes and hair remaining unruffled.

'It's making more noise than air.'

A magnificent scowl captivated Leon's face. 'Look, we're travelling. This is what it's like.'

'If you would listen for a second... I'm not bothered about the bartering or room.'

'What then?

'Flicking the money down the street. You humiliated that driver.'

'He humiliated us by ripping us off. It's the only way these people will learn. You know, I really worry for you when this is over and you need to go out into the real world.'

The real world. That one again. Number 8 in Leon bingo.

'OK, don't get too comfortable, it's only one o'clock,' Leon said. 'Let's go do something.'

'We got up really early and have had a long flight. Can we not just relax today?'

'You can relax when you die.'

Relax when you die. Another one of Leon's favourites. Number 3.

'Fine,' Josh said, 'but I want to go and see something official like a tourist attraction. I'm not going on one of your harebrained adventures.'

'Good, that's settled,' Leon said. 'I'll just cheer this place up a bit, have a quick shower and then we can head off to see the National Monument.'

Josh shut his eyes and tried to ignore the pain that groaned through his head. He didn't need to look to know what Leon was doing now; emptying the contents of his rucksack on the floor: three t-shirts and two pairs of shorts, hooded top, rain jacket, three pairs of socks, boxer shorts, wash bag, knife, water bottle, medical kit, travel towel, malaria pills, mosquito repellent, Sony Discman, trainers, flip-flops, the book he had been agonising over since Ho Chi Minh City. Next, he placed his possessions in what he called their 'rightful positions.'

Routine complete, he commenced the next one: decorating the room with various objects collected during their six month tour of Asia. He found a location for the engraved stone he'd stolen from Angkor Watt in Cambodia; took out his enamel coffee pot from Malaysia; rolled out the bamboo mat from Laos; lit his Chinese incense sticks; moaned when his Thai lantern didn't work.

Josh couldn't be bothered fulfilling his role in the ritual that day.

Why are you doing that?

To make the place like home.

You don't do this in your home.

What do you care?

What about my space?

Fine. Leon would say, picking up his things and placing them on his side, taking care to push them that extra inch over the imaginary line in the centre of the room. Happy?

'Naked man alert,' Leon called, getting ready for his shower; clothes dropping to the floor; strutting around tensing his muscles; scratching his mosquito bites whilst swearing. The patter of bare feet. Slam: the door closing. Wait for it. 'Awww the water's freezing.'

Every day travelling was different: every day was the same.

*

Ahmad knew that he should have said, 'No,' the moment he saw the old man limping across the train station concourse towards his barber's shop. He was already running late.

That morning his daughter had told him that she was working late. She'd been busy recently and it wasn't unusual for her to work overtime. But as the day progressed something nagged at him. Perhaps it was the way she'd said it so quickly and changed the subject afterwards. Maybe it was how specific she'd been with the 7 p.m. pick up time. Usually she'd call him when she was ready. Either way she was up to something.

Ahmad had decided to shut up early to find out what.

But when the old man entered the shop and greeted Ahmad and his wife and two daughters, he also knew that he had no choice but to accept his custom: the old man was local and came each fortnight and despite his complaints and weary conversation he paid and never asked for credit.

The old man picked his way towards the chair and lowered himself on to the seat. Ahmad spread a towel over his shoulders, picked up the water spray and squirted a fine mist over the old man's thinning hair. The old man swivelled in the chair, 'I told you last week. No spray.'

Ignoring him, Ahmad lifted his scissors and began to cut. He was sure the old man only came back so he could criticise his every action.

As he trimmed his hair, the scissor handles dug into the calluses on Ahmad's fingers. The old man, as was his way, wriggled in the seat.

'Please can you sit still?'

'It is too hot in here.' The old man gestured with his

forehead to the wooden top under the mirror. 'Doesn't that fan work?'

Ahmad lowered his scissors, rounded the seat and plugged in the fan. The blades picked up speed and currents of air blustered through the old man's shirt. Although the motor drowned out the noise, Ahmad could see in the reflection of the mirror that his two daughters had started to fight. In the corner, their mother's vacant eyes followed the smoke that curled from her cigarette. Ahmad clicked his fingers and motioned in the direction of the girls. His wife's eyes remained fixed on the smoke. Despite the fan, the girls, the outside traffic, no noise was as clear as the single tut released by the old man.

Ahmad glared at the old man but muttered to himself, 'Do your work. Get rid of him. Go and pick up your daughter.'

His scissors barely paused between each snip. In his haste, the blades nipped a pocket of skin that sagged behind the old man's ear. He yelped and grabbed at his neck, 'What are you doing? Trying to cut off my head?'

A train passed above. The light bulb swung on its cable, blinked and gave up. The familiar rattle of his spare scissors, the girls crying in the dark, the sporadic glow of his wife's cigarette – the lack of customers, the memory of the magnificence of his father's shop, the shame of the bolt hole underneath the train tracks he was now stuck in, all vibrating through the dark.

The light blinked back on, the bare bulb accentuating the ridges of the old man's scowling face. 'This place is a joke. I don't know why I come here any longer.'

Ahmad's tongue pressed against his lower teeth. The glint of the scissors. The outline of the veins in the back of the old man's neck. He gripped the handle and pointed the blades forward. His hand trembled and dropped. He sucked in a deep breath, wiped his hands across his t-shirt and lifted the scissors back to the old man's hair.

*

Josh looked beyond the vehicles that streamed from eight different directions across the intersection to a monument in the centre: a topless man wearing a conical hat with a gun slung over his shoulder. 'Is that the Farmer's statue, again?'

'Nah, it's a different statute,' Leon said, with a quick, definitive shake of his head.

'It's definitely the same one. Your sense of direction is terrible.'

'How dare you criticise my –'

Josh grabbed the Periplus map from Leon, flipped over the yellow cover and opened it. 'OK, you said we were going to that National Monument. We started here and wanted to go there... so that means... we've been going in a circle.'

Leon snatched the map back. 'No, we haven't.'

'Give it here.'

'Don't, you'll rip it.'

Josh released his grip. 'OK, you hold it then but listen. We wanted to go this way.' He ran his finger along their intended route. 'Directly north. Now look where the sun is.' He stepped back and pointed upwards. 'We've been heading east.'

Leon's head moved up and down the street. 'This map is rubbish. They've put it the wrong way up,' he looked up to the sky accusingly, 'or maybe the sun is in a different position in the Southern hemisphere.'

'We're lost and you know it.'

'Yes...' Leon said, massaging his chin. 'OK, we might need someone to take us there. Don't worry I'll sort this out.'

*

Leon stood by the side of the road and contemplated his options. He needed to make a decision, Josh was becoming suspicious.

Three vehicles hovered in front of him. A driver leant out of a blue car flapping his hand and yelling, 'Taxi.' Behind the taxi lingered a motorised rickshaw with a multi-coloured metal frame, three wheels and a small cab from which the driver called, '*Bajaj*.' On the pavement, a helmetless man on a black Honda motorbike, tapped the back of his saddle and shouted, '*Ojek*.'

The taxi would be the safest and most reliable. It would also be Josh's preference. Leon instantly ruled it out. The *ojek* ride would be fun and the cheapest. The *bajaj* the most exotic and daring.

Leon stole a look at Josh. He was moping under the shade of a tree, sweating in that disgusting way of his, still transfixed with the map. He'd hate the *bajaj*... that sealed it. Leon walked to the *bajaj*, opened the door and lowered himself on to the plastic leather seat. He put his thumb and index finger in his mouth and blew. The shrill blast made Josh look up. Josh approached the *bajaj*, hesitantly got inside and squeezed next to Leon.

Leon leant towards the cab and spoke to the driver. 'We want to go to a *pasar gila*. Understand? A *pasar gila*.'

The driver looked back and licked his lower lip. '*Pasar gila*?'

'Yes.'

The driver smiled, faced forward, gripped the throttle and twisted. The *bajaj* rumbled into the centre of the six lane road, the 60cc engine roaring like a departing aircraft. Leon turned to Josh and gave him a triumphant nod.

Josh stared back at him. 'You think I don't know we are in a *tuk-tuk*? I told you in Thailand that I don't want to travel in these death traps.'

'Actually it's not a *tuk-tuk*. It's a *bajaj*.'

'*Bajaj* is clearly just the Indonesian name for *tuk-tuk*.'

'How could that be?'

'Because they have a different language.'

Leon made a clucking noise with his tongue. 'Well that's true... but I don't know how you can compare this fine vehicle with those *tuk-tuks* in Thailand. These are much safer. Look at this body.' He rapped his knuckles against the frame producing a tinny sound. Flakes of paint crumbled on to the floor. '...and look, it's also got windows.'

Josh twisted around and prodded the clear tarpaulin that covered the back windscreen, 'And what will that protect us against?'

'Rain?'

Not a flicker of amusement touched Josh's face. Leon knew he was pushing his luck. He looked around for inspiration and found it across the street. 'Hey Josh, look at that,' he said, pointing at reams of barbed wire meshed atop a green barricade. 'Driver, what's that?'

The driver glanced to his left before quickly looking away. 'American Embassy.'

He sped up as they passed an entrance guarded by a tank and two armed soldiers.

'It looks like they're ready for war,' said Leon, sticking

his head out the window. He dropped back inside and faced Josh, 'I said, "It looks like –'

'I heard you.'

'Well, why didn't you answer?'

'Because you're trying to change the subject. What does *pasar gila* mean?'

'What?'

'The words you said to the driver when he got in.'

'Oh that. It means... market... small market.'

'You better be joking! We agreed to go to the National Monument and then back to the hotel. A nice relaxing first day.'

'This is relaxing.'

'You know how much I hate markets...' a sudden sternness took over Josh's face. 'That's why you had us walking around in circles earlier, wasn't it? You were looking for this market.'

*

Ahmad drew the shutters down to meet the hasp, slipped the padlock shackle through the breach and pressed it until the mechanism locked. He took a step back and studied the shop facade before turning to leave.

He paced along the mustard-coloured tiles of Gondangdia station nodding to his fellow *warung* owners without registering a face. Had he heard the padlock click? Were the shutters fully pulled down? When his wife left earlier she'd taken the spare key, hadn't she? The last thing he needed was another robbery. Should he return to check? His pace slowed. Probably. He glanced at his watch. Half past five. He winced as he recalled his lateness and dismissed the idea. If he went back, he might lose his chance at finding out what his daughter was up to. He jogged out of the main entrance, acknowledging the *bajaj* and *ojek* drivers waiting under the station bridge, and turned to his immediate left down a narrow *gang*.

He reached his car, got in, started the engine and drove until he met Jalan Wahid Hasyim. He arrived at the crossroads and, without the time or patience to wait, he shunted out, his bumper barging other vehicles out of the way. His car was already battered so he didn't need to follow the one rule of Jakarta's roads: if you have a nice car... watch it. After little more than a hundred metres he reached the Farmer's statue. In the distance a black veil crawled across the city. Lightening crackled, white and clear. Thunder rumbled seconds later. The rest of Jakarta knew, like him, what was coming. The road that everyone had taken to came to a standstill.

*

Josh gripped a random strap that hung from the canvas roof of the *bajaj*. He pointed his knees inwards, drew his shoulders up and murmured a prayer for this journey to end.

Next to him, Leon hung out of the window, the petrol-filled air ruffling through his blonde hair. Each time the *bajaj* bounced over a pothole or swerved around a stray dog or nearly hit a child, he'd drop back inside and grin at Josh.

They slowed and stopped at a red light. Two youths dodged through the grid of vehicles towards them. Both had guitars slung over their shoulders. They reached the *bajaj* and burst into song. The clamour attracted other sellers. When Leon bought a watermelon, the sight of his money stirred a greater frenzy. The guitarists sped up and wailed the lyrics with increased gusto. The hawkers dangled their products and chirped, 'cheap, cheap, cheap.'

Around them the dozens of mopeds, buses and cars waited for the release of the green light. Revs of anticipation; a cacophony of horns; the race began. The guitar players pressed forward, their hands outstretched, palms open. Leon slapped a 50,000 rupiah note into a guitarist's hand and the *bajaj* spluttered away.

'That was a bit generous, wasn't it?' Josh said.

'Well, you gotta give the kids a chance.'

Leon reclined in his seat and bit into his watermelon. Occasionally, he interrupted his chewing to spit a pip out of the corner of his mouth. Josh watched him and wondered how someone who would refuse to pay a penny extra if it offended one of his many principles, could be at the same time so frivolous. He inwardly shrugged. He'd long given up trying to analyse Leon: you had to know him to understand him and if you knew him as well as Josh you didn't understand him at all.

They drove on for a further ten minutes before pulling into the side of the road. Leon paid the driver and they stepped out of the *bajaj*. They faced a sprawl of plastic awnings and metal poles.

'Now this is what I'm talking about,' said Leon, displaying the expression he pulled when he became bewildered by, and in awe of, his own good fortune.

Josh trailed him towards a walkway, two metres wide, packed with people squeezing into the market. They stopped at the entrance.

'What's wrong? Leon said.

'What do you think is wrong? You tricked me into coming here and –'

'What did we say before we left?'

Josh sighed through his nose. 'Never be lame. Live every moment.'

Leon had been using this promise against him for months.

'And what are you doing now? Come on,' Leon said stepping into the murky scene. Josh took a deep breath and followed.

Hit by a swathe of heat, everything slowed, stilled, and then burst into life; relentless noise; people everywhere; pulling, pushing, bartering, buying, selling, stealing, fighting. The traders' excitement increased when they saw the white men with their curious faces and leather wallets. Cries followed their path, 'Tony Blair', 'George Bush', '*bule, bule, bullllleeee.*'

They followed the arc of the passage. A woman wearing a multicoloured dress wrapped a sari around Josh's waist and twirled him on the spot. Dizzy, he stumbled down the narrow passage passing ducks and chickens hopelessly flapping inside their cages.

On they went, through a crowd swarming around three great pots of rice; some buying a few ounces; others lugging away great sacks. Passing a bread stall, the sweet smell vanishing into a deeper aroma. Eyes watering, dozens of pots of spice, all different colours, all in demand, delicately served by a bearded old man. The passage narrowed: food stalls, garlic, onions, potatoes, red chilli, boiling chicken broths. A man peeling cassavas; a deafening clang as a woman mashed them in a giant steel drum. Plastic stools filled with hungry patrons; steam rising from the vats of fried vegetables. The market widened into a ring, the outer perimeter lined with scores of fish in buckets and giant bovine carcasses hanging from metal hooks.

'I've got to leave,' said Josh.

'What did you say?'

'I HAVE TO LEAVE. SEE YOU OUTSIDE.'

'We are outside. Wait, where are you going?'

Stuck in the crowd, everyone pressing in, their breath hot, elbows sharp. Trying to escape, wading towards the light. Store owners tugging his arm, shouting in his face. Colliding with a man carrying two buckets of fish. The memory of being forced to eat mackerel as a child. Saliva lining his mouth. Stomach retching. Vision unclear. Taking the final few steps out of the market and staggering towards a shop. Sitting down and resting against its facade.

*

The precipitation beat a furious rhythm on Ahmad's windscreen. He could hear the Maghrib call to prayer from the nearby Mesjid Istiqlal. It was almost six o'clock. His destination was Jalan Jaksa: the home of foreign backpackers and their entourage of whores, drug dealers and other affiliated scum. If his daughter had lied she was probably in a bar with her cousin Elok surrounded by such people. If she hadn't lied to him she might be alone in the office with her boss, Jusuf. He didn't know which option was worse. He thumped the steering wheel with his fist. Still the traffic didn't move.

*

Cinta pushed open the front door of the shop and peered onto the street. People scuttled past, glowering up at the sky. A stall owner rolled tarpaulin over his *warung*. He stepped aside to avoid a group of women who spilled out of the adjacent bar. She recognized the group as her work colleagues. They must be switching locations before the rain came. She studied the six figures hurrying down the street and listened to their boisterous voices and felt certain Elok wasn't with them. Maybe she'd waited in the bar for her. She glanced at her watch. Six o'clock already. Her father was coming to pick her up at seven.

She closed the door, turned the lock and made her way back to her desk. Ten more minutes' work, finish the task and then go, she told herself.

She switched on the desk lamp and began work on the four remaining receipts. The rustle of paper. The scratch of her pen. A boom of thunder in the distance. She rose and picked up the bucket and positioned it under the leak in the roof. Single drops fell five seconds apart, clanking into the rusted metal. She returned to her seat.

The front door opened. A torrent of wind screamed through the entrance. The door slammed shut. A figure approached and crouched over her, blocking out the light of the lamp. 'Hello Cinta. Are you still working?'

'Yes, but I've almost finished.'

Jusuf walked to his desk. He picked up a receipt from the pile and studied it, 'What are these?'

'The receipts I couldn't read.'

He gathered the pile, returned to her desk and dropped them on the surface. 'Well, please try again.'

'Did you speak with Elok?'

'About what?'

'She was going to ask you something... it doesn't matter.'

Cinta rotated her chair to face away from him and glared at the returned receipts. They were as illegible as the first three times she'd tried to read them.

Jusuf remained behind her chair, his pupils, those

miniscule black dots, penetrating the back of her head. 'You work very hard.' Thin streams of nasal breath on her neck. 'Not like all the other girls.'

'Thank you.'

He rounded her chair, cupped her jaw and lifted her face to meet his eyes. Old cigarettes on his fingers. Her eyes flitted to the door. His eyes followed. 'I see... you want to meet the other girls? I know they've gone out.'

'I thought you hadn't spoken to Elok?'

'I must have forgotten.' He smiled in that sneering way of his. 'OK, you can leave but only because you're my favourite.'

'Thank you,' Cinta mumbled. She got to her feet, put on her coat, grabbed her bag and hastened to the door. She yanked it open. Spray blew into her face. Water roared along the gutters. The smell of earth and chalk.

She turned back to the warmth of the office. Jusuf rested on her desk watching her with his hands clasped.

She shut the door firmly and set off down Jalan Jaksa using the shop fronts as shelter from the rain. She got to the bar in which she'd agreed to meet Elok within thirty seconds but hesitated when she reached the entrance. A board to her right said, 'Happy Hour,' in English and listed a series of drinks she didn't know. Three red-faced men wearing t-shirts and stinking of alcohol staggered past her seeming not to notice that they'd almost knocked her over or that it was bucketing it down outside.

She peered through the window of the front door and saw Elok and her friend, Soraya, perched on stools at the bar. Every few months Elok would find herself a new best friend. They would be inseparable for a few weeks before falling out when Elok found someone more interesting.

Her latest soul mate, Soraya, featured in most of Elok's recent stories. These stories had a similar theme. They involved Elok and Soraya tricking men, usually rich white men, into paying for dinners, drink, taxis and hotels. They invented names for themselves and characters with back stories. Watches and wallets sometimes went missing. All of that was Soraya, of course; Elok just went along for a laugh. She did have a new phone though. But that was a present.

Cinta watched them swoon as a group of foreign men approached them and felt herself backing away. Yes, she wanted to meet a man, to talk to and practice her English and maybe something else. But a nice man. Not a man who hung around in bars looking for girls like Soraya. Maybe her father was right all along. Maybe a girl like her shouldn't go to places like that.

She trudged back up the street and sat on a wooden bench under the shelter of a deserted street stall.

*

Josh remained anchored to the grime-scarred pavement staring at the entrance to the market and trying to control his breathing. After what seemed an eternity, Leon emerged carrying two cages, an air rifle and a stuffed hawk. When he reached Josh, an expression of deep concern consumed his face. He settled his cages on the ground, crouched down and rested his hand on the middle of Josh's back, 'You look awful.'

'I told you I get panicky in markets. That was the worst one yet.'

'What was wrong with it?

'The heat. The hassle. The noise!'

Leon's features scrunched up, 'That's what's good

about it.'

'What the hell have you bought now?' Josh said. He pinched the velvet cover of one of the cages and was about to lift it and look inside.

'Don't. I can't show you until we get back to the room.' Leon tapped his right nostril whilst winking his left eye, 'The stall owner made me promise.'

'OK, I understand,' Josh said, mimicking Leon's nose tapping with as much sarcasm as his condition would allow.

'Right, if you're feeling better, let's go.'

Josh accepted Leon's hand and allowed himself to be yanked to his feet. Leon attempted to release his hand but Josh held on. 'Before we go.... I've got a question.' He squeezed a little tighter. 'What does *pasar gila* really mean?'

Leon slipped his hand free. 'I told you.'

'I know you did but what does it really mean?'

Leon threw his hands up in defeat. 'It means crazy market.'

'So let me get this straight... you asked the driver to take us to a crazy market... in Jakarta?'

'I didn't think you'd almost faint,' Leon said. 'Come on buddy, I'll make it up to you. There's a station near to here. We'll catch a train back, get changed and go out and find you a girl.'

'Where?'

'There are loads of bars on that Jalan Jaksa near our hotel.' Leon stepped closer, grabbed Josh's ear and tweaked it. 'Look at your face. I knew that would cheer you up.'

'Get off,' Josh said, swatting away Leon's hand.

'Can't stay mad at me for long, can you? I'm too

likeable.'

Josh watched Leon pick up his cages, air rifle and stuffed hawk and saunter towards the train station. Despite his best efforts he couldn't stop himself from smiling.

*

Cinta remained crouched on the wooden bench of the street stall. Damp had crept through her shoes and up her trouser leg. The product Elok had given her to 'stop her hair looking so flat,' dripped down her face. It tasted more like congealed fat than the promised coconut milk.

She looked up to the source of the relentless drumming. Above, the plastic sheet sagged under the weight of the gathering water, threatening a greater soaking. Her eyes wandered back to Jaksa Travel. A faint glow lit the office. She looked at her watch: 6.10 pm. Fifty minutes until her father would arrive. Fifty minutes in the rain or fifty minutes with Jusuf. Fifty minutes in the rain. No contest.

She sighed and thought back to the start, only a few months before, when she used to look forward to going to work; before the incident with the trousers; before the dispute that would never end.

She'd heard about the job from Elok. At the time, they were eating at their favourite *warung* just off Jalan Haji Agus Salim. It was at the start of the rainy season. But no rain came that day. Instead the smog lifted and the blue seemed to reach up into the heavens. They ordered *mie bakso* and Coca-Cola and sat in silence watching the red embers of the late evening crackle across the Jakarta sky.

'You've left school, haven't you?' Elok said, still chewing. 'Do you have a job?'

'No.'

'But you got a good result for English, right?'

'Yes,' Cinta said. She shovelled a forkful of noodles into her mouth and tried not to smile. Elok knew! Everyone in her family must be talking about it.

The result had arrived a month before. Previously described as an average student, she'd received the best mark in her year for English. Validation for her work; for her love of the mysterious words and sounds; sounds that transported her to beautiful places; far away but perhaps no longer beyond her reach.

'Well,' Elok said, settling her fork on the plate, 'I think there is a job at Jaksa Travel. Most of the customers are foreign so we need people who speak English.'

'I don't think my father would like me working in the travellers' area.'

'You're a woman now. You don't need to ask him.'

'He's not like your dad.'

Elok flicked her hand in dismissal. 'Come to the shop tomorrow. I'll introduce you to my boss, Jusuf.'

The next night, Cinta pulled a chair from under the table and faced her father. The clink of plates and splashes of water told her that her mother was in the kitchen. Just say it, flashed through her mind. And she did. 'I've been offered a job working with Elok. I went for the interview today.'

He didn't look up from his paper. Minutes passed. He closed the paper and turned back to the front page but appeared not to focus on the words. She rose and pushed her chair back under the table, making sure the wood grated across the floor. She stormed up the stairs, flicked on the light of her room and threw herself onto her bed. Her twin sisters watched her with the wide eyes of those startled out of sleep.

They all lay awake for what felt like hours.

The activity in the kitchen ceased. A door shutting. A low mutter from downstairs.

She got up from her mattress, eyed her sisters and pressed her finger against her lips. She crept across the floor, out the door and down the stairs. She settled on the bottom step and listened. Muffled words behind the closed door. *Elok... Salim... Bule... Jaksa... Jusuf....* until one sentence rose above the rest, 'Only rich men can afford to be proud.'

Her family needed the money: working at Jaksa Travel paid well.

After six months, her father's begrudging acceptance was broken when Jusuf acquired a new uniform for the girls. Cinta remembered rising early that day, heading straight for the wardrobe, taking out the uniform and dressing. The blouse was tight-fitting - like the ones that Elok wore. It seemed to enhance her breasts and shrink her waist. She undid a couple of buttons. A hint of cleavage. Her eyes dropped to the navy-blue skirt. It covered her knees. Just. A honk of a horn outside. Her father waiting at the bottom of the street. With a smile, she attached her name badge and made her way to the car.

She got in the front seat and waited. She sensed him looking her up and down. A terrific heat exuded from his direction. Without a word, she opened the door and returned to the house to change.

When they arrived at Jaksa Travel, she chased after her father, grabbing his arm, begging him to stop. The door rebounded off its hinges as he entered. He marched behind the counter, reached Jusuf's desk and banged his knuckles off the surface. Coffee slopped over the edge of his cup. Jusuf peered at the brown line trickling through his papers and then up at her father. His face contorted - like he'd eaten something with a disgusting taste. 'Can I help you, *Bung* Ahmad?'

Her father shouted about the skirt, about Jusuf having no honour, about Jaksa Travel bringing shame to his family. Cinta knew why Jusuf smiled in response: he lived to shock people like her father; people of the old Indonesia, pious old men without the power or means to counter someone like him.

When Ahmad finished, Jusuf gave the hint of a shrug and said, 'Cinta can, of course, leave at anytime. Please take her if she is unhappy.'

Her father's head moved from Jusuf back to Cinta. He grabbed her wrist, his knuckles white and protruding, and led her from the shop.

When they reached the house Cinta ran to her room and sunk onto the bed. She wished the world was as black and as quiet as under her blanket. What would all the other girls at the shop think? What would Elok say? Cinta gripped the blanket tighter as she imagined the sneer on her face.

The next day she was awoken by her father's voice, 'Get up. You're late.'

'But you said I couldn't work there anymore.'

'We can't afford for you to live for free, Cinta. Put your old trousers on and go to work. If he asks you to wear that skirt, phone me straightaway,' he said, trying to salvage dignity from his retreat.

She reached work. Climbed out of the car. Paused outside. Her father looked on. No escape. She pushed open the shop door and entered. Her co-workers watched her soft steps across the floor. She rounded the counter and met Jusuf. His arms were folded; his broad smile didn't match the stillness of his eyes. 'Good morning Cinta. May we speak in private please?' he said, beckoning her into the back office.

He shut the door and viewed her trousers, 'Are you OK?'

'Yes, thank you.'

'I have some good news. I've decided to give you a pay rise...'

She didn't reply.

'Are you not happy?'

'Yes, of course. Thank you.'

But she wasn't. The pay rise wasn't a gesture of goodwill. It was a message to her father: that Jusuf could buy what stood in his way.

A series of blue flashes brought her back to present. A cavernous growl. The clouds spat with greater intensity. She remained under the shelter of the stall. And still her father didn't arrive. She rose from the bench. Drenched nylon trousers clung to her legs. Such a small garment: the source of so much unhappiness.

*

The crowd surged as the train pulled into the station and juddered to a halt. The doors snapped open: passengers spilled out; others pushed on.

Leon, usually in the centre of such melees, remained unmoved.

'What are you doing?' Josh said. 'We're going to miss it.'

Leon was aiming his rifle at his own face and

inspecting the barrel. 'Let everyone get on first and then we'll use the windows to get up.'

'Get up where?'

He lowered the rifle. 'The roof.'

Josh looked back to the train. Lines of people hunched on the roof, inches below the electrical cable. 'Are you serious?'

'Always.' Leon walked over to the carriage and set his things down on the platform. 'OK, give me a punt and when I'm up I'll pull you up.'

Josh studied the muddle of limbs dangling over the side of the carriage. 'Do you have any idea how dangerous it is up there?'

'Why do you think I'm doing it?'

Leon planted his foot on the window ledge and, with the help of an out-stretched hand of a fellow roof-rider, clambered up. He shuffled into a pocket of space and looked back down at Josh. 'Right, pass up the rifle and the hawk. You can keep the cages for now.'

'Why do you need a stuffed bird and an air rifle up there?'

'It's my style that's why. Come up. It's free.'

'Dying is always free.'

'Don't be stupid,' Leon said, his face animated with a deep scorn. 'People like me don't die.'

A whistle blasted from the far side of the deserted platform. Josh picked up the rifle and the stuffed bird, rose to his tiptoes and bundled them up to Leon. He snatched the cages, clattered along the platform and dodged inside the carriage, the door almost clamping him in its vice.

When they arrived at Gondangdia station, Josh hastened onto the platform and walked backwards gazing at the roof. Not for the first time on the trip, he found himself in complete awe of the audacity of his travelling companion. Leon was perched on the edge of the roof pointing his rifle and pretending to shoot Josh. His fellow roof-riders were viewing him with a mixture of bemusement and fascination. He shook their hands, chucked his rifle and hawk to Josh and jumped down.

'Man, that was really something. You missed out big style. At one point...'

Josh followed Leon's gaze to the tops of the highest palm trees blustering below the blackened sky. Leon looked at Josh and then back to the train. 'Shit! Get down,' he said, motioning to the passengers on the roof.

The passengers remained on the roof as the train pulled away. Leon jogged and then sprinted in pursuit. 'Rain. Electrocution. Get down,' he shouted.

Leon slowed down and stopped as the train leave the station. Around him, raindrops spotted the platform. Josh reached him, 'What's wrong?'

'Those poor bastards. With that rain and those electric wires...'

Josh resisted the urge to ask why Leon valued the lives of strangers more than his own and instead put his hand on Leon's shoulder and said, 'They'll be fine.'

*

Ahmad drew the car to a halt halfway down Jalan Jaksa. An orange glow lit the shop. A shadow passed before the window and formed a silhouette. Broad-shouldered. Thick-headed. Tall. Ahmad kept the engine running and flicked his headlights to full-beam. The figure receded and then disappeared.

Thirty metres away on the other side of the road, the

headlights caught a person huddled under the plastic cover of a street stall. She shielded her eyes and peered at the vehicle. Her hand dropped and she sprung to her feet and splashed towards the car. She opened the door, got inside and greeted him like everything was normal.

'Why are you not in the office?' Ahmad said.

'It's closed.'

Ahmad's eyes flitted to the shop and then rested back on his daughter.

'Maybe someone left the light on,' Cinta said softly.

Ahmad nodded to himself. Sitting outside in the rain. The smudged eyeliner. The scent of perfume. He'd been right. 'Have you been to a bar with Elok?'

Cinta reached to her left, drew her seatbelt across and buckled. 'No.'

'So if I go into that bar Elok won't be there?'

'What are you going to do if she is? Nothing! Because Elok can do what she wants... unlike me.'

The phrases he knew so well, *Elok can do what she wants* or *Uncle Salim lets Elok*. When Cinta said those words he wanted to grab her and ask her why she thought that was. Was it because Salim was a better father? Was it because he loved Elok more?

Cinta's hand reached for the dial on the radio and lowered the *keroncong* music that she so hated. 'Come on. Tell me. Why can Elok go to bars and I can't?'

He gripped the cuff of his shirt in his fist and cleared the fogged windows with the forearm of his sleeve. Outside, thousands of aquatic nails rattled down onto that godforsaken street. 'Elok is different.'

'We are cousins. Why is she different?'

'Because...'

Because what, Ahmad? he thought. Because your brother, Salim, drives a Mercedes car and lives in the Pondok Indah. Because his money had sent Elok to the best schools and to university. Because Elok had been brought up around the progeny of actors, artists, doctors and politicians.

'Because?' she repeated. Her eyes glinted in the gloom. Eyes that had looked up to Elok since she was a little girl.

How could he tell her the truth? That in Jakarta people like Elok could do what they wanted; that people like her couldn't.

'Because she's not my daughter.'

'That's not a reason.'

Ahmad lowered the handbrake. 'Well, it will have to be,' he said, as they pulled out.

They drove a hundred metres before the headlights met two travellers strolling across the road. Two *hujan* boys held golf-umbrellas above their heads.

Later, Ahmad could not explain his reaction. Was it the argument with Cinta or a feeling embedded deep in his genetic memory? He didn't know. But the image of the two boys, no more than six years old, dressed in oversized t-shirts and sandals, drenched by the rain whilst escorting two bone-dry white men, for probably as little as 500 rupiah, roused an unknown ferocity.

He accelerated towards them. A jolt of panic. Fear overcoming instinct. He stamped on the brake. The car skidded to a stop. Ahmad was propelled forward before his belt twanged him back to his seat. Next to him, Cinta clutched the back of her neck, '*Pak*, what are you doing?'

The two men remained in the centre of the road; the umbrella boys had run away. The tall one with blonde hair was the first to recover. He picked up the two cages that he'd dropped, replaced their felt covers, and stepped towards the car. He began to shout. The words made no sense: the sentiment was clear. The smaller man's eyes shifted from Ahmad to the passenger seat and settled on Cinta. She returned his attention; her look intense and unflinching.

With a surge of anger, Ahmad pressed down on the accelerator once again. The tyres kicked up spray and then gripped. Churning through the grey swathes towards the two travellers. They leapt out of the way, just in time, only a glimpse of their wide-eyed fear visible from the speeding vehicle.

*

Josh followed Leon into their room and shut the door behind them, 'Can you believe that guy?'

'I know what an idiot,' Leon said, resting the two cages on the bed. 'He could've damaged my things.'

'I was more worried about us than your things.'

Leon readjusted the velvet covers on the cages. 'Right, close your eyes and I'll unveil the great mystery of what's inside.'

Josh stared at Leon.

'What?'

'Nothing,' Josh said. Leon clearly wasn't going to let someone nearly running him over steal the limelight away from the ridiculous things he'd bought. Giving in, Josh shut his eyes.

'Tighter,' Leon said. 'No peeking.'

'Just get on with it.'

'OK, ready.... tah-dah!'

Josh opened his eyes. Two cages sat on the Leon's

bed: a small snake in one; a turtle with a jagged shell in the other.

Looking at the turtle. Then the snake. Then at the beaming idiot, arms at full-span standing next to them.

Leon picked up the cages and thrust them towards Josh. 'Imagine trying to buy these in England,'

'Alright, not so close,' Josh said, shuffling along the bed.

'You don't like them?'

'Yes, they're great and everything but do you not think it'll be a bit of a hindrance backpacking, you know, with PETS?'

Leon lowered the cages back onto the bed. 'I hadn't thought about it.'

'Of course you hadn't. I guarantee you'll just end up having to leave them here.'

'Then I'll just give them to someone I meet like I did with Mr Woof in China. It'll be like a sacred gift to my favourite person in Indonesia.'

'You were made to leave "Mr Woof" with the immigration officer who caught you smuggling him into Vietnam,' Josh said. 'I'd hardly call that giving a sacred gift.'

'He was a nice guy.'

'You weren't saying that when you were calling him every name under the sun.'

'I warmed to him in the end.'

Josh picked up the guidebook from the floor and flopped back onto the bed. He opened the still-glossy cover, rested the book on his chest and began to read. There was really no point. Whatever the conception of their debate, all their quarrels evolved into the same seven disputes that would never be settled: the idiocy of the "Mr Woof" scenario; the bar fight in Vietnam; the burglary in Cambodia; their night in the police cells in Bangkok; the motorbike crash in Ko Samui; Josh's lack of adventure; women.

'Those bars on Jalan Jaksa looked quite busy when we passed. Shall we go for that beer I promised you?' Leon said, who could forget an argument as quickly as he could start one.

'Let me just read this for a bit first.'

'Should we leave the animals here or take them with us to the bar?'

Josh dropped the book on to the mattress. His eyes shot upwards, searching for something, anything, which could explain the perplexities of this man.

*

Ahmad sat at his dinner table alone. 'Cinta, I've already told you twice,' he shouted in the direction of the stairs. 'Dinner is ready.'

Cinta hadn't spoken in the car after the incident with the foreigners. She'd disappeared upstairs the moment they arrived home. Now she was ignoring him.

He glared at the stairs. If he had to go up there and get her... he heard the sound of her coming down the stairs. She entered the room and mooched over to the table. Shoulder-length hair. V-neck white top with a slogan in English. Navy blue jeans clinging to her legs.

Her twin sisters Nur and Rani followed her to the table and took their places. The moment they'd settled the kitchen door burst open and their mother, Wening, bustled over to the table. Two plates clattered onto its surface. Ahmad watched his wife hurry back into the kitchen and come back with two more plates. She put the food in front of the twins and left again. She returned, dropping a handful of knives and forks onto the centre of the table.

Ahmad took a fork and held it up to the light. A brown stain ran down the central tine. He glanced up to see his wife hustling back towards the kitchen, 'Wening...'

She flinched, perhaps contemplating looking back, but went on into the kitchen. The door shut.

Ahmad thrust his chair back, slapped his hands on his knees and prepared to rise. Then he stopped. Would the forks in the drawer be clean? Would they even be in the drawer? Of course not. His eyes circled the table. Four servings of *nasi goreng*: leftover rice, scraps of chicken, a puddle of soya sauce. Steamless. Odourless. Untouched.

'Eat your food,' he said to Cinta and the twins.

A collective groan.

He put a forkful of rice in his mouth to show the way. Cold and crunchy. Closing his eyes and swallowing. The darkness filled with his earlier desires. The thought of cutting the old man. The eyes of the two tourists as he drove at them. Never a violent man: now not so sure.

'Why are you sleeping at the table?' Cinta said.

His eyes shot open. 'I wasn't sleeping. I was thinking.'

Cinta's eyes rolling back to the fork she was using to push her food around her plate. The twins watched on, doing what four years olds did – copying the adults. Not eating. Not talking. Not happy.

The fifth place at the table was directly across from him. Not even set. No food. No fork. No wife. Silence radiated from the kitchen. What did she do in there? Did she stare through the wall at them? Did she ever think of joining them? Did she think about them at all?

Ahmad took a long drink of his warm water, set his glass on the table and contemplated another mouthful of rice. He'd trained himself to ignore the lack of conversation, the grate of cutlery, the click of Cinta's jaw, the empty chair, but there was one thing that he couldn't avoid: the way it made him feel.

*

Josh waited outside their guest house room and watched Leon follow him out. He wore a leather band on his right wrist; rings on his fingers; a shark tooth necklace around his neck. During their six months travelling his skin had turned a rich brown. His hair was long, matted and sun-bleached. He looked like a traveller.

Josh's hair was mousey-brown and cropped. He wore no accessories except his digital watch. He looked down at his sweat drenched t-shirt and khaki trousers. He looked like he'd just stepped off the tourist bus with his grandparents.

He waited until Leon locked the door and said, 'Hand it over.'

Leon slapped the key into Josh's palm. 'One mistake and I'm not allowed to look after a key ever again?' Leon said, stalking off.

Josh picked up their laundry bag and jogged after him into the reception where they found the owner on his knees scrubbing the floor. He noticed them and clambered to his feet. 'Hello, Mister Lion and Joss,' he said, removing his glasses and rubbing the lenses on his vest. Sweat gushed down his face. The smell of chlorine emanated from his body. He replaced his spectacles back on his face. 'You have good day?'

'Yes, very good thank you,' Josh said.

'*Hujan*,' he fluttered his fingers and made a swooshing sound. 'How you say?'

'The rain?'

'Yes, today very bad. But you lucky because now it stop. Where you go?'

'To some bars, I think.'

'Oh very good, misters,' the owner said, transferring his eyes to Leon. 'But not come back too late. Two strong boys need sleep.' He reached out and touched Leon's shoulder. His hand moved down to his bicep. 'Yes, strong boys.'

Josh saw the disgust on Leon's face and thought about Leon's ridiculously overplayed homophobia and pressed his hand against his mouth and a stifled chuckle.

'You are OK?' the owner said.

'Sorry, I thought I was going to sneeze.'

'What bars you go? You need a guide, perhaps? Nothing is too much.'

The friendly pats on Leon's arm had merged into strokes.

'Right Josh. Give him the washing and we'll go.'

'I think we could do with a guide though,' Josh said. 'It's a very kind offer...'

Leon snatched the laundry bag from Josh, stuffed it in the owner's wandering hands and strode out the front door.

The owner peered over the bundle at Josh. His expression had morphed from cheerfulness to confusion. 'I say something bad?'

Outside, Leon leant against a wall. A lengthy draw of his cigarette illuminated his scowl.

'Why did you leave so quickly? You were getting on so

well...'

'Piss off,' Leon said, smoke billowing from his mouth. 'Did you see him touching me up? And I thought you were safe from them in this country.'

'Leon, gay people aren't dangerous.'

He dropped his cigarette and ground it into the pavement with his foot. 'Maybe not to you,' he muttered.

*

She listened to her husband call upstairs for the third time and prayed that Cinta would continue to ignore him. Then she heard movement on the stairs. The sound of the twins in the living room. The scrape of chairs being pulled out at the table.

She stared down at the food she'd prepared. No more excuses or delays. The time had arrived to serve it.

She fought the tremors and picked up the plates. Her hand gripped the porcelain. Receptors triggered. A cold and hard flash. A memory. Rejection. Her grip loosened. The plates dropped.

She stood there looking at the food. Looking at nothing. A moth's wings battered against the window. Mosquitoes zizzed and pinched in the stale light. The last line of steam tapered from the rice. No one spoke in the other room but she knew they were waiting. Waiting for food they didn't want. Waiting for her to fail again.

Her eyes scanned the kitchen. Scattered utensils. Rice everywhere. Dirty knives. Chicken bones. How was she going to clean this place up?

A fresh wave of exhaustion. Hands on her knees. Black spots splodging across her lens. She needed her *jamu*. That made it better. For a while.

Her eyes rested on the green bottle wrapped in a

brown paper. She seized it, twisted the cap and drew it to her mouth. Cold liquid burning down her throat. Thick and sour. The sting of chilli humming behind her eyes.

She took one more gulp, set the bottle down and for that one glorious moment felt renewed. She drew herself up, picked up two plates, pushed the door open with her foot and hurried into the living room. Her shivers hit as she reached the table. Rattling through her spine and down her arms. She dropped the plates onto the table. Rice spilt over the side. No time or correction that could be made. Back to the kitchen picking up the two smaller plates. Returning and blundering them in front of the twins. More spillage. Into the kitchen for a final time. Knives and forks clasped in one hand. Hurrying back to the table and dropping them in the centre. She spun around and could see inside the kitchen: she could see the end. That was when Ahmad called her name. But she couldn't answer. She just couldn't.

She shut the door and slipped down its surface. Back pressed against the wood, she listened but heard only the thudding of her heart. What did he want? Was something wrong?

Next door she heard the scrape of a chair. A pain deep in her chest. Was he going to come in? Would he see the mess inside and her on the floor and think she was crazier than he already did?

'Eat your food,' she heard him command. A loud groan from the girls. She knew they hated the food. Or was it the person who cooked it? A succession of images engulfing her mind. The twins sick and poisoned by what she'd produced. The quiet disappointment of Cinta. The look on Ahmad's face.

Tears wet her cheeks. Or was it sweat? Her heart roared and blackness encircled and all breath was sucked from her lungs. The small, airless room, dimly lit and without escape, enclosed and concaved. Draped in bleakness, she longed for relief from this harrowing loneliness but feared nothing more than the presence of others.

*

Josh took a gulp of his Bintang beer and set it on the table. Across from him Leon was in full-rant mode, dissecting each and every moment of the day. Josh's father called Leon, "The Radio." It wasn't apt. There was no off button.

At intervals of thirty seconds or so, Leon would stutter over his words and gasp inwards, like he'd suddenly remembered to breathe, an inconvenience for which he apparently hadn't accounted.

Josh followed the beads of perspiration cracking through the icy coat of his bottle and tried to tune out.

The back of Leon's hand slapped against his bicep. 'Are you listening?'

'Intently.'

'What was I saying?'

'What weren't you saying?'

'Very funny. Right, listen up. I promised to find us some girls tonight and that's what I will do.'

'And where do you suggest we find these girls?'

'Behind you.'

Josh adjusted his position and pretended to study the drinks selection behind the bar. Out of the corner of his eye, he could see two young women stealing glances in their direction. His gaze rested on the woman that faced him. She perched on a bar stool, legs crossed, feet high-heeled, ankle bones slender and protruding. He moved up her body until their eyes met. A jump of embarrassment. He swivelled back to face Leon.

Leon's eyebrows knitted. 'Could you make it any more obvious?'

'Sorry,' Josh said, still visualising her legs. 'I doubt they'd be interested in us, anyway.'

Women fascinated and scared him in equal measure. On the trip, he'd been more popular with foreign woman than he'd been with the girls back home - probably because they couldn't understand, let alone be put off by, his clumsy attempts at chatting them up.

'We're western,' Leon said. 'They're sitting on Jalan Jaksa. They can't stop looking at us. Of course they'll be interested.'

'Maybe.'

'Don't look so worried. I'm not going to ask them over.'

'Good.'

'They're coming over by themselves.'

All his remaining breath whistled out of his nose. Peeking to his left, Josh discerned the movement of two objects – a blur of rich brown skin, layers of hair, swivelling hips. The clip of their heels, the sweetness of their perfume, the scrape of two chairs.

'Hello. Can we sit?' asked one of the already seated women.

'Please do... Hi, I'm Leon.'

'Layan? I say right?'

'Lee-on. Like a lion,' he said, making a clawing gesture with his hand. Josh had heard this line hundreds of times, in various locations, throughout the globe. He'd found it vomit-inducing the first time.

'My name is Laura.'

'What's your real name?'

'Laura is my real name.'

'And your friend?'

'She is my sister. Her name is Tina.'

Tina lifted her eyes from her drink and smiled.

'I'm Josh by the way.'

Neither woman even acknowledged that the sound had reached their ears. 'What is your country?' Laura asked Leon.

'England.'

'I know it,' Laura said. 'I live in Germany for a long time.'

'Why?'

'I marry to a German man. But he very bad man. He crazy *bule* and drink and he no good in bed and fat. Now we divorce.'

'What a lovely story...' Leon said, glancing at Josh and lifting his eyebrows a touch. 'So, I suppose you've got yourself a nice new Indonesian man?'

'No,' Laura said, holding Leon's stare.

'How about you, Tina?' Leon asked, thumbing in Josh's direction and winking.

'I am a virgin.'

'How noble,' Leon said with a barely concealed smirk.

'Never mind, you're still young. There's plenty of time,' said Josh, relieved he'd finally thought of something to say: disappointed at what he'd actually said.

*

Ahmad lowered himself onto the bed, his weight

pinging through the springs of the mattress. He took off his shirt, wiped it across his brow and dropped the damp rag to the floor. He removed his shoes and peeled back his socks and dropped them next to his shirt. A starchy, damp odour rose; a smell that would have disgusted Ahmad had it not come from his own body.

From his trouser pocket he removed an article clipped from that day's paper. He unfolded it and smoothed it out.

President Megawati Backs Stability over Principle with New Compromises

Throughout his life his father had collected, articles, papers and speeches. After his father's imprisonment, Ahmad had started his own book, cutting and saving the things he knew that his father would have been interested in. He'd been collecting cuttings for over thirty-six years. His father had never read the book.

He usually glued the articles into the book and hurried it back under the bed. His family already accused him of living in the past. The last thing he needed was for them to see the scrapbook.

As he placed the scrapbook back under the bed that night, he noticed the corner of his father's wooden trunk peeking out. He dragged it outwards, lugged it up onto the bed and settled it next to him. The trunk contained the remnants of his father's life.

He'd long thought that the truth behind his father's capture probably lay inside that trunk. Perhaps that was why he'd never opened it.

Outside, the evening call to prayer bellowed across the *kampung*. Ahmad pressed his hands on his ears and closed his eyes and waited for the beckoning to cease. Although he normally ignored the cry of the *muezzin*, he always attended Mesjid Istiqlal on Friday to pray for his family. But it wasn't enough. Maybe if he'd been a better Muslim and a stricter father, it would have been different. He smiled in resignation because he was torturing himself with fancy - if he couldn't make his own wife wear a veil, fast during Ramadan and go to the mosque twenty years ago, what chance did he have with his own daughter in modern Jakarta.

He glowered at the trunk and was glad that his father was dead, so he couldn't see how little control he had over his own wife and daughters; so he couldn't see him being abused in his own shop; so he couldn't witness his wavering faith.

With a trigger of defiance, Ahmad threw back the lid of the trunk. A musky smell met his nose, like he'd removed a novel from an old bookcase. The learned odour of his father seeping out and kissing him with its scent. He began to lift the contents out of the trunk: a beige uniform; bamboo spear; half-singed Dutch flag, maybe collected after the Jakarta riots of 1948. He pressed the flag to his face and still tasted the gasoline. He replaced it in the trunk and saw a photo of his father with the first President of the nation, Soekarno. The same photo used to hang in the living room of their house in Menteng.

Ahmad noticed a photo of baby Cinta and was about to take it out of the trunk when his eyes fell upon an object wrapped in a red cloth. He picked it up, unravelled the cloth and laid the contents on the mattress. A revolver and a case that contained six bullets. Ahmad lifted the revolver up, blew the dust from the surface and rotated it in the light.

His eyes shot to the door. Through the wall, Cinta was reading the twins to sleep. Their giggles and questions sounded sharp, like the story had just begun. Nothing moved downstairs. When Wening finishes her chores she doesn't call anyone or watch TV or go out or entertain visitors. She sits. Very still. You can't hear her, but you feel her presence. A tension that radiates. A pulse which says she's waiting. Waiting until the light goes out and he falls asleep; until she can creep into bed; until she can turn her back and spend one more loveless night next to him.

Ahmad raised the gun up level with his chin and flicked back the hammer. He shut one eye, pointed it down to the kitchen at the point that he imagined that his wife would be standing. He pulled the trigger. Click. The empty chamber revolved.

He allowed himself a smile before lowering the weapon and settling it back on the red cloth. Slowly, he burrowed his left hand to the bottom of the trunk until he met a rough cold texture. He'd found what he was looking for. He gripped the leather binding and fished out his father's own scrapbook. In it his father kept records of his correspondence and speeches. His father's friends had always said that the attention of the regime had fallen on his father after correspondence with, or a speech given to, foreign journalists. The theory said that the journalist wasn't a journalist but a spy.

Ahmad opened the book at the first page. After all those years, maybe he'd finally find out the truth.

*

As the conversation continued, Josh watched the sisters relaxing into their respective roles. Laura screeched with laughter, opened her mouth in shock, frowned with every muscle of her face. Tina spoke when addressed, her face inexpressive, demeanour calm. Laura ordered cocktails. Tina sipped on a coke. Laura directed her conversation at Leon. Tina ignored Josh.

After a quick glance, the two females excused themselves and went to the toilet.

'Right, quick before they get back,' Leon said. 'What do you think about them?'

'Well, they're nice and –'

'Yes, obviously but do you think they're prostitutes?'

Josh's eyes rolled skywards. 'Why do you ask that every time we talk to locals?'

'That's exactly why I ask. Because they're talking to us.'

'So every woman that talks to us must be a prostitute?'

'They aren't two women working in the market or walking down the street. One,' the index finger of Leon's left hand slapped the palm of his right, 'they're in a bar on the main street of the traveller area. Two,' two fingers aloft: both slapped against his palm, 'they've given themselves ridiculous English names. Three, they're out drinking on a Tuesday.'

Evidence totted up, three fingers thrust in front of Josh's face.

'The chatty one is pretty confident,' Josh said. 'Maybe she's a... you know.'

Leon couldn't finish the swig of his beer quick enough. 'Don't be daft. She's far too loud. Prostitutes don't have that amount of energy. It's the other one.'

'Her sister, Tina?'

'Yes, of course... hang on,' Leon wiping away the splutter from around his mouth. 'She's not her sister! And her name's not Tina either! And don't tell me you believed that virgin nonsense?'

'Why wouldn't I?'

'Because it's obviously bullshit! Who just announces to two strangers they are a virgin? Like that's some kind of normal small talk.'

'What does it matter? She isn't a prostitute. She's far too sweet.'

'Oh not this...you better not pull that Pretty Women shit again.'

'What are you talking about?'

'Meeting some local bird and getting all loved up and thinking you can save her.'

'That happened once.'

'Twice. Plus don't think I don't know you still email them both.'

'So what if I do?'

'It's a waste of time. You'll never see them again.'

'I might do...'

'You're a mug. Any girl that acts even a little bit bashful and you think they're some sort of princess. Trust me, that Tina girl, or whatever her real name is, has had plenty of men. The type that pay. It's a set up.'

'No, it's not,' Josh said.

'I haven't seen a performance as well rehearsed as this since Riverdance. That shy one is one hundred per cent hooker if I –'

'Heads up,' Josh said, spotting the girls' return. 'Just give them a chance. OK?'

'Fine,' Leon said, adjusting the flow of his hair, 'but I'm on the loud one.'

*

Outside, the *kampung* rocked to the nightly buzz. Those long, dry season nights where women congregated outside houses; children tore through the streets; men retreated into the long shadows and gambled away the ghosts of boredom.

And as the cockroaches zinged, Cinta's soft voice read to the twins and plates clattered downstairs, Ahmad crouched on his bed in the last wash of light, staring at the scrapbook of his dead father.

He folded back the cover, pinched the first page and turned it over. His index print greased the decaying paper. That small destruction almost made him stop, until he saw his father's scrawl and the date at the top of the page:

28 September 1955

Almost forty seven years before. When he was more or less the age of the twins next door. Although he strained to remember specific events, something he wouldn't forget was the feeling. A time of hope and urgency; visits from important-looking people; furrowed brows and late night debates. It was also a time of uncertainty and social unrest. But in the house Ahmad felt sheltered from the rioting; the thousands of hungry and poor camped outside the train station; the swells of people moving down the street, shouting and chanting, wielding placards, ribbons and banners.

He licked his finger, turned the page and started to read a copy of a letter his dad had addressed to a man named Rahim Sulai, of Singapore:

Dear Rahim,

Thank you for your letter and kind words. It heartens me that you show such interest in our country at this historic time. I will endeavour to answer your

questions about both myself and my country and hopefully enlighten you as to our years of struggle. I write on the eve of Indonesia's first democratic elections. Tomorrow millions of people will vote to elect members of the People's Representative Council.

After years of war and disputes, victories and defeats, we as a nation stand on the precipice of democracy. The moment has come for self-rule. I hope we shall prove ready for this task.

As I mentioned in my previous letter I was born in 1921, deep into the long and, at times, oppressive rule of the Dutch. This day, for me, and many of my generation, appeared unattainable. In the late 1930s, our underground movement foresaw a future where the Dutch Indies would become its own country with one motherland, one people, one language: Indonesia. Through the long years of the War of Independence we fought for this future without knowing if the next day would come. But to die for its conception was preferred to living without its hope.

The word choice, the cadence, the optimism. His father at the dinner table sermonising; sitting on his knee whilst his father told historic tales of their great land; those long, boring speeches his mother would take them to watch in must-filled auditoriums. A big sickening mass formed in his throat; the mass that choked him each time his father came alive in his mind; that choked him still, all those years after their parting.

In those days, and throughout World War II, the nationalist movement was underground and orchestrated by radical youth groups. Politically and spiritually naive we made few gains until the historical fluke that led us to this point today: the Japanese invasion during World War II. The Japanese forces expelled the Dutch, occupied the Dutch Indies and promised independence within the Japanese empire. Although many of us doubted this promise, their resolve was never tested as the events of Hiroshima and Nagasaki led the Japanese to surrender the Pacific and withdraw from Indonesia.

Mobilised and ready, we, the nationalists, took advantage of the power vacuum that existed between the Japanese exit and the Allied Forces arrival. On 17th August 1945 the leaders of our movement, Soekarno and Mohammad Hatta, declared an independent Indonesia.

This declaration was not recognised by the Dutch who tried to reclaim their former colony. Yet, in the post-nuclear world the Dutch found a different land to the one that they had left a few years previously. Throughout the islands across the archipelago, the people revolted against their return. For many Merdeka Atau Mati (Freedom or Death) was not merely a slogan but their destiny. I saw friends injured and family members die for the cause. After nearly four years of guerrilla warfare, in 1949, the Dutch surrendered and the nation of Indonesia was officially born. Despite the victory, the toughest battles for this fledgling nation had yet to be fought.

However, with these difficulties came hope and

nothing brings hope like renewal. In 1950, nearly a year after the declaration of Independence was recognised, my first son, Ahmad, was born. He was followed a year later by a brother, Salim, and just last year by our first daughter, Misbah. They, like millions of others born after Independence, form a new generation; children of the revolution; the first Indonesians.

This should bring us strength. This is the generation that will take our country forward and establish what we have long known: that this is among the finest lands on Earth.

Ahmad put the book down on the mustard-coloured blanket. How disappointed his father would be to see the country now.

*

Leon and Laura left the bar linking arms. Josh and Tina followed behind. They reached an intersection and gazed at the electrifying skyline. Neon whizzed across the billboards. Cathedrals of commerce smouldered orange into the blackness above.

They dashed across a road lit by hundreds of car lights, passed a queue, nodded to the doorman and entered the Hard Rock Café.

Inside, Josh, Leon and Laura sat at a table next to the dance floor while Tina excused herself and approached a group of young females. She greeted them without affection. They didn't speak but instead grouped together and scanned the bar area. Their attention fixed upon a group of older white men seated nearby. A man with a pot belly and white moustache clambered to his feet. The girls closed inwards; eyes elsewhere; indifference personified. The man lumbered over to Tina and kissed her on the neck. She jumped with feigned surprise.

Josh swivelled in his seat, 'Are you watching this?'

Leon was disappearing into the cloak of dry ice, hand in hand with Laura. Josh scanned the empty table before springing to his feet. He wasn't going to be alone again whilst Leon went home with another woman. He walked up to Tina and tapped her on the shoulder. She halted her conversation with the moustached man and turned around. No glimmer of recognition or interest touched her face. The man wrapped his arm round her, eyeballed Josh and led her away. They settled in a padded and snuggled together.

Josh felt a prod in his ribs and turned to meet Leon's mirthful eyes. 'Where did you come from?'

'I was getting us a drink when I saw you sleazing. Gunned down again?'

Josh scratched his jaw and looked away.

'Come on,' Leon said. 'Don't tell me you're going to get down about this like you always do?'

'I might do...'

'Listen, Laura just told me that Tina fleeces old guys.' Leon looked Josh up and down. 'And, let's be honest, you don't exactly look like you're worth a lot.'

'Thanks...'

'What I mean is it's nothing to do with you except you're not rich and old.'

'And how do you know Laura isn't going to fleece you?'

'Fleece me of what?' Leon said. 'The five quid I've got in my pocket?'

'It doesn't work like that and you know it.'

'Nah, she works in a travel agent's near here apparently. She's got her own money.'

'I take it you're going to be with her for the rest of the night?'

'Hopefully.'

'Fine, I'll leave you to it.'

'No, you don't need to do that,' Leon said, his encouraging pats on the back feeling more like pushes towards the exit.

*

Each time Ahmad heard a creak, his eyes shot to the door to check that it wasn't his wife or daughter. Yet through these sound hallucinations he searched his father's scrapbook for the reason for his capture.

He turned the crumbling pages, pausing to scan things that caught his eye or to recall a headline or a photograph. He didn't linger long. What he sought, he found amongst the material from 1967. A speech to a group of foreign journalists investigating the turmoil that engulfed the state. Ahmad read the words for the first time:

Good evening and thank you for coming. Firstly, and with the knowledge that many of your colleagues have long since fled the country, I would like to salute your bravery in attending tonight's speech.

Last week, the March 11 Decree made official what had been the reality for months: that General Suharto now governs Indonesia. This brings to an end over twenty years of rule by our founding father and first president, Soekarno.

It took the Dutch centuries of extraction and extortion, battles and bargaining to collect the 17,000

islands, coral reefs and rocks that make up Indonesia – a land mass that spans over an eighth of the equator. Their withdrawal in 1949 led to the amalgamation of three hundred ethnic groups who spoke more than two hundred different languages. The Muslims of Java, Animists of Papua, Christians of Flores, Hindus of Bali and many others became officially, one. For two decades President Soekarno, the fabled orator, master propagandist, idol and demogogue, has preached unifying ideology to these diverse religions, cultures and ethnicities. He battled to keep this country together: building monuments; hailing the heroes of the revolution; decrying our former colonial masters; fighting off attempts to set up Islamic states in west Java, Aceh and south Sulawesi; even surviving a CIA sponsored coup.

Yet in 1959, under strain from these competing interests and the perceived inefficiency of parliament, Soekarno introduced "Guided Democracy" - a move labelled as the creation of a dictatorship by his opponents. I concede that in the following years, his rule became increasingly defiant. As you may be aware he increased anti- western rhetoric, removed Indonesia from the UN and started a confrontation with the newly-formed republic of Malaysia.

His detractors claimed Soekarno's foreign policy merely diverted attention from the failing economy and the increasing influence of the Communist Party of Indonesia, the PKI. Surging inflation, poverty and starvation were attributed to the rising membership of the Communist Party – which at its peak had over three and a half million members, making it, at the time, the largest communist party outside Russia and China. Soekarno, whose beliefs mix nationalism, religion and communism (in an ideology he called Nas-A-Kom) moved closer to the Communist Party– a position which, at the height of the Cold War, did not go unnoticed by the USA and her allies.

It is believed that the President's increasingly erratic behaviour and rumours of his ill-health led the competing international and nation factions to ready themselves for a seizure of power.

Yet ultimately Soekarno's downfall was triggered by the events of 30 September 1965. In the early hours of the morning, six of the most senior Indonesian army generals were assassinated. Subsequently, two battalions advanced and occupied Merdeka Square in Central Jakarta. They took control of the radio station and announced that they had saved President Soekarno from an attempted coup masterminded by these slain army generals. Their opponents claimed that in reality it was the battalions and their supporters who were attempting a coup and not the dead generals. As confusion reigned, a lesser-known general called Suharto stepped forward. By the end of the day, Suharto had managed to regain control of the army and remove the occupiers of Merdeka Square.

While to many a reasoned judge, this affair was merely an internal army dispute, the official story has become that General Suharto saved the land from a communist coup. Although such assertions are still subject to claim and counter-claim, what has followed is not open to debate: the armed militias, the hunt for communists, the indiscriminate beatings, the rounding up of both Communist Party members and non-supporters, the disappearance of friends, civil servants, activists, trade unionists and teachers. All of this approved and encouraged by the supposed saviour of our nation, Suharto.

I am here today to beseech you to focus on what is happening in our country. The massacres in the past and those yet to come. All against an enemy conveniently created and fictitious in substance. These crimes do not rid our country of enemies or conspirators or communists, but of innocent people: put to death in order to increase the power of President Suharto, a man not fit to govern this or any other nation.

Ahmad slapped the cover of the scrapbook shut. So this was the speech that many years later his father's friends had speculated caused his downfall. Ahmad had recently read that it was estimated that the anti-communist *pogroms* killed half a million people over an eighteen month period between 1965 and 1967. His father had made that speech well over a year into that craze.

Ahmad pounded his fist on the mattress. Why did his father utter those words in public after Suharto had taken power? Did he think of his family before he did it? What other speeches had he made? Did he see himself as a martyr or did he have a death wish?

Ahmad was sixteen when they took him away. His

father, despite not being a member of the PKI, a communist or a sympathiser was placed into category B with other ambassadors, cabinet ministers and journalists loyal to Soekarno. In many ways he was fortunate: his classification led to imprisonment and torture, rather than death.

As members of his party were eliminated or imprisoned, the deposed President Soekarno died under house arrest in 1970, unreported and without mourning, his dream of Indonesia lost and forgotten in a swathe of fear and violence. Suharto did not attend the funeral.

A week after his father was taken away the men with the suits came around. They were polite but firm.

Ahmad father's role in the war of Independence and loyalty to President Soekarno had been rewarded with a high ranking position in the civil service and a house in the administrative district of Menteng. His father's punishment for his loyalty to President Soekarno was Ahmad, his two siblings, Salim and Misbah, and his mum carrying boxes out of their house, along those manicured lawns to a waiting minibus. Inside neighbouring houses, government officials and foreign dignitaries sat and watched and wondered who was next.

They moved in with an elderly uncle of his mother, who lived alone in the Sumur Batu area of central Jakarta. The house had a single living room and kitchen, a bedroom and an outside toilet. It baked in the dry season; flooded in the wet season. The house was less than two kilometres away but for Ahmad it could've been another world. After growing up in an elite area of Menteng, he found it difficult to adjust to the complex life of the *kampung*. Outsiders were treated with suspicion -

particularly those who were 'communists.' In the urban village doors remained open; all business was known and openly discussed. But with the lack of privacy came community and with community came loyalty and, in time, acceptance.

Four months after their arrival, his mother's uncle died. They decided to stay a bit longer. On a temporary basis, of course, until their father returned.

Ahmad was sat in that same house more than thirty years later.

A brisk knock at the door. It opened before he had the time to respond. Cinta stood in the breach. Her brow furrowed as she inspected him and the contents of the room.

*

On stage a man dressed in a sparkling black cat suit played an electric guitar. He dropped to his knees and leant back; his body moving in unison with his instrument; great licks of sound blasting from the amplifiers. Leon watched Laura dancing and gazing at him, her expression sensual, almost pleading. With the final chord swirling around the room, she collapsed onto the seat next to him, flicked back her hair and leaned in until her lips brushed his cheek. 'We go to your hotel?'

'My hotel?' His throat contracted into a slow gulp. 'We can't.'

'Why?'

'Because... Josh will be in the room.'

'No problem.' Her foot ran up his calf. 'I know another place.'

*

Back in the guest house, Josh stood in that stale

sweatbox of a bathroom with its tin door and rope for a lock and scrubbed his teeth and glared at the mirror and despised what he saw. He wasn't the best looking, and didn't have Leon's confidence or charisma, but didn't understand why women never wanted him. He threw his brush into the sink and spat the white froth down the drain. As he left the bathroom, he heard the grate of a key in the lock.

The door opened. In came Leon. He walked straight to his bag and started rattling through its contents. 'Quick. Help me find a condom.'

'I'm not in the mood tonight. I've got a headache.'

'Not funny,' Leon said, on his hands and knees searching under the bed. 'Help me, please.'

'Is it not in its *rightful place*?'

'Stop it.'

Josh picked up his backpack, unzipped the front pocket, rummaged around, found two condoms and threw them to Leon, 'There.'

Leon caught them up and studied the packet.

'What are you doing?' Josh said.

'Checking the sell by date.'

Josh stalked across the room and tried to rip the packet from Leon's hand. They wrestled on the floor.

'Gwwff offff,' Leon said, from under Josh's armpit.

'Give them back now,' Josh said, squeezing his grip tighter round Leon's neck.

Leon kicked his legs and managed to gain the leverage to wriggle free. He scampered across the room, crouched on his haunches and scrutinised his assailant. One hand rubbed his head; the other clasped the condom packet. 'What the hell is wrong with you?'

'Why should I give you a condom when all you do is take the piss?' Josh said.

'I wasn't taking the piss. It's just you've had them since the beginning of the trip and God knows how long you before that. I'm not taking any risks.'

Josh took two steps back and sat on his bed. 'Well, I don't blame you... where is she?'

'Outside. If she's gone, I blame you.'

'Where are you going?'

'She knows a hotel that does rooms by the hour.'

'Classy,' said Josh, watching him head towards the door.

'Leon.'

'What?'

'Be careful.'

Leon nodded and went out the door.

*

Cinta stepped inside the bedroom and shut the door. Ahmad watched her eyes complete a slow lap of the room and pictured the scene from her perspective. A bare-chested man, overweight and old, a wooden trunk next to him, its contents spilled across the bed.

Her hard, beautiful features tensed in disapproval. Hundreds of events from the pretty girl beaming in the photo that lay next to him.

'What are you doing?' Cinta said.

Ahmad glanced down to the red cloth next to him and remembered the revolver. He picked up a photo of her as a child and handed it to her. She stepped into the room hesitantly, seemed to cough and cover her nose, before taking the picture from him. He drew red cloth and closer to his right thigh and out of her sight. 'You've changed a lot since then?'

She glanced at the picture before laying it face down on the bed. 'Why are you looking through grandfather's stuff?'

'I'm not.' Ahmad heard the defensiveness in his tone. 'I'm just tidying up.'

'Still putting articles into that scrapbook?'

'You know about that?'

'Why should I put the twins to bed while you sit in here reminiscing? And what about,' her arm flailed towards downstairs, 'her?'

'Cinta, remember to whom you speak.'

A long, cold stare. She turned and left, failing to close the door on her way out.

*

Leon tiptoed across the reception of the hotel, trying not to awake the owner, who was curled up on a rug, his belly rising with each sleep-filled breath.

Outside Laura waited, one hand draped on her hip, her heeled foot pressed against the wall. She pushed off the brick, tottered two small steps, rose to her tiptoes and kissed his cheek.

They went down the lane in silence, touching but not holding hands. Water ran through the gutters, slithering in the moonlight, murky and grey. The odour of urine and stagnant water. Two rats darted across their path. A girl crouched under a porch light in front of a closed gate, white make-up masking her brown skin. As they passed, she sucked her teeth making a wet-sounding hiss.

Laura's nose scrunched up in disgust. 'I hate that tramp,'

'How do you know that word?'

She pinched his hand. 'I know many things.'

They stepped onto the Jalan Jaksa. Laura pointed to a single-story building across the road. 'We go there.'

They walked parallel to the spiked iron perimeter, went through a gate to a doorway, crossed a grimy floor and stopped at a desk. One man leant against its top. Another sat behind it. They stared at the couple.

Laura spoke in Indonesian, exchanging sharp words with the man behind the desk. She turned to Leon, 'The room is 25,000 rupiah for one hour.'

Leon dug his hand into his jeans pocket, took out the money and dropped it on the desk. The man behind the desk held the keys out, his expression a mixture of a grimace and a grin. The other man, who had not taken his eyes off Laura, stretched forward and took the keys. Overweight with deep stubble burrowing into his face, he dangled the keys in front of her, his hazel eyes leering with delight. Laura snatched the keys, clasped Leon's hand and led him to the stairs. Laughter followed their ascent.

They sat on the solitary bed in a windowless room.

'Who was that?' asked Leon.

'I work in a travel agent. He is my boss, Jusuf.'

'He doesn't look Indonesian.'

'He is born here but some blood is Arab. This makes him very proud. He own half this street.'

'What did he want?

'He wants me... he gets me sometimes,' her legs crossing and uncrossing, fingers curling her hair, 'when I want something.'

'What is it you want from me?'

She moved in and kissed his neck. Her tongue worked its way down to his chest. She withdrew and looked at him, her eyes two saucers of darkness. 'You will see.'

She climbed on top of him, straddling his waist. Her weight pressed down on him and she clasped the back of his hair before drawing her nails down his back. Her kisses moulded into faint bites, great gusts of passion panting from her mouth.

'Wait,' Leon said, his hand flapping towards the door. 'Is it locked?'

She slapped his arm down and gripped his biceps and pushed him back onto the bed. He thudded back on to the mattress, the smell of damp wood and old cushion hitting his nose. She rose and took two steps backwards. Her skirt dropped to the floor. She pivoted and eased out of her underwear, looking back towards him, her back arching as she returned to upright. She waited, staring at him with an overbearing intensity. Leon studied her and couldn't meet her eyes and pleaded for her to break the impasse.

'You say nothing?' she said.

'What should I say?'

'Tell me to come to you. Tell me you need me.'

Leon adjusted his position and swallowed. 'Come to me.'

She strode to the bed and stood over him. 'Tell me.'

'... come to me... I need you.'

Her hand slapped off his thigh. 'Take off your clothes.'

Leon looked down at his clothes and back at her. He sat up and pulled off his t-shirt over his head and dropped it on the floor.

'Everything.'

Leon undid the buckle of his belt, yanked down his shorts and boxers and kicked them off. His heart roared as he watched her taking in his body, her upper teeth biting down upon her bottom lip. A film of sweat glistened on her skin as she crawled on top of him. She pinned his wrists over his head and reached down and gripped him tightly, her hand easing up and down.

'Laura... wait.'

Her finger rested against his lips. She hovered over him before gradually easing him inside her.

Crouched over him, her hips raised and dropped, each impact rattling through her torso, rippling up to her breasts. 'Stop,' Leon said. 'Condom...' his words lost in the frenzy.

He tried to think of anything but the tight wet grip; her body; the slap of their flesh colliding. Rolling his eyes back into his head, he clenched, like his survival depended on it.

A sudden rush; an anguished cry; his body juddered and relaxed. Laura slowed and then stopped. Released from their clench, he rolled over.

'Finished already?' she said.

The haze lifted, he felt like he'd spat out a great joy. He tried to ignore the clarity of his thoughts as he got to his feet. How long might he regret what he'd just done?

He put on his shorts and flip-flops and picked up his t-shirt.

'Leon, what you do?' Laura asked from the bed.

'I've got to go,' he said. Still topless, he staggered out of the door.

*

The door slammed. Heavy footsteps and curses in the dark. A click. A flash of brilliant white. Squinting through his sleep-filled eyes, Josh saw Leon's face six inches away, his skin translucent, beads of sweat bubbling from his forehead.

'What the fuck?' Josh said, rolling over and reclosing his eyes.

Two hands tugged at his shoulder. 'Get up.'

Josh huffed and sat up and rested on his elbows. 'What time is it?'

'I've got AIDs. She knew the guys in the hotel. Who the hell knows people in hotels? Shit, we booked the room by the hour. Who does that? Prostitutes that's who. Fuck I was wrong. I thought she was real. Oh fuck. Oh fuck. Oh fuck. I'm dead... dead.'

'What are you talking about dead?'

'I didn't wear a condom.'

'You came back here for one.'

'I couldn't stop her she was like a wild animal. Then I messed it up... again.' Leon stood up and paced the gap between their beds. 'Like I do every time. Finished before it had barely started. Three women. I've only slept with three women... and now I'm going to die. That's so unfair. Some have tens... hundreds... and I get three.'

'Three? What about all those girls you went back with?'

'Sometimes I get nervous and nothing happens. Why am I telling you this?' Leon said, kicking his bamboo matt, scattering his things over the imaginary line in the middle of the room.

Into the bathroom, swearing, the tap running, an unabated scrubbing grating through the room for the next fifteen minutes.

Josh removed the travel pillow he'd pressed against his ears and sat up again. 'What are you doing?'

'Remember that guy we met in Cambodia?' Leon said, coming out the bathroom, his genitals covered by a mass of foam. 'Said that he had been sleeping with girls there for years. Never worn a condom: never got AIDs.'

'Yes, he was an absolute sleazebag.'

'Yeah, well after you left he told me his secret - he scrubbed his dick with soap for hours after he did it,' Leon said, going back into the bathroom.

'What a load of bullshit.'

'It's not.'

'OK, believe what you want... just one thing before I try and get back to sleep'

'What?' Leon said, reappearing in the doorway mid-scrub.

'You know the next time you need to scrub your dick?'

'Yep.'

'Shut the fucking door.'

11 August 2002

Ahmad placed the rice in his mouth, chewed it into a cold mush and washed it down with a swig of water. It tasted worse than the previous night. His fork was halfway to his mouth again when the front door opened. Strong light. Thin morning air. Cinta, one foot inside, one outside the house. 'Are you ready?'

'Did you take the twins to school?'

'They finish earlier today, so you need to collect them.'

'Me?'

'Yes, mum was late last week and forgot the week before. Their teachers are asking questions.'

'I can't shut the shop early.'

'Pak, it's getting embarrassing.'

Ahmad threw his hands up in surrender. 'OK, fine... I'll pick them up.'

'Where is mum?'

'Still in bed.'

Cinta took a step into the house towards him. 'Why?'

'She's tired.'

'It's been two months. The last time she was better you said it was over.'

'It was. But it comes back sometimes. She's been to the *dukun* and has her *jamu* now.'

'She doesn't need magic potions. She needs a real doctor. Real medicine.'

'Haj Gut has treated this family for years. He treated your grandfather.'

'Grandfather's dead.'

Ahmad's eyes shot to his daughter. She bit her lip. Her voice softened. 'Sorry, I just can't do anything when she's like this. I can't see my friends. I can't practise my English. I can't –'

'Enough,' Ahmad picked up his plate and car keys and strode past Cinta, through the door and down the street. He heard the door close behind him and the patter of Cinta's flat-soled shoes following him down the *gang*.

She caught up with him. 'Why do you have the plate with you?'

'Because I don't want your mother to know that I don't want to eat her food.'

Ahmad tossed the contents amongst a pile of refuse, the residue of the brown sauce dripping from the plate swinging in his left hand.

'Perhaps it'll help if she knows.'

He stopped and faced her. 'Of course it wouldn't!'

A shadow appeared at a window above. Two women next to the drain wrung out their clothes; not looking; not missing a thing. Grasping his daughter by the forearm and leading her away. 'Don't speak about your mother like that. Not out here.'

She removed her arm with a frown and rubbed her wrist, '... sorry.'

They turned left onto a side street traipsing past lines of parked cars. They reached the car, split off to either side and climbed inside.

Ahmad put the keys in the ignition and turned. The engine spluttered but didn't start. He'd replaced the coil last month. The mechanic had also told him the starter connection was corroded but he didn't have the money to replace both.

He turned the keys again. Still it failed to fire. He glanced at Cinta. Her face remained even. He turned the key again. The engine started up and revved. He quickly put the car into gear before the engine cut out again. He reversed out and swung the car parallel to the curb and accelerated away.

Cinta turned the dial on the radio and said nothing. No sound came.

Ahmad tutted. 'If there is one more problem with this car, I'll buy another one.'

Cinta again said nothing.

They both knew he wouldn't.

*

Josh sat on a bench, sipping ice cool water and squinting through the morning glare across Merdeka Square. An outdoor exercise class squatted and lunged behind them. Men with wicker brushes swept up litter, whilst others watered the lawns. No one tried to sell or talk or bother them. 'It's nice when it's like this isn't it?' Josh said.

Leon slouched next to him picking at his fingernails and didn't reply.

Knowing that Leon's bouts of introspection usually lasted for a few minutes, Josh decided to take advantage. He slowly unzipped his bag and took out his diary. The smell of the leather binding was no less rich after six months on the road. He laid it on his lap and detached a pencil that he kept in the inside cover.

Leon's attention remained upon his fingernails. The previous night's events must have affected him if he couldn't muster a comment on the hated diary. *Put it away... If you think I came all this way to watch you scribble in a book... Don't think I don't know it's just an excuse to show off all those big words you think you know... It's worse than that reading you do...*

Despite this, Josh knew that Leon read the diary when

he wasn't around. As a consequence, writing it had become a fine balance between accurately recording what they'd been doing and winding up Leon in the process. Recognising the rawness of the events of the previous night, Josh decided to not include the details. He'd try to be nice to Leon in this entry.

11:00, 11 August 2002, Jakarta, Indonesia

Arrived yesterday on a flight from Bangkok. We got to the airport a couple of hours early. While we waited, a girl came to talk to us. Leon was joking with her (as he does) and it was hilarious.

Josh laid down his pencil. This being nice to Leon was going to be difficult. Josh glanced across at him. He looked like a drama student in his first week asked to pull a sad face. Experiencing the unusual sensation of feeling sympathy for him, Josh continued,

She asked Leon for his address. I think Thai girls do this so they can write and perhaps entice a wedding proposal. Leon gave his address as 8 London Road, London, England... which was very funny. Leon cheers up most of my days with humour like this.

Josh paused. He hoped he'd never read this and believe it was the truth.

I managed to get Leon up nice and early this morning despite his supposed hangover. I'm now sitting in Merdeka Square, which is a park in the centre of the city. We've just been up the National Monument, which is a large phallic-like object made of white marble. We went up an elevator to the observation deck. Around us sprawled Jakarta, the view through the smog extending for at least a

hundred yards. I read on a plaque (in somewhat questionable English) that the tower was commissioned by Soekarno, who was the first President of Indonesia. Apparently, the current president, Megawati, is Soekarno's daughter. She has big glasses. I don't know if people like her because the only Indonesians I talk to are trying to sell me something. You can be in a country so long and know nothing about it.

When we arrived yesterday we had time to do a bit of sightseeing. We went to a local market – an experience I'd write about if it didn't involve me reliving the experience. Leon (of course) loved it and bought the most ridiculous things he has ever purchased, which is saying something.

On the way back to the guest house we took a train. It was a busier carriage than even the hard seat section on the Chinese trains. Leon sat on the roof and seemed to make quite a few friends. I would have gone up myself... if it wasn't for the speed, the electric wire and the fact it was a MOVING TRAIN.

That wasn't even the most dangerous part of our trip back. We were crossing Jalan Jaksa (which is just your run of the mill, cheap, sleazy, backpacker street) and further down the street a man pulled out in a car. He was driving too fast in the first place and I'm sure he sped up when he saw us before braking at the last moment. There was hate in his eyes. His daughter looked petrified. Leon said that he was probably just having a bad day but I don't know. I'm still not sure if Indonesians are fascinated by us or resent us or both. I suppose we will find out as the trip continues.

We are staying at a fairly standard guest house. The owner is clearly in the closet. He doesn't take much notice of me but has taken a real liking to Leon. Leon pretends he doesn't like the owner of the hotel but I can see chemistry between them. They would make a really cute couple.

Although he recognised the last section was fairly childish and negated all the previous niceties, the thought of Leon's face when he read it, was too amusing for Josh to remove it.

Josh settled his diary back in his bag and did up the zip. 'Come on then,' he said to Leon. 'What can we do to cheer you up?'

'Nothing. I want to go home.'

'To the guest house?'

'No, to England.'

Josh smiled. 'I don't think that's possible right now.'

'More's the pity...'

'Do you want to talk about it?'

'No!'

'Sorry for asking.'

'Do you have any idea how hungover I am?'

'Are you sure it's not the AIDs kicking in?'

'That's it,' Leon said, slapping both hands on the bench and pushing himself onto his feet. He strode off through a gaggle of passing school kids. Boys in brown trousers and orange shirts leapt out of the way. A separate line of girls wearing white-head scarves giggled in polite amusement as he stormed past. Josh ran through the void created, smiling and apologising to the children on the way through. He caught Leon near the entrance to the park. 'Slow down, will you? I was only joking. There's no way you've got AIDs.'

Leon stopped and spun around, 'You think?

'One hundred percent. Listen, why don't we eat in that café that you've been going on about?'

'The one under the underpass? You said that you didn't know where it was.'

'I only said that because I didn't want to go.'

'But you do now?'

'If it cheers you up.'

'Ah, thanks Josh,' Leon said, rubbing his hands together. 'What do you think they sell?'

Josh watched the grimace on Leon's face warming into the widest of grins – the cure for AIDs found in a Jakartan café.

*

The outdoor café amounted to a smattering of plastic stools nestled in deep shade. The ceiling, six feet above, rose diagonally until it met a stanchion which supported the concrete expressway that passed above. Outside, the bright contrast of the morning sun hid the details of the street. The triangular enclave reverberated with chatter; the hiss of the food; the vibrations of the traffic above.

To the passing Jakartans, the patrons of this establishment were probably unremarkable. A ragtag of *tukang jalan*: drivers, street sellers, storeowners and hustlers. To Leon and Josh they were the daring and daunting; the exotic and masculine; the real men of Jakarta. Likewise, in England Josh and Leon were two nineteen year-olds with without jobs, qualifications or money. But to the *tukang jalan* they were *orang asings* - tall, rich people of the West.

Each group stared at the other with the affectionate fascination that unfamiliarity brings; two gas cylinders and a wooden stall the centrepiece of the impromptu party.

Josh joined the queue behind two other men and looked for a menu, a card, a board – anything which might give him an idea as to what he was about to eat.

Leon clapped his hands together. 'Ready to order?'

A sea of oil bubbled in a black iron wok. Condensation dripped from the ceiling. Flies crept across the raw meat that lay exposed on the counter. Josh's brow lowered, 'How do we know what we'll be eating?'

'We won't. That's the exciting part.'

The two men in front took their food and departed. The cook, illuminated by the blue roar of the stove, nodded a greeting. '*Sop ayam*?' he said, shielding his eyes from the spitting fat.

'Yes, *dua*,' said Leon, holding up two fingers.

'*Tahu goreng*?'

'Yes, *dua*.'

'*Mie bakso*?'

'Yes, *dua*.'

'*Kopi*?' the cook asked, his smile broadening with each of Leon's confirmations.

'Yes, *dua*.'

Josh elbowed Leon in the ribs. 'Stop it. '

'Stop what?'

'Yes *dua*, yes *dua*, yes *dua*,.... "Want some rat?" Yes *dua*... "How about a punch?" Yes *dua*.'

'Listen, we've got to take advantage – you won't get food like this when we go home.'

Without a further word, Josh watched Leon (the man who could turn meals into feasts, walks into quests, shopping trips into sprees) gather up his food and set off in search of a spare plastic stool.

They devoured their chicken soup, fried tofu and rice, meatballs and noodles before resting their empty plastic containers at their feet.

'Well, what did you think?' Leon said.

'I'll let you know tomorrow...'

'Just admit it was great.'

'OK,' Josh said. 'I admit it. It was great.'

Josh picked up his coffee from under the stool and took a sip. He didn't mind that the glass stung his touch, that the liquid was unnaturally sweet or that the granules stuck between his teeth. It was moments like this that he regretted the relentless call of the road. His joy weakened to contentment and then faded into contemplation.

'I know what you're thinking,' Leon said, studying Josh's face. 'We need to get out of here.'

'Well, the opposite actually.'

'Yeah, I'm getting to like this place but you know... we should leave tomorrow.'

Josh exhaled upwards, ruffling the hair of his fringe. 'Can't we just slow down for once? You know enjoy a place, maybe meet some people...'

'We've only got two months until we go home. We won't be able to go sailing with the Bugis pirates, go to a Toraja funeral or whale hunting in Lembata if we stick around here too long.'

'Been reading the guidebook, by any chance?'

'Of course.' Leon took a final glug of his coffee and put the glass at his feet. 'Right, we go home from Sydney on the 14th October. So we should book a flight from Bali to Sydney on the 13th.'

'Don't you want to spend any time in Australia?'

'I'm an explorer not a tourist.'

'Sorry, I forgot...'

'I saw a travel agent's on Jalan Jaksa. Let's go there after we finish here and get the flight booked while it's still cheap.'

'OK' Josh said quietly.

'October the 13th...' Leon made a clucking sound out of the corner of his mouth. 'Man, that's going to be the most depressing day of our lives. Do you think we'll just go home and end up working in offices and being boring like our dads?'

'Our dads don't work in offices.'

'You know what I mean. Will we become, you know, *those guys*?'

Josh gave Leon a long sideways look. Wild unkempt hair. Eyes roaming from one point of interest to the next. Restless limbs jiggling. 'I'm sure *you* won't, Leon.'

*

Cinta stapled the receipt to the photocopy of the ticket and laid it in her filing tray. If she finished this set, she might be able to finally get around to organising the brochures strewn across the customers' waiting area. No one else seemed concerned about them: they must create such a bad first impression.

She glanced up and noticed Jusuf striding towards her. Gravity sunk to the pit of her stomach. She looked back down at her desk and awaited the inevitable: a lecture about the work she'd failed to process the night before and still hadn't done.

'Hello Cinta.'

She daren't look up – like the very sight of her features

might remind him of her incomplete task.

'I want you to do something for me.'

'Yes, I will start them –'

'Go to the front desk, there is no one there.'

She looked into his eyes searching for the joke but for once he wasn't smirking. 'Me?'

'Yes.'

She didn't serve customers. That was the job of Elok or another of the 'pretty ones.' She fumbled around her desk and located a notepad.

'You don't need that. Just go.'

Cinta rose from her chair and rushed to the counter that ran the breadth of the shop front. Her breath quickened as she waited. Finally she might get a chance to practise her English.

She rested her arms on the counter and leant forward. Too casual. She stepped back and folded her arms. Too standoffish.

A couple ambled past the window. Her stance forgotten, Cinta watched them stop next to the entrance. The woman removed her sunhat, tied back her auburn hair and put the hat back on her head. She linked her partner's arm and they carried on down the street.

Hands behind the back. Too exposed. Intertwined at the front. Too prudish.

The crow of that unmistakeable laugh. Cinta peeked over her shoulder. Elok, glowing from her latest re-application of make-up, had returned and was talking to Jusuf. She left him with a lingering smile and sauntered over to relieve Cinta.

The door jangled and two men entered the shop. A tall man with blonde hair led the way. He bounded towards the desk, his green eyes curious, head twitching as he took in the shop. Behind him, followed a smaller man with light, brown hair. He looked up only when he reached the counter, his features soft, eyes light blue.

Cinta stepped forward and opened her mouth. No words came. The waft of orchid perfume. High-heels on tiled floor. Elok rounded the counter and walked to them in that way of hers – that strut which drew attention to all the right parts of her body. She approached the blonde man, skipped the last metre and launched herself into his arms. He returned her hug, freed himself from her clasp and took two steps back. Crimson burned away his earlier confidence. The smaller man viewed their clinch with an amused expression. He stole a glance in her direction and became more serious. He looked down and then looked again. She held his gaze. Recognition - but from where?

He cleared his throat, 'Hi, I'm Josh.'

'My name is Cinta. It is my pleasure to meet with you,' she said, her English sounding stilted to her own ear. She urged herself to relax, which made her increasingly tense.

'Have we met before?'

'I am not sure.'

'You look familiar.' His eyes opened wider. 'You were in a car with an older man. Yes, yesterday. Just outside here on this street... he kind of drove at us.'

The sounds replayed in her head and separated into words and the clearest phrase, 'drove at us,' registered and connected with the heavenly face before her. 'Oh *maaf*... I mean, I am so sorry. He is a bad driver.'

'It's fine. No harm done.'

Cinta brushed her hands down her clothes and said, 'I am sorry again, Mr Josh.'

'No problem. Really...' He eyes lowered to a map of Jakarta laid out on the counter. 'Can I ask you something about the city?'

'Of course.'

He opened his left hand, which had been clamped shut by his side, and put a piece of paper on the counter. She lifted it up. It was still warm from his touch.

'Can you tell me where this place is and how to get there?'

'OK. I try.' She focused on the sweat stained writing and resisted the strange urge to press it to her nose. 'Taman Mini park? You have very bad writing, no?'

'Yes,' Josh said, returning her smile.

She took out a pen from her pocket. 'OK, you are here,' she said, touching the map with the lid. 'Taman Mini is here. It is very good. I have more information here.'

She reached across and lifted a leaflet from the rack on the adjoining wall. She put the glossy paper on the desk and opened it. 'Look, there are traditional houses from all Indonesia's islands. Also there are museums and cultural performances. Will you go this afternoon?'

'If we have time.'

'You can go with the bus. But I recommend, if you have less time and maybe a bit more money, to take a taxi. It is safer also.'

'Safer?'

'Yes. We recommend Blue Bird.'

'Is Jakarta not safe?'

'In some places no. Where do you go already?'

'The usual. Merdeka Square, the National Monument... some market. I don't know the name. It was around about,' his finger circled before jabbing against the map, 'here.'

'You go here? Why? It is not safe for tourists. There are *preman* ... how you say in English? Bad people?'

'Criminals?'

'Yes, criminals. Please also don't go here... and here... and here,' she said, her pen shooting across the map.

'Is anywhere safe?'

'Yes, most places.'

She went through the map with him circling areas of interest. She spoke in English and felt it flow and her confidence grew. When he asked a question, she understood him and answered and after she'd overcome her initial nerves it felt like a normal conversation.

'You know a lot about the city,' he said.

'Well, I live here my whole life.'

'Maybe you should be my guide...'

'Yes,' she said, the answer out her mouth before the appropriateness registered. 'Sorry, I mean if you want.'

'I'd like that,' he said.

Behind the veil of the counter, she pinched the skin on her forearm and tried not to show him how pleased that made her, 'OK, good. I do not work tomorrow.'

'Yes, that would be nice.'

Cinta looked over to the blonde man who had entered with Josh. He was taking out a credit card. He gave it to Elok who was now behind the counter in full sales mode. 'Do you need to ask your brother first?'

A look of amusement spread across Josh's face. 'He's not my brother.'

'Does he know my cousin Elok?'

'I thought her name was Laura.'

'No.'

'Has she lived in Germany?'

She laughed, 'No, she tells that to *bules*... visitors. Is she friends with your friend?'

'In a way.'

'Elok is...' She checked to her right and leaned forward over the counter until only the tips of her toes brushed the floor.

'Yes?' his breath kissing her face.

'Elok is friends with many *bules*.'

'I think that is what Leon was afraid of.'

'I am not like her.'

'I'm not like him either.'

Their eyes met and wandered nowhere else.

'Hello, how are you?' boomed a male voice.

They both jumped back from the counter. On the customer side, next to Josh, stood Jusuf. Cinta reacted first. 'I am fine, Jusuf... I mean, Mr Jusuf.'

'Not you Cinta. The gentleman customer... hello I'm the manager.'

'Hello, I'm Josh. Pleased to meet you.'

Cinta watched Josh's hand disappeared into Jusuf's fat palm.

'And how can we help you today?' Jusuf said, leaning back against the counter.

'I'm looking for a flight to Sydney from Bali,' Josh said, his voice deeper than when he'd spoken to her.

'And I am most certain Cinta has given you all the information.'

'No, we hadn't talked about it yet.'

'I am sorry sir. Cinta is... how do you say? She is a little slow.'

Josh held Jusuf's stare, his expression unflinching and

earnest. 'She's been very helpful.'

'OK, I understand,' Jusuf said. 'You are like your friend, huh? You like the Indonesian girls.'

'I don't think that has anything to do with you.'

Jusuf turned to Cinta, 'His friend was with Elok last night in my hotel.'

'In a hotel?' Cinta said.

'Yes, your cousin and that man in a hotel,' Jusuf said, his voice slow and measured, like he wanted to gauge her reaction to each word. 'My hotel. How about you?' Jusuf said, his nose crinkling as he sized Josh up and down. 'No bar girls for you last night?'

'No, of course not.'

'Mister Josh, please. We are all friends in this shop. You can tell us.'

'There's nothing to tell.'

'Let's ask Cinta,' Jusuf said with a smile. 'Do you believe him?'

She felt both their sets of eyes on her and looked down at the piece of paper with Josh's handwriting on it and knew she couldn't show any sign that contradicted the word of her boss but inside her head screamed that, 'Yes! She did believe him.'

'Sorry,' Jusuf said to Josh. 'Cinta is what we say in Indonesian, *pemalu* - very shy. Anyway, Mister Josh your friend already bought your tickets and left. Maybe you should run after him.'

Josh looked towards where his friend had stood and muttered. 'Nice of him to tell me.'

His Adam's apple lifted and dropped and met Cinta's eyes. The truth that they'd no excuse to continue their conversation passed between them but his eyes lingered and seemed to ask for something more.

Josh slowly opened his shoulders, 'OK... well... goodbye.'

'Goodbye,' Jusuf said.

Cinta looked down at her trousers and murmured the same. She couldn't bear to look up but heard his slow footsteps and the soft closing of the door.

'Cinta...' Jusuf said.

Their meeting tomorrow... she hadn't given him her phone number.

'...Cinta.'

'Yes.'

'Back to work.' Jusuf clapped his hands. 'Now!'

She returned back to her desk not feeling any regret or anger but an acceptance that this was how her life was going to be: taken for granted and demeaned; longing and missed opportunities.

She stopped. Why should it be? Because she was Indonesian? Because she was a woman? Because her father and Jusuf would disapprove?

She grabbed the nearest notepad, tore off a sheet of paper, scribbled down her number, ducked under the counter and ran out the shop onto the street.

Left then right. Nothing. Once again. Two men, disappearing down a lane. Maybe. She ran after them.

*

Ahmad reached the corner of Jalan Sumur Batu, the thoroughfare which cut through his *kampung*. He hesitated and looked down the street. To pick up his daughters he'd need to do something he avoided at all costs: walking down that street. But what was he meant to say when Cinta asked him? That he couldn't walk down the street to their school? That it hurt too much.

He tugged his cuff up and studied his watch. 'Don't be late.' Cinta's words in the house that morning, dragging him down that abyss. The pavements were littered with parked motorbikes, crates of Coca-Cola, green gas canisters, rolled up carpets and textiles. Blasts of music accompanied the unremitting whirr of passing cars.

He walked on and rubbed his temple but the throbbing didn't abate. Ten steps on, he reached the spot. The location of the old barber's shop. The memory of the lather, dust and hair; the glint of a razor; the buzz of the waiting customers. The scent of sandalwood shaving cream, freshly laundered towels and stings of aftershave. The smell of men. The smell of another time.

An image of his father. Long sleeves and trousers covering his body, only the scars across his knuckles and cheeks hinting at what he had suffered in prison. As he hurried around the shop his breath was quick and sharp, like he was trying to pant away the pain that shot through his limbs. But he didn't stop. Well, not until the shutters came down and he sank into his chair. Skin hung from his gaunt cheekbones. Eyes dull and retreated into his skull. You didn't speak to him then. What could you say anyway? You cleaned up and you went home.

It was 1979 when his father was finally released. He never spoke of his ordeal.

Ahmad stepped around in a circle. The Gado-Gado Betawi restaurant, the Rendra brothers' motorbike repair shop, Mela's laundrette, Ongky's carpet trade. People and businesses. Grandfather, father and son. The same families, the same shops, who all those years ago, had refused to give work to his father on his release. The same people who labelled his father an enemy of the nation he'd helped to form.

That was when his father started to leave the house late at night. He'd return in the morning, distant, tired, regretful. No-one knew where he went. What he did. What he gave up. But whatever it was, when he'd saved enough money, his father opened a barber's shop on the very street that had rejected him, taking his two sons out of the factories and employing them himself.

At first only their close friends would come to the shop, loyal yet scared. But his father gradually built the business under the watchful eye of the local police. When they came to collect on Monday afternoons his father would pay without complaint; the twitch below his left eye the solitary sign of his inner torment.

All that work, all the strength of character, to set up a business, run into the ground by his son within three years of him taking him over. Strangers inside stripping out the teak wood fittings, carrying out the leather chairs and white laundered towels. The humiliation of his wife in her own *kampung*. Her barely disguised scorn. Perhaps the start of it all.

Fifteen years ago. He knew he should have let it go. But how could he stop all those thoughts, mastering him with their grim reality, as he stood there looking into what should still be his? When instead he was met with unfamiliar faces and wafts of cheap plastic. Kids, just kids, selling fake rucksacks and fake handbags and fake trainers; bringing it all back again, in sharp pincers of pain.

He looked at the shop a final time and set off towards the school.

*

Josh stalked after Leon along Jalan Jaksa and right down the side street that led to their guest house. The moment they turned the corner, Leon spun around and danced backwards. Josh watched this great burst of idiotic joy and said, 'What are you so pleased about?'

'She really does work in a travel agent.' His dimples bit into his cheeks; the ones the girls at school liked so much. 'I told you that she wasn't a prostitute.'

'No, it was *me* who told *you* that she wasn't a prostitute.'

'Who cares? I'm free again.'

'Why did you leave the shop without telling me?' Josh said.

'Why do you think?'

'Because you embarrassed yourself last night?'

'I can't have embarrassed myself that much,' Leon said, wafting a piece of paper, 'considering she gave me her number.'

'You left pretty sharp after you booked those tickets.'

'That creepy boss guy was eyeballing me. Apparently he's some sort of gangster.'

'Who would waste his time on you because?'

'I was with Laura in his hotel last night.'

'Why would he care?'

'Because he gets it on with her as well.'

Josh stopped walking. '*She* sleeps with *him*.'

'They all do apparently.'

'Not all of them I'm sure.'

'You mean not the one you were talking to?'

'Well... yes.'

'OK, everyone but her if it makes you feel better.'

'I don't get it. I mean he's a total sleazebag.'

'Not everyone is like you Josh. You know, some guys actually get laid.'

'But that Elok or Laura, or whatever her name is, is totally gorgeous.'

'I know isn't she? Great moves from me, pulling her. Put it there my man.'

Josh ignored Leon's outstretched hand. 'What are you going to do with her number?'

'This.' Leon ripped the paper in two. The pieces met the ground and drifted back towards Jalan Jaksa. 'She's already had the pleasure...'

'What for thirty seconds?'

Ignoring him, Leon rounded a mobile food car and set off down the street. 'We're leaving tomorrow anyway.'

Josh followed. 'I suppose.'

They were about to turn left into the alley towards their guest house, when Josh heard a shout. It sounded like his name. Another call. Definitely his name. He squinted back down the lane. A diminutive figure ran through the low-hanging haze, becoming clearer with each step. An electrifying shudder.

'One second,' he said to Leon. He walked towards her until they met.

'You forget your receipt,' Cinta said, pressing a piece of paper into his hand. 'Please do not forget to use it. Use it tomorrow morning.'

Josh watched her hurray back towards Jalan Jaksa. He looked down at his fist and opened his hand. A ball of paper sat on his palm.

*

A further hundred metres down the road, Ahmad reached the *taman kanak-kanak* pre-school provided by the local mosque. The spiral of the minaret. The curve of the dome. Clouds flickering shadows onto the playground floor. No uniforms, fees or curriculum here. Just a space for parents to leave their children, whilst they tried to earn enough to feed them.

Through the rails of the yard, two girls played alone on the ash black tarmac. They hopped along invisible lines, arms up in celebration, winning a game to which only they knew the rules. Rani, older by ten minutes, ran ahead chased by Nur. Hair billowing and falling down to their waists. When did it grow so long?

It was a little more than four years since their birth. They couldn't afford a night in a *Rumah Sakit Bersalin*, so two of Wening's elderly aunts delivered them in their bedroom. Ahmad sat in the next room listening to the rhythmic wails and felt useless. When he did enter the room, the aunts shooed him out, but not before he saw his wife's sweat-drenched face or her nails biting into the sheets as she wriggled in exquisite agony.

Eighteen hours after her waters had broken he was called into the room. To his surprise two daughters were placed into his arms: twins! Fighting tears, he'd gazed down at his wife lying on the bed. Her face was pallid; her body lifeless and defeated by the pain.

He'd thought that the distress of the long labour was why she initially appeared disinterested in the welfare of the girls she'd just birthed. But after several days of recovery she still didn't want to hold her babies. She took no interest in the celebratory *Ari-Ari*, after-birth ceremony or in choosing their names. She ignored their crying and refused to feed or care for them. Ahmad tried persuasion, shouting, ignoring her, veiled and explicit threats, but her demeanour remained unchanged.

Time passed. Months. Then years. She continued to avoid the twins. The girls accepted this as only children could. What other reality did they know? At what age would they realise that this wasn't normal? Would they ever?

Rani noticed him first. Then Nur. They consulted through a shared look of surprise and looked back at him. It was at that moment that he realised he'd never picked them up before. Their amazement at seeing him there shamed him.

Rani took her sister's hand and together they ran towards the gates.

*

Josh lay on his bed watching Leon stuff his possessions into his backpack.

'Listen, I was thinking...'

Leon turned out the pockets of his pair of jeans and, finding nothing, folded them in two and started to roll them up. 'What?'

'I don't know.'

'Of course you do.' Leon dropped the jeans and folded his arms. 'You've been building up to something for about thirty minutes. Lying there biting your nails, doing that disgusting heavy breathing thing. Just spit it out will you. And don't say what I think you're going to say.'

'Can we stay in Jakarta for a few more days?'

'Well isn't that a surprise. Now let me see...' Leon drummed his fingers on his chin, '...no.'

'There's still a lot more to see.'

'Like?'

'Sights...and... you know... other things.'

'Josh, come on man,' Leon said, placing his palms together and rocking them back and forth. 'We talked about this. It's been a good couple of days but I want to see coffee fields, rice paddies, volcanoes. Not pollution, rats and prostitutes. I'm here for the *real* Indonesia. I won't find it here.'

'What do you know about the real anything?'

'Oh right like that is it? At least what I say is real.'

'What does that mean?'

'You said there are a lot of sights still to see but I'm not sure. Is there another reason you want to stay?'

'You know fine well there is. I want to stay to meet up with Cinta.'

'Cinta? Wow you've even swapped names. That's cute.'

'It's not something trivial.'

'Of course it is. You met her for five minutes.'

'She gave me her number.'

'Her phone number? Whoop-di-fucking-doo! Pull yourself together, man. First time in your life you get some attention from a girl and you want to ruin the whole trip?'

'You've ruined the trip every day for me,' Josh said quietly.

'Oh it's all coming out now isn't it? Do you know the amount of people that would give their left leg to travel with me?'

'But don't you see Leon... they wouldn't... which is why you had to go with me. No one else would put up with you.'

'We're leaving tomorrow,' he crouched back down next to his bag, 'and that's the end of it.'

Josh rolled over on the bed to face away from him. 'I

don't see why you should dictate this whole holiday. It's about me as well.'

A clatter as if something was thrown. 'Well I'll leave alone then.'

A knot twisted in Josh's throat. He lay still whilst fighting his desperate need to gulp.

'Fine just ignore me then.' Feet scuffing. Objects scattering. A hand on his shoulder hauling him over. Leon leaning over him. 'And what is all this shit about me and the owner of this place?'

'What?'

Leon's finger wagged in his face. 'Saying that me and this guy make a good couple and that I'm gay.'

Josh slapped his hand away and sprung to his feet. 'What were you doing reading my diary?'

He faced his best friend, their chests touching, breath intermingling.

'Come on then.' Leon jutted out his chin, enclosing the space, eye-pressingly close. 'What you going to do?'

Josh met his fierce eyes. He knew he wasn't going to do anything: Leon knew he wasn't going to do anything. Self-consciousness overcame his anger. He slowly lowered himself back onto the edge of the mattress and looked down at his bare feet. Leon released a derisory snort and retreated to his side of the room.

'I only wrote that stuff because I knew you were reading it. And you only read it in the first place so you could laugh at me... like you've been doing your whole life,' Josh said, each word feeling like it broke a deep silence. 'Why shouldn't I have some fun at your expense for once?'

Without reply, Leon went back to packing his bag. Josh watched him pack his mementos from the places they'd visited together and glanced over to his own meagre possessions, scattered at the bottom of his bed.

12 August 2002

Josh opened his eyes and pressed the light on his Casio digital watch. It read 05:30. The door crept open. A shadow lugged objects out of the room. It carried the final item into the hall. The figure returned and checked the corners of the room before lingering at the foot of his bed. Josh clamped his eyes shut and held his breath. A pause. A deep sigh. Footsteps. The door shut, painting the room black.

*

He put the bottle on his lips and tilted back his head. No beer appeared in his mouth. He put it down on the table and pushed it towards the other empty bottle. A low clinking collision. The glint of the sun on the glass. He watched the green reflection glimmering across his vest-top and tried to avoid looking at the internet café across the street.

He took out Cinta's 'receipt' from his pocket and flattened it onto the trestle-like table. His eyes followed the pinpointed curl of words and numbers that by now he knew off by heart.

He'd been putting off calling her for over an hour and a half. One more beer then he'd do it. His hand lifted to signal to the waiter. It fell back down to his side. It wouldn't help. He hauled himself up, trapped a 20,000 note under the ash tray and left.

He waited on the pavement looking left, then right, down that long replicating street. No cars gave him the excuse he needed not to cross. After a long, deep breath, he set off across the black tarmac, knowing if he paused he would lose his nerve. He entered the internet café and met the front desk. 'Hello, can I use the phone, please?'

The receptionist lifted her head and gave him a well-practised look of utter dispassion.

'Phone... can I use?'

Her face grew blanker. Josh gestured to the vacant booth. Her head didn't move.

Josh's hand balled around the 'receipt' in his pocket. Cinta's words, 'Use it tomorrow morning,' drilling in his mind. The clock above the desk ticked further away from noon. Frustration trembling through his body, he moved closer and stuck out his thumb and little finger and waved an imaginary phone inches in front of the receptionist's face. Her eyes widened as if to say, you should have said before.

She rose and led him to the wooden booth. He stepped inside and closed the door. The dryness of the plywood cubicle. The taste of sawdust. A sliver of sweat meandered down his face. He stared at the receipt, lifted the receiver and pressed its grease-licked surface against his ear. His heart rate increased with the tap of each digit. A second passed. A scratch-filled ringing.

'Halo, Ahmad,' a man's voice said.

The words he'd rehearsed trapped in his voice box.

'Halo, Ahmad,' the man repeated.

'Yes, hello,' scraped out of his mouth, 'can I speak to Cinta, please?'

A pause. A grating sound like the grinding of teeth.

'Hello? Cinta? Can I speak to Cinta, please'

Breath the only reply.

'Hello?'

He withdrew the receiver, studied it and placed it against his ear. The drill of the dialling tone. He held the paper up to the sooty yellow light and dialled again.

Twenty long rings: no answer. She'd given him the wrong number.

The recollection like a trance. Pushing open the door; out the internet café forgetting to pay; meeting the terrifying brightness of the day. Across the road without looking and into Jaksa Travel. The cool of the air conditioning, the force of attention, twenty eyes, ten silent mouths, drawn to the manager leaning on the counter.

'Hello, is Cinta here?'

Jusuf's brow lowered. 'Cinta?'His fingers drummed on the newspaper that lay before him. 'Oh yes Cinta. Small girl. Like a child. She works... sorry excuse my English. I make so many errors. I mean, she worked here.'

'She worked here?'

'That is correct, no? In the past tense. When something ends. How do you say?' He formed a two-fingered gun with his hand, pursed his lips and puffed out a bang.

'You fired her?'

'Yes, that is it. Yesterday, she went outside without my permission.'

'You mean after I left?'

He picked up his newspaper and folded it into a single page. 'Yes, it may have been that time.'

'She was giving me a receipt.'

'This is what she said. But I know more, you see. Cinta did not have a receipt because it was Elok who sold the ticket. Liars cannot work here.'

'She left for a minute. You can't sack her for that.'

'Yes, I can.' He quartered the page, lifted the newspaper up and studied the print. He peered over the top, a smirk dancing across his face. 'Can I help you with anything more?'

*

Josh returned to the internet café to pay for the phone call and for thirty minutes internet time. He took the nearest spare computer, logged onto his email and addressed a message to Leon. 'Sorry,' he wrote in the subject box. Almost instantly his finger jammed down on the delete key. He clicked back to his inbox. He saw a new email from his mum.

From: Lucy Beckford
[mailto:lovelylucy1961@hotmail.com]
Sent: 12 August 2002 14:34
To: Josh Beckford
Subject: Hello!!!

Hi Josh,

How are you? I wish you'd write more often. Everything is fine here back here in Gloucester. Your gran is in hospital again but don't worry it's just an infection and nothing serious. The big news on the street is that Claire from next door is leaving Jack. Apparently she's been having an affair with someone from work. The house is up for sale and everything. Your father is worried that some immigrants might move in. He said that you should be good at handling them after all your travels!

Hope Leon is OK. I was talking to his mother about you two the other day and how much fun you are both having.

Anyway best be off and make the tea because your aunt is coming round and you know how demanding she can be!

Write back soon!

Love Mum xxx

Josh left the internet café and sat on the pavement, alone and eight thousand miles from home. He'd never felt so lonely.

BOOK 2: A SHADOW REVOLUTION

12 August 2002

The heat of the glass stung Leon's hand as he slid it down the train window. Warm air, sweetened by the lush vegetation and volcanic soil, drifted through the carriage. He lifted his camera from his lap, peered through the lens and scanned the surrounding fields. A dozen or so people squatted beneath a palm tree watching the train pass. Click. Two children broke from the group and ran alongside the tracks waving at the passengers. Leon angled the camera but the children faded from view before he could capture their chase. He searched upwards, focusing on the layers of flattened ledges that clung to the hillside. Figures dotted across the terraces tending to their crops, their backs bent, their conical hats bobbing up and down. Click.

Leon lowered the camera and gazed out at the countryside. They'd been in Asia for six months. Nothing had been as grey as Jakarta: nothing as green as the rural amphitheatres of West Java.

Inspired by the terrain, Leon took the guidebook out of the bag and flicked to section about his destination.

YOGYAKARTA

Pop 700,000

The city of Yogyakarta is located in the south of central Java, two hundred and seventy miles east of Jakarta. To the outsider, the city is often characterised as being the protector of traditional Javanese life, a cultural haven, which possesses the island's soul. Whilst the north of the city is every bit as modern and chaotic as Jakarta, when a visitor looks back on their time in Yogyakarta they remember the Kraton Palace at its centre; the mysterious tales of princes and sultans; the narrow streets and dilapidated chic of the old city; the batik fabrics and engraved silver; the Javanese dance and *wayang kulit* puppet shows.

Sultans, palaces, old cities... he liked the sound of this place. Now that Josh wasn't there to hold him back he could really take the adventure up a notch.

He read on and daydreamed about his future adventures as the train clattered west to the city of Cirebon before angling north to navigate the flats of the central Java plain. Soon the water buffalos dragging wooden ploughs and women planting rice shoots receded and the train approached a cluster of adobe roofed houses. They entered a white-tiled station and creaked to a halt. A station guard with a red fez-like hat, grey shirt and black tie whistled and waved instructions to the general disinterest of everyone. Those who had reached their destination picked up their bags, chicken cages, rice sacks, bicycles and farming equipment and exited. Newcomers replaced them carrying more of the same.

A young family crowded next to Leon. The pregnant mother lowered herself onto the floor while the father lugged their belongings onto the racks above, his slight frame keeling under their weight. Two little girls rested against their mother, their eyes big and round, their attention directed towards Leon.

'First time they see *bule*,' said a man who had been sat next to Leon since Jakarta. Throughout, he'd maintained an erect posture with his head slightly tilted back. 'The country people are not like people in Jakarta. They not see many things before. *Bules*,' the man said, brushing some non-existent dust off his blue-suit jacket. 'Yes, I see many –'

He lurched forward as a passing hawker knocked into his arm. Without looking back, the salesman trampled over those scattered in the aisles, whilst yelling out the name of his product. Others followed ferrying plastic containers, cardboard boxes, buckets, trolleys, palm leaves, and woven baskets. As the calls of, "*nasi-nasi-nasi*", "*Kompas-Kompas-Kompas*" "*pop mie-pop mie-pop mie*", "*agua-agua-agua*" faded, more hawkers appeared, selling snacks, fruit, magazines and biscuits.

Blue Suit flagged down a woman, removed a leather wallet from the inner lining of his jacket, and purchased a packet of sweets. On the floor, one of the little girls stretched out her arm and opened and closed her palm whilst saying, '*Gula-gula*.'

The mother, horrified by her daughter's plea, drew her child back towards her. The little girl crouched back down and sucked her thumb, her eyes not moving from the sweets. Blue Suit, seemingly immune to anything beneath his eye-line, offered Leon the packet. Leon dipped his hand inside, picked out a couple of sweets and offered them to the little girl. She looked to her mother for assurance before lifting a sweet from his palm. Leon gave the other to her sister.

Blue Suit ran his finger across his well-trimmed moustache and said in a voice so calm it dripped with anger, 'They are a gift to you.'

'I thought the children would want them more than me.'

'I do not waste gifts on them,' Blue Suit said, gesturing at the family with his chin like they weren't worth a movement of his arm. He crossed his right arm over his left and readjusted his position to face the aisle.

Leon glared at the back of the Blue Suit's head, the mark of every comb tooth visible throughout his side-parted hair. This would show him.

Leon got up, squeezed past Blue Suit into the aisle and offered the pregnant woman his seat. She touched her cheek, batted her eyes downwards and shook her head. Leon tapped her husband's arm, pointed to his wife and back towards his now vacant seat. The husband looked at Leon and then his wife and nodded. Leon helped her to her feet, across the scowling Blue Suit and onto the window seat. He looked down to the two young girls. Further inspiration struck. He reached up to the overhead rack and brought down his two cages and dangled them in front of them. 'Meet Terry the turtle and Simon the snake.'

The girls eyed the cages like he were a thousand packets of the sweets. With great ceremony, Leon displayed the cages. The line of sellers halted. People shuffled in their seats. Some stood to gain a better vantage point. Leon cleared his throat and addressed the audience, 'I now bequeath these animals to your family as a sacred gift. Please take good care of them until death or fate leads you to part ways.'

He handed the two cages to the father and bowed. The expression of bemusement on the father's face was replaced by a smile. He shook Leon's hand while the other passengers cheered and clapped.

Basking in their warmth, Leon held the father's arm aloft like a referee awarding a bout to a prize fighter. As he turned to acknowledge the other side of the carriage, a SCCCHHHHHH!!!!! exploded in his ears. A thousand nails on a thousand blackboards. The cages crashed from his grip. His body thudded on to the floor. Sharp impacts all over his body. The screech died and with a violent lurch all motion ceased.

Everything lay still.

A child crying. Her body trembling against his yet sounding so distant. The larger body of an adult wriggling from under his legs. A faint murmur rousing into a panicked chatter. Movement all around: people disentangling limbs, lifting bags off those on the ground, yanking each other free.

A curdling wail from outside. A female passenger looked out the window. She slapped her hand over her mouth and averted her eyes. Others turned away to face the inner carriage.

Blue Suit got to his feet, not a single-hair displaced, and went towards the vestibule. He returned five minutes later.

Leon stopped rubbing his neck and looked up, 'What

happened?'

'A boy is hit by the train,' Blue Suit said, the palm of his hand slapping the tops of his fingers. 'Dead now.'

'Why are you smiling?'

'You not understand? He walk in front of train. So stupid.'

Before Leon could respond, he felt the slow vibration of the wheels grinding upon the track.

'What's happening now?'

'We go.'

'What about the boy?'

'He not important,' Blue Suit said, retaking his seat. 'He only a local child.'

Leon rose to his tiptoes, using the seat headrests to leverage his view. The train picked up momentum and passed a group gathered around an obscured object. A woman, who must have fainted, was being fanned by another. Three men gripped each other. Two others had sunk to their knees, foreheads pressed against the floor in prayer. The "local child" seemed important to them.

*

A faint orange glow lit a classroom at the end of a narrow corridor. Inside, a man lay on a mattress staring at the bare wires that crawled along the ceiling. It was two o'clock in the morning, yet he hadn't contemplated sleep.

He got to his feet, picked up an oil lamp and used it to guide his way through the paints and stencils scattered across the floorboards. He reached his workstation and set the lamp upon it. From the wooden surface, he lifted a quadrant of stretched buffalo hide to his mouth and sucked in the odour of the sweet, dried leather. The musk took him back to the day he'd bought it. Trundling in his old van from Yogyakarta to the neighbouring city of Solo. Reaching the old warehouse and meeting Mr Prabukusumo. He'd shaken his hand and saw the undiluted trust in Prab's eyes that comes when your fathers did business and your fathers' fathers and theirs likewise. Prab led him past the rolls of buffalo hide on general sale to the back of the dust-filled workshop. He lifted a roll and gave it to him, touch alone revealing its quality.

During the long year since, he'd spent hours dividing the leather into hundreds of pieces; bathing them in *rempah rempah* spices; stretching, cutting, chiselling and shaping. The results hung in front of him: nineteen characters strung across the back wall. One space remained.

Refocusing on the workstation, he lifted the final piece and balanced it flat on his left palm. His eyes closed. The penetrating light of the screen. The waiting orchestra. The murmur of the crowd. He opened his eyes and exhaled. Forty hours to go; forty hours until the moment he'd contemplated since the age of fourteen.

He bore the character to the wall and clipped it to the one remaining space on the metallic line. Above the line, he saw the audience list pinned to the wall. He scanned the names. Different ages, religions, ethnicities and ideologies. A powder keg of people designed to create the chaos, he sought. One key ingredient was missing: *bules*. He smiled to himself. No anarchy was complete in Indonesia without a bit of foreign intervention.

He went back to his desk, opened the drawer and looked down at a stack of flyers he'd had printed in English. The heading said, THE LAST DALANG: A SHADOW REVOLUTION. Tomorrow he'd give them to some tourists. This would certainly give them a cultural experience they'd never forget.

He shut the drawer, took a cigarette from behind his ear and lit. The roll-up dangled out the corner of his mouth, flaring and burning, as he paced the length of the line to the piece he'd just hung up.

He studied it for a long time. Something wasn't right.

He unclipped it, took it back to the workstation and held it to the lamp. A craggy shadow crept across the rotten plaster. He lowered the character and put it on the work station. From an open drawer below, he removed a pouch and rolled it out. Thirty chisels, different sizes, descending right to left. He selected the finest chisel and positioned it against the corner of the character's mouth. He took his hammer and tapped the chisel. He lifted the character up to the light and studied the shadow created.

From sinister to pure evil: the effect of a single incision.

*

Leon lugged his backpacks down from the train and dropped them onto the platform. He felt a double-shoot of pain in his hamstrings. He'd been on the train for twelve hours. The ticket seller in Jakarta had told him it would take six. With a grunt, he hoisted a bag onto each shoulder and returned to the upright.

The departing train gained momentum. Guidebook in his left hand, finger trapped inside the requisite page, he returned the waved farewells of the father, pregnant wife and their daughters with his right. The locomotive vanished into the eastern darkness.

He stood alone on the platform. The only light the glow of the surrounding city. All visible signs in Indonesian. No idea where to go. No one to ask. The familiar feel of the unknown producing a mixture of exhilaration and doubt.

To his left, what looked like a tunnel. He shuffled through it both hands stretched out ahead. After twenty paces he saw a fissure of light. No longer concerned about the uncertainty of his tread, his pace quickened as the faint light ahead expanded.

He burst into the open. Dark blue replaced pitch black. Rain slashed diagonally across a square plastering his clothes to his skin. An intake of breath. Getting ready for the rush: the offers of cheap hotels, free rides, guided tours... nothing but a single taxi; the driver not giving him a second glance. Experience told Leon that these were exactly the type of people he wanted to travel with. He dashed across the concourse, opened the door and leant in, causing the driver sit up and stiffen. 'Is this Yogyakarta?'

Rain blew over his shoulder and into the interior. The driver wiped some spray off his cheek, blinked and beckoned him inside. Leon shook his head, showering more water onto the passenger seat. He knew the rules: never get into a car with someone before you've sussed them out; always get a price before you leave; never pay until you get there. 'Yog-ya-kar-ta?'

The driver's face relaxed with recognition. 'Jog-ja-kar-ta.'

'Can you,' Leon pointed to the driver, 'take,' pointing to the car and making a steering motion, 'me,' pointing to himself, 'to Sosrowijayan,' pointing to the map in his travel book.

The driver's eyebrows dropped. He crooked his ear closer to Leon's mouth.

'Sos-rowi-jay-an.'

'Ah Sosrowijayan,' the driver said, his pronunciation again markedly different. He made a scuttling motion with his fingers in the direction of a nearby lane.

Leon gestured towards the lane and then back to the map, his raised eyebrows signifying that he was asking a question. The driver confirmed the earnestness of his directions with a single nod.

'Thank you,' Leon said, patting the top of the driver's arm. He stepped back out the car, shut the door and dashed towards the alley, vaulting the streams of water that cut across his path. He reached the street, ducked under the shelter of a doorway and surveyed the scene. A stray cat appeared to be his only company. He dipped his hand inside his pocket and took out three crumbled notes. Just 30,000 rupiah left. Why did he give so much money to that family on the train? Where was he going to find an ATM around there?

Twenty metres down the lane, a sign read *Losmen* in faded red paint. One front window was boarded up; a grille protected the other. He had no choice. He splashed through the puddles to the entrance. An investigatory push. The door crept open. The musk of rotten wood. Sparse light. A small reception. He stuttered to a desk-shaped shadow. 'Hello?'

As he groped across the surface, his hand knocked a bell causing a tingle. He hit it again but harder this time. A groan followed by a rustling. A click. Faint-yellow light. A man emerged from the back room, rubbing his eyes.

'Hello, do you have any spare rooms?'

The man held up a single finger. He detached a key from a hook, rounded the counter and led Leon down a corridor. They passed twenty doors and stopped at the end of the passage. The man pushed the door open, reached back and flicked on a light that illuminated the back lot. Leon trailed him towards what looked like some sort of shack. Rain cut across their path blurring a door spanning the breadth of the structure. The man tugged it open to reveal a bed pressed against three graffiti smeared walls. A pool of water covered the solitary patch of visible floor.

'You must be joking?'

The man looked at him impassively.

'Toilet?'

The man signalled to a cement block to their right. Its door swung open and shut in the wind.

'How much?'

'50,000 rupiah.'

'What a rip off.'

The man stifled a yawn with the back of his hand.

'30,000 rupiah,' Leon said.

'OK.'

Shit, he'd agreed too quickly. '20,000.'

The man shook his head. Leon looked at him, blinking away the rainwater that seeped into his eyes. He knew when he'd lost. He'd said a higher price and was going nowhere at midnight, in this rain, in a strange city, with no money.

'Here,' said Leon, slapping a note into the man's hand. 'Just give me the key.'

13 August 2002

Ahmad's eyes snapped open. Blue, sombre light. He lifted his arm and squinted at the alarm clock on the bedside cabinet: 6.26 in throbbing red-lights. He'd woken, as always, four minutes before the alarm.

He gradually sat up, manoeuvred his legs to the left, and rested his forearms on his knees. A bead of sweat trickled down his forehead. A scorching dryness encircled his throat. He reached to his left, located the glass of water and drained the remains. Warm, repulsive, not enough.

He battled the urge to shut his eyes. Nothing had been thicker than the air in their room last night. Hot and pointless attempts at sleep. The sweat soaked bedding. His wife's raspy voice calling out to unseen terrors.

He rotated his body and looked at her. Knees up to her chest, eyes open, stillborn in the breaking light. 'Wening, it's six thirty.'

She lifted her head. Pillow marks on her face.

'You need to get up if you want to take the girls to school.'

She murmured, tossed over and tugged the sheet up and over her head. The torture of sleep chosen over the torture of life.

He stared at the torpid, grey mound next to him and rubbed the back of his neck in slow circular patterns. He got to his feet and paced to the window and looked down on the street where they'd met.

Ahmad was eighteen when his family moved to the *kampung*. Back then, Wening was just another child who lived in the neighbourhood. Over the years that followed he'd watched his wife grow from a girl to a woman.

He'd mainly see her on the way to work sitting outside her parents' house next to her mother and aunt. When she was around fourteen, he started to steal glances as he passed. Each time he'd spot another feature he liked. Her large, charcoal eyes. Her small, straight nose. The dimple on her chin. Her heart-shaped face. It was incredible that the little girl, who lived eight doors down, was turning into such a beautiful woman.

He followed the same route to work day after week; month after year. Not once did she look back at him, not even for a millisecond.

When she turned sixteen rumours crept around the *kampung* of potential suitors for marriage. Ahmad's name was not mentioned. Yet still he looked to her, urging for eye contact, a glance, anything, which told him that she knew he was alive.

He leant on the window sill, all those years later, and fixed upon the spot where it had happened and his skin prickled like it had that day. She'd swept her hair to the side, looked up at him for less than a second before lowering her head and smiling. Coy, juvenile, playful, secretive.

He knew that that glance and those that followed were her promises that she'd wait for him. And wait she did. It was the thought of her and her alone that made those long, sweat-filled days in the factory almost bearable.

By 1980, his father had been released from prison and the barber's shop set up. His father had taken Ahmad out the factory and he now had a business to inherit. Yes, Ahmad was thirty-one and Wening seventeen. But the age gap was not the problem. Her father was.

An image of his father going towards Wening's house to make arrangements. Ahmad had stood at that same window and watched in the knowledge that his father didn't walk there as a war hero or a man who had repelled a brutal dictator. He walked there as a former prisoner; an outsider; a communist.

Wening's father answered the door and his father entered. Hours later it opened again. A formal handshake. His father's return. A slight hop to his limp. A single look up to Ahmad at the window. A nod.

Joy.

Pure joy.

Sinking.

After all their setbacks what had his father given up this time?

Ahmad ran downstairs and met his father at the door. His father grasped his hands and pressed them together and gave him the biggest smile since his release from prison.

Ahmad didn't smile back. Wening's father considered the match beneath his daughter. A significant dowry was required. One they couldn't afford.

His father searched Ahmad's face, his smile fading. 'It wasn't so bad.'

His father read his thoughts like that. They seemed to be nothing he could hide.

'If it is too much we can wait,' Ahmad said.

His father let go of his hands, turned and closed the door. He stepped towards his son, put his hand behind the back of his neck and looked at him evenly. 'We've lost enough time already.'

A high-pitched beeping brought him back to the present. Six thirty. He cast one last look towards Wening's family home. The doors closed; windows shut; her relatives mere memories, flickers of light that ghosted now and then through the minds of those left behind. He paced to the bedside table and pressed the alarm off.

He heard a flurry of high-pitched voices, next door. Cinta waking up her sisters. The mound on the bed stirred, muttered something and stilled again.

His eyes wandered to a frame perched next to the alarm. He picked up the photo, his thumb-print displacing the dust on the frame. In the picture on the right, Wening carried Cinta in a *selendang* sling. Focusing on his daughter's soft, round head and tiny eyes. What your children couldn't comprehend. That you'd lived without them. That you remembered what they didn't. When they were young. When they needed you. When that was enough.

His attention moved to Wening's face in the photo. Her chin up and proud. Her beautiful smile as she nurtured her daughter. Different from that luscious smile she used to give him when Cinta was fed and asleep and she could commence her nightly quest to produce more.

It wasn't until a year after Cinta's birth that the questions from family and friends started: when will you have more children? Does Cinta not want any sisters? What about a boy? Or would you prefer a girl?

Wening started to receive gifts of fertility: tens of bottles of *jamu* to drink, sniff or rub on her stomach, back and genitals. An uncle of hers gave Ahmad discrete packages of *obat pria* pills designed to boost his virility. When that didn't work, an aunt of Wening's travelled to Pulua Madura in north-east Java to pick up a potion called *jamu madura*. She claimed her side of the family had been using the remedy for generations and it worked without failure. Ahmad, usually dubious of the suspicions and fables of the urban village, tried the fluid, part out of guilt for the aunt's arduous journey, part out of desperation. He vomited within thirty minutes.

A sickly metallic taste developed in his mouth at the memory of the whole humiliation.

He replaced the picture on the cabinet, facing it away towards the wall, and rounded the bed. Next to the wardrobe, he picked up his trousers from the place he'd dropped them the night before and put them on. From the wardrobe he selected a brown shirt at random and pressed it against his mouth. Salt and dried soap. He drew it back and held it the distance any customer would be from him. Could he still smell the shirt or was that his body? What did it matter? He wrestled his arms into the sleeves and started to do up the buttons.

Water splashed downstairs. The playful screams of the twins. The motherly commands of Cinta. Eyes back to the mound in the bed. He wanted to grab her and shake her. Shake her until she awoke. Shake her and say: I gave you what you wanted, didn't I? Listen to them downstairs. Listen to them.

Two sets of feet padded up the stairs followed by a slower and heavier pair.

That double knock on the door that came every day. An impatient rap. Like Cinta didn't trust him to get up. Like he was her child.

He opened the door and looked at her. 'Good morning.'

She didn't reply. The mirror of her mother in expression and movement, the familiarity of her scorn was almost haunting. The look on his wife's face when the barber shop closed; that fleeting glance, she'd given him when they told her father the news; when another month passed and they hadn't conceived; looks his daughter replicated years later when he refused her requests to go to bars and nightclubs; looks now replicated when he said, 'Good morning.'

*

Leon sat in a café flicking through the menu. A waiter brushed past him on the way to the adjacent table. First the clink of the plates and then the smell. Shrimp paste searing through his nasal cavity. Two local men next to him hunched over their meals. He'd long become used to such odours in the restaurants of the East. But not in the morning. Not at this time.

Leon lifted his t-shirt over nose, slumped down in the seat and shut his eyes. A silhouette of a plane flying across a red sky; a train gliding through green English fields; nestling in his own seat; no one on the floor; no hawkers; not one person looking his way. His mother waiting at the station; sitting at his place at the table; the smell of crisp fried bacon; the splurge of the brown sauce; vinegary and fine. Walking in the fields near his home through the wet tangled grass; a cool breeze prickles his skin; a fine rain kisses his brow. He takes the shortcut back through the woods; the deep smell of the bark; bracken cracking beneath his tread. He arrives home and goes upstairs to his room and sinks into lavender-scented sheets –

A touch on his elbow. 'Mister... you are OK?'

Leon opened his eyes. Indonesia slowly returned. 'Not really.'

'Good,' the waiter said, his answer clearly pre-programmed to deal selectively with positive responses. He turned to the page in the menu that Leon would require and stepped back. The first line read:

Banana pancake......................6,000 RP

Leon looked up at the waiter and then back at the page headed, 'Tourist Food.' He scowled at the intimation before looking back down at the page. The lingering smell of the shrimp paste... the ache his back... screw it, he'd break the rules this once; there was no way he was having local food that morning. 'Banana pancake and a coke.'

'Of course,' the waiter said with a smile. He took the menu and headed towards the kitchen. On the way, he skirted around a man loitering next to the notice board. Tall for an Indonesian, he was wearing jeans, a plain white t-shirt and sandals, yet somehow still looked managed to look incredibly smart. He waited until the waiter disappeared, slipped a poster from his satchel and pinned it to the wall. He stepped back and surveyed the café. He was younger than he looked from behind perhaps early twenties. His skin shone. His cheek bones were impossibly high. Leon caught himself staring and looked down at the table. His eyes fixed on a knot in the wood yet he sensed the man's approach. A light-brown arm stretched into his vision. A flyer dropped in front of him. Leon slapped his hand on the flyer and thrust it back across the tabletop. The man put his hand on top of it and guided it back.

The crash of a door, opened without care. The waiter appeared, cut in front of the man and put a banana pancake on the table and a bottle of coke next to it. He made to leave, glanced at the man and froze mid-step. His mouth searched for either words or air. The man cocked his jaw. An acknowledgement: perhaps a dismissal. The waiter bowed slightly and scuttled off back into the kitchen.

Leon watched him go. 'What was that all about?'

The man didn't reply.

Leon sighed. Why did he even bother?

'Look, you clearly don't have a clue what I am saying and I don't want what you're selling so can you kindly take your flyer and fuck off.'

'Where should I go?'

'Oh... you speak English?'

'Yes.'

'So you understood what I just said?'

The man nodded.

Leon tucked his hands under his arm-pits and leant back in his chair. 'Well, I still don't want what you're selling.'

'You appear angry. What is wrong?'

'Why should I tell you?'

'Because I gave you a flyer for my performance tonight and you told me to fuck off. Many people would be angry. Instead I am asking a polite question.'

Leon ducked forward, crunched the plastic straw between his teeth and swigged the coke. He looked back at the man and winced. 'OK, fair enough... I'm a bit tired. That's all.'

'Tired of what?'

'Of travelling'

'How can you be tired of travelling?'

'You can. Believe me. It took me twelve hours to get here and I slept in a hut last night.'

'But that is normal for you backpackers, no?'

'Yes but I'd read some amazing things about this place. That Java was the biggest island in Indonesia and that if you want to know this island that you must know this city and all that. But so far it's been the same bullshit –

horrible hostels and people ripping me off and fucking banana pancakes for breakfast.'

'If you look beyond what is in front of you maybe you shall discover want you seek.'

'What does that mean?'

'Become Java and Java becomes you.'

'How do I do that?'

The man shrugged and began to walk away, 'That is what you need to discover.'

Leon watched him head towards the exit. 'Why don't you help me?'

The man turned and smiled at him. 'I already tried,' he said, pointing at the flyer.

'Can you try again?'

'Come to the Kraton Palace in the old city this afternoon and maybe I will.'

'How will I find you?

'I do not know. But you will.'

He slung the strap of his satchel over his shoulder and was gone. Leon looked back down to his pancake. Not a hint of steam emanated from its flat body. Next to it sat the flyer. Two black silhouetted characters: crooked, cragged, cruel. The heading bold and in English: THE LAST DALANG: A SHADOW REVOLUTION.

*

Cinta opened the door of her father's car and got out. She circled the bonnet and stepped onto the pavement. With exaggerated care, she crouched to search in her bag. The car didn't move. She stood upright, fastened the clasp and placed her bag back over her shoulder. Ten deliberate steps. The hum of the stationary vehicle. She twisted her upper body and waved. Through the windscreen, her father looked surprised and then pleased and then waved back and smiled. It was the first time she'd seen him smile in weeks. Why did he need to do it today?

Another wave. Another wave returned. Why wouldn't he leave?

On she stuttered towards Jaksa Travel. She was going to have to go inside. Ten metres to go. Nine. Eight. The engine revved. She held her breath. The noise grew fainter. She dared to look. Her father's car disappearing down the street. She blew all the air out of her lungs, shielded her face and dashed past the shop facade.

*

Leon headed south under a covered walkway that sheltered a line of market stalls displaying the obligatory fake belts, sunglasses, wallets, handbags and watches. Yet no one tried to sell him any of those things. Instead a new word rung around the enclosed space. It sounded like '*bateek*' or '*batick*' but he couldn't be sure. What he was sure of was that this same word was coming out of the mouth of almost every person and each time this word was uttered it was directed to him.

He sidestepped out of the main passage and leant against a concrete stanchion. Steaming, eastern air. People pressing in. All those eyes. Looking. Searching. Straining. Wanting.

His body filmed with sweat. People blurred and sound flattened. He felt himself fall forward and lurched in surprise only to come around and notice he hadn't moved.

He clenched his fist and punched his palms and muttered to himself, 'Man up, boy, you're getting like Josh. Don't let this place defeat you.' He shut his eyes and the words of the man in the café ghosted into his mind.

'Become Java and Java becomes you.'

He punched his palm again, this time harder, and opened his eyes. Time to adapt. Time to take control. Time to become Java.

Taking a travel book out in such circumstances was known suicide. But that's what he did. He flicked to the back and ran through the Yogyakarta index until his finger pressed down on, 'Batik p376.' He found the page and scan read the section: *The fabled cloth of Java... old Javanese word meaning to dot... natural waxes... dyes... hand-painted cloth... used to make shirts, sarongs, kebayas... popular in Yogyakarta.*

Leon glanced up into the nearby shops. Cloth hung from the rafters. Textiles piled metres high teeming with colour: violet, scarlet, pink and purple. So that's what they kept saying.

He drew the book away from the peering eyes and read on: *Batik is at its cheapest in markets, especially Pasar Beringharjo.*

He studied the map on the next page. Bingo. Five minutes down the road and on the way to the Kraton Palace, where he'd said he'd meet the guy from the café. He snapped the book shut and dropped it in his rucksack.

He walked across a single lane reserved for horses and carts and bicycle rickshaws. Across the road, a hulking peach-coloured building bore a series of enormous billboards. The words 'Maliboro Mall' ran the length of its edifice.

Within five hundred metres he reached Pasar Beringharjo. He jogged up twelve steps and entered the indoor market.

Become Java and Java becomes you.

He hurried to the first stall and after a few minutes of

haggling purchased a long-sleeved batik shirt with a zig-zagged gold and brown design, matching fez-like hat, and a pair of beige trousers. He took off his t-shirt, discarded it in the stall owner's bin and replaced it with the shirt. He then removed his shorts and stepped into the legs of his new trousers and hitched them up. He somehow forced the waist button through the hole. The zip reached little more than halfway up the fly. He kicked off his flip-flops and signalled to the beaten brown sandals worn by the stall owner.

The scene, as with any street theatre in Java, had attracted an audience. The gasps that accompanied Leon's strip had been replaced by fascination as to whether the stall owner would accept the shoe trade. Perhaps caught up in the drama, the stall owner unfastened his sandals, held them aloft and gauged the opinion of the assembled throng. In response to their cheered encouragement, he laid his palms out flat with the sandals atop and offered them to Leon with a slight bow. Leon took the sandals with one hand and gave the man his flip-flops with the other. The crowd hooted with increasing delight as Leon put on the sandals, which were at least two sizes too small, paid the stall-owner and hobbled from the building.

*

Ahmad drove to the end of Jalan Jaksa and reached Jalan Wahid Hasyim. A line of cars streamed past, not a bumper's length apart. He glanced down at his wrist: 8.34.

He was late. *Late for what? Sitting by yourself?* A gap appeared in the traffic. *How many people came to the shop yesterday?* The gap closed. *No one will come today either.* Ahmad hit the left indicator and edged out. *People will walk past and look inside and see no customers and give you that face.* A pedestrian hurried in front of the bonnet. *That look lower than pity.* A rage of horns amplified tens of cars back. *The way you look at a dog in the street.* Ahmad cancelled his signal. *Then your wife will come. You won't hear her but she'll be there. Sitting in the corner wallowing in all her sorrow.*

He tugged the wheel in the opposite direction and forged through a narrow gap. He blocked the first lane to a standstill, accelerated across the traffic flow and turned right, away from his work, towards Sarinah Mall. A hundred metres down the street he saw a space between two cars at the side of the road and pulled in.

He sat for a long time inside the vehicle. He thought of Cinta, in her office a few hundred metres away; about his wife; about the twins. He thought of the rent and the food and the repairs needed to fix the car but still he couldn't go to the shop that day.

He unbuckled the seatbelt, removed the keys and got out of the car. He walked to the front of the vehicle and saw the tops of the skyscrapers peaking over the low-rise buildings in the foreground. Towards them suited men marched; shiny boots clomping towards the towers of blackened glass.

Ahmad traced the tops of the urban temples, a crooked smile creeping across his face. He remembered their construction in the early 1990s; another economic miracle; a further triumph for the Republic. He started laughing. He saw suited people glaring at the grubby old man sat on his battered car chuckling to himself, but still he continued. Suharto. That old bastard. Too busy looking up rather than down. Because as those skyscrapers and malls were being erected, something else was rising in Jakarta and beyond: popular discontent.

That glorious year of 1998. A time known simply as *Krismon.* When the spiralling national debt, banking crisis and increased fuel prices led to something unknown in the rule of Suharto: mass protest. The security forces responded in type: shooting dead four students. Rather than quell the anger the deaths increased activism. Students first stormed and then occupied the MPR parliament building. The army, defeated by popular consent and sympathy for the cause, failed to intervene. Anarchy spread across the city: riots in Ketapang; widespread looting; the burning of the ethnic Chinese area of Glodok. Ahmad, remembering anti-communist pogroms, barricaded his family in their house.

Then nine days after the "Semanggi shootings" the unthinkable happened: after thirty-one years, Suharto resigned. As if a curse had been lifted, six weeks later Ahmad and Wening conceived. Wening, who at thirty-seven had given up hope, bloomed with pregnancy. Her cheeks flushed, hair shone, eyes sparkled. It should have been the start a new era.

A moustached man hobbled along the pavement, a bundle of newspapers folded over his arm. He dropped a single paper on the rusted bonnet, wiped his hand on his muck-covered *Kompas* bib, took Ahmad's payment, readjusted his hat and trooped on.

Ahmad unfolded the paper and looked at a picture of a middle-aged, bespectacled woman glibly pointing into the distance. The headline said:

The President Defends her Record:
Compromise Brings Stability.

He remembered watching her inauguration on a black and white television in the *warung* next door to his shop.

July 2001: him and his fellow shopkeepers huddling inside Gondangdia station looking on in disbelief, as Megawati Soekernoputri, daughter of his father's hero Soekarno, was sworn in as President - a result that was unimaginable during the Suharto rule. The joy as he walked back to his shop. Thinking of his father. Thinking they'd won at last.

A year had passed since then.

Ahmad's fingers curled around the paper, scrunching up the sheets. He ripped out the picture of Megawati, folded it and dropped it in the top pocket of his shirt. He threw the rest of paper on the ground and stalked back towards Jalan Jaksa.

*

When Cinta felt sure her father had left she took the first left off Jalan Jaksa onto the backstreet Jalan Kebon Sirih: Barat I. She hid behind a large white van, pressed her back against a wall and took a deep breath inwards. Like yesterday, she'd pretended to him that she was going to work. What else could she do? Tell him she'd lost her job chasing after a man? And not just any man: a white man.

She dug her hand in the pocket of her trousers and removed a piece of paper. Last night, she'd sat in her room, pen in hand, longing for a rush of inspiration. After hours of deliberation, she'd narrowed her options and resulting consequences down to the page in front of her:

> ***Choice 1**: Lie to my father and say I've been dismissed for another reason.*
> ***Reaction 1**: My father will confront Jusuf, who will reveal my indiscretion.*
> ***Outcome 1**: My father will kill me.*

***Choice 2**: Beg Jusuf for my job back.*
***Reaction 2**: He'd take me back and then torment me even more than before.*
***Outcome 2**: I would kill myself.*

***Choice 3**: Continue to pretend to go to work and hide in the nearby mall.*
***Reaction 3**: If I haven't been caught before, I will be when my father demands half my salary at the end of the month.*
***Outcome 3**: My father will kill me.*

Each outcome was the same and every reaction as bad and they'd all surely result in her death at the tender age of nineteen.

Anyway, it all seemed trivial in comparison to the REAL problem in her life: Why had Josh not called? The thing that her mind returned to over and over again.

Today would be different. Instead of letting thoughts of him consume her, she'd find him: whatever it took. And when she did, they'd leave together to somewhere far away. She tried not to contemplate what it would do to her father but she could no longer live under his rule. Her mother wouldn't care - since the birth of the twins she hadn't cared about anyone or anything, let alone Cinta. Sure, she'd miss her sisters but they'd understand when they were her age and weren't allowed to hope or live or love or do ANYTHING.

She paced down the street and stopped at the spot where she'd given Josh her number. Her heart rate quickened as their conversation replayed in her head and she groaned at the effect he could have on her after only one meeting. The same questions came but the answers were still no clearer: Had she made it clear to phone only in the morning? Had her English been correct when she explained? He was happy when she gave him the paper, wasn't he? Or had she been wrong?

No! her mind screamed defiantly. He felt it too. He must have.

Following the path, she shielded her mouth and tried not to inhale the acrid air. She couldn't understand why *bules*, whose plane tickets cost more than her yearly wage, stayed in such an overpriced and disgusting area. Apparently, a book called The Lonely Planet had told them it was the best place to stay. A tourist had once told her that The Lonely Planet was like the Koran for travellers. When she hadn't responded, he'd laughed nervously and told her that it was a joke. She didn't have the confidence to tell him that maybe such jokes wouldn't be found funny in Indonesia. She was sure Josh wouldn't tell jokes like that.

Further down the *gang*, she passed the girl who Elok called the 'tramp' - an insult she'd picked up from one of her *bule* friends. The *tramp* lingered around Jalan Jaksa day and night. She'd prowl the street; gyrate against lamp posts; rub her crotch against anything in sight; sit on the pavement, her legs fully spread, yelling at passersby. When she saw other Indonesian girls she hissed like an animal warning competitors off its prey. They said she was retarded and had been disowned by her parents at a young age. Cinta felt sorry for her and prayed for her soul. Yet, whenever she encountered her, fear instantly quelled her pity.

The *tramp* wore the usual: black hot pants, heeled

shoes and a stained vest top. The white make-up plastered on her face clashed with her dark, sun-scarred arms. Cinta rushed past, keeping her head down and hoping that the *tramp* didn't notice her.

Wwwaaa! the *tramp* leapt in front of Cinta, arms out-stretched, fingers splayed.

Cinta stumbled backwards and over-balanced towards the adjacent wall. A hot, concrete burn scraped down her elbow. The *tramp*'s eyes bulged. Her mouth formed a hideous grin. Spotting an escape, Cinta dodged to her right. A cackling laugh chased her as she ran right and left and then straight on until fatigue overcame her legs. Panting, unsure if the *tramp* was still in pursuit, she stole into the nearest guest house.

*

Leon walked under an archway and into a labyrinth of side streets. The trees that crept up between the single-storey houses had sprinkled dead leaves over the red tiled roofs. An old woman wrung out her washing; children played football in the street; a man cleaned his windows. Within fifty metres, the road widened and opened into an expanse of grassless scrub-land. The glimpse of everyday Indonesia gone as the next wave of touts descended upon him.

He walked on, avoiding the loose stones and tangles of scorched weeds that blighted the bleak expanse. A stray dog limped by his side. As Leon surged ahead, it stopped, sniffed at his trail before crabbing sideways in laboured pursuit. Six touts joined the chase, deluging him with offers, their short, quick steps kicking dust up into his face. He covered his mouth and joined a long, straight road. The midday sun beat down upon the tarmac and scalded the balls of his feet as he followed the path to a black gate. Beyond the wrought iron barrier stood a white pavilion displaying a golden coat of arms.

'See mister? I tell to you. Kraton Palace closes today. Come my *batik* workshop. Very cheap prices,' pattered one of the touts.

Leon looked at the man and didn't record his face or his personality or consider who he was or the reason that he followed him. All he saw was another cheat trying to get his money. He barged past the man and followed the outer wall until he met another archway. He ducked under the low entrance, passed a row of souvenir stalls and reached what looked like the official entrance desk. Behind it sat a man wearing black turban. The name tag, 'WS. Saygota' was pinned to his blue tunic. Two stern-faced sentries flanked him; daggers tucked in their belts; their eyes trained straight ahead. The attendant pointed to the sign which read Admission Price: 10,000 rupiah. Leon laid the money on the desk, took his ticket and sarcastically waved goodbye to the pack of guides.

Inside, those fabled and holy grounds, the illusion of the East tranquilised him and removed all thoughts of the heat and the hassle and home. A dream wander of Java: a gravelled path, French bandstands, marble floors, tiered roofs and teak pillars. A pavilion: two thrones; a gold-leaf roof carved with swirls and flows; black pillars and gilded light enhancing the luminescent glow. Walls and courtyards inside walls and courtyards; smaller and more ornate as he fell deeper into their charm.

Across a sheltered walk into the Sultan's tea room. Viewing the relics of the East India Trading company: porcelain from China, tankards from Holland, teapots from England. Into an adjoining room; portraits of the former Sultans, their great moustaches curling at the edges; pictures of grandiose weddings; displays of heirlooms; a complete family tree. Islamic writings; a bronze Buddha; the aura of Hinduism; the essence of Java.

The circle complete, he returned to the first courtyard. A crowd of seated tourists watched an illuminated cotton screen set up in front of a stage. A shadow puppet show. One spindly cragged shadow faced another. Unknown words and harsh intonation. The implication of deep conflict yet to pass.

Leon watched the show unfold. Absorption led to intrigue. Who moved the shadows? What was the source of that beautiful music? What passed behind that cotton screen?

Leon rounded the stage, ducked under a red rope and perched on a tiled ledge under the shade of a Banyan tree. His position revealed the secrets of the show in all their splendour. The music, soft and arrhythmic like the flow of a stream, was created by a hidden fourteen-piece orchestra. Wearing orange shirts, turbans and sarongs, the orchestra hit gongs, hand drums and xylophones with mallets, batons and drumsticks. They were accompanied by two flutists and three female singers.

At the fore, a green log stretched along the base of the screen. Dozens of puppets were stuck into its bark by their stems, their design displaying intricacies of incomprehensible detail. In the centre, the puppet master sat cross-legged. It was he who voiced the characters; his voice deep and haunting one moment, gentle and contemplative the next. It was he who conducted the orchestra, controlled the puppets, narrated the dialogue, led the song.

The final scene approached. The orchestra's tempo increased; the sound transformed from the lap of water to a cascade. On screen, two puppets faced each other. The audience hushed. Swords appeared. The puppets soared and swooped and attacked. They intermingled and exchanged blows. The master wailed. A crash of percussion; the fall of a character; the shadows faded from the screen.

The crowd gave a standing ovation before filing to the exit. The orchestra packed up their things and followed. Yet, the master remained in the same position, unnaturally still, like a deep trance chained him to the screen.

Finally, he stirred, tapped the golden dagger tucked into his belt three times. He muttered to himself, touched his forehead and rose. On his feet, his legs buckled and he stumbled. He steadied himself against the log and lifted his head and saw Leon. To Leon's dismay, he made his way towards him, across the sunlit courtyard, his shoeless feet barely leaving a print upon the gravel. He rested on the ledge next to him.

Leon looked at the man but his proximity prevented any focus. 'Do I know you?'

'Yes, from earlier...'

Leon leaned back and studied the man. He recalled his chiselled features and the depth of his eyes but otherwise he looked like a different person. His plain white t-shirt and jeans were gone. A turban hid his pristine side-parted hair. His black tailored suit buttoned up to the collar made him look broader and more imposing.

The brilliant man who led the show was that beautiful man he spoke to in the café.

*

Cinta closed the door of the guest house and pressed her back against its cold surface. She listened but couldn't hear anything. She must have lost the *tramp*. She wasn't ready to go outside to test the theory. Instead she allowed her eyes to accustom to the sparse light. She touched her elbow. A sticky fluid met her palm. She'd forgotten she'd scraped it on the wall. The creak of an opening door rendered her static.

A rotund figure emerged from behind the front desk. 'Hello, what do you want?'

'I'm looking for my friend Josh.'

The skin around his eyes, magnified by his spectacles, tightened, 'I don't know any Josh.'

'Please, he's my friend.'

'I can't give you information about my guests.'

'So he is a guest here?'

'Please leave.'

'OK,' she said, taking a pen and paper from her bag, 'but please give him this message for me.'

She pressed against the wall and wrote,

Hello, I came to find you. Email me at cinta.cantik19@yahoo.com Write soon. I will come back tomorrow to find you and next day also. Love Cinta

She folded the paper and handed it to the man, who took it with a slight raise of his left eyebrow. Cinta understood his caution. When had an Indonesian girl looking for a *bule* in his guesthouse ever been good news?

Outside, she hid behind the fence that guarded the entrance. Peeking around the corner through the open door into the reception, she could see the owner had already opened her letter and was holding it up to the light. After a brief read, he screwed it up and dropped it out of sight.

*

They sat in the flickering shade of the Banyan leaves, alone in the vast courtyard of the ancient palace. The sun beat through the tree and not a whisper of breeze touched the browning leaves. The man unravelled his turban and placed it on his lap. 'I concentrate so much that when I finish I need time to recover.'

'I saw,' Leon said.

'Why did you sit in a place where you cannot see?'

'I thought behind the screen was more interesting than in front of it.'

'It always is. In life as well.'

They sat on the ledge shoulders brushing both facing forward. Leon rubbed his nose and stole a glance out of the corner of his eye. 'I didn't recognise you in those clothes.'

'I'm the *dalang* or as you say the puppet master of the palace. It is my costume.'

'The *dalang*?' Leon pressed his hands in his pockets and pulled out the flyer that the man had given him in the café. He unfolded it to reveal the red heading: THE LAST DALANG: A SHADOW REVOLUTION. 'Was this for the performance I just watched?'

The man snatched the flyer and thrust it down the front of his shirt. He gripped Leon's knee and hissed through his teeth. 'Not here.'

'Sorry, I didn't know...'

The man got to his feet, touching Leon under the elbow as he rose. 'Come with me. We cannot talk of this in the palace.'

*

Josh had a final look around the room, trudged out the door and made his way into the reception, his movement impeded by his twenty kilogram backpack. The owner sat behind the desk.

'Mister Joss, halo.' The owner lowered his specs and studied him. 'You look very white... more white than normal I mean. You look very sick.'

'I'm fine, just a bit nervous about my journey.'

'Where you go?'

'I'll decide when I get to the train station.'

'Where is Mister Lion.'

'To be honest I don't care.'

'You have argument?'

'Yes.'

'You be friends soon. Mister Lion is a very nice man.'

'Sure...' Josh raised an eyebrow and walked backwards towards the door. 'Anyway, thanks again.'

'Goodbye, Mister Joss. Please return soon.'

Through the entrance and turning left, Josh stumbled over the legs of a girl who was sitting on a wall. He mumbled, 'Sorry,' and went on.

'Josh?'

He turned and reality slowed and then stopped. It was her.

*

They sat at the summit of a stone staircase looking down upon the thousands of red tiled houses below. Leon gestured to the sandstone tower behind them. 'Where are we?'

'It is called the *waterkasteel* in Dutch; the water castle in

English.'

'And in Indonesian.'

'*Taman Sari.*'

Leon's eyes wandered down and to the east. 'And what's down there?'

'That is the old city,' the man said, his finger tracing the outline of the city walls. 'In the ancient times only the servants of the Sultan lived in these grounds.'

Leon shielded his eyes and viewed a shimmering, white building in the centre of the old city. 'Is that where we have just come from?'

'Yes. The Kraton Palace. Home to the Sultan of Yogyakarta.'

'What could you not tell me inside?'

'I am not certain...'

Their eyes met. The bore of the man's stare spread goose bumps down Leon's arms but he didn't look away. 'Not certain of what?'

'If I am able to trust you.'

'You can.'

'I do not know your name.'

'Leon.'

'I am Zak. It is not my birth name, of course. My friends call me it.'

Leon lifted his hand to shake and dropped it by his side. It felt ridiculous to do so now.

Zak removed a battered tin from his belt. He opened it, took out a roll-up and lit. 'I only have *sigaret kretek*.'

Leon took the tin and studied the filter-less roll ups inside. 'Is it good shit?'

'*Kretek* is not drugs. It is tobacco and cloves.'

'Yeah, I know...'

'They are called *kretek*, because when you smoke the sound it makes is *kretek, kretek*. Listen,' Zak took a draw. The end of the cigarette crackled. He exhaled slowly. A silver mist engulfed his face before circling and fading into the air above.

'I've been smoking it since I got here,' said Leon, fishing a cigarette out of the tin. He lit it and took a long draw and listened to the crackling sound and let the dense, sweet scent of the cloves burn into his nostrils. Then the smoke hit his lungs. He jerked forward, slapped his hand on his chest and barked a cough.

Zak rubbed his back in circular motions. 'I did not say *kretek* is strong –'

'You're not kidding.'

'– because you said you smoked many before.'

Leon shrugged off Zak's touch and held the cigarette vertically in front of his face. He stared it down and muttered to himself and drew it to his lips. He took a deep lungful, reclined on his elbows and blustered the smoke out of his nose. He gave Zak a triumphant nod and resisted the urge to splutter. 'See, no problem.'

'OK...' Zak said, his eye moving up and down Leon's torso. 'May I ask you something?'

'What?'

'What you are wearing?'

Leon glanced down at his batik shirt and the tight, brown trousers hitched halfway up his calf. He took off his *peci* hat and wiped his brow. 'I took your advice, "Become Java and it becomes you." I wanted to blend in.'

'Did you?'

'No. I caused a scene in the market and then got even more attention when I left.'

'You do not like attention?'

'Not from the people that give it to me,' Leon said, flicking the ash off his cigarette in five-second intervals. 'At least I got a real batik shirt for my collection, I suppose.'

Zak rubbed his mouth and looked away.

'What?'

'Real batik is made by hand and takes months to produce. This,' Zak rubbed the sleeve of Leon's shirt between his thumb and forefinger, 'is printed in five minutes.'

'Typical.' Leon dropped his cigarette to the floor and ground it into the stairs with his sandal. 'You know I've been away from home for six months?'

'A long time.'

'This is my last place before I go home. My mate thought it was too dangerous but I insisted we came. Like I told you in the café. I thought this would be my country.'

'It could be.'

'No, it's just like everywhere else. The only people that talk to me either try to rip me off or lie to me.'

'They are poor. They do not have any other hope.'

'It's not just here; it's everywhere,' Leon said. 'You go to these places that a guidebook tells you and you take a picture and you go to the next place. People who want something talk to you and you talk back if they have something to give you.'

'Is this not life in general?'

'Yeah but I thought travelling would be different. It's like everything that is really happening in a place is not happening to me. Like I'm an actor with no lines.'

'It is not that way.'

'Of course it is. I can walk around all day sightseeing but the truth is that I don't really see anything. Nothing real. . Take those *kretek* cigarettes... I haven't smoked them before. I hadn't even heard of them.'

Zak nodded.

'You knew?'

He nodded again.

'It was a lie. My whole experience is a lie. Just like this shirt.' Leon undid the buttons, tore the shirt off, screwed it into a ball and threw it from the ledge. It caught the breeze, billowed and floated into the streets below.

No one spoke. The sound of footsteps broke the impasse. A child scurried up the steps clasping Leon's shirt. He looked about four years old. He leapt up the final two stairs and panted as he presented Leon with the shirt. Leon took it, burned a deep pink and thanked the child.

The child lingered, his eyes big and hungry. Zak held out a note. The child snatched it, descended, reached the bottom and gave the money to a woman, who was waiting for him.

*

The buzz of the traffic, the howls of distant dogs, a child's laugher, a ball thud, thud, thudding off a wall. Jakarta spoke to him a thousand sounds but only they inhabited that dusty alley.

She walked forward and stopped before reaching touching distance. A hot breeze dusted past, flapping through the laundry strung between the two-storey buildings.

'Josh,' she said, in a voice so tender that he found himself stepping towards her. He took her by the lower back and moved in to meet her lips.

Her face turned: her forearm thudded into his ribcage. 'Josh, are you crazy? This is Indonesia. It is bad if we talk in the street. I cannot kiss you.'

'Who's going to see?'

She froze, her eyes following something behind them. Josh turned to see a middle-aged man sidling down the street. He slowed as he drew level with them. Knowing eyes of gleaming imagination. He grinned and slunk onwards. Cinta waited until he was twenty metres away, 'People see like this man.'

'But who cares if he does?'

Cinta backed away, her hands flapping like she was trying to grasp the words out of the air. 'Josh, please, there is no time. Where do you go now?' she said, gesturing to his backpack.

'I was leaving.'

'Without me?'

'Without you?'

'Why you not call me? I waited by the phone all morning.'

'The thing is... I didn't call until the afternoon.'

The skin above the bridge of her nose pinched together. 'Why?'

'I was nervous.'

'Josh!' she bounced on the spot, her hands making strangling motions. 'I tell you. Call in the morning. Who answered the phone?'

'A man said, "No, Cinta" and hung up.'

Her hand shot up to her mouth. 'My father... I hate him!' her full lips parted and she smiled dimples into her flushed cheeks. 'But you called me?'

'Yes.'

She held his stare and radiated a look of intense affection. 'I have a plan. I meet you in McDonalds in Sarinah Mall at one o'clock.'

Josh looked at his watch. It read twelve fifteen.

'If I do not come, it is because I cannot,' Cinta said. 'If I come we have four hours only.'

She turned and rushed back towards Jalan Jaksa. He studied her bum pressed against her black trousers and felt his teeth grind in anticipation. He straightened his backpack and returned to the guesthouse.

A shadow moved away from the glass door. He entered. The owner lumbering back around his desk. 'Hello, Mr Joss. Back again?' he said, feigning surprise through a hitch-pitch tone.

*

Leon put his arms through the sleeves of his shirt and did up the buttons and sat down. He glanced at Zak who tugged a fold of skin under his chin and looked straight ahead. Leon waited for him to say something about his shirt throwing tantrum but he didn't speak.

Finally, he shifted, removing the battered tin from his pocket and lit another cigarette, this time failing to offer one to Leon. He snapped the tin shut.

Leon squeezed his fists together and tried not to but had to break the silence, 'Why are you not saying anything?'

'You are not talking but I am still listening.'

'I've got nothing more to say...'

Zak took a draw an exhaled the smoke out the corner of his mouth and away from Leon. 'Before I can help. I need to know what you want. I mean, what you really want.'

'I don't know what I want that's the problem.'

'Ok, during your time travelling how many temples, museums and markets have you seen?'

'Hundreds.'

'How many souvenirs have you bought?'

'I've two bags worth already.'

'How many friends have you made from the countries you have visited?'

Leon fell silent. All he could think of were guides or hotel owners he'd liked.

'You say the only people who talk to you are trying to sell you something,' Zak said. 'But I think you only speak to people from who you want to buy something.'

'Is that bad?'

'No, but it is stopping you finding what you really want.'

Leon shuffled closer to him, 'What's that?'

'I think you want to make a connection with a place. To experience something different.'

'Yes! Exactly.'

'But you seek that only in places and goods,' Zak said. 'Wood, stone and metal. Buildings, clothes and food. To truly experience a place you must do so spiritually as well as materially.'

'How can I do that?'

'Through the people you meet as well as the things you obtain.'

'That's exactly what Josh said.' Leon swallowed and felt a pang of regret. 'In fact, I suppose that's exactly what he's been saying the whole time.'

'Where is this Josh now?'

'In Jakarta... we had a fight.'

'About a girl?'

'Yes but it wasn't like that. I wasn't interested. She's really plain and looks about twelve. But we said some stuff and I got angry but this time he didn't back down. He stayed in Jakarta to be with her rather than come with me. It was weird. It is weird.'

Leon silenced and looked beyond the city to the faint-blue cone that peaked through the distant mist.

'Gunung Merapi,' Zak said. 'Fire Mountain. The most active volcano in the world.'

'How close is it?'

'Far enough for Yogya to be safe. But we feel its power in the air and water. In 1994 it killed many people from the villages on its slopes. The cold ash blew to Yogya. It fell like snow. Cold lava came down the Code River to the city. My friends and I rode in old tyres and rings. There was no school and we were happy. We knew nothing of the death and pain. We were too young.'

'Why do people live on the slopes?'

'It is where they have always lived. They know nothing more. They go to the peak and give offers to the God of the Mountain. No man can control what happens above or below. But still the people try. It is all they have. It allows them to sleep at night'

Leon nodded and discerned no change of subject. 'I can't apologise to Josh.'

'No, not yet.'

*

As the light failed the earliest stars burned through the blue of the stratosphere. Below, the orioles, turtle doves and wood pigeons of the *Pasar Ngasem* bird market, cried out to the faraway skies that they'd neither see nor soar over again. And Zak, who had sat for what seemed hours, listened to Leon talk about the places he'd been to and the places he was going to and about things he'd bought and given away.

As Zak listened he studied Leon's barely visible face and his expressions and movements. He talked with great pace, his arms animated by his enthusiasm, his entire body involved in the narrative.

'What is the worst thing in the world?' he said to Zak, who gave no reply because he knew Leon didn't want one. 'The time... '

'What about it?' Zak said.

'It passes.'

'Time does not exist. We created this concept. Minutes, hours, days. Like all moments are the same. In reality, they can go as quick or as slow as you want and you never know how much you have.'

'If there is no time, what is there?'

'There are two times only. When you are born and when you die. The rest is life.'

'I like that,' murmured Leon. 'Yes, I like that a lot.'

Below, house lights switched off one by one. Smoke rose and they were met by the smell of extinguished charcoal. A motorbike roared by. Above, a myriad of constellations speckled the true blackness.

'I have thought about this a lot and I will trust you,' Zak said.

'Even after the *kretek* thing?'

'Yes.' Zak turned to Leon and looked at the black outline of his face. 'There is nothing more honest than to say you have lied.'

*

The previous two nights Josh had eaten dinner alone. Both times he'd felt that everyone was watching him and he hadn't known where to look. With no one to share his thoughts - simple things like commenting on the food or a good looking girl that passed – he'd pretended to look busy by reading a book or studying the menu.

That night he ate alone again. Yet, when he entered the restaurant he didn't choose a corner table or sit facing the wall. He wasn't conscious of where he was looking or who was looking at him or what he ordered or the sound of his own chewing. When he finished his food, he delayed getting the bill, ordered a coffee and took out his diary. He hadn't written in it for days.

13th August 2002

Leon left three days ago.

At the time I was shocked but now, when I think about it, I'm amazed that he didn't go before. It'd been building.

The thing about Leon is that he's a control freak. As soon as he lost control of our plans he left. The only reason he didn't leave earlier was because I was perfect for him. Sure he didn't want a complete walk over (because he loves arguing too much) but he knew that I'd usually give in to keep him happy. And for a while it worked. His personality and drive would make me do things I'd never have considered alone. The pay off was I had to put up with his ego, mood swings and bouts of depression. It's weird because he combines tremendous arrogance with massive insecurity. Like when he looks in the mirror and says

"I look great today" before turning around and asking "don't I?"

We've been friends our whole lives but I wonder how much of that is because we grew up on the same street. The whole time I've known him we've had different groups of friends. He hangs around with people like himself who think I'm boring and a nerd. I hang around with "nerds" who think Leon is a total prick. When I stick up for him, I tell them that his persona is a mask. Unfortunately, he's been wearing it for so long it has become his real face. When he does let it slip and admits that he is not invincible (like when he admitted he messed up with Elok and that he hadn't slept with many women) he denies it later - even though he must know that he can tell me things like that and it won't matter.

My mum will inevitably find out about this on the grapevine and get upset about it. She sees the good in everyone and loves Leon. He was always around our house eating the meals that weren't being cooked at home. I'll never forget my dad's face when he used to come home to find Leon at the table– failing to see why he should work all day to feed the cocky kid from down the street, whose own dad was nowhere to be seen. Leon's dream is for my dad to take him on as an apprentice in the plumbing business. I doubt that will happen.

I'll stop the amateur psychology soon but I think it's because of his mum. When he was younger she wouldn't let him do anything in case he left her like his dad did. Now he's an adult and finally has some freedom he's like a wasp in September – buzzing around like crazy, stinging anything that gets in his way.

But the time has come for me to admit to myself (despite all the mitigating factors) that Leon is a "total prick" and move on. It refocuses me and makes me want to do more. It sounds pathetic but I want to show him that I can travel without him.

The reason Leon left was because I wanted to stay in Jakarta to meet up with a girl I met called Cinta. Leon went up the wall when I told him and he said he wasn't going to change his plans for the sake of 'some girl' that I had just met. I can kind of understand what he meant because it does seem stupid but I felt from the moment I saw her that she wasn't just some girl. And yes I only had her number and yes I'd only spoken to her for five minutes but it meant so much more. So he left and I stayed. At first I did feel lonely and young and afraid but also hopeful and excited. OK, this does sound crazy now - which is strange because everyone always says that I am too rational.

Of course, nothing in this saga was simple. When I called Cinta, a man (who turned out to be her father) told me I had the wrong number. It was my fault because I didn't have the bottle to call in the morning like she'd told me to. So I went back into the travel agent's to find her, only to be told by her creepy boss that she'd been fired for leaving the shop when she ran out to give me her number the day before. I walked out in a daze and sat down and told myself it was fine because I could find her somehow and it had all been a mistake. I told myself that at the time and I told myself that when I was still awake at three in the morning.

Yesterday, I went around in circles: I felt guilty for contributing to her losing her job and then angry that she'd given me the wrong number and then regretful that I'd made the classic mistake of choosing a girl over my supposed best mate.

So today I packed my things and was ready to leave. I hadn't even considered where I was going. As I left the guest house I tripped over a girl sitting outside. It was Cinta! She'd come to find me. I knew I should have trusted my instincts!

Of course, I didn't hide my surprise and play it cool. No instead I lunged in for a kiss. Maybe somewhere in my demented thought process I decided this might be somewhat of a suave manoeuvre. In reality, a local girl seen kissing a white man down a back alley doesn't look so good.

This was only the start of my ignorance. Today, I must have heard the expression, 'Josh, it is different in this country,' accompanied with a bewildered smile about ten times - and I consider myself to be quite culturally aware. Can you imagine all the rules that Leon is breaking?

Cinta suggested that we meet in McDonald's in Sarinah Mall. As a meeting place I thought it was a bit strange. I remember a guy at my school that took a girl on a date to Burger King and got crucified for it. I also thought it was strange that she brought her cousin Elok/ Laura (the girl who Leon got it on with). This wasn't weird just because of Elok's personality in general (more on that later) but due to the question of who brings their cousin on a date? The answer: everyone here! If a female Muslim in this country meets with a man in public the custom is they must bring a family member with them. Cinta's only option was Elok.

So why McDonald's? Well, like everything else it is viewed a bit differently over here. For many kids, the West (whatever that means... isn't everywhere west of something?) is the coolest place around and what symbolises the West more than McDonalds? Another thing is that only the richest people eat in these places. The meals are about a fifth of the cost of the ones in the UK, which sounds cheap until you consider that everything else is about a twentieth of the cost. Hence McDonalds = privilege. The type of people that go there aren't going to frown and gossip about someone meeting a white man especially if accompanied by a female relative.

We finished our food and got into Elok's car – a Mercedes with tinted windows, air conditioning and leather seats. We drove for a while then stopped at a petrol station. Elok got out to fill up. Suddenly, my seatbelt was released. I turned to see Cinta's face inches away from mine, her expression intense and lustful. Before I could comprehend the transformation, her lips pressed against mine.

There was something different about her kiss compared the other ones I've had. It felt like she was kissing me for a reason - like it was her only explanation of how she felt. It was natural and meaningful, like it is meant to be. She pulled away and gazed at me. I thought that wasn't allowed, I said. She smiled and tapped the tinted windows. I'm not saying this culture is perfect but one of the reasons the kiss was so special was that people here hold something back. They don't get hammered every Saturday and snog anything that's passing or sleep with people they've just met... well most of them don't.

Anyway, speaking of which the car door opened and Elok got back into the driver's seat. Cinta pretended to continue a conversation that had never started. Josh, she said, looking at me with a bashful expression. No vest tomorrow, OK? Wear a shirt.

Why? I said playing along.

In Indonesia it is not right to wear such things in public.

Shut up, Cinta. You sound like your dad! Elok butted-in.

That was typical of the way Elok spoke to Cinta all day. You can tell she thinks she is above Cinta and, in turn, that Cinta is slightly in awe of her. In general, their relationship is a bit strange. I mean, for example, Cinta won't have a word said against Elok but Elok has said nothing about the way Cinta has been treated by their boss Jusuf and still works there –

which is especially weird in a culture so obsessed with family.

Elok is the biggest show off, attention seeker and most melodramatic person you'll ever meet. To be fair, she's very entertaining – especially her one of a kind, Indo-glish accent. She constantly talks about her white friends. Every sentence either starts or ends in the word bule. Put it this way, in her life the sun rises in the West.

Almost every time Cinta spoke to me, Elok interrupted and started flirting with me. She wouldn't have given me a second thought (like that night when she was pretending to be called Laura) if she hadn't been so put out by Cinta (for once) getting more attention than her.

Although I find Cinta more beautiful, I can see from other men's reactions that Elok is preferred. But I think it's like blondes and brunettes. If you have a blonde and a brunette of equal attraction and you look at them both once, you'll prefer the blonde. Look at them ten times and you'll prefer the brunette. That is the thing with Elok: she makes herself noticed straight away. She has long flowing hair, wears tight clothes and permanently has her massive breasts on display. No wonder an untrained eye like Leon was a sucker for this! If you look at Cinta once, she blends in. But get close and look and look again and there is so much beauty there and more to come. She is short, perhaps only 5ft 3inches. Her eyes are dark and almond-shaped. The touch of her skin is like... I can't think of any other way to put it... silk. Perfect, unmarked and smooth. It is chestnut-coloured - much to Elok's delight (who is far paler). Over here, the lighter your skin the more attractive you are. Women will do anything to avoid the sun and wear this bizarre whitening cream. It's like the reverse of fake tan and foundation. We yearn for a tan: they yearn for pale. It goes to show that people only want what they don't have.

After the petrol station, we drove around a bit and then went to a mall. I bought Cinta a mobile phone – they are so cheap here – so that I wouldn't have to call her house again. At first she refused but I could tell she really wanted it. Afterwards we sat down for a drink and talked about England, my family, Leon and why he left, and where I'd been travelling. She told me about her upbringing and her relationship with her father. This was when I learned she had still not told him that she'd lost her job. She's been pretending to go to work in the morning and meets him outside Jaksa Travel at night. I said that she should tell him and that it wouldn't be as bad as she thought and that he'd understand and would still love her no matter what – he is her father after all. She looked at me like I was mad, laughed and then assured me I was very much mistaken in that prediction.

She said that her father doesn't like bules and thinks there was an on-going conspiracy to re-colonise the island. There probably is! I suggested. She slapped me on the arm, Don't say that, you are meant to be on my side. Why does he let you work on Jalan Jaksa then? I asked. Because we need the money, she said flushing red. If he knew I lost my job chasing the bule then he will be so crazy, she said, her smile vanishing.

And you know what? I completely understand. He should be against her hooking up with me. I'm odds on to be some guy out here trying to get it on with a local just so I can boast about it to all my mates back home (I'm not but how the hell would he know that?).

It's funny because it makes Cinta angry that her father is critical of foreigners' role in Indonesia but if anything I don't understand why they don't hate us more. Look at what we have done to Asia. In Vietnam the children chased our motorbikes, smiling and waving. Why don't they despise us? Didn't the white face kill their ancestors? Or are they so beaten down they now accept it? In reality rather than resent us, a lot of them are in awe of us like we are a superior race – which only goes to show that they understand as little about us as we understand about them.

When it was time for Cinta to be picked up by her father they dropped me off near to my guest house. When I got out of the car, Cinta wound down the window, grabbed my hand and mouthed to me, 'I love you.' I leaned in closer, sure I had misunderstood and then she said it again – but actually said it out loud this time! And what did I say? Thank you. Of course I did. Who says thank you when a girl tells them that? Me that's who. And did I correct myself? Of course not. I said thank you and shuffled away.

And now it's all I can think about. No one (other than my mum!) has said that to me before. I keep telling myself she doesn't know what it means and it has been lost in translation and then I think perhaps it's true. Maybe people here do love at first sight and aren't as cynical or as scientific as us and are more in touch with their emotions... OK, she didn't understand but it still felt good!

Josh laid down his pencil and finished his coffee. Despite the caffeine hit, he felt exhausted. He yawned and unfurled the note Cinta had slipped into his hand as he left the car. It was the plan for tomorrow. It read like an espionage mission.

Tomorrow, 14 August 2002

1. *Go to Gambir station at 9.30 am.*
2. *Buy a ticket for the 9.44 am train to Bogor.*
3. *Arrive at 10.45 am.*
4. *Walk outside the station. Catch bus number 4 with me but do not talk to me.*
5. *Follow me from the bus but you do not talk to me until we enter to the Kebun Raya Gardens.*
6. *We walk together.*
7. *Kiss me again*

*

Leon sat on the stairs of the Water Castle in the near pitch black next to a man he'd met but a few hours earlier and waited for whatever truth he had to share. Suddenly, as if awoken from a trance, Zak sat upright and spoke, his voice low and growling. 'Seven generations of my family have lived here, in the *Kraton,* in the same quarters. Seven puppet-masters – one for each sultan. From birth this was my destiny. I have studied the Javanese language, traditions and etiquette; learned *Kawi*, an ancient language spoken only in the performances; learned English and Dutch since before I could walk.

I learned all of this because my family knew that one day I would be the *dalang* of the Kraton, like my father and his father and his. I knew by the age of fourteen that this was not my life. Ten years later I decided to tell my father. Before I could, he became ill last year. Now I am the Sultan's *dalang*. This became news across all of Java. I am the youngest puppet master to play for a Sultan in the Kraton.'

'Ever?'

'Yes. I have no brothers and my father is still sick. He will never perform for the Sultan again. After today neither shall I.'

A rattling sound, followed by a scrape and a burst of orange light. Zak held a match up illuminating the flyer he had taken from Leon earlier.

'The Last Dalang,' Leon read.

'Me,' he said, tapping his heart. 'I am leaving the Kraton to do my own shadow puppet performances. Tomorrow night is my first.'

'That was why you didn't want the flyer in the Kraton?'

'Yes. If the Sultan knows about the content of my performance it does not happen. Maybe I do not happen.'

Leon didn't know what the final part meant but decided it didn't sound good. 'Does your father know?

'He does not understand anything. He will die before

the end of the year.'

'Sorry.'

'He has less to fear in death than some of us in life.' Leon could sense Zak's stare. 'That is what you need Leon: to fear less.'

'I don't fear anything.'

'You do. You fear wasting your experience. But I can cure your fear. I can take you on a journey.'

'Where?'

'Come to our compound tomorrow. There I will explain...'

'Compound?'

'It is late now. I will explain tomorrow. But listen,' Zak said, his stare radiated through the gloaming, 'when you come you will need to be ready. You will need to be brave.'

'Why?'

Zak's fingers gripped Leon's forearm, the calloused skin of his hand in contrast to the smoothness of his unblemished face. 'My actions of the next days will shake this city. It will never be the same again.'

14 August 2002

Josh stretched onto his tiptoes and scanned the length of the platform. A white and blue train hurtled towards him. He lowered himself back onto his heels and checked his watch. His eyes moved to his ticket, to the platform number above and then to the tracks. Where was Cinta?

The howl of the brakes signalled the train's arrival. Josh followed the front carriage, breaking into a jog as the train overtook him. He reached the doors as they slid open. He waited until all passengers got on or off and placed one foot inside the carriage and kept one foot on the platform. Those who had disembarked disappeared down the exit steps. A man in a blue uniform strode in Josh's direction, his footsteps dominating the empty platform. He waved Josh inside and blasted his whistle. Josh searched a final time and, defeated, stepped back inside the carriage. The doors clamped shut.

He walked through the train, his head darting from side to side. Drawn curtains, blackened windows, seats facing inwards. Nothing but strangers, wide-eyed curiosity and welcoming smiles. He halted at the end of the final carriage in a rectangle of natural light provided by the window of the sliding doors.

A screech and a sway. Josh grabbed a metal pole to his right and steadied himself. The festering sweat of previous passengers greased his palm and he removed his hand and wiped it on his shorts. Outside, shacks lined the tracks, their roofs varying from sheets of iron to sheets of tarpaulin. On the margins, people with carts competed with packs of dogs, scavenging through the piles of rubbish that filled the unkempt foliage.

On a parallel line, another train headed in the opposite direction. He watched it pass. Standing room only, people spilling from every crevice of the grey vehicle. The train passed and they commenced a slow climb. The shacks and garbage and people lessened and the tropics thickened. His breath grew shorter. A black wraith of clouds sped to the South. The wet tracks shimmered under the lights of the train. They entered the city of Bogor, perhaps having missed the storm by minutes. The train eased into the station and terminated.

Josh stepped onto the black platform and waited until all passengers had passed and still didn't see her. He took a deep breath and set off to their meeting point, unsure what he would find.

*

Leon perched next to Zak on a fifteen-foot mound of rubble piled in the corner of a courtyard and gazed wondrously at his surroundings. Next to them, an abandoned bus sparkled with rust and multi-coloured patterns. There were sculptures; all weird and wonderful; none more so than the collection of pink traffic bollards with bike wheels attached, the spokes painted gold, all spinning in kinetic splendour. Above, banners and flags stretched from window to window across the buildings that enclosed the square. 'Now this is what I'm talking about,' Leon said, slapping the back of his hand off his palm.

'I thought you would like it,' Zak said.

Leon turned to the posters plastered on the wall behind. 'Who are those people?'

Zak glanced back at the gallery of frayed depictions griming the brick, 'Our heroes: Rousseau, Voltaire, Garibaldi, Jefferson, Vivekananda...'

'Love those guys,' Leon said, whilst wondering who

the hell they were. 'And this place... do you live here?'

'Yes.'

'Like a squat?'

A slight nod of his head.

'Why don't people try to kick you out?'

'They do. Then we return.'

'Who are we?'

'The *Taring Padi*.'

'The what?

'You ask many questions,' Zak said, fixing his attention on a group huddled around a rusted metal drum in the centre of the yard.

'What are they up to?' Leon said, noting their low voices and severe expressions.

'Talking.'

'Are they conspirators? Can we join them?'

'No.'

Zak hunched forward and narrowed his eyes and appeared to study a man spray-painting a mural on the far wall. A serpent slivered out of the picture, mouth agape, teeth venomous. The artist filled in a white speech bubble emanating from the serpent's mouth. In the gap in English he wrote, 'KILL YOUR EGO,' in green letters. He outlined the speech bubble with one red sweep. He lay down his can, stepped back and inspected his work, before hitching up his baggy jeans and sallying over towards them. He picked his way up through the rubble, his black knee-high boots, with their luminous green laces, unsuited to the climb. He reached the top of the mound and said something in Indonesian to Zak, who looked away with a faint scowl and didn't reply.

'Hai bro,' the man said, slapping his hand into Leon's.

'Aji.'

'Leon.'

'Aji, I present you Leon, who is a traveller interested in our projects and our country,' Zak said, his voice dull and without intonation as he formalised the introductions. 'Leon please meet Aji, who is an artist that –'

'Designer.'

'... an artist who lives here. As you can hear, he speaks English. He spent two years in Australia.'

Aji lowered himself onto a flat rock, re-spiked the green prongs on the top of his head and smiled at Leon, his teeth gold and silver or missing. 'What's up?' he asked.

'Not much,' Leon said, looking to Aji and then Zak with his brown trousers, batik shirt and neatly trimmed hair. 'I take it you two don't have the same stylist?'

'Yeah we totally do. But now he's on holiday,' Aji said, returning Leon's grin.

Leon shuffled towards him. First he tried on Aji's thick-rimmed black glasses held together by white plasters at the hinges and then his jacket. He got to his feet, and spun around. Two rocks displaced, rattled down the heap, crashed to the floor and bounced along the stone surface. The conspirators halted their chat, looking round to the stranger dancing on a pile of rubble in a silver jacket.

'Leon, please sit down,' Zak hissed, his eyes darting from the conspirators to the windows above. 'Please sit down now.'

Leon took the jacket off and handed it back to Aji. A wind picked up. Dust shifted and swirled across the cement floor. Above, a pale white sun burned through the smog. The hot air knitted tight around Leon like a jumper he couldn't remove. He met Aji's eyes, raised his eyebrows and gestured to Zak with his head.

Aji picked up a stone, tossed it up and caught it. 'Today, he is very angry.'

Zak turned to face them, 'Who is?'

'No-one...' Aji said, tossing the stone and catching it again. 'Leon tell me, how did you meet Zak?'

'He gave me flyer in a café for his performance tonight.'

Aji dropped the stone. 'You said you only invite people you know,' he said, slapping Zak's bicep with the back of his hand. The blow lacked power but not meaning.

'Why is it important?' Zak said.

'Because you can't lose control of this performance.' Aji's eyes shifted with speed-filled agitation. 'Why do you want to waste your talent?'

'Talent should not be a cage. It should be your wings,' Zak said.

Aji and Zak stared at each other and didn't speak or break eye contact or move.

*

Josh followed the flow of passengers through a metallic barrier. Outside, the street was black and wet. Grey water steamed through the gutters. Tens of bicycle taxis eased through the puddles in the station forecourt.

The walkway contained the same stalls, products and faces as Jakarta but with more space and less desperation. After one hundred metres of relatively little hassle, the market widened into a concourse that was circled by twenty green and blue minibuses. Conductors hung out the doors, hailing numbers and destinations. An empty bus manoeuvred through the disarray. Its boyish conductor hung out the passenger window and called to Josh.

'Number 4, mister?'

Josh pointed to the side of the bus, 'It says number 3 not 4. '

'Yes, the bus normally number 3. But now number 4 to Kebun Raya, the great gardens. Good price for you. No local people. Me and you only. Best friends.'

'I'm meeting someone.'

The conductor rubbed his tinted-blonde hair and grinned. 'A girl?'

'Maybe.'

'Very lucky. No local girl love me. Only the *bule*,' he said, rubbing his eyes in mock sadness. The minibus wove on through the cluster of vehicles and passed a stationary number 4. Beside it waited a girl with her back to him. She craned her neck and watched the exodus of people from the market.

A bullet of adrenaline.

He flattened his hair with the palm of his hand and walked towards her. He reached her and touched her back just above her waist. She stiffened and turned to face him. A loud blast of a horn. The number 3 bus swung past. The driver flashed the lights: the conductor stuck a thumb out of the window. 'I tell you! They only love the *bule*,' he called.

Cinta watched the bus drive away. Her features tautened. 'Why does he say that?'

'I didn't say anything. It was him–'

She cut off his explanation by stepping away and getting on the bus. Josh winced as he watched her shimmy beyond an old woman and sit next to the window in the front row. That hadn't looked good. He followed her inside and wedged himself between Cinta and the woman.

'Why you sit here?' Cinta said in a hissed whisper.

'Why wouldn't I?'

'I tell you not to. Also do not speak to me here.'

'OK... just one thing. I didn't say anything to that bus conductor. He –'

A heel dug into his leg. She lifted her index finger and pressed it firmly against her lips before crossing her left leg over her right and facing out of the window.

The minibus waited for the final seat to be filled and set off. In three hundred metres they came to a red-light and stopped. A giant tree loomed to their left, its hundreds of aerial roots swaying in the light breeze. A boy with a guitar rested against its vast trunk. He wore a pink t-shirt, red-rimmed shades and demeanour that said he didn't really care. He spied the bus, got up and jogged towards it. The traffic light turned green and the bus accelerated away. The boy caught the moving vehicle, grabbed the rail and ducked into the cab. He began to strum and sing, his position blocking the exit and creating both a silhouette and a bubble of intense sound.

When the bus slowed and stopped at another traffic light, the music ceased mid-song. The guitarist scrambled about his being, located a brown envelope and passed it between the passengers. Coins jangled inside. Josh added his own contribution and passed it back to the boy who winked at him. He hopped off the bus and scampered in the direction of the next vehicle that he intended to commandeer.

Josh leant his body against Cinta and whispered, 'What a job. So romantic.'

Her eyes didn't move from the outer perimeter of the gardens.

After a further two hundred metres, she tapped the driver's shoulder and he pulled over. The conductor pointed at Josh and Cinta, '*Dua*?'

'Yes,' said Josh. He handed him 5,000 rupiah note and dismissed the offer of change. He got off first and held out his hand to support Cinta onto the pavement. She ignored his offer, stepped down and strode away. He caught up with her, dodged in front and obstructed her path with his body 'Cinta, what's wrong with you?'

Her head flitting from passing traffic and back to Josh. 'I tell you in the note I give yesterday. We cannot be together until the park.'

He ran his hands down her arms. 'This is ridiculous.'

She closed her eyes and let him continue before stepping back with a quick shake of her head. 'Josh stop it. Not here.'

With those words she set off. She came to an enormous trunk that occupied two-thirds of the pavement and slipped through the gap. Josh tried to follow but three people that entered from the other direction blocked his passage. He waited until they passed and ducked through the gap, the damp bark brushing crimson stains onto his white t-shirt. He reached the other side and studied the curve of the road. She was gone.

*

Zak got to his feet and brushed the sandstone from his backside. 'Leon, I am going to make my final preparations. Please, can you stay with Aji and I will see you at the performance,' his eyes flashed to Aji, 'as my guest.'

He climbed down the mound and paused at the bottom and looked back to Leon. 'I am going on a journey for a couple of days after the performance until everything calms down. Do you want to come?'

'Where are you going?'

'I am also organising a protest on Indonesian Independence Day. I need to go to the countryside to think about things and to organise some protection for us.'

'I'm not sure...'

'Yesterday, you said you wanted a different experience. On this trip you will see things that you did not know existed. Remember, become Java and it becomes you.'

'OK, well if you put it like that then... yes.'

'I will meet you tomorrow morning at ten outside the café where we met.'

Zak strode across the courtyard, passed the conspirators, who watched him in an almost reverent silence, and jogged up the steps into the building.

Leon turned to Aji. 'What does he mean leave, "until everything calms down"? What protest? And what does he need protection for?'

The door Zak had entered swung shut. Aji stroked his six-inch, matted beard and murmured, 'I think it is better we talk somewhere more private.'

*

Josh stood by the perimeter fence of the gardens, cast in the shade of the tree canopy and searched for Cinta. In the centre of the six-lane road, a man with an eighteen foot stick tried to re-erect a fallen electricity wire. Motorbikes and green minibuses veered around the man like he was a traffic bollard.

Josh took in the scene and didn't know what was crazier: a man fixing an electric wire barehanded in the spitting rain or the fact he was stood there watching him, when he should have been chasing a girl that he'd known for two days and agreed to meet in an unknown Indonesian town and who now, every time he tried to speak to her, ran away.

He mumbled some self-encouragement and set off again. He followed the road up the hill and passed through a roadside bazaar that sold cages of rabbits. He pondered if the animals were on sale as pets or for food and decided on the latter and looked at their pink noses and doe-eyes and shuddered and hurried onwards.

At the brow of the hill, he met a granite building with the words Kebun Raya Gardens engraved in the stone. He ascended some stairs between two black lions that guarded the gate and followed the *Masuk* – Entrance signs to a counter inside. He paid 5,000 rupiah and received a map and welcoming giggles from the three young women wearing headscarves.

He took ten slow steps down the stairs and reached a fork in the road. All three directions led into dense forest. One led to Cinta.

*

Aji returned through the door carrying an oil lamp. He placed it on the floorboards and crouched to blow the dust off the glass. 'Soon it'll be brighter,' he said. 'You want a drink?'

'Sure.'

He searched the floor with his feet, kicking aside half-sown garments and spray cans and stencils and pens. Next to a sink disconnected from the wall, he located two bottles of Bintang beer. He picked one up and positioned it on the edge of his desk and jammed down with his hand. The cap displaced with a fizz and beer foamed over the top. He handed the bottle to Leon, its surface sticky and warm, and repeated the action with the other.

'Sorry, it's not cold,' he said. The mattress groaned as he eased his weight on to its edge.

'A beer's a beer,' Leon said, offering the neck of his bottle to Aji and clinking. He took a long swig, set his bottle down and looked at Aji. 'So what's going on with Zak?'

'I think he's nervous about his performance this night. It's a big day for us.'

'Who are us?'

'*Taring Padi*.'

'What does that mean?'

'There is an article on the wall about us in English. Probably it tells you better than me.'

Leon picked up the oil lamp, got to his feet and side-stepped along the edge of the wall. Posters and flyers and sketches were attached to its crumbling surface. He pulled out a pin and removed a torn piece of yellowing paper. The decaying carbon and ink instantly smudged his hand. 'This?'

'An Australian came to visit here last year. She was a journalist.'

He held it to the light and read.

The Art of Peaceful Protest
by Ruthie Wilson

The city of Yogyakarta is often characterised as the home of Javanese culture, the soul of an ancient island and civilisation. Yet, whilst the city closely guards its traditions, its inhabitants are the first to revolt against the aspects of Javanese life they do not hold so dear. Throughout the 20th century the

city, renowned for its social philosophers and artists, has been a focal point of radical protest and revolutionary struggle – from the Republican resistance during the war of independence in the 1940s to the youth groups instrumental in the overthrow of the New Order regime in the late 1990s.

Following President Suharto's departure in 1998 a number of these radical youth groups formed a network called the *Taring Padi*, a group which embodies both the sense of nostalgia and the revolutionary undercurrent that runs through the city.

The phrase *Taring Padi* in its literal sense means the fang or sharp tip of a rice grain but to its members has come to symbolise the process of the people biting back against oppression. The artists have embraced traditional as well as contemporary art forms to champion various social justice and ecological causes. They challenge groups such as the Indonesian military police and the International Monetary Fund through designing and dispensing controversial and colourful posters, pamphlets, flyers, postcards, books and matchboxes. The group's resistance also goes beyond artistic empathy and embraces direct action such as the organisation of sit-ins, marches and protests.

Spread throughout the city, the group had no cohesive base until 2001, when the Institute of Indonesian Art's visual art campus moved to a different location. The *Taring Padi* took over the vacated space and sometimes up to thirty-five artists squat inside the disused building.

It was in these confines that I first encountered the group –

The sound of footsteps in the corridor. Leon lowered

the article. Torch beams slanted into the room. Voices but no people. The lights extinguished. Two men appeared at the doorway.

*

They walked along a trail that undulated and curved through dense and dark foliage. Spots of light flickered through the high canopy, where birds perched and bats screeched. They passed a sign which read 'Mexican section' in flaked paint and the path became marked and pebbled. They reached a patch of sunlight and stopped and faced each other through the dusty glare.

Cinta looked down and studied the outline of their combined shadow. The crunch of pebbles. His hand met her upper arm, 'What's wrong with you, today?'

She dropped her shoulder and his hand fell.

'Why were you not on the train?' Josh said.

'I told you in the note I gave you yesterday. We meet in Bogor not Jakarta.'

'I was worried I was on the wrong train or you weren't going to come.'

'You do not trust me?'

'Do you know the amount of times I've been to meet girls and they haven't turned up?'

She adjusted and readjusted the bracelet on her wrist. 'That is not my fault.'

'Why didn't you at least wave at me from a distance or something? I almost didn't come.'

'My train does not leave from Gambir station.'

'Your train?'

She focused on the clusters of moss that sprouted between the stones and roots. 'The *ekonomi* train.'

'What train was mine?'

'*Eksekutif*-class trains - the Pakuan Express.'

'You should have said. I don't mind travelling in economy.'

'You cannot travel in *ekonomi*,' she said, shaking her head rapidly. 'It is hot and very busy and there are thieves and you cannot sit. It is not for *bules*.'

'I could've given you the money for the executive train.'

'I do not want your money.'

He nodded slowly and toed a stone with his foot. 'Why did you not speak to me on the bus?'

She stepped to him and lifted her hands and drummed her fists off his chest. 'Why you not understand? I cannot sit on a train with you. I cannot laugh when the bus driver shouts jokes. I cannot walk in the street and hold your hand.'

'Why not?'

'Because I lose my job and do not tell my father. Because we not married. Because I am Muslim. Because we are in Indonesia.'

'You keep telling me this. But we were in Indonesia when Elok slept with Leon after meeting him three hours before.'

'Elok is not Indonesia. Why you not understand? If people see me in Bogor with a white man I am out of my family. This is not a holiday for me, Josh. This is my life.'

*

Leon watched the smaller man, who wore an eye patch, cross the room. He walked past Leon like he didn't exist, reached Aji's desk, swept the contents to the floor, perched on it edge and looked down at Aji sitting on the mattress. The other man stood motionless, his tattooed arms gripping the doorframe.

Eye Patch spoke in Javanese, his words urgent and angry. Aji replied, his voice softer and less certain. Occasionally Eye Patch laughed but to Leon's ear it seemed mocking.

And on Eye Patch went on. Aji peeled the label from his beer bottle and listened and tried to interject by lifting his hand. When this action failed for a third time, Aji got to his feet and raised his voice. At first Eye Patch didn't move. Then his chair rocketed back, hit the desk and deflected onto the floor. He took two steps towards Aji and placed both hands around his throat and squeezed. Aji tried to wrench the man's arms open. As his energy faded he gasped, his arms whirring, landing soft blows on Eye Patch's tensed arms.

He tightened his grip further. Aji sunk to one knee. Tattoo at the door turned his head to check the corridor. Leon saw his chance. He crept over to the edge of the desk. The arteries of the Eye Patch's neck bulged in the light of the oil lamp. He gripped his t-shirt, smashed his bottle against the desk and held the glass against his neck. Tattoo's head snapped back to the room. He advanced a little, seemed to notice the bottle pressed against Eye Patch's neck, and halted. Eye Patch's hands were still around Aji's throat.

'Let him go,' Leon said. He could smell the sweat exuding from the man's body. 'Let him go or I'll cut you.'

Eye Patch loosened his hold. Aji crumpled to the floor. Leon gripped his t-shirt, dug his forearm into the Eye Patch's back and marched him towards the door with the bottle's edge still touching his neck. Blood marked the end of the shard. He reached the doorframe and pushed

Eye Patch back to Tattoo and retreated back into the room.

The four men faced each other.

Eye Patch growled and picked up a stray piece of wood from the ground. He sucked in a deep breath and stalked forward, his attention honed upon Aji. Leon stepped in front of Aji. Eye Patch lunged forward and lifted his hand. A wooden blur swiped through the air. His hand stopped the moment before impact. Eye Patch held his pose, the stick six inches from Leon's nose. He slowly lowered the stick, spat at Leon's feet and walked backwards without breaking eye contact. He pointed at Aji with the stick, hissed a threat and strode out the door followed by Tattoo.

*

They followed the descent of the track and met a drawbridge. The old boards creaked under their tread and the structure swung as they sought balance on the side ropes. Underneath, the *Ciliwung* River raged, smashing off the rocks, brown and white and grey.

On the other side, they came to a wide avenue lined with Javanese cotton trees over forty metres high. The wind picked up and ruffled through the trees and released a shower of fluffy kapok seeds. They floated through the shadows and flickered like an elliptical snow storm and sank and settled on the road which was straight and stretched for what seemed like miles. Josh and Cinta walked along it; the only souls who touched its path.

After five hundred metres they turned right, their feet squelching through the shallow bog and releasing the stench of peaty decay. They passed rhododendrons and giant terrestrial ferns and came to a clearing. Before them, a manicured lawn rolled upwards. They circled a lotus pond and rested on a bench.

'Is it always this quiet?' Josh said.

'On Sundays no. Thousands of people come. You see the café,' Cinta said, gesturing to a wooden-structure on the brow of the hill, 'it is always full.'

Josh placed his hand on the bench in the gap between them. 'Are we friends?'

'Yes,' she said, resting her hand on his but not closing her palm. She looked at him and smiled but the smile was thin.

And there they sat. On the bench, watching the clouds rolling shadows up the lime green lawns.

Josh faced her and spoke - because he felt uncomfortable in the silence not because he had anything to say. 'I thought the journey here would be more scenic. Fewer houses and more tropical like this.'

She lifted her shoulders and lowered the corners of her mouth. 'Many people in Java live near railway lines.'

'Why?'

'Hope.'

'What hope?'

'That other places exist.'

'I hadn't thought about it like that,' Josh said. 'Some houses didn't have roofs.'

'I know.'

'It's strange because in my country if you are poor you still have a chance to have a house, clean water, a fridge and television.'

'But are they happy?'

'Not necessarily.'

'To be poor is not what you have or do not have. It is

a feeling.'

'Maybe,' Josh said, staring at the slow movement of the lotus in the waters of the pond.

*

Leon pushed the desk towards the entrance, an abrasive howl piercing the silence. He muscled it in front of the closed door and sat on it. He looked at Aji, who was sagged in the desk chair, his right hand pressed against his temple, his left massaging his throat and said,
'It's not perfect but it'll give us time if they come back.'

Aji looked up and removed his hand to reveal circular contusions on his neck.

'Are you OK?'

'Yes, I'm fine. My neck is a bit sore. That's all.'

'What the hell was that all about?'

Globules of hair wax sweated over Aji's brow. 'Do not ask,' he said, blinking rapidly.

'Tell me again who you are? I mean the *Taring Padi.*'

'A group of artists who fight,' he said, his voice hollow and croaking. 'I don't know... injustice with art.'

'Injustice? That's quite a big thing to fight with art.' Leon got up from the desk and picked up the article from the floor. He stepped towards Aji and reread the headline, 'The Art of Peaceful Protest.'

Aji winced as he nodded.

'Do you think I'm fucking stupid? Stupid like,' he held the article up and read, 'Ruthie Wilson?'

Leon screwed up the article into a ball and threw it at Aji. It deflected off him and fell to the floor.

Aji looked down to his crumpled paper and back to Leon. 'What are you doing?'

'I'll ask you again. What was that all about?'

'And I'll say again: don't ask.'

'I will ask. That guy could've cracked my skull with that stick.'

'OK... I will tell you.' Aji's eyes fixed on Leon. 'But it's much more complicated than you think.'

*

They left the bench and went across the lawn towards the Orchid House. Inside, they walked slowly around the high ceiled greenhouse and viewed the single and multi-stemmed flowers. Josh paused and took a particularly beautiful flower, its lilac sepals and inner petals contrasting with the deep orange of its stigma, and cupped its head and smelt the sweet, floral odour that was so familiar yet elusive. He felt a tap on his shoulder and turned. In front of him was Cinta, framed by the flowers that tangled around them.

'What you said earlier about Elok,' she said, her voice barely audible. 'Did she ML with your friend?'

'ML?'

She whispered. 'Make love.'

'Yes.'

'I thought my boss Arief lies.' She tapped her lip with her index finger. 'Have you ML to many women?'

'No.'

'How many?'

'Three.'

'Three.' Her hand gripped his wrist. 'It is many.'

'Not in my country... how about you?'

Her cheeks reddened and her head shook, 'No. This is why I tell you that Elok is not normal.'

'Well, that's true.'

'You do not like her?'

Josh paused for a little too long.

'Why?'

'No, I mean, she is beautiful and everything... what's wrong?'

'I make a plan for you to meet her tomorrow.'

'With you as well?'

'Tomorrow is my father's birthday. I cannot see you. I feel bad so I organised for Elok to do something with you.'

'What?'

'She has a car and I do not. She can give you a tour of Jakarta. You will see many things and in less time. Then the day after is a party at her house for Indonesian Independence Day.'

'Will you be there?'

'No, my father does not allow me. But you must go to see. For a tourist it is very interesting. It is the party of the year.'

Josh signed through his nose. 'I'm not sure about that... I mean, she's quite intense and I don't really know her and –'

'She is this way for a reason. When you know her she is different.'

'In what way?'

'When she born her mother died. Her father, my Uncle Salim, never is married again or have more children. He gives everything to Elok to stop his sadness but nothing works. He makes a lot of money. Elok goes to best schools with very important people. But they are horrible to her and bully her because she is a *orang kaya baru*... it is difficult to say in English. They say that her money is new and dirty.'

'I understand.'

'They also say she killed her mother. They call her the witch. People think because Elok has all the money and jewellery and good-looking and has an easy life but she has hard times. She has no mother. Her father work all the time and takes no help from the family. The closest Elok had to a mother was her *pembantu*... her father's servant. Before she has a car she had her own *sopir* to drive her everywhere. For many years he was Elok's best friend. When she is older she changes and become more beautiful and men like her and she feels very different to school. Now many girls want to be like her. She comes very confident. Maybe she is different now but I think the real Elok will return soon and be happy. Like when we were young and we played together.'

'Some people don't change,' Josh said.

'That is what my father says. He does not like. He says she only goes to university because of *nepotisme* – her father Salim have many important friends.'

'Salim is your father's brother.'

She contemplated the question. 'Yes. But they do not talk now. They had a barber shop together for some time but there were problems. So Salim left the shop. Still he and my father do not talk. Now Salim has a lot of money and we...,' she intertwined her fingers and stopped talking.

'So this is why Elok drives the fancy cars and has all the clothes?'

Cinta took his hand, touching only his fingertips. 'So, tomorrow and the Independence Day party? I think you enjoy very much. Also Elok can be important to us.'

'Well, OK but I'd rather meet you.'

She lowered her eyelids, 'Not many men say that.'

*

They faced each other in the mustard light of the oil lamp. Leon on the mattress: Aji on the chair.

'They wanted to know about Zak's performance tonight,' Aji said.

'What about it?'

Aji adjusted his position in the seat. His t-shirt hung limp around his neck. The front green spike of his hair was splayed across his forehead. His eyes didn't leave the desk that covered the door. 'Where it happens, what it be about it... I cannot talk English now.'

'Did you tell them anything?'

'No. Zak hasn't told to anyone nothing about this story. Even the orchestra only know the music.'

'He attacked you because you wouldn't tell him?'

'They wanted to know about the protest too.'

'Who are they?'

Aji's eyes moved to the door. 'I don't know.'

'Of course you do.'

Aji shrugged, 'These people that came now, they aren't official – they are *preman*. Who pays them to make these visits, these threats...maybe the secret police or special army forces... again, I don't know.'

'Why would the secret police be interested in a shadow puppet show and a protest?'

'What do you already know about Zak?'

'That his family have been the puppet-masters to the sultans for years but Zak is quitting to do his own thing.'

'You don't know who Zak is, do you?'

'Yes.'

'No, I mean who he *really* is.'

*

Josh and Cinta headed across the park and re-crossed the river. Giant palm trees towered above information plaques that revealed the species were from Sulawesi, Maluku, Kalimantan and Irian Jaya. They reached a clearing and followed a path that wound down to a pond.

'The Governor's residence,' Cinta said, pointing to a white-pillared house across the water. A herd of deer grazed on the lawn in front of the stately building. 'What are the animals?' she said.

'Deer.'

'I never see them before. There are many in your country?'

'I suppose so.'

'Do you see the *layang layang*? We played with them when we were younger.'

Josh looked up to the speck-like kites controlled by two children far below.

'Can you take a picture and send it to me when you go home?' Cinta said.

He positioned Cinta in the foreground, with the pond and water lilies in the middle, the deer and palace in the background and the kites above. She smiled and he snapped and could tell from the view through the lens what a beautiful picture it would be.

As he placed his camera back in his pocket, a splodge of rain plopped onto his forehead. More thick droplets followed. In the West a grey gauze of rain crept nearer.

Cinta scrambled in her bag and removed a see-through poncho. She struggled into it and looked at Josh. 'You do not have?'

'No.'

'This is Bogor. *Kota Hujan*. The City of Rain,' she said,

grabbing his hand and laughing. 'You *bule gila.*'

'How was I meant to know? As you keep telling me – I'm not Indonesian.'

'So now you use being a *bule* for your advantage.' She grasped his hand tighter and led him back towards the forest.

The rain crashed down through the trees and erupted as it hit the tarmac floor. They hurdled a temporary stream gushing along the edge of the boulevard and sought refuge amongst the roots of a giant tree. Josh wedged himself in the hollow and Cinta, with her back to him, rested against him. He lowered his hands and gripped her hips and drew her closer and felt no resistance. Wet bark on his back. The scent of orchids on her neck. The thump, thump of the rain.

After a few short minutes, a white truck pulled up next to them. It had a blue and red siren on its roof. The door swung open. Cinta broke their clinch with a jolt. A uniformed man jumped out and rushed to them. He spoke in Indonesian, his face stern, words urgent. He beckoned them towards the car with exaggerated movement.

*

Aji got up from the chair and settled next to Leon on the mattress. He looked into his eyes and didn't look away. 'To understand this, you need to know about the history of this city and the belief of the people. Only then will you see the craziness of what Zak is doing.'

Leon watched the shadows of his face and saw the tension and recognised the sincerity in his voice and nodded for him to continue.

'This region is the only kingdom in Indonesia – they say it is a kingdom in the sea of republic. The previous

Sultan of Yogyakarta, Hamengkubuwono IX, was one of the most important men in the history of this country. He was also one of the most intelligent.

After World War II the Indonesian nationalists declared independence. The Dutch didn't accept it. The Sultan of Yogyakarta had two choices: support Soekarno and the rebels or support the imperial Dutch. He chose Soekarno.

This was a very important for Soekarno and the rebels and maybe why they won. The Sultan also offered Yogyakarta as the new capital city during the war. The Dutch wouldn't fight the Sultan or attack the palace – they knew what he meant to the people. The Sultan also gave the royal soldiers to the fight. These soldiers weren't farmers with guns like the other rebels. They were professionals. This made a big difference. In 1949, the royal soldiers won a famous victory against the Dutch in a battle known as March 1 Attack. When independence was won and Soekarno became the first president he returned the capital to Batavia and renamed it Jakarta. But Soekarno had a big debt to this city. So when Indonesia was created it was a republic except for –'

'Yogyakarta.'

'Exactly. Hamengkubuwono IX received his reward for his war efforts. He was made the Sultan and the Governor of Yogyakarta. Later he became the vice-president of Indonesia. When he died, his son Hamengkubuwono X became Sultan and is now also the Governor of Yogyakarta. And guess who is his favourite puppet master is?'

'I get it. Zak is quitting an important job for an important person.'

'He's more than an important person. The people in Yogyakarta believe that the Sultan is the Shadow of God on Earth.'

Leon studied Aji for a flicker of the hyperbole in his expression. It didn't come.

*

Sat in the back of the van staring out at the dark green streaming past the windows. Rain smacking off the body of the car. The windscreen wipers on full pelt but unable to clear the water.

Josh wiped the rain from his face and looked at Cinta, who looked straight ahead. 'What's the problem?'

'He say there is lightening and it may hit the trees which can fall on us. We must hurry. They close the park.'

'Where now?'

'Jakarta.'

'Can we take the train back together?'

'OK, but we cannot talk.'

Josh smiled. Each concession felt like a small gift.

*

'The people think that the Sultan is the Shadow of God on Earth? I don't believe you,' Leon said.

Aji ruffled his hands through his hair, dismantling another green spike. 'Yes, many people do. The indigenous faith in Yogya is Javanism. It's a form of Islam but it is different to any other in the world. Before Islam the Javanese people believed in Hinduism and Buddhism. We also had animist traditions. How do you say? Like pagans. Then Islam came. It did not replace but added to our spirituality. We created our own form of Javanese Islam.'

'How do you know all this?'

'Everyone knows. I also studied English and Javanese

history at Gadjah Mada University. I dropped out after six months.'

'Why?'

'I guess I had too many opinions for formal education.' Aji's metallic teeth flashed in the light of the lamp. 'Anyway, Javanese Islam has three very important places: the volcano *Gunung* Merapi, the South Seas and the Kraton Palace –'

'I saw Volcano Merapi yesterday. Zak told me it was the most active volcano in the world.'

'People believe that there is a line which starts at the peak of *Gunung* Merapi, passes through the Kraton and ends in the coast of the south,' said Aji, his jewellery rattling as his hand dropped down in a diagonal flourish. 'Merapi is the home of Sunan Merapi, a powerful Muslim spirit. In the depths of the sea of the south coast lives Nyai Loro Kidul, the Queen of the Southern Oceans. Like Sunan Merapi she's very dangerous. The sea in south Java is very rough. She's taken many victims.

The people of Yogya believe that on the day of judgement there will be an explosion and lava will flow from Merapi, down through the Kraton Palace, kill the Sultan and end in Nyai Loro Kidul's domain in the South Seas.'

'The apocalypse?'

'The Sultan's job is to protect us from this. Only through devotion and sacrifice can this day be stopped. He prays to Allah and other spirits. On his birthday he sends offerings to Merapi to offer peace to the mountain. During the festival of *Labuhan* in the South Seas he also sends offers to the sacred point at Parangkusumo.

To fulfil his role the Sultan has to be very spiritual. An

important part of that spirituality is *wayang kulit.* In Java, shadow puppets are one of the oldest and most prestigious art forms. Certain puppets in certain stories can bring protection – to a village, to a rice crop, to a person. Zak's performances bring protection to the Sultan. They bring protection to everyone. Zak's family hold secrets about the art and the royal court that no one else knows. Now do you see?'

'I think so'

'The Taring Padi fights the establishment. Zak is the establishment. He can't be a member of this group. He can't quit the Kraton. He can't waste his family name to do his own performance. And mainly he can't organise protests on Independence Day.'

'OK, that is why they don't want him to do it. What's your problem with it?'

Aji rested his head in his hands and focused upon the newspaper article screwed up next to the seat. 'Tonight you will see the finest display of *wayang kulit* in Java. In a small theatre with seventy people. A performance fit for any Sultan this land has ever had. Zak is a genius.'

'But he doesn't want to use his genius in that way. As he said, "Talent should be your wings not your cage." '

'It will be his cage though, Leon. Can you not see? It will be all our cages.'

*

They walked ten feet apart and didn't speak but were together - not in the eyes of those passing but in the eyes of each other and for Josh that was all that mattered.

They rounded the outer edge of the park, sheltering under the branches that stooped over the path. The street lights shone and the odd motorbike passed with its light on half-beam and the town seemed to settle and wait for the rain to stop and for the night to come alive in the way only an Indonesian evening can.

As they reached the turning for the train station, Cinta peered through the gloom back towards the park. A man sat on a plastic seat receiving a haircut from another man. A sheet of tarpaulin, tied to the park railings and held aloft by two wooden sticks, covered them.

'What's wrong?' Josh said.

'My father has some problems. Maybe soon we are like that man.'

'At least he has a customer.'

'You do not understand. You look at everything with a full stomach.'

'What do you mean?'

'The man who receives the hair cut waits until evening because he knows that the other man needs to eat tonight and will take a lower price. He knows the hairdresser must say, "Yes."'

'What else have I looked at with a "full stomach"?' Josh said.

'Like earlier on the bus. You think the singers are romantic but they cannot read or write. They fall off the buses. They leave school early. They cannot even sing or play. They beg with a guitar and make only enough to eat.'

Josh stared into the rain that battered into his face. 'Well, that isn't my fault.'

'I do not say it was your fault.'

'Well you –'

'I cannot speak about it here.'

'Of course not,' Josh said, crossing the deserted street without her.

*

They sat and smoked until they had no cigarettes left. From time to time, Aji moved his head from side to side and clutched at his throat. When Leon caught him touching it, Aji would shift his hand and pretended to rub his stubble or the back of his hair.

'Are you OK?' Leon said.

'Yes.'

'It's OK to say you aren't?'

'I know.'

Aji stood and walked to the corner of the room, his tread careful and slow. He crouched down and slid aside part of the floorboard and dug his hand inside the hole created. He pulled out a battered leather wallet, replaced the floorboard and stood up. 'I need to make some phone calls,' he said, passing Leon on his way to the door. 'There is a *wartel* across the road. Want to come? You can check the internet.'

Leon rose and followed Aji to the door. They lifted the desk back across the room. Leon went back towards the door but Aji remained next to the desk. 'Do you think it was wrong of me to tell Zak he was ruining his life?'

'Is Zak your best friend?'

'Yes, I suppose he is.'

'Sometimes you need to tell them things they don't want to hear. Even if they hate you for it later.'

'You are very wise, do you know that.'

'Well...' said Leon, straining every sinew and muscle and nerve in his body to try to mask how happy that comment made him. 'Some people say that.'

*

The streams of water gushed down windows clouded

by the breath of the passengers. The wet tracks shimmered in the lamplight. Figures huddled outside under tarpaulin; beneath trees; inside abandoned cars. The tracks diverged and the train screeched to the right. In the carriage, a forest of arms and legs swayed with the movement. Through their midst Josh disappeared and appeared from her vision.

Closing her eyes and thinking about their kiss in the car; the bristle of his boyish moustache; the softness of his lips; the way he opened his eyes so slowly when it finished.

Yesterday, the feeling building all day. In McDonalds and the mall and the car she found deep affection and meaning in his every action. His gait. The constant blinking. The way he spoke slowly so she could understand. His nervous laugh when he repeated a question or she didn't understand. His lies that her English was perfect. His interest in her family and country and life. Her words when he left the car; a whisper at first; repeated with conviction; an urge she couldn't control. She loved him. His reaction and surprise and embarrassment as he left. In the car alone; trapped with feelings that she knew wouldn't go away.

The night before, she'd dreamt of them lying on a beach together. Waves lapping over their naked bodies. Him tugging back her hair and kissing her neck. His body smothering hers. Sinking into the wet sand. Waking and realising she'd been asleep and pulling up the sheet and snuggling under it and feeling an unknown warmth and shutting her eyes and drifting off to another place where they could be together.

The drilled reality of the alarm clock. The silence at breakfast. Plain left-over rice and water. The car journey to work. The horror of awaiting her father's departure. The relief of his departure. Overwhelming guilt. The walk to the station. Not daring to lift her head, to meet an eye, to chance a sighting.

Waiting on the platform. What was she doing? Pausing before she got on the train and thinking about the consequences: of those little girls she cared for; of the bitter old man whose life she could ruin; of the old woman possessed by a sadness that no one could reach. Stepping on the train to Bogor telling herself to control the previous day's excesses.

Reaching Bogor. Across the station concourse and waiting by the minibuses. The eagerness of his approach. The insensitivity of his affection. The humiliation of the bus journey: him sitting next to her; talking to her; paying the driver for both of them and refusing the change. The pounding of her heart as she got off the bus. The heat of his pursuit. His gentleness lost in anticipation. The bile and the sick and the fear as she reached the gates of the garden.

The peace of the park. Realising that she'd need to tell this beautiful man the truth: that she'd think of him always but that it wouldn't work. About to tell him when the rain came.

His wonder at the downpour and their run and laughter and hiding under the tree.
His body touching against hers. Whispering into her ear. The words tingling down her spine. Pushing back and feeling his body and with that contact all her restraint and negativity dissipating. Disparate imagines of purity and shared love exploded in her mind. A fantasy of their future. Sharing food in a restaurant, their legs brushing under the table. Shopping in the mall. Bringing him to her

friends' houses. Everyone marvelled at the handsome *bule*. Her handsome *bule*. Living together. Her making the food when he returned from work; Indonesian dishes; not too hot; that he'd grow to love. Spending the weekends in the park; planning a trip across the islands.

Those few minutes of dense entanglement under the ancient tree ended by the lightening. The white truck taking them out the park; taking him away.

That poor man cutting hair outside the park. Josh's comments. Her over-reaction. Thinking of her harsh words. So out of character; so uncontrolled; so rude.

She sat on the train, haunted by his sullen face and knew there was no way back.

*

In the *wartel* while Aji made a series of frantic phone calls, Leon sat down at the nearest computer and opened an internet window. He checked his email. A few from the lads back home. Five from his mum. One for each day since he last contacted her. He logged onto MSN Messenger.

*

The train ground to a halt. They filed out the exit. Josh brushed past her. He pressed ahead and looked over his shoulder and she saw his face and didn't know what she saw. Was it disappointment? Anger? Longing? Fear?

Over the next day she replayed that look over and over again; each time his features distorted in her reflective memory and provided a different answer.

*

Josh got off the train and walked towards the exit. He told himself not to look back at Cinta but he couldn't stop himself. He caught her eye and felt her rejection and turned and hurried out of the station and crossed the road without looking back again. He walked quickly towards Jalan Jaksa trying to stride away all his frustration. He passed an internet café and decided to go inside to cool down and take his mind off her. He went in, sat down at the computer closest to the fan and flung his bag on the floor. He logged onto his Hotmail account and signed into MSN Messenger. He'd received no emails. He opened the Independent website. The headline story read, 'The Return to Afghanistan: Americans Begin to Suffer Grim and Bloody Backlash.'

*

A message appeared in the bottom right hand corner of Leon's screen: Josh has signed in. Leon watched the icon lower and then disappear.

*

Josh read about the Americans being attacked by guerrilla forces; of American soldiers shot in Kabul and Kandahar; of the Americans bombing a wedding party and killing 55 people; of the fury of the Pashtuns at the US troops preventing survivors from helping the wounded; of the false allegations of US troops taking naked pictures of Afghan women; of the aid agencies' fear of being associated with the soldiers. He stopped before he reached the end of the article.

If he wasn't depressed before he was now.

He glanced at his watch and decided to leave. Before he logged off he maximised his MSN page. Only one person was online – Leon. His throat contracted. He clicked back on the Independent and waited for Leon to initiate contact.

He read the whole Sports section. Then the Comment

section. Then Motoring. He didn't even like cars. This was stupid. Leon was probably doing the same thing. Why was he so nervous about messaging someone he'd known since he was a child? He clicked on Leon's green icon and wrote.

Josh said:
How's things?

Leon said:
great... you?

Josh said:
Yes, good thanks.

Leon said:
where r you?

Josh said:
I'm Jakarta still. And you?

Leon said:
Yogyakarta

Josh said:
What are you doing?

Leon said:
I ve met this guy who's the puppet master to the sultan of Yogyakarta. This boy is top dog. You wont know this but the sultan here is mega powerful. He s like only king left in Indonesia, the unelected mayor and a messenger from god.

Josh said:
A messenger from God?

Leon said:
yeah him and some woman who lives in the sea and a volcano spirit. They protect this land from disaster

Josh said:
Where are you getting this information?

Leon said:
its what they believe here. Special sort of Islam. anyway Zaks family have been the royal puppet masters for hundreds of centuries but he wants out. hes quittin and doing his own show. the first one is tonight. man its ruffling some feathers round here. he lives in this squat with other artists. theyre revolutionists

Josh said:
You mean revolutionaries?

Leon said:
this Zak guy is amazing. yesterday i just spent hours talking to the guy. hes like the leader of this group of artists. They re called the paring tandi or something like that

Josh said:
What are they trying to revolutionise?

Leon said:
i dunno. problems that are happening in the world

Josh said:
So basically they told you and you didn't listen?

Leon said:
it's just you i don't listen to. i listen to everything Zak says

Josh said:
You're terrible at listening to foreigners and being patient with their English.

Leon said:
Zak's english is better than yours

Josh said:
And yours as well then.

Leon said:
actually someone was just telling me that im 1 of the smarter people theyve met and brave also and they could do with my sort in the struggle thats 2 follow

Josh said
Sure Leon. In fact, I bet they have been waiting for someone just like you. Are you the final piece in the jigsaw?

Leon said:
yeah im like that Lawrence guy in the film who goes to

another country and gathers up the locals and fights the police

Josh said:
The police? Also did you just compare yourself to TE Lawrence?

Leon said:
no lawrence of arabia you div

Josh said:
Just get on with your story.

Leon said:
OK, just then some people broke into their compound and tried to shake down one of their members to get some info about this performance tonight and this big protest thats going down on independence day. one of these guys was practically killing Zak's mate Aji when suddenly I stepped in and scared these guys away

Josh said:
Who were they?

Leon said:
Spies or somethin

Josh said:
You stepped in and scared off two spies?

Leon said:

no big deal

Josh said:
Anyway back on planet earth... what are your plans?

Leon said:
see what goes down tonight then head to the countryside to lay low and prepare for this protest.

Josh said:
My trip is going really well btw. Thanks for asking.

Leon said:
yeah what the hell have you been doing since i left? I guess looking around museums and chatting to french people in hostels about fossils?

Josh said:
I don't even know what that means.

Leon said:
that bird binned you off yet?

Josh said:
We looked around Jakarta yesterday and went to Bogor today.

Leon said:
shagged her yet?

Josh said:
I wondered how long it would take you to ask that.

No!

Leon said:
come on stop being a pussy as usual and make a move!!!

Josh said:
You're an idiot. You have no idea. It's different around here. You don't just do that with girls when you first meet them.

Leon said:
why not?

Josh said:
There are like rules that we didn't even know about and I don't mean the bar girls before you starting talking about Elok/ Laura. You have to go out on dates and be chaperoned by family members. For example, today we had to go all the way to Bogor just not to be seen.

Leon said:
which is why i told u not 2waste ur time with that girl and come with me instead

Josh said:
So it's all a waste of time if you don't get laid? It's always the same macho bullshit with you, Leon. Do you not think it's a bit romantic?

Leon said:

look you re going to be here for a few weeks max. sure its romantic but remember the only thing possible is a holiday romance and your not even having that = its a waste of time

Josh said:
I'm sure it was you who said that just because they say no at the start of the night doesn't mean they'll say no at the end.

Leon said:
sounds like your night ended days ago and your alone on the dance floor. remember that book you gave me that you were always slagging me off about cos ive been readin it for months and not finishing it

Josh said:
The God of Small Things

Leon said:
its got that character father mulligan from ireland who the pakistan woman falls in love with but nothing can happen and he knows nothing can happen the whole time but then he totally plays it and just leaves and she ends up alone thinking about him for the rest of her life?

Josh said:
Well it wasn't exactly like that...

Leon said:
well add it together. You're just leading on some local

girl. a proper nice one by the sounds of it. then you're going to leave. You're father mulligan!

Josh said:
How does this advice add up with all YOUR supposed womanising on this trip?

Leon said:
ive been getting it on with travellers and locals on the scene... ive not been dipping into real lives. nothing changes... if it wasn't me it would be someone else...

Josh said:
That's convenient

Leon said:
why don't you just give it up and come here? if you get a train in the morning you ll get here by night. you ll meet the coolest people and get involved in this massive protest. imagine that? 2 bules marching down the street, placks, fighting the police, proper revolutionists, like Che

Josh said:
I can't tomorrow I've agreed to meet Elok or Laura as you know her.

Leon said:
whhhhaaattt???!!! u little player. mayb ive not been giving you enough credit

Josh said:

It's not like that. It's Cinta's dad's birthday and she can't spend the day with me so Elok's taking me out instead.

Leon said:
good!! well put some moves on her. shes proper easy. all you need to do is buy her a couple of drinks and you re in. no payback... your down here the next day with a notch on your bedpost to go with the other one and we re all happy...

Josh said:
Right Leon very good. I'll speak to you later.

Leon said:
Josh, listen. Fuck all the chat, just be careful alright – we're miles from home and you don't know what you re messing with here.

Before he could send the message, he saw Josh had signed out.

*

Josh logged off MSN and put, "Paring Tadi" and Yogyakarta into Google. He searched the first five pages of results. There was nothing about any underground artistic group. For a moment he forgot about Cinta and laughed out loud, drawing the attention of some teenage gamers playing Medal of Honour.

Typical Leon. He was probably sitting in some café by himself, full of energy and lonely because he'd had no one to vent upon for about half an hour. Yet even in Leon's world of exaggeration this story of the Sultan's servant rising up against the city in an artistic revolution was farfetched. His imagination was truly incredible. And to think during their conversation that he'd actually compared himself to Lawrence of Arabia and Che Guevara. Josh laughed again, logged off, left the café and headed back towards the guest house.

*

Leon watched Aji leave the phone booth and come over to his computer.

'Why are you smiling?' Aji said.

'I was just chatting to my mate Josh. He's stayed back in Jakarta to be with a girl.'

'An Indonesian girl?' Aji expression was part grin and part grimace.

'Yes but she's not some bar girl. She's like a really traditional girl who still lives at home with her parents.'

'Does he know that every Indonesian girl has hundreds of fathers, brothers and cousins waiting for boyfriends to make a mistake? Man, when the guy is a foreigner everyone she knows is her uncle.'

'I've told him. Thing is, he's never had a girlfriend before. He wants some sort of little romance like off the movies with popcorn and nachos and dips and dinner dates and all that shit.'

'You should tell him to be careful.'

'He won't do anything bad. He's too much of a pussy. All he'll do is waste another couple of weeks of his holiday before he realises he's wasting his time.'

'Come on.' Aji said, slapping Leon's back. 'Let's go back. The party has started.'

'There's a party?'

'Of course. With the *Taring Padi* there always is.'

*

And so Leon's first interaction with the *Taring Padi* began. Through the compound's corridors they went, handshakes and smiles, broken English and offers of cigarettes. Into an artist's room, marvelling at his posters and paintings. Being shown how to print pictures; rolling the ink on the *cukil* wood; pressing it onto the canvas; Leon's first attempt drawing hilarity from the onlookers; his second, admiration and praise.

Back into the courtyard. The conspirators in the centre had more than doubled to twenty. Shouting replaced the earlier whispers: the music had started. There were fifty people; soon seventy; singing, clapping and dancing. The women took it in turns to teach Leon Javanese dance. He twirled and spun and laughed and thought that this was turning into the best night of his life.

*

As they trooped down the street towards the theatre people stopped to study the mohawks, hair dye, piercings, tattoos and studded necklaces that decorated the group. Bottles and joints where passed amongst the revellers. Impromptu sing-a-longs accompanied the excited chatter. Leon was in the centre, a fully-fledged member of the group of artists - and he couldn't draw a stick man.

*

Leon and Aji descended the stairs and stopped at a row near the front. They clambered towards two spare seats, avoiding bags and feet, and sat down.

'It's very busy,' Aji said to Leon.

'Is that a bad thing?'

'Yes,' Aji said, scanning the auditorium. 'The audience is very different to what I expect. Zak told me it was friends only. I can see some *dalangs* over there. Yes, there are many... and one of Zak's teachers is here... some elders from his Mosque... those young men with beards and the same t-shirts must be some young Islamic society or something... his friends from school... I think that's his family over there.... yes, it is... oh shit it's those guys!'

'What guys?'

'The ones who came to my room.'

'They aren't going to do anything to us here.'

A sudden blast of music accompanied the separation of the curtains. The main lights cut and the glare of the screen bathed the audience in a brilliant white light. The screen darkened and a shadow puppet appeared. The audience roared with delight.

To Leon, the production was markedly different to the previous day in the Kraton. The orchestra sounded the same but the rhythm and structure was more modern. The puppets' designs were more elaborate and grandiose. The screen was larger - almost cinematic. The scenes were a third of the length; the action more frequent and greater in its intensity.

Despite the language barrier, Leon discerned that the story was based around a young couple who, although they didn't love each other, were preparing for a wedding arranged by their parents. Their wealth and stature were as transparent as their unhappiness. The groom was chastised by his strict father while the bride cried and sang high-pitched songs that explored her inner pain.

A few moments of light relief came from the groom's best friend, who cheered up his companion with various songs and dances.

At the culmination of each scene a tree fluttered

across the scene.

'What's wrong with you?' asked Leon, viewing the furrow of Aji's brow.

'That's called the tree of life. It separates the scenes. It has two sides: heaven and hell. It shows the future of the story. Every time it shows hell.'

Leon listened to Zak's despondent lilt accompanied by the harsh rattle of the mallets upon the gongs. 'You can tell.'

The song faded. The audience sat in a contemplative hush, engrossed in the story's slow yet gripping development. The wedding day had arrived. The groom and his best friend were alone in a room. After two dramatic speeches, the best friend sank to his knees and declared his love for the groom. The couple started to kiss. The groom's father entered the room and yelled with horror.

Aji had shuffled so far down that his bottom no longer touched the seat. Leon could hear seats hitting the backrests, footsteps in the semi-dark, shouts in Indonesian, the opening and shutting of the entrance door.

Back on stage a battle ensued between the groom's best friend and his father; great booms of the bass symbolising each blow.

Some that had stayed booed. Others rose to their feet to cheer in support.

With a mighty crash the best friend knocked the father to the ground and towered over him victoriously. The bride screamed with delight realising she'd been released her from her fate. She gave her ring to the best friend, who placed it on the groom's finger. The couple were declared man and man.

A battle between applause and jeers commenced. A minute of bedlam later there was still no victor. The lights blinked on. A variety of missiles including lighters and coins rained down upon the stage. A scuffle broke out near the front. It spread to the rows behind like a Mexican wave of violence. Pandemonium. Wrestling in aisles. A shrieking call to arms. The thwack of knuckle on skin.

As the auditorium erupted, Leon clambered over the rows of seats. Gasping for air, he tried to barge his way to the exit. A blue spark flashed in his eye as an object hit his head. The cacophony dulled and a sharp ring whined through his head. He stumbled back into the theatre and tasted a saline liquid in his mouth. An unmanned confectionary stall provided temporary support as he regained his balance. A group of young men surged past him, broken chair legs and other makeshift weapons in their hands. Their attack was repelled by a counter surge from a group that manned the door.

With no escape, Leon glanced to each side and measured a small run-up. Four quick paces. He vaulted the stall's serving hatch, caught his ankle on the way over and landed on his hands and knees. Groaning in pain, he crawled into an open cupboard and pulled the door shut. Everything turned black.

*

Zak ran from the stage, dodging the missiles and abuse that followed his departure. Along the corridor he went, unable to see more than a foot ahead. He stumbled across the unseen undulations of the floor until he collided with a flat surface. His hand shot up, hitting what felt like a handle. He lowered it and opened the door and slipped inside. His left hand groped the wall. Where the hell was the light? No time. He thrust his hand in his pocket, found a key and removed it.

He jabbed the key against the door but was unable to locate the keyhole. Was this even his dressing room?

Voices echoed along the corridor. Footsteps becoming clearer. He dropped the key. A high-pitched rattle.

'Shit, shit, shit, shit,' he whispered, scrambling on the floor trying to find it. His hand hit cold metal. He picked up the key, got to his feet, grabbed the handle and jabbed the key towards the door. The key slipped straight into the hole. He jiggled it inside, straining for the correct fit. With a turn to the right, the key located the mechanism and clicked.

He pressed his back against the door with his arms outspread. Was it locked? Voices getting closer. Unable to check. Their footsteps ceased. Heavy breath on the other side of the wood. The sound of the handle lowering. The door gave. Slightly. He squeezed his eyes shut. The door jarred. A kick vibrated through the wood. The handle snapped upwards. Pacing outside. A momentary silence. The footsteps became distant and then faded.

Zak slid down the doorframe and sagged onto the floor. Alone in the dark, he could hear his heartbeat and the intake of each sharp breath. He clamped his eyes shut and tried to soothe his body into submission. But the feeling wouldn't go away. He sprung to his feet. Why did he want it to? Was this not why he created the play and handpicked the audience in the first place?

He unlocked the door and strode back towards the action. Halfway down the corridor he banged into another person. 'Zak?' a familiar voice said.

His hand traced the outline of the figure's features.

'Aji?'

'Where are you going?'

'Back to the stage.'

'No, don't be stupid,' fingers gripping his wrist. 'We've just managed to calm everything down. It'll start again if you go back.'

'Let them try. Why should I hide?'

Zak shrugged off Aji and hurried on.

*

Out in the main theatre, the lights shone brightly over the stage. Missiles littered the boards. Members of the *Taring Padi* manned the main door, great slams coming from the outside.

The whole night had felt like a dream but as he stood there looking at the aftermath of the chaos everything became clear and he realised that all of the last two years' work had been worth it. Towards him walked Aji. Zak gave him an ecstatic smile – one which Aji failed to return.

'What did you think of the performance?'

'I think you are selfish and crazy and insane. Why did you do it?'

'You know how important this issue is,' Zak said. 'Indonesia needs to face this. It needs to change.'

'You've ruined your career. You know that the other *dalangs* were here? Why did you let me invite them?'

Zak ran his hand down Aji's arm. 'To educate them about us.'

'Don't touch me,' Aji said, stepping away. 'I'm not ready for this.'

'We can't be scared for the rest of our lives.'

'Yes, we can. Two men came to my room earlier. They were asking me about your performance and about the protest. They threatened and attacked me. If Leon hadn't been there...'

'Who are they?' Zak said.

'I don't know. They were here tonight.'

'You think they started the trouble?'

'Definitely! You know how important you are in this city. Do you think you can just quit the Kraton and do performances like this? Do you think you can organise a protest for thousands of people on the most important day of the year and no one will do anything? You actually think they don't know? That they haven't been watching you? This is why I told you not to do this. They won't let you. You won't win.'

Zak lowered his head.

'They told me to cancel the protest or there would be trouble,' Aji said. 'If you do what they say and you might be OK.'

'I have people coming from all over Java - farmers, workers and students. It's their day.'

'Are you sure it's not *your* day? Like tonight... did you invite all these people on purpose because you knew that this would happen?

'Of course not.'

'I don't think tonight was about art or making a point about the issue,' Aji said. 'I think it was about you.'

'Don't be angry with me. Be angry with them - the people who won't accept us for who we are.'

'I am angry with them but I'm also angry with you. I'm not coming on the trip tomorrow.'

'Fine... I'll go alone with Leon. He has courage... unlike you.'

Aji's finger poked into his chest. 'This may be a game

to you but this is my life.'

'Don't touch me like that.' Zak slapped Aji's hand away. 'You spend your life fighting for the poor of this country. But you'll do nothing to stand up for yourself. You know what you are?'

'Tell me.'

'A coward.'

Zak watched his boyfriend take a step towards him, his eyes burning with fury.

*

Leon pushed open the door with a tentative poke and peered out. He clambered out of the cupboard and crawled under the latch of the stall to reach the back row of seats. Voices boomed off the ceiling and echoed back down. He peeked over the seats and saw fifteen to twenty people gathered on stage. The group reconstructed the riot by mimicking the punches and kicks they'd given and received.

In the corner, isolated from the main inquest, the Puppet Master and the Punk were deep in conversation. Aji delivered his words with an almost exaggerated vehemence. His finger prodded into Zak's chest. Zak slapped it away. Aji looked down at his hand then back to Zak before grabbing him and slamming him against the wall. He pressed his tattooed forearm across Zak's chest, held him for a second, before letting go. Zak slumped to the floor, his turban knocked off his head. The group rushed over before splitting into two sub-groups, each one consoling a different party.

Taking advantage of the distraction, Leon decided to slip out while he could. As he rushed towards the exit, he felt conflicted: delighted to be leaving this freak show;

daunted by what he may find outside.

15 August 2002

The blackness starts the moment she opens her eyes. The curtains and bed sheets are black. The wardrobe and her clothes are black. Everything is black. Or white. White like the incarnations of the night. White like the light of the morning. The white is worse than the black. The blackness hides you in its abyss. The white opens you. It shows the world, how thin and miserable and pathetic you are.

She got up and stumbled over to the curtains and tugged them closed. Exhausted by her trip to the window, she fell back on the bed. A solitary line of white still slit across the ceiling. She pulled the sheet over her head and lay there. Downstairs, through the buzzing in her ears, she could hear her husband. Rustling, restless, waiting.

She tapped herself on the forehead. Harder and harder. Get up. Tap. Get up. Tap.

But she couldn't get up on a normal day. Yes, a normal day - when she waited until everyone left before she got up. Where the top of the stairs felt like a precipice. One step at a time, convinced they would disintegrate and that she'd fall onto their sharp edges. A normal day, when the first thing she did downstairs was rush to the door to see if it was locked. A normal day, when she jumped each time the phone went. When she didn't answer the door. When she put it off for hours and then ate her first meal. Fear, pure fear, that each unendurable swallow would get stuck in her throat, choking her, leaving her dying and alone.

Or those other normal days when he made her go to his shop and she sat in the blackest corner knowing that every customer looked at her and wanted her to leave.

Today wasn't a normal day. It was worse than a

normal day. The worst day of the year: her husband's birthday. The day when she wore that ridiculous *kebaya* and put on all that jewellery and make-up and faced herself in the mirror and realised how ugly she was. The day that he insisted they all spent together, cooped up and strangled in that small room.

The dress, the make-up, the misery of the company, she could handle. The cooking she couldn't. He wanted her to cook his favourite dishes, like she did when they first met; when it was light; when they were young; perhaps even happy. How could she? How could she cook it like back then when she was like this now? Why did he ask her to do it anyway? To show everyone how pathetic and useless she'd become? To humiliate her and make her even sicker and make that kitchen smaller and darker than it already was?

Last year, she did as he wanted. But how? How did she get dressed and cook that food and sit there all day? Why could she do it then but she couldn't do it now? Was she getting worse? Slipping deeper into it? Trapped and never to return?

She couldn't control her tears. Stop, please stop, she begged herself but her body sobbed on. Footsteps outside. Here he came. To get her up. Like last year. But this year she couldn't do as he said. She just couldn't. The door slowly opened.

A black figure in the doorway. It clicked on the light. Deathly white. Footsteps to the bed. He leaned over her. Knees up to her chest. Heart pounding. A blackness gripping her throat. Opening her eyes to face him.

Cinta's face two feet away. She moaned with relief and reached up and hugged her. She gripped and didn't let go, trembling in her daughter's arms.

*

Josh sat on the wall outside the restaurant where they'd agreed to meet and stared at his watch. She was an hour late. He'd have left but he was expecting nothing else from Elok.

Ten minutes later, at the very moment he'd decided to leave, a silver Mercedes screeched around the corner and hurtled towards him. It pulled in, mounted the pavement and braked sharply. Josh scrambled out of the way, narrowly avoiding the front bumper. The window lowered and Elok's face appeared. She beamed at Josh and released a great blast of the horn. He yanked open the door and got in the passenger seat, 'Why the hell did you beep the horn?'

'I show I am here.'

'I'd noticed – you almost ran over my feet. You didn't need to deafen me as well.'

She laughed and held her ears, 'Oh poor me. I hurt my ears! I deaf! Me deaf *bule*!'

'What time do you call this anyway? You're over an hour late.'

Elok batted down the sunshade and inspected herself in the mirror. '*Jam karet*.'

'Eh?'

'Rubber time, *bule*.' She reapplied lipstick to her already red, glossy lips and twisted the stick shut. With a last longing look at herself, she flicked up the visor and, using every modicum of the car's powerful engine, accelerated away.

The car swerved to the left before careering towards a stationary lorry. Josh shut his eyes, pushed back with his feet and waited for the impact. Nothing came. Opening one eye, he watched the car speed towards the next hazard.

*

Leon went under the arched entrance of Gang II and left behind the side-alleys and rats and stench of untreated sewage of Yogya's backpacker ghetto. He turned right along Jalan Sosrowijayan and passed the horses and carts and bicycle pedi-cabs and restaurants offering burgers and pizzas and cold beers and crossed the road and walked on until he reached a brown Suzuki camper van. It looked like it had been used as an instrument in the previous night's *gamelan* such were the array of dents and fissures that scarred its body. Leon rounded the vehicle, creaked open the door and climbed into the three person front seat. The van smelt of damp leather, turpentine, dried dust and old sweat: the van smelt of the *Taring Padi.*

'How are you?' Zak said.

'OK.' Leon swivelled in his seat and flung his rucksack into the back amongst the paints and half-finished puppets that littered the back of the van. 'Is this banger yours?' he said.

'What's a banger?'

Leon reached to his left, tugged the seat belt across his torso and saw there was no holder to buckle. 'This is a banger.'

Their eyes met. 'You have a problem?'

'No... let's go.'

Zak shrugged, wrestled the gear stick into first and set off. 'So are you ready for a journey of a lifetime?'

'Where are we going?'

'It is a surprise. All I can say is that today you will experience the spirit, brilliance and deep sadness that is

Java.'

'I thought you said you needed somewhere to lay low after the show and to get some protection before the protest.'

'Yes, that also.'

Leon wanted to say well make your mind up but managed to stop himself.

'Last night was brilliant, wasn't it?' Zak said.

Leon looked out the passenger window and didn't reply.

'Remember, I told you how art can change the world and how it can...'

They left the Sosrowijayan area and took a right. The road dipped and they went under a bridge, crossed the railway tracks and turned left. The road led them west out of Yogyakarta towards the plains and mountains beyond. As they drove, Leon caught various parts of Zak's speech, *I cannot believe the performance attracted such strong feelings on both sides.... it shows what art can do for this country.... it can start discussions about topics and feelings that we are too scared to talk about...* but on the whole tried not to listen. He wound down the window and let the air hit his face but found his neck getting hotter and hotter as Zak's sermon, delivered in his annoying over-formal English, went on and on.

'You're unreal you know that?' Leon said, unable to hold it in any longer.

'Thank you.'

'It wasn't a compliment. It's called sarcasm. What the hell happened last night?'

'You mean the small fight at the end?'

'Small fight?!'

'There were many different people at the

performance,' Zak said, one hand on the steering wheel, the other hanging out of the open window casual as you like. 'A great mix of people with different opinions. I thought you would like the action. You said you wanted some adventures.'

'Not adventures like that.'

'You didn't enjoy the performance?' Zak said, in high-pitched surprise like hadn't even contemplated the possibility.

'I enjoyed some of it.'

'What parts did you not enjoy?'

'All the bender parts?'

'Bender parts? What are these?'

'All that gay shit with those two guys. What was the point of it?'

'The point was it was the theme and the story. It is a theme that means a lot to me.'

'I don't understand?'

'Because of the way I am and the way I live. Do you understand now?'

'No.'

'What would you say if I said it was important to me because I am gay and Aji is my boyfriend?'

'I'd say stop the van and let me out.'

They drove on, passing bike repair shops, roadside stalls and shack-like houses. Motorbikes roared past, zipping into and out of the small pockets of space. Zak wove amongst them, speeding up and slowing down, the perturbed look on his face becoming more pronounced.

'...OK,' he said, indicating and pulling over at the side of the road, his movements performed with exaggerated control. He brought the van to a halt, leant across Leon and opened the passenger door. 'Goodbye.'

'Goodbye?'

'Please get out.'

Leon stuck his head out of the door and looked out at the street. 'Where am I?'

'About 5 kilometres from your hotel. You are in a dangerous area but maybe it is not as dangerous as sitting in a car with a "bender" like me.'

A group of youths slunk past, jostling and laughing. A woman, perched on an upturned bucket, vigorously scratched her lower calf whilst glaring at the van. A stall owner dropped his cigarette and ground it into the pavement with his foot.

'Alright Zak point proven.'

'Is it? I thought you would understand.' Zak said, his finger jabbing into Leon's arm in rhythm with each word. 'That is why I invited you last night. That is why I told you my secret now.'

'Well you should've warned me earlier...'

'Warned you? To be gay is not a disease.'

'Is that why you sneak around disused buildings and dark theatres?'

'No, I do it because people in this country are as small-minded as you.' Zak faced the road, eyes following the passing cars, his Adam's apple rising and dropping.

Leon exhaled, 'Listen, I didn't mean to be a bad guy. It's just that I've never hung out with a ben.. I mean... a homo... I mean, what do you call yourself?'

'Humans.'

'Well, I've never hung around with one before, you see, and it'll just take some getting used to that's all.' Leon removed his hand from Zak's shoulder. 'You do know I'm not one right?'

'GET OUT,' Zak said, his vehemence so soon after his calm causing Leon to jump. Zak unfastened his seatbelt and tore it away from his body. His eyes glowed like those of a feral cat. 'I spent every day for two years making that play and I will not have it ruined by you or Aji or those people last night.'

'Fine by me... psychopath,' Leon said. One foot on the pavement, gripping the door panel for leverage, Zak's foot pushed hard into his back. He stumbled and fell onto the street. A rock dug into his ribs. The door slammed shut and the van drove away.

Leon pushed himself up to his feet, scooped up the rock and sprinted after the vehicle. Failing to make any ground, he hurled the rock in its direction. It looped and dipped before crunching through the back window. The van veered out of control and collided with a nearby stall.

*

Cinta cradled her and lowered her back down upon the mattress. Wening lay there and looked up at her daughter and felt like Cinta was her mother and not the other way round.

'What's wrong?' Cinta said.

'I'm feeling a bit tired today.'

You do that. Make excuses. Tell people the problem is temporary and small. Sometimes you tell yourself that too. Sometimes you believe it. Most of the time you don't.

'What has happened?' Cinta said, stroking her arm.

That is what they thought. That it was one thing that made her like that and when that one thing was fixed she'd be OK. Like repairing a car or a bike.

How could she tell them it wasn't like that? That she

didn't know why she felt that way so how could they?

'It's because of father's birthday, isn't it?' Cinta said.

They did that as well. Liked to attach it to an event or news. Like when they argued with a friend or had a bad day at work and they felt a bit down. Something they could put into a category and understand.

'Yes. It's today,' Wening said, because it was today. But it was also yesterday and the day before and tomorrow and next week. 'I can't do it. I can't get up and cook for him.'

'What has father done?'

That was something else they couldn't understand. That it wasn't the things they did or didn't do or anything they could or couldn't do. It was her. All her.

'Mum, you didn't use to be like this.'

Sometimes hearing what she used to be like made her feel worse: sometimes it gave her hope. Mostly it did both.

'Remember when we got our first television and we'd sit and watch it and I'd sit on the floor and you and father would sit on the sofa and you'd fall asleep on him. Or when your parents came around and you used to sing and grandfather made you do that dance you did as a girl.' Cinta's strokes on her arm increased in pace as did the speed of her speech. 'Yes, and you used to dance and go all red and look at father to see his reaction. But he never laughed at you. He just watched you and smiled. Like he was proud. So proud.'

'Do you remember the picnics in Merdeka square?' Wening heard herself say.

'Remember when you bought me a Coca-Cola and father was so angry?'

The memory made Wening smile. Cinta bounced up

and ran out of the room. At first she thought Cinta had gone and wasn't going to come back. But she returned and silently shut the door and sat back on the bed. It seemed strange but she missed her during those thirty seconds. Missed her so much. Through the sheet she could feel Cinta's body touching hers and she wanted to clasp and hold her. As if reading her mind, Cinta searched under the duvet and took her hand. Her touch was warm. So warm. She rested a picture on her stomach. 'I found this.'

The picture was black and white but coloured in her mind. Sat on golden thrones. Ahmad wore a white shirt and turban. A *kris* dagger, owned by his great-grandfather and used by his father in the War of Independence, was tucked into his batik sarong. She wore a golden lace *kebaya*, silver high-heeled shoes and a silk gown. Jewellery passed down through generations of her family adorned her wrists, ears and neck. Their wedding day. Traditional Javanese – lavish, opulent and unaffordable.

'Where did you find that?' Wening said.

'Father had it the other day. I picked it up when he finished.'

Wening pushed herself up onto her elbows and studied the picture. 'We had to sit on those thrones for hours. Hundreds of people were passing us. We must have heard *selamat menempuh* or *selamat bahagia* a thousand times. I remember we hardly knew any of the guests. We were looking at each other and saying, "who was that?" or "what are their names again?" In the end, we started laughing and couldn't stop. But no one said anything. Maybe they thought we were so happy that we couldn't contain it.'

'Were you?' Cinta said.

'I think we were.'

Cinta placed another photo on her lap. 'And this.'

A makeshift marquee tied to the houses on the opposite sides of the street. 'That was the reception,' Wening said. 'It was on this street. Almost everyone in the *kampung* came. Ahmad's father gave a speech saying although the start had been difficult that his family now felt welcomed into the community.'

Cinta frowned. 'Why?'

'They weren't from here and your grandfather was a communist.'

'Father says he wasn't –'

'I know what he says.' Wening sat up further and whispered. 'Your father doesn't know this but the only reason my father agreed to the match was that the dowry was publically doubled. My father returned half the sum out of the sight of the *kampung*. It was so his family could afford the wedding; so my family could save face.'

'Why save face?'

'His father was a prisoner...they had no money... it was a different time.'

'That's wrong.'

'You shouldn't tell that to father.'

'I wouldn't. Ever.' Cinta shuffled on the bed. 'Why did you tell me?'

'I don't know.'

Cinta's hand rubbed up and down her back. 'You can tell me things.'

'I know.'

'About today –'

'Stop.'

'You have to,' Cinta said, her eyes imploring in the

way only a daughter can. 'It's important to him.'

'Do you know when you want to do something important but you just can't?'

Cinta's eyes glazed and she looked down at the pictures on her lap and nodded.

'That's how I feel.'

'We'll do it together, OK?' Cinta moved in and hugged her. 'First we'll make the food and then we'll get you dressed. I'll ask father to go out so we can prepare.'

'Yes,' Wening said, hugging Cinta so tight that she thought her ribs would crack. 'Yes. Please, let's do that.'

*

'Drive faster!' Leon yelled, gripping the headrest and looking out of the back of the van.

'I'm trying,' Zak said, his old van reaching the unfamiliar realm of top gear. 'Where are they?'

'Right behind us.'

After Leon had hit his van with the rock, Zak lost control and all but destroyed a clothes stall. The furious owner refused Zak's money and apologies. A crowd gathered. They started rocking the van in an attempt to tip it. Zak and Leon jumped inside; trying to save the van; trying to save themselves. The stall owner booted the van's body. Others joined in. Zak floored the pedal, scattered the mob and accelerated away. Just when they thought they were safe, they noticed a motorbike carrying two passengers following them.

Ten minutes later and the pursuit continued, the bike snaking between the pieces of leather and paper that flew out the smashed, back-window and onto the road. The passenger held an object by his side which glinted in the light.

Leon adjusted the rear-view mirror. 'Is that a machete or a sword he has?'

'What?' Torrents of wind blustered through the back window. 'I cannot hear you.'

To their right, a wagon reversed from an alley across the street and into their path. Zak swerved left but the driver-side wing mirror clipped its tailgate. It hung limply, attached only by its wires.

'Shit,' Zak said, looking back at the truck.

'It's OK,' Leon said. 'I think we have lost them.'

'I do not think we have.'

'Why?'

'Red light,' Zak said, slowing down as he approached a line of stationary traffic.

*

'Ok, today Cinta is busy with the birthday of her dad,' Elok said, chatting away, taking in the sights of the city, concentrating on anything but her driving. 'So she tells me to take this *bule* around Jakarta and show him some things he like to see.'

'Yes, she told me.'

'I show you many things. You are with the correct person. You know the Stadium?'

'No. Watch that car!'

'It is big club with seven floors. Is amazing. Best club in Jakarta. I take you tomorrow night.'

'Elok brake. BRAKE!'

'Why?'

'You almost hit that bike.'

'Why *bule* so scared in car?'

'Because you're driving it?'

'Funny *bule*, no? Very funny Josh *bule*.'

Josh clasped hands together on his lap and inwardly begged for the journey to end. 'Are we almost there?' he said.

'Not close yet. Josh get boring, yes? It take too long? OK we drive faster.'

'No!'

Elok careered across a junction towards a man wearing a beret hat, beige shirt and brown trousers. He stood next to a black motorbike, the word, "Polisi" etched across the windshield in yellow writing. He saw the silver Mercedes driving straight for him, stopped waving through the other lane of traffic and froze.

Elok brought the car to a halt two feet away from his cowering body. She wound down the window and they proceeded to have a terse exchange. While Elok threw her arms around like a chastised child, the *polisi* had regained both his composure and authority. After much debate, Elok pulled some money from her purse and slapped it into his gloved hand and drove away - her brush with the law having no effect upon the speed of her driving or speech.

'Fuck the *polisi*! *Maling*! Did you see this? He say I pay fine. Fine into your pocket, I say. Proper fine, he say. Do you know who I am? I say. I make problem for you Mr *Polisi*. Big problem. He is scared...very scared.'

'If he's so scared why did you pay the fine?'

'You know this days you have fine for anything. My friend Simon. He *bule*. Simon had a lot of drug for ten maybe fifteen people for one night in the Stadium. He catched by *polisi* and you know what he get? Two million rupiah fine.'

'No jail? That was lucky.'

'Lucky? He no lucky.' She bawled into his ear. 'He lose all drugs and all money and you think he lucky?'

They reached an intersection with a constant flow of traffic in both directions. After two failed attempts to pull out, Elok wound down the window and called to a man wearing a luminous vest who lingered in the centre of the road. '*Kanan*!'

Without hesitation, the man stepped in front of an oncoming vehicle and raised his hand. The vehicle did an emergency stop and halted a few inches from the diminutive figure. Elok pulled out and crossed to the opposite side of the road in the gap he'd created. The man followed the car. Again, he stepped out, hand raised, stopping the traffic and waved Elok through. No one beeped or complained - such behaviour seemed to be the normal course of events. Elok leant out of the window, gave the man 2,000 rupiah and drove on.

'What the hell was that?'

'I pay 2,000 – one for each side of road.'

'Not the price... the whole thing?'

'That is his job. He is a *parkir penuh*.'

'Do they not get run over?'

'Of course.'

'Then what happens?'

'Someone else takes their place. Why you do this with your face?' Elok asked, twisting up her features.

'It seems strange that's all.'

'This is Jakarta. There is no traffic light so there is a problem. Someone with no money fix the problem for someone with more money. The person who fix the problem has money. Now he pays someone to fix his problems. Simple.'

*

The van slowed for the red light and became trapped inside the static chaos; black fumes spluttered from exhaust pipes; new smog mixed with old smog; pollution strangling the life out of the muggy day. Above, five rows of traffic to their fore, a traffic light displayed red numbers that counted down until the next green light.

Leon and Zak stared at the numbers. Fifty.... forty nine... forty eight... the figures felt disconnected from the reality of time.

'I can see them coming,' Leon said, looking in the rear view mirror. 'Yeah, it's definitely the stall owner. '

'How close?' Zak said, his head turning back and forth from the countdown to the traffic behind, like he was watching a game of tennis.

'Closer with every word,'

'Fifteen seconds.'

'Shit,' Leon hunkered down in his seat. 'I think he just pointed at us.'

'Five seconds.'

'They're riding towards us.'

Zak went on zero; his bumper practically touching the vehicle in front.

The bike rode to their rear left. One man was hunched forward over the handlebars: the other sat side-saddle. The bike accelerated until it was adjacent with the van. They rode four feet apart. Leon could see the detail of the men's faces. They were no longer an object chasing him but people and for that his heart roared ever the more.

The man riding side-saddle yelled and pointed the machete at Leon. Leon wanted to raise his hand up in apology or surrender but couldn't. You didn't do that. Not when it had gone this far - however wrong you were.

The bike homed into touching distance. Side-saddle lifted his arm and cracked the side window with the machete. The glass crystallised but didn't cave in. The second blow sent it scattering across the vehicle. Fragments battered into Leon's neck. Zak flinched and momentarily lost control and veered onto the other side of the road. A group of motorbikes dispersed. A truck's horn bellowed. Zak fought with the wheel and returned the van to the left-hand side and straightened to avoid the bike.

'What you doing? Knock them off the bike.'

Zak shook his head.

Leon lunged for the wheel but Zak blocked his attempt.

A screech and a spark to his left. The machete hitting the metal body of the car.

Leon steadied himself and took a deep breath. He was on his own now. He pulled the handle, unlatching the passenger door and let it rest on its hinges.

'What are you doing?' Zak said.

'Ending this.'

The motorbike drew level. The man sat side-saddle grasped the window-frame.

Leon laid his forearm flat on the armrest of the door and waited.

Side-saddle lifted his arm.

Leon placed his foot against the door.

The machete glinted above side-saddle's head.

In one violent motion, Leon kicked out and extended his arm. The door rocketed open and crunched into the motorbike.

'Go, go, go,' said Leon.

Zak drove on but then slowed and looked behind. 'Are they OK?'

'Who cares?'

'Tell me or I will return.'

Leon looked into the wing mirror back at the two men, dusting down their clothes whilst inspecting their overturned motorbike. 'They're fine. Now drive!'

*

Elok sped on for a couple more minutes before pulling into a free parking space. Josh climbed out, shut the door and leant against the side of the car. He felt ill and dizzy and tired but most of all he felt relieved.

High-heels clipped around the car. 'What wrong?' Elok touched the centre of his back before squealing. 'Ewww! Why you so wet?'

'I'm sweating because of your driving. It's the worst I've ever seen.'

She peered into the car at his seat. 'Yuk! Seat like river. What wrong with this *bule*?'

'I'm from a cold country. Plus leather makes you sweat.'

Elok's features scrunched up in disgust. She perched a sun umbrella on her shoulder and set off.

Josh followed her. 'Slow down. Where are we?'

'A port. It is soooo boring. But *bules* they like. They take lots of pictures.'

'Elok do you have to say *bule* every sentence.'

'You are *bule*. I say *bule*. What is the problem?'

Josh watched her sashay ahead, all teeth and lipstick and swivelling hips and wondering why he was so drawn to the negative charm that radiated from her mischievous smirk.

They crossed a bridge over a pool of stagnant water and a beach of washed up rubbish. As they neared the port the stench worsened until it became nearly unbearable. Aware of the attention they were receiving, Josh tried to subtly cover his mouth and not cough.

Elok wasn't as restrained. 'This place it stink. It stink worse than *bule*. The people that work here all live in that *kampung*,' Elok said, gesturing to a collection of buildings supported by stilts dug into the riverbank. From this shanty town, a rowing boat filled with people departed and made the short journey across to a pier. A man paddled them through a rainbow of effluent that polluted the water, his spit adding to the puddles of slime. Two children leaned over the prow of the small vessel, pointing at the dead fish that lapped on the surface. When they reached the pier, the children jumped out, their clothes ragged, their young faces radiant. Next, the women stepped out carrying bags of fish. The last off were the men; their skin dark and wrinkled; their gaits weary yet athletic.

'Their *kampung* get flooded all the time and still stupid persons live there. Why they not move to new home?'

'They probably don't have the money.'

'Yes, they have no money,' she said impatiently, 'because they need to make a new house every time it rain. *Bule* stupid like them.'

Josh began protest at the many aspects of her comment he found offensive but then stopped. With some people there was really no point.

They went on, passing a brown marble plaque that read, "Pelabuhan Sunda Kelpa", and walked onto a long wharf that stretched out to the sea. Docked at both sides of the marina was a fleet of wooden ships, their majestic sails flapping in the breeze. Barefooted men carried sacks down to the pier, the wooden gangways bending under the weight. Outside the boats, women laid out fish on blue tarpaulins, ready to spend another day in the sun hoping to make a sale to the hungry workers.

As they strolled along the wharf people stopped and gawped at the white man and the glamorous Jakartan with large sunglasses and a white sunshade elegantly balanced on her shoulder. When anyone approached to sell them souvenirs or to offer them a trip on the rowing boats they were shooed away by Elok, who appeared to have a talent for being dismissive.

One short, bald man, perhaps in his sixties, was more persistent than the rest. He followed them, unperturbed by the lack of response, telling Josh in broken English a series of facts about the port. *It was called Sunda Kelapa. It was home to Makassar sailing ships. The boats were world famous. They provided delivery between Jakarta and the whole of Asia. They carried wood across the South Seas for centuries...*

When they passed a schooner whose bow was painted yellow and white, the man beckoned Josh towards the ship. He looked at Elok who pulled an expression of disgust and shook her head. Deciding to rebel against her ignorance, he ducked under the mooring ropes and followed the man up the wooden gangway. As he stood on the deck looking out, he watched the crew throwing bags of rubbish overboard, the contents joining the plastic bottles and other debris that bobbed on the surface and thought of the harbour centuries ago before industrialisation and how different it must have been. His contemplation was cut short by the man ushering him below deck for the next round of his impromptu tour.

When he finally returned to land, some fifteen minutes later, Elok was perched regally on a wooden chair with a man next to her holding her sunshade. When she saw him, her body twisted into a knot of crossed arms and legs. 'Why so long Josh?'

'He wouldn't stop talking,' Josh said, nodding in the direction of the man who still lingered by his side.

'OK, pay him and we go.'

The old man stepped forward and held out his hand.

'Pay him? No way.'

'Yes, we not pay,' Elok said. She got to her feet and snatched her sunshade from the man who held it. They strode off triumphantly. 'Why I pay man to hold my umbrella and give me chair? If he gentleman he do anyway.'

'Exactly, I didn't ask that guy to give me a tour. I can't pay every person who follows me and starts to talk.'

'Fuck them!'

'Yes, fuck them,' Josh said, watching an expression of joyful superiority spreading across Elok's face. He'd seen that look before... but where? An image of Leon fired into his mind's eye. He stopped and looked back down the wharf.

'What wrong?'

Josh began jogging back in the direction he'd come.

'Where you go?' Elok called after him.

'To pay them,' Josh said, breaking into a run.

*

They sat on two rattan mats around a table made of two drinks crates, a wooden board and a plastic cover. Leon studied the inside of the café. 'How long will it be?'

'Ask the owner.'

'You know I can't.'

Zak trapped his hands under his armpits and faced the dusty cars and trucks and motorbikes trundling along the road. 'Perhaps you should learn...'

At that moment, the café owner brought their food and served it onto the table. They ate *mie goreng*, fried noodles, from plastic bowls with plastic forks. Leon finished his noodles, lifted his bowl to drink the remaining soup, returned it to the table, rested his hand on his overfull stomach and inhaled deeply through his nose. The smell of palm, fried oil, overripe bananas, diesel and fresh laundry hit his nose, yet he recognised only a single scent - Java. He shaded his eyes from the shards of sunlight which crept between the palm tree branches and looked at Zak, pushing his food around his plate, his eyes upon his van. 'Listen, I'll pay for the car windows.'

'No.'

'Why not?'

'That would allow you to think your money has changed something.'

'Well, what else do you want me to do?'

'To say sorry.'

'What for?'

'For damaging my van; for destroying that man's stall and bike; for the chase; for insulting my sexuality... have I forgotten anything?'

Leon sucked his teeth releasing a contemplative squeak. 'Thing is everyone is so obsessed with the word, sorry.'

'Allow me to guess - you aren't?'

'It's too easy. It doesn't change anything. Maybe I was

wrong but I know that if the same things happened again that I,' said Leon, thumping his palm off his chest, 'would do the same thing again. The wrong thing. But the same thing. How can I then say sorry later?'

'You cannot.'

'Don't look at me like that,' Leon said, feeling the rise of the anger that he was trying so hard to quell. 'What about you? Where's my apology?'

'For what?'

'I've been thinking about this... it's a bit strange that I met you in the backpacker area giving out flyers in English for your performance and I was the only white guy there.'

'What do you want to say?'

'That it was weird. The whole audience and the topic of the play. It was like you wanted the riot to happen.'

'I did.'

Leon opened his mouth to rebut Zak's denial but then realised that Zak had outright admitted to it. 'Why?'

'All revolutions start in chaos,' Zak said.

'And where did I fit in?'

'I wanted foreigners to witness it. To tell people from their country. I came to the backpacker area to find the right people. I gave a flyer to you and left.'

'Why?'

'You were enough. You seemed so different to other tourists I meet, like you really wanted to see something. I was wrong.'

Zak's words, 'You *seemed* so different,' and that he'd been 'wrong,' stung Leon like no others. This wouldn't do. Leon *was* different. Zak *wasn't* wrong. 'Look about last night...' he said. 'It was a shock. First, those guys in Aji's room and then the theatre. I thought I was going to see a nice little shadow play and then there was all that gay stuff and a riot. And then this morning you tell me you are gay and Aji's your boyfriend and... it was all too much.'

'Why is that so important to you?'

'I've never hung out with a gay guy before.'

'I will take you home. You are right. It was not fair to involve you in this.'

Leon tilted his empty glass and rotating in his hand, 'No, it's fine.'

'So you want to continue?'

'If you want to continue with me? I did kind of wreck your van?'

'It was wrecked anyway.'

Leon glanced at Zak to confirm their reconciliation but could not determine if his expression was a forced smile or if he was grimacing into the sun.

*

Walking through the alleys of the *kampung* to collect food from the shop. Sun-cracked pavements. A dry breeze. The smell of fish and oil. Washing water sloshing towards drains, smearing its filth across her path.

In the store. Chicken, eggs, peanuts, spice. How are your family? Great. Really great.

Carrying the shopping home. Refusing the help of Nurman, the neighbour's son, with his searching eyes and long stares. Like everything, she was doing this herself. Like she'd lifted her mother out of bed, herself. Like she dressed her in her *kebaya*. Like she told her a hundred times how beautiful she looked and how important this day was for her father. How it would be over soon and then she could go back to bed and shut the curtains and see no one for days.

What about next year? her mum said.

It's a year away.

A crooked smile. The promise of a year of darkness. That's what it took now. That's what it took.

Returning to the house and pushing open the door. Into that room with its crypt-like stench. Her father had done what he was told for once and left to allow "her mum" time to prepare the food.

Her mum was preparing by sitting on the bathroom floor crying. What do you say? You say nothing. You let them cry. That's all you can do. It lasted for ten minutes. Only for ten minutes. Good news in these times. Sometimes it lasted for hours.

Cinta finally coaxed her to her feet. Come on, mum. Keep going.

Her mother nodded and absently wiped her hands down her dress. She looked at her mascara-smudged hands and then down at the dress. Thin black lines of desolation smeared down the material.

I'm sorry, her mother said.

Don't worry, mum.

What about the dress?

You can't see it. It's fine.

You could see it. It wasn't fine. Running out the room to get a cloth. The twins on the floor of the hall. Dolls and little cars. I told you to get ready. She pointed at their dresses on the bed. Sheepish grins as they got to their feet.

Downstairs and into to the kitchen. Cutting up the vegetables and meat. Boiling the rice. The click of the front door. Out of the kitchen. What the hell was he doing back?

I told you to go out for the afternoon.

Yes, but I was bored.

Stepping to her father and taking his hand. Mother is in the kitchen cooking. She has a surprise for you. Please don't ruin it.

He turned and she pushed him, softly on his lower back, out of the door. He stepped onto the street and looked back to the house. A faint smile on his lips. She shut the door and returned to the kitchen. The girls scampering around upstairs. The faint sound of sobbing from the bathroom. The rice boiling over. Thinking that her father wouldn't be smiling if he knew the truth.

A thousand problems colliding in her head. She'd forgotten to clean her mother's dress. The girls were still not dressed. She had to put the meat on.

How do you cook a meal and dress two children and an adult at the same time? How do you dress yourself?

You don't think about it. You just do it: if that's what you've always done.

*

That afternoon Josh learned a bit about Indonesia, a bit about Jakarta and a lot about Elok. He learned that one hundred metres away from the grime and dirt and chaos was a gate. Inside that gate was a shiny, purpose-built complex. The gate was large and let anyone through. When he got inside he learned that the real gate that kept people out was money. He also learned that playing mini-golf and visiting an aquarium called Seaworld with exotic fish, and a theme park called Dreamland with rollercoasters and candyfloss, was as much fun in Jakarta as it was anywhere else.

He learned when he got back in the car that Elok could drive as fast as the rollercoaster. They went to the

Kota Square in the Old Town and saw all the Batavian architecture. He stared at the colonial facades and shuddered at the thought of the stories behind their presence and the wars and conflict and the lives ruined on both sides and all because of the greed of humanity. He learned that Elok didn't care about that topic or anything he had to say and all she wanted to do was to go to the Café Batavia. They entered to jazz music, passed a grand piano and ascended the great staircase, pausing halfway up to take in hundreds of pictures of the great and the good from Elton John and Audrey Hepburn to Soekarno and Mohammed Hatta. Upstairs he learned that Elok was not interested in the Java Teak wood fittings or the grandeur of the white table cloths and serviettes and wooden fans that hung from the rafters or his musings about how amazing to think that centuries ago Dutch colonists had drunk coffee in that very vicinity and that she was much more concerned with the cocktail menu.

After they had finished three drinks and left the café, he learned that the nearby China Town contained much beauty in the narrow winding streets with all the mini-pagodas and archways and market stalls. They walked amongst the closely-packed buildings and under the lanterns strung from house to house and visited the Vihara Dharma Bhatki Temple with its red pagodas and great batons of incense that burned like Olympic torches. When they walked through a market selling frogs stripped of their skin and locusts and fried birds and beetles and cockroaches Elok asked him triumphantly if he'd ever seen anything like it.

Yes.

Where?

In China.

After that exchange he learned that he was an ungrateful, selfish, arrogant *bule*.

He learned that China Town was beautiful but also home to a great sadness like the people sitting on the street helpless and hungry with towels on the floor but nothing to sell. He learned that Elok had no pity for such people because no one liked the Chinese because their eyes were slitty and they took all of the money and didn't mix. He learned that he had never considered that other races were racist against each other and that he thought all racism was perpetrated by white people against other ethnicities and then realised how stupid that belief was.

He learned that Elok didn't just dislike the Chinese but most other people in Jakarta. He learned no one in Jakarta came from Jakarta and that most people came from other parts of the archipelago. The only ethnic Jakartans were called Betawi. The Betawi had always been in Jakarta because they were too stupid to leave and they thought they were special but really they were all *malas* and *malings* (lazy and thieves). He learned that Elok was not only against the natives of the Jakarta but also those that had chosen to live there. They were all peasants and should *pulang kampung* (go home).

Elok also taught him about the many dangers of Jakarta which he hadn't previously seen nor comprehended. He learned that there were thieves on buses who hypnotised people and robbed them and that a *bule* should 'keep eyes to himself.' He also learned that each inch of the street was run by different gangs who competed for territory. They passed areas controlled by gangs such as the Christian Ambonese, East Nusa

Tenggara (NTT), Betawi Brother's Forum and Islamic Defenders Front. He learned to see the streets differently – about the battle for space and control of any opportunity. He learned that faced with such imperceptible dangers that the only way to defend yourself was to buy a gun. He thought that Elok was joking when she said she wanted one but realised she wasn't when she made him stand outside a shop while she argued with its owner over the price. When he did venture inside he learned that the shopkeeper was more than a match for Elok and that when she asked him if he knew who she was, that a reply that Elok didn't like was to be called "Jusuf's favourite prostitute."

He learned that with each passing moment he found Elok both more fascinating and infuriating, especially when she pressed the gun against his temple and clicked. She laughed when he jumped and told him it wasn't loaded and he got really angry and stormed off because she was fucking insane. She caught up with him and hugged him and said sorry and that he didn't need to worry about dying anyway because what is inside of us doesn't die but simply moves on. She then told him about all the ghosts she'd seen and that she talked to her mother, who died when she was born, every night and he thought she was really crazy and she thought he was because everyone had seen a ghost except the strange *bule* who also didn't believe in magic and the afterlife. It was when she said things like that that Josh learned that their entire belief systems were the product of seven thousand miles worth of distance and centuries of tradition and that even though they didn't understand each other's opinions and beliefs and found them equally ridiculous that that was half the fun.

Finally, he learned that none of the things he saw that day were weird or unusual or exotic in Indonesia but just the way things were.

And after all that, they sat in the car and he agreed to do something that (he didn't realise at the time but would learn later on) would change everything.

*

After Leon and Zak left the café they drove for over an hour before Zak parked the van on the side of the road. They got out, walked down a dirt track for fifty metres before Zak stopped under the shade of a tree.

'What are we doing here?' Leon said.

'I want to show you something.'

Leon's eye followed the track down to a field. Symmetrical rows of green bushes stretched to the horizon. 'What?'

'Be patient,' Zak said, taking out some papers from his pocket. He unfolded them and began to read out loud.

'What are you doing?'

Zak lowered the pages. 'Before the protest I will give a speech. I must practice. There will be many people watching.'

'Fine,' Leon said. He sat down and rested against the tree. He wriggled down the trunk until his head rested against a suitably shaped nub. 'OK, wake me up when you're finished.'

Zak settled next to him. 'Do not get too comfortable. We must arrive at my uncle's house before dark.'

Leon closed his eyes and listened to Zak's soothing voice practising his speech. As the orange glow of consciousness dimmed into a deep black, he was stirred by the vibration of the ground. Through half-closed eyes, he saw a group of thirty or more men walking towards them.

Zak stopped reading and tapped Leon's arm, 'OK, look. Do you remember you said you wanted to see the real Indonesia? This is why I brought you here. You see those dirty, sweaty men. That's the real Indonesia. Palm oil plantations, farming, tea-pickers, coffee growers, sun on their backs, hard work, no space, no food, no nothing.'

Leon reclosed his eyes. 'Yeah, I know it's bad but what can you do?'

'Look at them and realise it. Tell the people in your country about it. Tell them where all their luxuries and products come from. This is who we protest for. For the people who have nothing. That is what the *Taring Padi* is. That is why I have quit the Kraton. That is why I organize the protest.'

Leon opened one eye. 'You're shouting.'

'We all should be shouting!'

'They don't seem to be shouting and they're the ones affected by it.'

'That is because they do not know better.'

'So if they don't know any better what's the problem?'

'What do you mean what is the problem?'

'If they don't know any better, as you say, then they won't hate their lives. It's just their reality,' Leon said, sitting up as he became more interested in the debate.

'You see this land?' Zak's hand swept across their surroundings. 'Look how green. How fertile. You see these fields. They are coffee plantations now. Other plantations near here make palm oil, tobacco, tea. None of these things can be used by local people. Instead it is exported for cheap,' Zak said, waving the pages of his speech in front of Leon's face and his eyeballs bulging, lips quivering.

'Zak, are you OK?'

'Why?'

'When I met you, you were like the coolest guy around. Like proper ice... today, I don't know, you're acting a bit crazy.'

'You think today is normal day for me? That last night was easy?' With those words, the energy seemed to drain from Zak's body. He slumped forwards, 'Before, I tried to... what do you say? Show a good face.'

'Put on a brave face?'

'Yes. You know my performance last night took me two years to make. Not one person told me it was good.'

'Aji did.'

'No, Aji hated it.'

'He said that I'd see the finest display of shadow puppetry in Java and that you were a genius. I'd say that was pretty complimentary.'

'He said that? Really? .... but he does not understand,' Zak said, his gloom seeming to return as quickly as it lifted. 'You know every day I perform Javanese shows based on two ancient Indian stories the Ramayana and the Mahabharata. These stories have not changed for centuries. My performances are watched by royalty and tourists and people who have enough money to bring me to a wedding, a birthday or a *selamatan* feast. But young people... they do not care about *wayang kulit*. They watch TV, play computers, go on the internet. The art is dying and the power of the Sultan is too. Yes, seven generations of my family have performed in this way but it will not continue for seven generations more. Aji thinks that I fail my city and my family and my art. But he does not understand that I am doing this for my city, my family, my art.

The other artists protest through their mediums and still *wayang kulit* remains the same. *Wayang kulit* needs to change to be relevant now or it will fail. Like this country needs to change. The way I achieve both is the same. And now is the time to do it.'

'Aji thinks there are people in high positions trying to stop you?'

Zak smiled but his face didn't soften. 'People in high positions have stopped me my whole life. They've stopped us all.'

*

Josh trailed Elok through a back alley off the main street and into a labyrinth of connecting lanes and conjoined houses. Occasionally, he broke into a series of quick steps to catch up, only to fall behind soon after. 'Are you sure they won't mind us turning up?' he called after her.

'Why they mind?'

'Because Cinta said it's her father's birthday and it sounds like a family occasion.'

'It is my family also.'

Josh broke into a jog, caught Elok and blocked her path. She kept walking. Their bodies collided. Elok rubbed her chest and stared at him with those salacious eyes, 'Be careful.'

'Sorry,' Josh said, diverting his eyes. 'Listen I need to tell you something.'

'What?'

Josh looked inside the open door of a nearby house. Eight people crammed onto the floor, barefooted, legs crossed, eating. A twelve-inch black and white monitor blared out but no one watched it. The action on the street appeared better. 'Can we talk somewhere else?'

'No, tell me here.'

Josh listened to the TV and smelt the fried vegetables and steamed rice wafting from the house. He felt the washing, strung across the houses above, dripping on his head and all those eyes looking at him and wanted to run away but looked back to Elok and knew he wasn't going anywhere. 'The first time I met Cinta's father –'

'Why *bule* whisper you think they understand?'

'The first time I met Cinta's father... he tried to run me over.'

'He crazy.'

'The second time when I called up he hung up straight away.'

'So?'

'This is before he even knows about me and Cinta.'

'You and Cinta? What about you and Cinta? You don't do nothing. You probably never do nothing. Cinta she like little girl not woman.'

'You sound like Leon.'

'I sound like Leon?' Elok hands met her hips, pressing her waist inwards. 'You look like Leon.'

'No, I don't.'

'When I see you I think you twins. You have big nose like him.'

'I don't have a big nose.'

'You all have,' She started to walk away. 'I understand why you worry about Cinta father but come I show you something.'

He followed her deeper into the *kampung* until they

reached a small two-storey house. 'Here is Cinta home. Now listen, her family are poor people. They pee sunts.'

'Pee sunts?'

'Yes, no money.'

'Oh, you mean peasants?'

'Yes, pee sunts. They poor and live in a small house. My father Salim, he rich. He build Seaworld and the theme park you go today. Salim he grows up the same as Cinta father but he now better. So not worry about Cinta father. He not real man. If he say something to you I shoot him.' She laughed and put her arm around him and kissed him on the cheek.

She turned and strode to the door and let herself inside without knocking.

*

They drove along flat, straight roads framed by palm trees towards the green turrets on the horizon. The trees thickened and the forest enveloped and Zak lowered the gear and they started their ascent. As they spiralled up conjoined hairpins towards a solitary patch of blue, the road morphed from tarmac to rock and then dust. They drove through lunaresque potholes, the shards of broken glass sliding across the floor and pattering against the sides of the van like winter hail hitting a tin roof.

It was late afternoon when they pulled off the road. When they could advance no further, they left the car and hiked the final few hundred metres. Zak trampled ahead, hacking through the foliage, his machete clearing a temporary path. Shafts of dusty sunlight flickered through the leaves creating intricate patterns of light on the forest floor. They cracked through branches and tore through thorns to emerge by a wooden house.

Climbing up the staircase, Leon steadied himself on the banister, the termite ridden wood crumbling in his palm. He picked his way across a small veranda, avoided the vines that dangled from the thatched palm roof, and entered the single-roomed hut. The taste of rot: dense, thick, dust-filled air. The flash of Zak's torch; a billion golden particles; cobwebs, crickets, woodlice and flies; a single mattress; a gas stove; some pots; some pans. He barked a cough, chucked his rucksack inside and followed Zak back to the veranda.

The hut stood at the top of a hill. A single terraced field parted the forest. Like one side of a pyramid, the terraces were narrow at the top and widened as they descended. They were irrigated by a stream that trickled through the trees and reappeared in glistening splendour in the valley deep below.

'It belongs to my uncle but I come here when I need to think,' Zak said. 'Do you know about *feng shui*?'

'Pay someone thousands of pounds to point your furniture in the right direction.'

'That is the understanding from your country in the material sense. *Feng shui* is also an ancient Chinese philosophy. A way to live your life. Here, is what is called a dragonhead. It is located on a hill with a mountain behind it and a river and valley in front.'

'And how does that help?'

'You cannot feel the power?'

'Not really.'

'I think you need some help. When I come here I often have what I call the three tastes of Java.'

'Sounds interesting.'

'It is. Come with me.'

Leon followed Zak into the house. Together they dragged a gas stove out and then a black bag onto the veranda. Zak unzipped the bag and rummaged and removed a pot which he laid on top of the stove. He took out a water tankard and a brown paper bag. 'Right, fill the big bottle water from the stream. Light the gas. Put water on it. Get my knife from the bag. Cut these vegetables and add them to the boiling water,' Zak said. He descended the staircase, the entire structure creaking with his movement.

'Where are you going?'

'To get the special ingredient before it rains.'

Leon watched him hare off into the undergrowth and disappear into the forest. His mind raced with the endless possibilities of what the three tastes of Java could be. He'd already forgotten about the vegetables.

*

That year, Ahmad was fifty-two.

When he was young, his birthday used to be a major celebration. Falling two days before Independence Day, it was like a practice for the main event. Friends and family members would come from afar to attend the large get together at their house and to lavish gifts upon him –

That year, five people attended.

– As a child, Ahmad had thought that all the fuss was for his benefit but could now see that the day had signified something else. Here was a child born two years after the declaration of independence. It was as though his birth and life symbolised the hope that ran through his father's group –

That year, he invited his brother Salim out of courtesy. He, of course, declined.

– Ahmad looked back upon those early days with great

fondness. It was like a link to the past, maybe to the last time in his life that he was considered important. For that reason, he always insisted that his immediate family spend the day together. It was one of his few indulgences –

That year, he looked around the table at his wife, three daughters and sister, Misbah and smiled ruefully. He was the only man left.

– Throughout the preceding years the day had become so well established it had developed its own traditions. One ritual was Cinta's complaints at having to take a day off school or work to spend it with her family –

That year, curiously, there were no such protests.

– Another custom was for them to argue about their plans for Independence Day. It would be at his birthday meal that Cinta would request to go to Salim's house. It wasn't that Ahmad didn't understand why she'd want to attend the party of the year, where she would be waited upon by Salim's maids and enjoy a *selamatan* feast. He did. But still he couldn't let her go. When he refused she'd sulk for the rest of the day –

That year, even more curiously, she'd failed to even mention it.

– A further tradition was the clothes that they wore. Ahmad dressed in a sarong, a white shirt made from Bugis silk, a *baju koko* embroidered jacket, a woven prayer shawl and rimless *peci* hat. His three daughters wore matching gold lace *kebayas*, high-heels and red gowns. His wife and sister also wore *kebayas* but with blue sarongs. Jasmine and incense scented the house –

That year, they looked as beautiful as ever.

– Normally, Wening would make his favourite food: *bakso* (meatballs in noodle soup) followed by fresh rice and chicken *satay* in peanut sauce. When they were younger he'd told her that she made the best chicken *satay* in Java. In the past few years she'd made some of the worst –

That year, it was sumptuous.

As he ate, he glanced up and caught Wening watching him. She looked away. Not before he saw a glimpse of that adorable, almost embarrassed expression of pride that she pulled when she made him happy.

He allowed himself to smile. Yes, he knew Cinta had got her up and gone to the market and dressed her and cooked the meal. And he also knew that both of them would probably rather be somewhere else. But they weren't. And at the moment that was all he could ask.

He knew that his wife felt his stare but he didn't look away and for a moment, he looked beyond her greying hair and wrinkles that burrowed into her skin and saw the past: the dimpled girl with the devilish smile that he'd met all that time ago.

When they finished, his sister, Misbah cleared the table. Cinta joined her. They stood next to each other, the same height and shape, their faces mirrored, a few inches apart. Just like each other. Just like his mum.

Misbah grinned at him, 'What are you looking at?'

The youngest sibling. Devoid of malice or cynicism. The cleverest. The most vivacious. A life spent as a housewife to a dour, middle-ranking official in the civil service; the son of one of his father's friends. Three children. Two girls and a boy. All intelligent, high-achieving and well-behaved.

Misbah returned from the kitchen, set up the karaoke machine and playfully argued with the twins as to who would be the first to perform. The twins won. They were always going to.

That was when the door swung open and Elok burst in followed by a white man. Everyone stopped. She'd not been to their house in years.

*

Leon used Zak's pocket knife to cut up the cassava, carrots, potatoes and shallots. He added them to the pan of boiling water and stirred the thickening liquid. A line of ants scuttled between his feet. Dark clouds skimmed across the sky. The wind picked up, blustering up the ridge and ruffling through the green rice shoots. The trees heaved left and then right. A flock of birds flew low and west.

A figure emerged from the forest, leaping over roots, trampling through the clusters of wild orchids and dandelions. Zak reached the veranda and darted under the shelter of the palm and bamboo canopy.

The pressure dropped. The earth inhaled before emitting a cackle of deep thunder. A flash of electric blue followed by thick, heavy, rain.

'Just in time,' Leon said. 'I hope this "special ingredient" is worth it.'

'It... is...' said Zak, his ribcage heaving up and down. He opened the contents of his bag to reveal dozens of wild mushrooms. He went to the stove, scattered them into the pot, took the ladle from Leon and stirred. 'This is stage one.'

Leon took his eyes from the broth and gazed out at the jagged blue lightening. A chorus of thunder; the power of the rain; steam rising from the land. As dusk settled the blue flame of the stove taking over from the natural light.

They huddled close together and drank their soup and

listened to the patter of the rain on the canopy. The liquid was thick, the aftertaste pungent. Leon's lips moistened and his senses dulled. Life hazed and nothing seemed to matter much anymore. 'Those mushrooms really gave that thing some kick.'

'Stage one opens your imagination,' Zak said.

'What is stage two?'

'Coffee.'

Leon grinned. 'Shouldn't we do something a bit softer before the hardcore stuff?'

'You joke but I do not think you have tasted coffee.'

'I think you'll find I have.'

'Not real coffee. Not coffee that is picked fresh and pure. Coffee that has not been transported or frozen. Coffee that is so strong it will make you high.'

Zak got up and returned with a smaller pan filled with water, two metal cups and a clear plastic pouch. He unfastened the seal and sprinkled the black granules into the pan and rested it on the stove. Engulfed by the blue flames, the coffee came to boil. Zak removed the pan and poured the liquid into the cups. Leon lifted his cup and let the steam hit his face and the aroma burn into his nostrils. He let the drink cool, put the cup to his lips and drank. The thick texture smoothed and the taste took over. He perceived the liquid dispersing around his body and his eyes widened and mind pulsated. He looked at the black liquid and saw the moon in the cup and looked up. The sky had cleared.

*

Josh stepped into the house and saw six people sat at the table. They all stopped eating and looked at him. At first Cinta looked like she couldn't believe what she was seeing before an expression of sheer panic overtook her face. She blushed and started to frantically adjust her dress. The splendour of her attire; the sparkle of her jewellery... wary of staring at her too long, Josh's eyes moved around the table. Like Cinta, all family members wore traditional costumes, displaying a grandeur that looked so out of place in the small dark house off the back alley.

He lingered near to the doorway, wrung his hands and wondered what to do. Elok took his hand and made the decision for him. She led him to the edge of the table and there he stood. 'Sit,' she said, pushing him down onto a spare seat.

The inside of the house reminded him of an old photograph. The shutters on the windows blocked out any light. A single low-wattage bulb washed the scene with a dull yellow. Fissures cracked across the tiles on the floor. The wallpaper was peeling and stained. The little furniture they did possess was well worn.

Elok had, of course, appointed herself as the master of ceremonies. She introduced Cinta's mother and father, her aunt and Cinta's two younger sisters. Josh nodded and smiled and didn't know what to say. It seemed like they didn't either. But he certainly had their undivided attention - they all stared at him like they were watching the latest episode of their favourite TV programme.

Meanwhile, Elok circled the table inspecting the family's costumes and laughing. She appeared not to notice that no one laughed with her. Tiring of mocking their clothes, Elok pointed at Josh with exquisite pride like he was some prize game she'd captured. She spoke in Indonesian, the only discernible words 'Josh' and the ubiquitous *bule.* The aunt listened intently whilst smiling and winking at him. The two little girls gathered next to him, poking his arm and tugging at his shorts, like they were checking if he was real.

Not so in awe of, but no less interested in, his presence was Cinta's father. Josh recognised his intense eyes, low hanging brow and flared nostrils from their previous encounter on Jalan Jaksa. His expression, in the comfort of his own home, was no less stern. He certainly didn't look like the pushover Elok had described earlier. By way of contrast, the mother's expression was glazed almost stupefied. Not reacting to any social cue, she managed to look straight at him while also apparently looking at nothing at all.

The only person not gawping was Cinta. Instead, she faced away whilst fidgeting in her seat and wringing her hands. She appeared to be as mortified as he was with how this scene was developing. Josh glanced at the door. Escape was now impossible. Why did he let Elok talk him into this?

Elok crouched down next to him, jostling with the little girls as she tried to get closer. With a couple of elbows, neither particularly playful, she repelled the competition of the two children. 'Is *bule* hungry?'

'No. I'm fine.'

Elok turned to the mother, speaking in Indonesian and gesturing to the kitchen like she was ordering from a waitress. The mother creaked to her feet and shuffled off.

'No, please don't. ,' Josh called after her but to no avail.

She returned from the kitchen to the table and lowered the food, inch by inch, her hand unsteady. Eventually, the bowl met the table. In front of him, was what looked like the spicy meatball soup that he'd had in the café under the underpass with Leon and that had made him so ill the next day. He studied the food, shivered and felt like he'd returned to a scene of a crime.

Throughout, the father had been making a low grumbling sound and clearing his throat. Suddenly, he burst into a particularly loud fit of coughing. The family diverted their attention from Josh. The father glowered at the onlookers before dismissing their interest with an angry wave of his hand. He muttered something to the group; his voice harsh and monotone; his eyes shifting to and from Josh as he spoke.

This guy hates my guts, Josh thought. As far as I know that old nutcase has a gun upstairs just like that crazy bitch Elok has one in her car.

He glanced at Cinta. Blushed cheeks. Full lips. Blinking eyes. Gorgeous. But was this worth it?

Josh stirred the soup. The smell of meaty water. Saliva coagulating in the corners of his mouth. The mere smell making him nauseous.

And there they remained. Cinta saying nothing; the twins pulling at his arm; the aunt smiling; the mother gawping; Elok shouting; his bowl of meatball soup sitting untouched.

*

'Now for stage three,' Zak said, producing a ball of tightly wrapped cling film the size of a marble. He unravelled it to reveal a light brown powder, which he emptied onto a six-inch square of tin foil. He handed a thin plastic pipe about the length of his index finger to Leon. 'You first?'

'What do I do?'

'I will heat the powder and it will turn into liquid. Put the pipe in your mouth, follow the smoke and suck in.'

He clicked the lighter and the flame rippled under the foil. It crinkled and crackled. The powder liquefied and bubbled. A blob of the molten liquid condensed and ran across the foil. Leon followed the blob with the tube and inhaled the fumes.

'Yes follow it,' Zak said. 'Well done.'

The initial repugnance softened and returned in jolts of acidic venom; ink and tar melting into the aftertaste of bitter chocolate. Slightly choking, Leon waved his hand to Zak to indicate he was finished. He dropped back in his chair and watched Zak prepare the next batch. The edges of his vision blurred but the centre became clearer and he viewed everything anew. The sweat that trembled out of his pores was warm and light and he felt an inner contentment that was alien to him. He gazed at Zak and felt euphoric and thought that he loved him and his shitty little hut and this whole amazing adventure.

'Are you OK?'

'It's horrible but makes you feel great' Leon said, his words feeling tinny and unreal like what he'd said had become trapped in his own head. 'Can you hear me?'

'Yes.'

'I can hear you too. And man can I see. I can see better than ever before.'

'You are wasted.'

'I'm not,' Leon said, aiming a playful hit at Zak's arm. 'Look, the sky's cleared.'

'The stars are always there you just need to look for them,' Zak said. He lit the foil, followed the brown liquid and inhaled. He sprinkled more, lit and did it again. He laid down the kit and grabbed Leon's hand and led him down the steps into the dark. They collapsed onto the wet foliage. 'Look at the stars.'

'You're the one who's wasted. You're talking about the stars,' Leon said. 'Do you want to make objects out of the clouds too?'

'No, I mean really look at stars and think what they are and how far away they are. Then think that some are billions of miles closer than others and what we are seeing passed billions of years ago and what we are looking at may no longer exist and if something happened to them we would be dead for millions of years before the news arrived here. Then look at them in, how do you say? In three-dimensions and feel the depth and spirit of the universe.'

'You are so high,' Leon said. But despite his mockery he did study the sky and lay still and embraced the numbness that overtook his body and thought about all the things that came into his head every time he made the mistake of not distracting his mind in another way. Although he learned to suppress those thoughts, sometimes, mostly at night, he couldn't.

And that night those thoughts came all at once: the small and big things that saddened him equally and he didn't know why. He thought about his small terrace house in Gloucester and missed it; about his dad abandoning them and felt no anger. And then he thought of his youth: playing football in the park when he was ten, the bigger kids disallowing his goal; wetting himself on a school trip to Bristol zoo; his mum's tears when Josh and he were ten and got lost in the woods and came home three hours late; his brother joining the army; the helicopter crash; his brother's death; running in the park when him and Josh lost their kite; Josh finding it; Josh. He wondered what Josh was doing at that moment...

He opened his eyes and the darkened mass of trees merged together and he saw shapes forming in their midst. He shut his eyes and tried to escape it all. The dark rotated beneath his eyes. Then the colours came, spotting and twirling, rising and pirouetting. His body spiralled downwards and he fell into an endless chasm. The impact of the imaginary brought him back and he sat bolt upright. 'Let's go back,' he said to Zak. 'I don't like it here.'

*

Although he'd seen plenty, he'd never shared a room with a *bule*. Ahmad was fascinated. He tried not to stare but found his eyes drawn to the white man. Unable to properly observe him with his weak vision, he leaned forward in his seat and peered.

He thought of westerners as brash and loud due to their lack of custom and faith. He'd heard about their firm, impolite handshakes and sexual promiscuity. On television, and from a distance, they appeared too sure of themselves and over-confident.

While something about this man seemed familiar, he was so different. His frame was slight, his legs short. He had soft, doughy features, light brown hair and blue grey eyes; his hands were small and unfathomably pristine like he'd never done a day's work. Elok had said he was English. This certainly contradicted his father's description of a sturdy race built for war.

His family had been ganging up on the guest since he'd, rather tentatively, set foot in the house. When he sat down they clustered around him like he was an exhibit in a museum. Elok proceeded to mock him in a language he didn't understand; Misbah flicked her eyelashes and grinned, while his wife gave him nothing but her usual listless stare. The guest smiled at the women, looking at them for only as long as necessary, before casting his eyes back on the twins, who were clambering over him like he was a climbing frame in the park. Their behaviour was embarrassing but not without significance. Ahmad trusted the judgement of young children: they trusted the guest.

Despite her recent attempts to emulate her cousin, Cinta's reaction was also telling. Whereas Elok both touched and addressed the guest directly, Cinta, except for a brief acknowledgement when he'd first arrived, made no attempt to speak to or engage the stranger. Polite yet appropriate, she possessed a decorum that someone like Elok could only dream of.

When the guest eventually settled in his chair and stopped looking so uncomfortable, Elok insisted that he try the *Mie Bakso* soup. He sat pale and motionless, dismay displayed all over his face. It was obvious that he didn't want to eat the dish – it was probably so different to the food that he ate at home – but had been given no choice.

A cough erupted from Ahmad's mouth, burning a fire in his throat. He inwardly cursed the grime and pollution of Jakarta. He always dreamt of retiring outside the city. Now he doubted he'd retire at all. He lapsed into a prolonged fit of coughs. The attention of the room descended upon him. He waved away their attention. They all averted their eyes. All except Elok, who continued to stare with barely disguised disgust.

Why was she here anyway? It certainly wasn't to wish him happy birthday. Instead most likely she'd come around to sabotage it.

Anger throbbed through his head; anger that Elok was mocking this foreigner; anger that she was mocking them all.

He barked a final cough, thumped his fist off the centre of his chest and rose. He didn't accept this in his own house. He didn't accept this anywhere.

Two steps to the guest. He picked up the full plate, took it into the kitchen and slopped its contents into the bin. He returned to the room, strode towards the twins and scooped them up. One in each arm, he carried them out of the room and up the stairs receiving kicks and screams of complaint on the way. He took them to their room and dropped them on the bed. 'Play here for the rest of the night.'

They studied him to see if he meant it. The tone of his repeated demand left them in no doubt.

Downstairs, he returned to shocked faces and silence. 'I want you and your guest to leave,' he said to Elok. 'Please apologise to him.'

'I see,' Elok said. 'So now you hate *bules* too?'

'It's not him I have a problem with. If you came here to ruin my day you've succeeded. Now please go.'

'I brought him here so he could see a typical Jakarta house… you know, see how the normal people live.'

'To humiliate us.'

'Of course not,' Elok's mirthful expression made him follow the line of her sight to Cinta. 'OK, you want to know why I really brought him?

'No, I want you to–'

'I brought him here because he's Cinta's boyfriend.'

'Liar!' Ahmad's finger quivered as he pointed to the

door. 'Get out.'

'He isn't just her boyfriend. He's the reason why she has lost her job at Jaksa Travel. Yes, that's right. Perfect Cinta's been dismissed for chasing her *bule* boyfriend out of the shop without permission. How do you like that... uncle?' Elok's glare bore into the point between Ahmad's eyes. 'You don't believe me? Well ask your friend Jusuf. No, actually, why don't you ask Cinta? Do you see her deny it?'

'Cinta?' Ahmad said.

She lifted her head and breathed all the way in and all the way out.

'Well?'

She gave a solitary nod.

He looked to the *bule*. His eyes were wide open. Startled. Confused. That look. A look he'd seen before. The two men on Jalan Jaksa. The strange phone call the next day from a man repeating words he didn't understand and Cinta's name.

Ahmad steadied himself on the table. The room spun in two different directions. The last thing he remembered before he lost control was Elok's curdling laugh.

*

What happened next surprised Josh with its speed. When writing his diary later he remembered only fragments of action, unclear and fast, like a series of separate incidents.

He'd convinced himself to eat the food. Lifting his knife and fork. With no warning his plate was swept away. Cinta's father stomping into the kitchen. Returning and grabbing the twins; taking them out the room; sparing them from witnessing what was about to happen. Her father returned. An argument in Indonesian. An unknown revelation. Things quietened. Her father scarlet with rage. He walked towards me, his hand raised, his eyes possessed. I stood up, my seat crashing off the ground as I backed towards the door. Cinta screaming, pulling her father back. He shrugged her off. Elok grabbing my arm, 'leave... leave now.' Out the door. Falling on the way out. Elok dragging me to my feet. Hobbling down the lane towards the car. Glancing back. Her father at the door, his fist held in the air.

*

The car approached a security barrier. In a booth to their right a uniformed man guarded the gate. Elok lowered the window. No identification or searches needed. Just that smile – the one that exhilarated her through life. The barrier lifted upwards and she drove under it.

They entered an area of well-lit, deserted streets enclosed by walls. High walls that kept out the hawkers, the *ojeks*, the *bajajs*, the traffic jams, the buses, the horns, the begging, the shoving, the smiling, the living, the looking, the laughing, the hurrying. Walls that kept out Jakarta.

The car rolled soundlessly on, along a flat asphalt road lined with tall, dark trees. They reached a gate and stopped. Elok stretched her arm out of the window and tapped a four digit code into the keypad. The gates parted. The wheels scrunched over pebbles and they drew to a halt under the foliage of a canopy. Josh got out the car, closed the door and jumped as a figure emerged from the side of a BMW behind which they'd parked. He put what looked like a bucket on the ground, sloshed his hand inside, withdrew it and began to wipe the surface of the car. Elok rounded the bonnet without acknowledging the man.

'Where are we?' Josh said.

'My house,' she said, blustering past. He followed her up some steps, the shortness of his breath disproportionate to the difficulty of the climb. At the top, Elok stood between two pillars in a white marble porch and pressed the doorbell. Sound echoed through the three storeys of the detached house. The slap of bare feet behind the door. Four locks clicked. The giant oak door creaked open. A channel of cool air met Josh's skin. A face peered through the gap.

'Elok,' the man said. He opened the door fully, stepped aside and lowered his head. Elok passed him before he'd completed the bow.

Inside they walked across a patterned rug and entered what looked like a living room. The haze of cigar smoke. The taste of tar. Three men in the corner reclining in leather chairs. Sporadic eruptions of laughter. Appearance Indonesian. Speaking English.

A man shifted in his seat, spotted them and rose to his feet. A crisp white shirt. Tall and slim. A confident upright posture. 'Elok,' he said with a nod.

'Good evening, father,' Elok said, her voice lacking its usual crow. 'Please meet Josh. Josh please meet my father Salim.'

'How do you do?' Salim said. His hand descended from shoulder-height, met Josh's and shook. Arms outspread, body open. 'Meet my businesses partners Andrez and Ongky.'

Two men. Open-necked shirts. Brandy glasses in hand. Ice clinking off the crystal sides. Pleased to meet you and all the rest. All in English. All so smoothly done.

Salim unhooked his thumbs from his braces, twanging them back against his torso, and stepped across them, cutting the conversation short. 'Elok has told me a lot about you Josh... only good things of course.'

Josh wanted to smile. To show this man he was just as relaxed as he was. His face wouldn't move.

Salim's arm rested on his shoulder. Friendly. Welcoming. Controlling. 'So Elok, where did you take our guest tonight?'

'To uncle Ahmad's house.'

Salim's hand tensed, his thumb pressing into Josh's collarbone. 'And tell me why would you take a visitor there?'

Elok pressed her knees together and joined her hands and didn't reply. Yes, Elok. Speechless.

'I enjoyed it,' Josh said, lying to avoid confrontation.

'You are very noble. Too polite to say what you really think. Tell me, what country are you from?'

'England.'

'The country of gentlemen. Winston Churchill and Charles Dickens. I would expect no less politeness from you.' Salim glanced back at his two associates 'OK, it has been a pleasure to meet you. This area is called Pondok Indah. It is home to many ex-pats and diplomats. You are welcome to stay for as long as you require. You will find it much like your country in here. Elok will now show you the house.' He went back to his seat, sat down, picked up his brandy glass and took a slow sip.

Elok nodded to the door, her wide eyes emphasising the urgency of their departure. Josh hurried after her into the kitchen. Inside, two women peered through the door, ready to pounce should one of the businessmen require a top-up or another smoke. They jumped when they saw Elok, who passed without comment, oblivious to the effect her arrival had had upon them. She reached the back door and started yanking frantically at the bolt.

'What was that all about?' Josh said. 'I've never seen you like that. All quiet and –'

'My father is very important and have many meetings so we need to leave him alone. Come on, I show you the garden.'

'Wait, Elok, who are all these people? The guy by the car, the guy in the garden, those women.'

'At the gate is our *penjaga.* He guards the house. The man cleaning the car is our *sopir* – he drives. The man who answer door is *laki laki* - he make painting and he fixing things and help in house. In kitchen is Bi Mimi and Bi Dewi.'

'Do you really need all these people?'

Disgust. Pure disgust souring her face. 'And be so selfish and keep all the money? Bi Mimi and Dewi can send children to school and live in big house and be happy. What *laki laki* do without job here? He sells newspaper or beg on street. Here he has food, a house and friends.'

'If you have so much money and are so generous and Cinta's family are so poor why don't you give them the money?'

'We try but her father has a hard head. My father offer him job and money and new shop but he say, "No."' Elok unbolted the door. 'Come on. We make too much noise inside.'

They stepped out into a large floodlit garden. A lime green hedge ran around the outer perimeter. Symmetrical lines of flowerbeds displayed orange, blue, white, burgundy and red. They walked along a path lined with vases and exotic plants and over a wooden bridge. A waterfall feature whooshing beneath their feet. They reached a large cage-like structure with wooden foundations and meshed walls and Elok unlatched the door. Inside, a group of five dogs roused from their slumber and bounded into action causing the exotic birds perched on the rafters to flap around in panic. The dogs leapt upon Elok, clambering up her body, barking in excitement. She shooed them away and went to a smaller cage. Inside a monkey flipped around the confined space.

'That is so cruel,' Josh said.

'Of course it not cruel. He happy *monyet*.' She pressed her hand against the cage. 'So happy aren't you?' she said, in a voice like she was talking to a baby. The monkey responded by clawing at the cage causing Elok to snatch her hand away.

Josh thought about the faces of the employees as they'd passed and looked at Elok standing there in all her beauty surrounded by birds and dogs and monkeys and didn't know if this logic, this way of being, was hers or her family's or that of her culture. Whatever it was, it seemed to him like he was from another world. Perhaps he was. 'Why am I even talking with you about monkeys? I don't care. What the hell happened at Cinta's house?'

'I told to you. Cinta's father angry because you her boyfriend.'

'Which he knows because you told him!'

'I not tell him. Why I tell him? He guess and ask Cinta. She admit. You saw her face. All I do is try to stop him. He very angry saying he will kill *bule*.'

'Why did you take me there then?'

'I think it is fun. But Cinta's dad is very crazy. Difficult to guess his behaviour.'

'Before we went in the house you said he wasn't a real man and you weren't scared of him. Now you are saying he is crazy. None of this adds up. I want to speak with Cinta.'

'You must not!' Elok's hand slapping onto his wrist. Pink nails pinching his skin yellow. 'Cinta sends to me an SMS and says she beg you not to call her because her father is angry and he will kill her. Must listen to me Josh. She is in big trouble for having *bule* boyfriend. Do not make this worse for her. Do not be a selfish *bule*. This your fault already.'

The confusion and disorientation and build up of guilt hit him all at once and he felt tired. So tired. He should never have got mixed up with this. He'd already done enough to wreck Cinta's life. 'OK fine, I won't call her. But only because I don't want to make things worse.'

*

They lay on the single mattress in the hut. Leon lay on his front and listened to the murmur of Zak's sleeping breath. He couldn't keep it from him any longer. 'Zak, wake up. I have something to tell you.'

Zak didn't stir.

Leon took a deep breath. He opened his mouth to speak again but his courage failed him. This was not going to be easy.

*

Cinta lay on her bed staring at the mobile phone Josh had bought her. Downstairs things had gone quiet. She'd heard her mother creep to bed but hadn't heard the front door open or shut. Her father must be still in the living room with her aunt Misbah. If they were talking they were doing so very quietly.

She picked up the phone decided to contact her school friend Ryna. She was the most sensible of her group of friends. She'd know what to do.

Cinta glanced over to twins in their beds on the other side of the room. Their eyes were shut and their breath slow and regular. Despite their sleep and the silence from downstairs she couldn't risk a call. She unlocked the keypad and started to message, pressing the buttons as softly as she could.

Ryna it's Cinta. The worse thing happened
tonight. Please say you're still
awake? MSG BACK DON'T PHONE.

Sender: Cinta
Received: 22:49 15-08-2002

Yes still awake . What happened?
It is not so bad surely?

Sender: Ryna
Received: 22:56 15-08-2002

My father knows everything!
Elok brought Josh to my house
&she told him Josh is my boyfriend
and why I lost my job xx

Sender: Cinta
Received:23:01 15-08-2002

She told him bout job??! She told
bout Josh??!! Elok is a real bitch...
Ive told u before! What did ur
father do?

Sender: Ryna
Received:23:06 15-08-2002

I'm hiding in my
room now – my father was v angry
& threw Josh out the house

Sender: Cinta
Received:23:21 15-08-2002

It'll b OK. He'll forget soon.
Promise x

Sender: Ryna
Received:23:24 15-08-2002

Not my dad. And what about
JOSH?!He's now with Elok+she's
not answerin my msgs. She
wants Josh for herself. I cant speak
to him –he has no phone & I cant leave
to use the internet 2tell him about
Elok. xx

Sender: Cinta
Received: 23:32 15-08-2002

Give me his email. I ll tell him!!

Sender: Ryna
Received:23:36 17-08-2002

It is josh.beckford123@hotmail.com.
tell him about Elok. Tell him
I love him& to wait for me!!x

Sender: Cinta
Received:23:42 15-08-2002

I will email now. We're too
clever for that bitch Elok!! xx

Sender: Ryna
Received: 23:48 15-08-2002

*

It was 2 o'clock in the morning. Misbah remained in the house, sitting in the armchair across from her brother sat on the sofa. She was too scared to leave him alone. 'Ahmad....'

He cast his lifeless eyes upon her. 'What?'

'I don't like to see you sad. Remember, Cinta is still very young. It's normal that she makes some mistakes.'

'It's not only...' he trailed off, as though even completing a sentence was too painful. He'd been acting strangely all night. Erratic in his mannerisms: rude and irresponsive in interaction. The only times he'd spoken were to offer a series of terse rebukes. That was not to mention his treatment of Josh, who he'd stared at throughout his visit, seemingly unconcerned at the discomfort he was causing him.

Since the revelation about Cinta and his subsequent explosion, the barely concealed rage seemed to have drained from his body. He sagged into his chair, shirt untucked, spluttering and muttered about his cough killing him. The tic, which made the muscle under his eye spasm every few seconds, had also returned.

'It'll be OK,' she said

'But it won't, will it?'

She fought the great knot that twisted in her throat with a deep swallow. It was the best she could do not to cry. She hated to see her brother like this. Recently, it was like he'd become engulfed by a solitary mist, a deep loneliness that neither she nor anyone else could penetrate. 'Please tell me what is wrong.'

He didn't need to reply. She knew already. What was wrong wasn't only the revelation about Cinta's boyfriend but the shop and his lack of money and Wening's depression and his failing relationship with Cinta and their brother Salim. All of that was wrong. But mainly what was wrong was Ahmad had contemplated what was wrong and rather than trying to make it right, had started to pity himself instead. It would be painful and he'd probably react badly but someone needed to tell him the truth. It would have to be her. 'You know Cinta is the loveliest girl.'

'No, now she is like Elok and Salim.'

'She's not –'

'What would father say if he was still alive?'

She felt an intense frustration building deep inside. 'Ahmad, you talk about father a lot.'

'We should never forget him.'

'I don't want to forget him but you can't spend your life trying to emulate him.'

'Why not?'

'Because although he was a great man, he had his faults. Faults that you forget. In your head he was perfect and everything he stood for noble and correct. You won't fulfil his expectations because your memory of father is of someone who didn't exist.'

'Why are you making this point?'

'Because you are trying to stop Cinta living her life and you are justifying it by saying it is against what father would have wanted.'

'How can you say that?' Ahmad said, the sound of his fingers clawing on the sofa fabric sending a shudder through her. 'What do you think he'd have said if he knew his granddaughter had lost her job chasing a *bule*?'

'Have you forgotten so quickly? He never forced his opinions on others.'

'So you think that you should let someone make their own decision even if you know they are wrong?'

'We don't learn from others telling us not to do something. We learn by making our own mistakes.'

'We never learn from our mistakes! The Dutch pillaged us. We finally got rid of them and look at Jakarta now. When I drive to work what I see? Malls, corporations, designer shops, fast-food chains.'

'Things change.'

'But they don't! That's the point!' he sat bolt upright and widened his eyes. 'They never change. Why can't you see? Why doesn't anyone see? They are still taking money out of the country. And this time not behind the barrel of a gun but through the choice of our people. And President Megawati, she who should know better, she who saw her father's ruin, is welcoming this robbery.'

'She's moved on. Maybe you should.'

'I see you've been taken in by the same influences as them. Is this why you were flirting with the *bule*?'

Misbah guffawed, surprising herself with the cruelty of her laugh. 'I was having fun Ahmad. You remember what that is?'

His heavy and bloodshot eyes revealed a hurt deeper than any of his words could convey. 'I thought you were on my side.'

'It is not about taking sides. I do agree with you that Salim can be greedy and that Elok is brash and girls of Cinta's generation expect too many freedoms. But I also know that Salim, like us, grew up poor and has worked hard for what he has, that Elok will learn as she gets older and that the young girls today have different lives to when we were brought up. My daughters are just like Cinta and I don't like their clothes or make-up or boyfriends either. But I accept these changes because fighting them only brings misery in this short life.'

'And in eternity?'

Misbah blushed and looked away. She knew how much it upset him that neither she nor her husband followed Islam.

'I see your shame and I understand it. You can forgive Salim but you forget your father and your faith. You think only of yourself.'

'I'm thinking of you and Cinta. Do you not see she is still so young and insecure? Think about what it is like for a girl growing up now with all the pressures they have to face. Do you know how much it means for someone like Cinta to be noticed by any man, let alone a white man? You've seen how they watch the films and television and idolise them. Like I said, the only way that Cinta will learn that her feelings are merely a teenage crush, or that these men are no better or worse than any man in Indonesia, is through finding out herself. And I hope she doesn't discover any of that because it'll mean she's found happiness.'

'Again I ask you - what are you suggesting with all this talk?'

'That you stop all these problems and forgive.'

'What if I do not forgive him?' he said, his ever changing expression now displaying a twisted glee. 'What if I seek revenge instead?'

'You'd never do such a thing.'

'I've thought about it.' He heaved himself up and took three heavy steps over to her. He leaned over her and gripped the backrest of the armchair with both hands.

'You know that bule? I saw him in the street last week. I didn't know who he was but still I drove at him and his friend. But I stopped just before I hit them. You know why I braked?'

'Ahmad stop. Please stop.'

'Because I'm a weak man. Tonight, I pitied that *bule*. I even started to like him. I thought he was innocent and being used by Elok. But the whole time he was making a fool of me in my own house.'

'He wasn't –'

'I had the chance to kill him and I didn't do it. It was a sign from God that I didn't take. Now I'm too weak to even follow His will and He's paid me back by sending this *bule* to my home to humiliate me.'

'It's never God's will to kill.'

He grabbed her shoulder and pressed his thumb into her neck. 'What do you know of God's will?'

'Get off me.' Misbah dug her nails into his hand. 'Get off me now.'

He released his grip and stood before her, inspecting his hand, like it was a foreign object out of his control. Misbah got up and glared at her brother with revulsion that she hadn't experienced before.

*

Leon lay in the hut, aware of every sound: the zing of the grasshoppers; the croak of the frogs; the trickle of the river; the heave of the trees. But mostly he was aware of the peaceful breath of Zak's sleep.

'Zak, wake up!'

A hiss followed by a groan. 'Mmmm... what is it?'

'It's about earlier in the van.'

'Yeah?'

'I'm sorry.'

'I thought,' Zak said, the location of his voice revealing to Leon he was now propped upright, 'you never said sorry?'

'I'm serious,' said Leon, his hand groping the dark, trying to touch Zak, to make him feel his sincerity. 'I want you to know that I liked your performance. That I think it was brave. That I agree with your decision to quit the Kraton. That I wish I hadn't wrecked that stall and that I don't care that you are gay. I don't care at all. I'm alone in a room with you and I don't even care!'

'If it is not important I am gay, why did you say those things before?'

'Maybe because I felt I had to.'

'Why?'

Despite the dark, Leon felt Zak's eyes trained upon him. He stared back at him, their shared intensity penetrating the blackness. 'Do you know what my mates would say if they found out I was in the woods with a gay brown guy? At my school the worse thing in the world was to be gay. You don't know what it's like. The first thing they'll ask me when I get back is how many girls I've slept with when I was away.'

'Why does it matter what people thousands of miles away think about you?'

'I don't know why it did matter but it doesn't anymore.'

*

Ahmad sank back into his chair. His sister's words, the slam of the door, the expression on her face staying with him throughout the night until the grey of the morning.

16 August 2002

They walked along a raised embankment through wheat crops swaying luminously in the sharp morning night. Leon gave up squelching through wet soil, rested his hands on his knees and fought for breath.

'What is wrong with you, today?' Zak said.

'What do you mean?'

'It took you a long time to get up. You did not carry anything to the van and, mostly strangely, you did not talk on the drive here.'

'I think it was that stuff we had last night... man, it tripped me out... I was hallucinating with happiness... now I feel like someone has blended my brain. I've never smoked hash like that before.'

'Hash? It was opium.'

Leon's head shot up. 'You must be joking.'

'Do not tell me that you have never tried it?'

'Of course I haven't. What do you think I am? Some sort of druggie?'

'Poppy seeds have been used in Asia for centuries as medicine and remedies for –'

'If I'm addicted then I blame you.'

'How can you possibly be addicted?'

'You can get addicted from using heroin once you know?'

'Who told you this?'

'I've seen adverts on TV. Everyone knows that.'

'Maybe in your country. But that is your society. You do not know moderation. You get addicted to food, alcohol, drugs, sex... everything that is fun.'

'I'm not interested in your theories... Junkie!'

'What is a junkie?'

'People who take heroin and say it's for medicine.'

Zak laughed and set off walking again.

Leon trudged in his wake, shading his vision with a flat palm and scanned the surroundings. 'Where are we going anyway?'

'There,' Zak said, pointing at a wooden hut in the middle of the field.

'Why?'

'We will meet a man, a very special man, who will give us some protection for the protest tomorrow.'

'About time! Fire with fire and all that. Go to war on them.' said Leon, slapping the back of his hand into his palm. 'So who are we meeting? Is he a real thug... what do you call them *preman*?'

'The protection we will receive is a lot stronger than kicks and punches.'

They climbed two steps onto the hut's balcony. The first thing Leon noticed was a chessboard sat upon a table in the centre. Before he could comment on the strangeness of this sight, Zak had beckoned him to the door of the hut. He brushed the batik drape to one side and held it open for Leon to enter. Inside, they crept across floorboards to a corner.

The square-shaped room smelt of burnt embers. Geckos crawled along the walls made of matted bamboo. Above, a one metre square hole in the roof provided a source of light. Beneath it, illuminated by the solitary beam, an old man sat cross-legged on a rattan mat. He wore a batik cap and an embroidered gown which drowned his emaciated frame. Across from him lay a younger man, perhaps in his twenties, in a deep hypnosis. Leon breathed and watched and smelled and felt like he had entered another time.

The old man rose to his feet and lifted his hand above his head. Without touch or prompt, the younger man, staggered to his feet, his pupils rolled back into his forehead, his eyes white and deathly. The old man drew himself up to his full height and seemed to levitate as he rested his palm on the young man's forehead. The young man collapsed back to the floor, his limbs fitting like he'd received an electronic shock. The old man crouched over him, picked up an opaque bottle, uncorked it with a pop, dabbed a small brush inside, withdrew it and spattered water upon the younger man's bare torso. His hand hovered over the younger man's heart. The young man sat upright and blinked and came around. They faced one another; eye contact unbroken; no words exchanged. The young man rose and stumbled out of the door.

Zak and Leon stepped towards the old man and stopped five feet away. His body was stooped and curved like a bow; his eyes were wide and hollow; his mouth circular and permanently open. His face looked like a scrunched up piece of paper: every fissure, expression and feeling of a well-lived life was carved into his mahogany skin.

'Leon this is Pak Bok. Pak Bok: Leon.'

The old man held out his hand. His nails were four inches long, decaying and coloured a yellowish umber. Leon took his claw and shook it as gently as he could - scared that a heavier touch may lead to the man's disintegration.

'He asks us to wait. He needs to recover his energy.'

'What are you talking about?' Leon said. 'He didn't say anything.'

'To me he did.'

*

Cinta sat in her father's shop contemplating how long she could wait until she went to the toilet again. It was fifteen minutes since she last pretended to go. It was the only way she could check her phone and send messages to Ryna. If she went again her father might get suspicious but caution was no longer an option. She'd heard nothing from Josh or Elok. In her last message Ryna had said that she'd sent Josh an email explaining Elok's duplicity. She also said Josh hadn't replied. What was wrong with him? She thought that these travellers spent half their days on the internet?

Her father, in the absence of any customers, was brushing the floor for the third time in the past hour. His sweeping appeared to be arbitrary with certain spots being cleaned repetitively while others hadn't been touched. He looked withered and pale like he hadn't slept. Hair everywhere, unshaven, his shirt stained and not ironed. And he wondered why no one came to the shop. How could he expect other people to come for a haircut when his own appearance was so unkempt?

As if sensing her scrutiny, he paused and glanced up at her. Cinta averted her eyes but made sure he discerned her scowl. When he'd allowed her out of the house to come to the shop, she detected the implication that she should be grateful for such freedom – as if he hadn't brought her there just to keep an eye on her.

They'd all come together that morning. Her father driving; her mother in the front seat, Cinta between the twins in the back. Traffic jam after traffic jam. Like hours were passing. All trapped together. All hating it. All hating each other. Winding the window down to taste pollution.

Winding it up to trap the silence.

Arriving at the shop and decamping inside. The rattling as the trains passed; the flickering lights; the power cuts; the heat; the stifling claustrophobia; the roar of the traffic outside. She hated all of that but most of all she hated her father for making her be there.

It hadn't always been like this. She remembered the old shop - bright and spacious. She was brought up in that shop, playing for hours in the back lane and surrounding streets. Whenever a customer brought their children they'd be sent to play with Cinta; it almost became part of the service. By the age of eight, she played with a handful of children. By ten, she played alone. With the customers went her uncle Salim and with Salim went the premises.

It was then that the process of downsizing started. The next few years became a Russian doll of premises: each location smaller than the last; all capable of fitting inside the previous shop.

She looked around at the latest premises and concluded that it must be the worst shop in Jakarta. Surely, this was the smallest, innermost doll and they wouldn't sink any lower, she thought as she watched her two sisters playing on the floor, amongst the strangers' hair. They spend hours trapped in that place – there were no back streets, no customers' children to play with, and it was too dangerous to go out on the main road. And her father wondered why they were so disobedient? The only positive was that they were too young to comprehend that they were spending their childhoods in a cupboard underneath a railway station. Cinta felt her teeth grind as she thought about how out of touch he was with all their feelings.

Worst of all, tomorrow was Independence Day.

Tomorrow was the day that he was always at his most volatile. Tomorrow was the worst possible time that she could choose to challenge a man already on the brink. Tomorrow was the day that she was going to have to risk everything.

*

Leon huddled in the corner of the hut and watched the old man sat on his rattan mat, rearranging four opaque glass bottles, a mortar and pestle, a wok and a ladle and said to Zak. 'Who is he?'

'He is a *dukun*: a person with supernatural abilities.'

'Like a shaman?'

'I do not know this word. He is someone whose actions are not comprehensible by logic.'

'Now I know what you mean by protection,' Leon said. 'Are we here to voodoo those guys that attacked us?'

'No, he does not practise black magic.'

'What does he do?'

'He heals; he controls spirits; he tells you how to change your future.'

'He can tell the future?'

'No man can,' Zak said. 'But he can tell you what to expect and how to change the energy when the future arrives.'

'And what was he doing to that guy earlier?'

'Healing him.'

'It looked like torture.'

'All healing requires us to revisit the pain of our early life.'

'What by electrocuting him?'

'Each *dukun* has his methods. Pak manipulates the energy you cannot see. It is not something any person can do. He learned from his father in the jungles of Kalimantan. Still his grandson returns to the village. Days of walking in the forest to get the plants needed for Pak to continue. Pak works only in this house and only by the light of day.'

'How old is he?' Leon said.

'No one knows exactly but we do know that in your calendar this is the third century he has seen.'

'He's three hundred?'

'No, he was born before 1900.'

Leon counted on his fingers, 'Oh right... so well over a hundred.'

'Yes. Imagine he was over fifty before this nation was born.'

'Amazing,' Leon said, inspecting the old man like he was an incarnation from another life. 'So if we are not here to voodoo our enemies why are we here?'

'Tomorrow at the protest I will need the protection of the *dukun* from the spirits who guide me and from the spirits who guide others.'

The old man got up from his mat and stepped into the light. He held out both arms and directed his flattened palms to Leon.

'What's he doing now?'

Zak looked to the *dukun* and back to Leon. 'He wants you to come forward.'

'What happens if I say no?'

'Nothing.'

'Except bad luck and spirits and all that stuff.'

'Maybe.'

'I know what I just saw was pretty amazing but I'm not sure I believe in all this. Then again...' Leon gave a wry smile and breathed out through his nose. 'I'm not sure I don't believe in it.'

'Well?'

'Well, then,' Leon said, throwing up his hands in defeat. 'I'll have to do it then. It's too much of a risk not to.'

*

The midday light lasered through the glass roof and illuminated the patio. In a pocket of shade, three people gathered around a TV. Two more sat on beanbags reading. Another slept in a hammock. In the far corner, a staircase spiralled up to a square balcony, which ran around the perimeter of the patio. Off the balcony, inside one of the collection of bedrooms, Josh sat on a single bed next to Elok and her English friend, Simon.

Elok had woken Josh early that morning promising to drive him back to his hotel. On the way, they made a detour to Simon's house so that Josh could, 'meet some *bules* like him.' Elok had promised it would be a 'fast visit' and the people would be 'very exciting' to meet him.

When they arrived at the house the '*bules*' hanging around the patio weren't, 'very exciting' to meet him. A couple of people mumbled, 'Hello,' another simply said, 'He's upstairs.'

On the way up the stairs to Simon's room, Elok put this lack of enthusiasm down to the frequency of her visits. She wasn't amused by Josh's suggestion that they were probably sick of the sight of her.

Simon, on the other hand, couldn't have been more pleased to see them. After the briefest of introductions, Josh realised that Simon, in fact, couldn't have been more pleased to see Elok.

Simon wore glasses, under-sized shorts and an expression that said he couldn't believe his luck. He hung on every word Elok said: deeply affected by any negative news; overjoyed by anything positive. Throughout, he rubbed his patchy blond hair, which resembled the down of a newborn chicken, and grinned manically. The unlikely friendship began to make perfect sense: together they could talk about their favourite subject for hours on end - Elok.

Whilst the duo pondered the life and times of Elok, Josh's thoughts passed to the night before and his current situation. He'd barely slept. He didn't know where he was or even the day. Last night, Elok had told him that Cinta's dad had her phone and not to call her. Was this true? Maybe. Should he risk calling? Yes. But what if it made things worse? He could phone and hang up if her father answered. But wouldn't it be obvious that it was him? He'd also need to give Elok the slip and find a phone. If only he had his own mobile. He knew his no phone pact with Leon would backfire – another idealistic concept of travelling... like the temporary tattoos in Thailand and the septic ear piercing incident in China.

Deciding to wait and see what happened, Josh gradually tuned back into the conversation. Elok was telling Simon about the events that had occurred at Cinta's house the previous night. As she went through the Elok version (not letting the truth get in the way of a good story) Simon shook his vast cranium whilst releasing great exhalations of sympathy. 'You poor thing. Are you OK?' he kept repeating.

Josh rolled his eyes. He didn't know how much more of this he could take.

'Simon,' a female voice called from the corridor. 'It's that woman for you again.'

'Great...' Simon's nostrils flared in feigned angst.

'What did you say about her? Josh listen. Simon so funny.'

'I called her a "Monet" because she looks good from a distance but not up close.'

Elok cackled and her head lolled around before her eyes fell upon Josh. She became serious. 'Why you not laugh?'

Josh wanted to say because I've heard the joke about a hundred times but couldn't bring himself to humiliate Simon in front of Elok.

'Simon,' shouted the same female voice from the balcony. 'Are you going to speak to her or not?'

'Cynthia, I've told you a million times, no calls from girls when I'm with Elok.'

'See all *bule* popular in Indonesia,' Elok whispered to Josh.

'Oi! I heard that.' Simon folded his arms across his belly. 'What does that mean?'
That if I'm popular every *bule* must be?'

'Of course not,' Elok beamed a sexless smile and buried herself in his torso like she was cuddling a big tame bear. 'Siimmoonn,' she said, in her most childlike voice, 'Can I borrow some money?'

He released her from the hug. 'You already owe me like a million rupiah.'

'But you have so many money. I need it for important things.' She flicked her hair from her face. Large brown eyes implored. Moist lips pursed. Josh's eyes traced the contours of her face and he recognised how beautiful she was and charming she could be and knew Simon had no chance.

'But your father is one of the richest men in Jakarta,' said Simon.

'Indonesia,' Elok corrected. 'But he very horrible to me. No money for Elok.'

Simon sighed. He was convincing no one - especially himself. He rifled in his pocket and produced a handful of 100,000 rupiah notes with pretend reluctance. Elok took the notes and didn't hug him this time but instead planted a kiss on his cheek. He shut his eyes, seemingly luxuriating in the memory of her very touch.

'OK, we go to the Stadium tonight,' Elok said. 'Big party. Night before Independence Day.'

'What's the Stadium?' Josh said.

'I tell you already. One billion times. The best club in Jakarta. OK, I have a plan. First we drive to the outdoor bars. There you see many cool people Josh and big cars. Then we go to Stadium.'

'I thought you had no money,' Josh said.

Elok wafted the money that Simon had just given her in front of Josh's face.

'You said that you needed that for important things.'

'Shut up Josh. Stadium is important. Tell him Simon.'

'Certainly is,' Simon said. He adjusted his jam and gave Josh a lop-sided grin, which seemed to say, 'Come on mate what would you have done?'

*

Leon rested his head on a pillow. A white sheet was draped over his body and covered his face. The padding sound of bare feet. The shadow of the *dukun*'s hand. The sheet filled with static and prickled against his skin before being flung away. The *dukun* gripped his jawbone and fixed his grey eyes upon him.

The room hazed. Silver smoke curling up the shaft of light to the freedom of outside. Zak sat in the corner, distant and alone. Suddenly, hands pressed against Leon's chest, sucking all the air from his lungs. A further touch sent an impulse through Leon's temple. Needles prickled through his blood vessels. Liquid sprinkled on his torso. Either boiling or freezing. The claw lingered over him. The liquid dispersed without touch.

Zak sat next to him now but was still so far away. The *dukun* spoke, his voice coming from somewhere deep within his hunched frame, the words barely audible yet deeply grave.

'He says that you have had a troubled past,' Zak translated.

'No,' Leon yelled, with a kick of his right leg.

'Do not speak. Just listen and trust. It is very important.'

'He sees problems with your family. That your brother is lost.'

Leon stirred but remained quiet.

'He will not return in this life although you desire it every day. But he will return to you later in a different place.'

Sweat drowning his face. Vision blurring. How could this man pry into the depths of his soul and talk about that which he would let no one else touch?

'In your future, you must forgive those who you love like your brother but expect no forgiveness in return. It may come but that is not for you or your spirits to control. He sees a big problem in your future. The event is a catastrophe. You cannot stop it. No one can and it will happen. You will know not when the moment has come until it passes. All you can do is follow your path and your instinct.'

The *dukun* rested one hand on Leon's heart and the other on his upper arm and guided him into a sitting position. The objects of the room started to form and shape. Leon lay back down and rolled onto his side and drew his knees up and covered his eyes with his hands and couldn't bear to see nor touch nor talk to another person.

After a long time, Zak helped him to his feet and out to the balcony. Leon slumped on a stool and rested his forearms on the table with the chessboard. Zak opened his flask of water and offered it to him. Leon took a long swig, wiped his mouth, lifted the flask back to his lips and drained the remainder of the bottle. He blinked and looked to Zak, 'How long was I under?'

'I could not say.'

'It was intense.'

'It always is.'

'I will go in now but you must wait here.'

'Why?'

'I do not want you to see what I am about to face.'

*

Leon sat on the balcony and watched a group of labourers transporting huge, white sacks on their heads. They staggered across the verges, disturbing a flock of birds that flapped in panicked retreat before soaring up and beyond the field towards the dark green hills in the south.

A child aged about eight or nine, who had been playing in the field, spotted Leon and skipped onto the balcony. He hesitated six feet away, shyness overcoming his initial curiosity. Leon smiled and beckoned him closer. The child shuffled along the rotting boards. Leon ruffled his hair and tickled his lower ribs and made him giggle. The child lowered his chin and batted his long lashes. 'Mister, *gula-gula*?' he said, presenting an open palm.

Leon fished in his pocket and produced a boiled sweet. The child took it, popped it in his mouth and perched on the other stool across the table.

'You play?' Leon asked, pointing to the chessboard sat upon the table.

The child nodded.

'OK, if you win I give you all these *gulas*.' Leon laid ten sweets on the table. The child looked at Leon and back at the sweets. His eyes glowed. He knew what was at stake.

As the game commenced, Leon heard a deep groan emanating from inside the house and shuddered at the thought of what Zak was going through. The child sat unmoved – oblivious to everything but the sweets and the board.

*

Zak emerged out of the hut as the child placed Leon into checkmate. The *dukun* padded after him. He stopped, rested his hand against the outer rail of the balcony and blinked at the sun as if he hadn't seen it in years.

'You have lost to a child.'

'I let him win.'

Zak looked at him sceptically.

'I did!' Leon said. 'What happened in there?'

'I cannot say. I do not even know myself.'

The *dukun* lowered himself onto the seat vacated by the child. His eyes met Leon's. The amber light of the late afternoon hit his skeletal, almost extra-terrestrial presence, and seemed to radiate a celestial beauty beyond Leon's comprehension.

'He wants to play you,' Zak said.

'He knows about everything that has happened to me in the past and all that's going to happen in the future.'

'Yes?'

'So I'm not playing him at chess,' Leon said. 'He will trounce me. If he knows about my brother he probably knows my moves already.'

'Well, use that to your advantage not his.'

*

Leon lined up his eight pawns, two bishops, two knights and two rooks. He lifted his queen and kissed her as was his superstition and positioned her back on the board. He surveyed the eight ranks and files of the chequered grid and concentrated on hiding his thoughts from the *dukun*.

The opening was as unconventional as Leon had experienced. The *dukun* appeared to have no discernible strategy. Leon pressed forward with his standard opening, concentrating on developing his pieces and gaining board position.

With an exchange of pawns and a knight, the game opened into the middle section. Leon had the key squares, the central position and had castled his king, yet felt no control over the game. As the middle exchanges developed the *dukun* played seemingly without regard for piece value. He sacrificed his rook and pawn in return for a solitary pawn of Leon's and to no perceivable advantage to his board position. His game was a contradiction. He picked up pieces without thought or indecision and placed them in innocuous positions but with the conviction of that being the only place that the piece belonged.

They entered the endgame. Leon's pieces both outnumbered and ranked those of Pak Bok's. It appeared the *dukun*'s last hope was when he moved his remaining pawn onto the eighth rank on Leon's side of the board. Yet, rather than upgrade to a queen or even a knight he under-promoted to a rook.

Leon looked up at Zak and frowned. Leon noted nothing at the time but when he thought about it later Zak's expression had seemed knowing.

Six moves later the *dukun*'s decision made sense. A further five and the whole game made sense. Like the *dukun* had planned every move in advance to get to this point. With his king controlling the middle of the board, within a further ten moves he had Leon in checkmate.

Leon knocked over his king with the back of his hand and stared at the board. 'I thought it was impossible to win from there.'

The old man laughed and shook Leon's hand and spoke to Zak.

'He says you play very well. It was his hardest game for five years.'

'Who has he been playing with?' Leon muttered. 'That kid?'

*

They gathered their things together and bade the *dukun* farewell. Before they left the *dukun* clasped Leon's arm and examined his face and spoke. Zak translated, 'He says earlier that he saw a terrible event in your future. Now he sees some hope if you listen to his advice. You have strength and energy but you cannot control your gifts.

That is why you become angry and anger others. You should learn from your game with him. He tells you not to believe chess to be a game separate from life. All life is chess. The endgame develops and is formed by all that has passed before. You may lose the beginning and also the middle but still win in the end. You must play with the harmony that allows you to make clearer decisions in this world and the next. If you control your life and energy like you control the chessboard you will win at both.'

*

Leon didn't speak as they walked to the van. When they reached it he opened the door and looked back to the house in the centre of the golden field.

'Now we travel to final and best part of the journey,' Zak said. 'The best part of Java.'

'OK.'

'OK? Is that all you say?'

'Yeah sorry... I was just thinking that's all.'

'What do you think about?'

'Do you think Pak Bok played that entire game to teach me a lesson?'

'I have seen him do it before. You played well.'

'Not that well.'

'He is the best player in this land. People come from Yogya to lose to him. I have seen him put good players in checkmate in 20 moves. He has played for years and his powers are divine. You won his respect. For a man this wise that is greater than to win a match.'

'What about the bad thing he said would happen?'

'I told you, he cannot see the future. He has a feeling. That is all. If you follow his advice and control your energy, he sees hope for you yet.'

'I hope I can listen to his words.'

'Do not change too much there is nothing wrong with the way you are.'

'Really you think that?' Leon said.

'Yes, I did not imagine you would be good at chess.'

'Why not?'

'You do not appear to have the patience.'

'After my dad left home I used to go to visit him...' Leon looked down and drew circles in the gravel with his big toe.

'Tell me.'

'It was like... chess was the only thing we'd do together. Think it was so we didn't need to think of anything to say to each other. Also he could drink when he was playing. He used to say to me, "Wait, Leon. Wait," because he knew I wanted to win straight away. It was just that I wanted to beat him so much. You know, to show him that I wasn't all bad...' Leon opened the passenger door and got inside.

Zak joined him but didn't start the engine. 'Do not stop.'

'He used to buy me a chess book every year for Christmas... and I used to read them. One year I studied it really hard. Learned about standard openings and solving problems. Thing is I don't tell anyone because chess is a bit nerdy and all that. A lad at our school got to the English championships. Played him just before he went and beat him and he looks at me all suspicious like this guy must have cheated. I didn't want to exactly go around boasting about it around school though and he certainly didn't want to tell anyone.'

'Do you still play?'

'I used to play Josh on this trip and let him win and then call him a geek. Made me laugh every time. This one time he had me down to like my king, a knight and pawn or something and he just couldn't lose. It was really similar to a problem I'd read about before and I knew how to solve it. He couldn't believe it when I won but I made it out as dumb luck and then lost the next game to prove it.'

'So you never told your best friend about your passion?'

'It's not really a passion. Just something to do. Anyway, I can't exactly spend all day calling him a geek if he finds out I'm into chess.

'Maybe your problem was you were not honest together.'

'Or that we just liked to wind each other up. He did the same to me. I used to read his diary and see all this bad stuff he'd written about me. I couldn't exactly say anything because I shouldn't have been reading it in the first place. It made me angry for ages. I'm not good at bottling stuff up. Then he wrote this one thing that was too far... that was one of the reasons I decided to leave. Then I found out he knew I was reading it all along and that's why he was writing it. It's quite funny in a way. It kind of sums us both up.'

'Why did you not stay when you discovered he did it with intention?'

'Like Pak Bok said,' Leon drew his seatbelt across his body and clicked it into the buckle. 'Maybe I was too proud to lose position in the middle even if it would have given me a better end.'

*

They drove. Street lights dim and disappearing. Pallid

houses. Padlocked garages. Rutted roads bouncing them around the interior. A wind picked up. All that moved was the garbage. Garbage and them. Wheels and waste echoing through the black emptiness.

When a faint glow kindled the horizon, Elok slowed and parked. She pulled down the sun-visor and re-applied her lipstick and adjusted her hair. She slapped both hands on the wheel and faced the neon mist beyond. Blue, yellow and red lights sparkled across her face and then were gone. A second of ink blackness. Breath hissed in and out of Simon's nose in the back seat.

'Ready? Elok asked.

'Yes,' said Josh, not sure what he was meant to be ready for.

They accelerated towards the lights and music. The road cut through rows of shimmering automobiles and their equally decadent owners. Some revved their engines, showing off the horsepower to anyone who cared to listen and many who didn't; others leaned against their bonnets, encircled by admirers, scoffing at the inferiority of the passing vehicles.

Elok lowered her window. Ringed fingers reaching out and twinkling hellos. No one in the crowd missed a single movement: no one saw a thing.

They circled. Not a space in sight until a red reverse light crept across their path. Elok allowed the departing car to reverse out and manoeuvred in the vacated space. They left the car and went towards a wooden-framed bar.

Elok flicked her hand at some vacant plastic seats. 'Sit there.'

'What do you want to drink?' Simon said.

'Nothing. Back soon.'

Josh and Simon silently watched her curve out of their view. Their eyes met and maybe they shared the same thought but both looked away and didn't voice it.

Simon's dull eyes set on the bar. 'I'll get the drinks. I would ask you what you want but there isn't much choice. Down here they do... cocktails I suppose you would call them.'

Simon went to the bar, returned and placed the glasses on the table. Josh inspected the luminous liquid before taking a measured swig. He resisted the urge to spit it out. 'Man, that's strong.'

'Sure is,' said Simon

Around them, collections of youths on plastic chairs drank from polystyrene cups and blasted clouds of tobacco into the night sky.

Josh risked another swig, wincing through the fiery sensation in his throat. 'How long have you lived in here?' he said to Simon.

'Four years, mate.'

'What do you do?'

'I'm an English teacher.'

'You must know a lot about Indonesia.'

'Yeah, well you get to learn a few things...'

'What's the story with this place?'

'It is actually illegal,' Simon said. 'The police let it build up for about a month and then when it reaches maximum popularity they come down and bust people for drugs and lack of licences and drunk driving and arrest all the bar owners. When everyone has paid their bribes and fines it starts all over again. Quiet at the start because people know about the bust but then getting busier as people forget.'

'What stage is it at the moment?'

'They did a bust about a week ago - so it's safe for now. This is the only time I come down. If I was here when they did one I would be the first one arrested.'

'Why?'

'My skin colour. You must have noticed that they think we're all rich?'

'Elok certainly does.'

'Where is she, anyway? 'Josh watched Simon clamber to his feet and realised that despite his infatuation with Elok and all his insecure traits like strapping 'mate' onto the end of every sentence, all Simon wanted to do was make people like him. And Josh could certainly empathise with that. It was easy for those like Elok and Leon to dismiss people because there would always be someone new coming along in their place. Those like he and Simon didn't have that luxury. But whereas Josh tried to be popular by blending into the crowd and befriending the most popular people, Simon strived to be popular in his own right. Josh watched Simon's bulbous head turning as he scanned the crowd and feared that in a world of superficiality and snap judgements that popularity was something Simon was never going to achieve.

At that moment, Simon began to rub his hands together and bounce on the spot. 'Here, she comes. Elok over here. Let me get you a chair.'

'No, I take your chair,' Elok said.

'Why?'

'I find your friends for you Simon,' she said, pointing to a group of white men, whose sudden appearance had coincided with her return.

'I'll go and say hello later.'

'It took me a long time to find them.' Elok widened her eyes and nodded. 'You go to say hello now.'

'I'm fine here.'

'Just go,' said Elok, dropping all subtlety.

'Alright... fine.' Simon tugged his t-shirt down, picked up his drink and left. On the short trip to his friends he cast two glances back to Elok.

'How long did it take you to find his friends?' Josh said.

'Not long.'

'It's lucky they were here so you could get rid of him.'

'Yes.'

Josh studied her. No expression passed across her face. 'Elok, I was joking.'

'What joke?'

'He obviously likes you. You shouldn't treat him badly.'

'When I treat him badly?'

'Like when you manipulated him for the money?'

'Manipul...mated...what that mean?'

'Strange how your English fails you when –'

'Shut up for one minute Josh. I need to speak you about Cinta.'

Josh sat forward, 'What about her?'

'I speak with her before but do not want to make you sad.'

'What did she say?' Josh said, feeling the shot of energy that overtakes your body when you realise that your fate depends on the words of another.

'She not want to see you again.'

'What... but...' Josh said, the electric tremble of his lips preventing him from phrasing the question.

'She say she not want trouble with her father. She not like you so much to make the risk.'
Elok dragged her seat closer, draped her arms over him and squeezed him against her chest. 'I am sorry.'
*

It was dark when Zak and Leon entered the town, driving along the main road past the hotels and restaurants. They took a sharp right and continued for a couple of miles. The houses decreased. Hundreds of flies swarmed around the headlights. A man walked past shielding his eyes. The road narrowed and they drove into a clearing with rice paddies on either side. The water that irrigated the fields shimmered in the light of the near full moon.

Zak cut the engine and switched off the lights and everything became quiet and still and it felt like they were the only people in the world. They stepped out of the car. Through the mist that crept across the top of the coconut grove, a floodlight lit a single bell-like dome, the silhouettes of the palm leaves flickering in its wake.

'What is that?' Leon said, his voice husky and breathless.

'Lord Buddha of Borobudur. Tomorrow you shall meet him.'

*

As Elok pressed against his ribcage, Josh became conscious of his erratic breathing and recognised how embarrassing his reaction to Cinta's rejection had been. He withdrew from her grasp and proceeded to handle the situation like any man would: he pretended he wasn't upset in the slightest.

Elok tilted her head to meet his eyes. 'Are you OK?

'Yeah. I'm fine.'

'Josh you not OK. Eyes like this.' She peeled back her lids to reveal the whites of her eyeballs. 'And *bule* shaking like he very cold.'

She slipped her hand into his. He took it and trapped it with his other hand.

'I not tell you this before so don't be angry. Promise? I could not say because she my cousin and I love her.'

Josh continued to nod - like he was trying to convince himself he wanted to hear what she was going to say.

'She is not what you think. She pretend to be nice little girl but she not nice. She has an Indonesian boyfriend. Her father likes him and soon they marry.'

Josh released her hand and shoved Elok away. She rocked back in her seat and almost fell off. He looked at her eyes, all big and shocked.

A hand grabbed the back of his t-shirt and twisted. 'What the hell are you doing?' Simon's voice in his ear.

'Simon, stop,' Elok said, on her feet, slapping at his arm. 'It is OK.'

Simon released him. 'It's not Elok. He shouldn't push you. What if you fell over?'

He seemed more upset than angry: he seemed more upset than Elok.

'Look I'm sorry OK,' Josh said. 'She told me something about Cinta which is untrue.'

'It true,' Elok said. 'Ask Simon!'

Josh faced Simon, 'Does Cinta have a boyfriend?'

Simon looked at Elok and back at him and licked his lips.

'Simon, answer the question.'

Simon adjusted his glasses and flinched. 'Yes, I heard

she does.'

Josh turned and staggered away towards a tree. He rested against the trunk, its shadow offering the only privacy he could find. Heart pounding, throat closing, his head fell into his hands.

*

Zak and Leon drove out of the clearing and climbed deeper into the forest. After five minutes, Zak pulled off the road and killed the engine.

They slept in the back of his van.

It was still dark when Zak woke him. Leon opened his eyes and adrenaline burned through the tiredness and without a word he sat up and crawled out of the back of the van. Zak flicked on the torch and they began their descent.

Bracken cracked beneath their feet. Vines clung to their bodies and lashed their skin. The air was thick with mosquitoes. They slipped and scrambled and stamped and kicked their way through the dense undergrowth. Ignoring the unbearable itches developing on their cut, stung and bitten skin, they blundered towards the bright light that signified the clearing ahead. Their pace quickened to a canter and then to a run. They burst out of the forest and onto the grass before stopping dead, rendered immobile by the magnificence in front of them. A floodlit pyramid made up of a series of ever decreasing square terraces stood before them. To Leon's eye, the side of the base he could see must have measured more than one hundred metres in width. The pinnacle of the pyramid rose to maybe forty metres from the ground. Even from more than a hundred metres away the detail of the architecture and carving could be discerned.

'I don't know what to say...' Leon said.

'I can never find the words. It is too perfect. My favourite description is the jewel of Java.'

'I like that.'

'Its real name is Borobudur. It is the largest Buddhist temple in the world. We will be the only people at the summit when the sun rises. It is how I start every Independence Day.'

Leon walked towards it almost in a trance.

Zak's outstretched forearm halted him. 'You cannot go now. We will be seen. We have a small opportunity. They turn the spotlights off half an hour before dawn. We use the dark to reach the monument. We follow the security guard who opens the gates on each level to the top and wait until he leaves. Then the natural light comes and we are on the pinnacle watching the dawn.'

'What happens if we get caught?'

'We will be arrested for breaking into the most precious monument on the island.'

*

Simon watched Josh almost stagger away in the direction of a tree some thirty metres away. He slumped against the trunk and drew his knees up to his chest.

'I don't think you should have put me in that position,' Simon said to Elok.

'Why?'

'Because I don't know if Cinta has a boyfriend or not. I mean, you only told me two hours ago she was with someone.'

'You think I lie?' Elok said, stepping closer, her thumbs tucked into her belt, her chest thrust forward.

'Of course not. But I have just told Josh something

that has upset him and I have nothing to prove it.'

'Yes but you know you can trust me. Simon, if you not trust me we never speak again... you understand?'

Simon slid his feet into and out of his loose fitting trainers and looked down. 'Yes.'

'OK you stay here and say nothing. I go to speak to poor Josh. '

She went off towards Josh leaving him alone with the drinks and table.

*

As they waited, Zak regaled the story of the beautiful structure in a mellifluous whisper. The Borobudur temple was built in the 9th century by the Sailendra dynasty. It is decorated by stone relief carvings that depict Buddha's own search for enlightenment. There are over 2,500 of these relief panels, each telling a different story. There are also over 500 statutes of Buddha. The five terraces that make up the pyramid-shaped temple represent *mandala*, a symbol of harmony in the universe. Bell-shaped stone objects called *stupas* are found across the terraces. Some say that the *stupas* symbolise the souls of the dead Buddhas; others that they represent the tears of the thousands of stonecutters, sculptors and builders who died during the years of construction. The path to the summit is stained with the blood of our ancestors. The tears of their fatigue a gift to their un-named island. At the summit, a gigantic *stupa* sits on a lotus-shaped base half a metre thick. This *stupa* is known as Lord Buddha. This was the Buddha they'd seen from the clearing the night before.

As the tale developed, the royal puppeteer's hands and arms illustrated his words and his voice grew louder and faster. As the low hanging mist rose, Zak explained that when the Buddhist empire was overthrown and Islam came to Java, the temple was forgotten. Centuries of neglect led the surrounding forest, and volcanic ash blown from nearby Gunung Merapi, to bury the wonder. It was only when Simon Raffles, the British founder of Singapore, came to administer Java that Borobudur was re-discovered. As well as building botanical gardens in Bogor, Raffles highlighted Borobudur's existence to the world, initiating its gradual restoration.

Twelve hundred years after it was built, it stood before them: immortal and abiding, withstanding volcanic eruptions, earthquakes, ignorance, ruin, looting, terrorism and war.

The floodlights extinguished. Zak beckoned Leon forth. They ran across the plane to the hulking black edifice.

*

Josh heard someone approach and crouch next to him. He knew it was her even before her sweet smell hit his nose. It reminded him of the orchids in Bogor. He lifted his head and offered her a conciliatory smile. 'I'm sorry.'

'Why?'

'For getting angry with you. It's not your fault.'

'No problem,' her soft words wrapping around him like a freshly laundered towel. 'Please do not be sad. She not deserve you.'

'Maybe...'

'No maybe. Why you with Cinta anyway? She like little child and not pretty. You are best looking *bule* I know. '

'If I'm the best looking *bule* why did you choose Leon on the first night we met?'

'Leon? Please! He nothing to you. He bad in bed and not strong man like you.'

'You're just saying that...'

'No, I am not. You are too good for Cinta and Leon. We are too good! We do not need these losers, OK?'

'I suppose not.'

'I said we do not need these losers, OK?

'YES.'

'OK. Get up.'

He met her wild eyes and, infected by all their wants, got to his feet and allowed her to take his hand.

'Tonight we go to the Stadium and we forget them. We forget them together.'

*

They stood at the base of the pyramid and watched a flashlight bounce up the stairs until it reached a white gate. The jangle of keys, the click of the mechanism, the door creaked open. Zak waited for a moment and then ushered Leon forth. They crept up the stairs through the gate and ascended to the fourth terrace. The guard's footsteps ceased. The light flashed in their direction. They ducked to their right behind the wall and tried not to breathe.

Zak pressed his chest against the stone's chest pressed against the detailed carvings; the lines of relief panels that illustrated tales of love and war; the story of man through every age always returning to the same primitive beginnings.

They waited until the footsteps had gone and took to the stairs again. It was dark when they reached the top. The moon had fallen and the stars dimmed and not a flicker of light was seen from the forthcoming dawn. They stumbled across to the Lord Buddha in the centre of the terrace and sat down next to him. 'Do you feel the spirituality?' Zak whispered to Leon.

'I told you before I'm not sure I believe in all that stuff.'

Zak watched the light flickering on the rim of the horizon. 'This is the difference between east and west. You think we are crazy for believing anything that cannot be rationalised or demonstrated by science and we think you are crazy in the belief that humans know everything.'

'So you feel something here?'

'This is my most spiritual place.'

'But you told me you were a Muslim earlier and that this is a Buddhist temple...'

'Yes, but Islam is different in Java. The Holy Koran arrived in the 12th century with the Arab traders. And when it came we mixed the teachings with native beliefs. In Java we have our own history, architecture, names, dance and music. Traditional Javanese Islam embraces our Hindu and Buddhist past. It does not try to replace it.'

'How can you say you are a Muslim when you drink, smoke, don't pray and are gay? I'm no expert but I'd say your entire lifestyle is an example of exactly how not to be a Muslim.'

'I am a Muslim for me. Not for anyone else. Because I worship Allah why can I also not worship life, the soul, the human body, wisdom and truth?'

'So basically, Java has chosen its own version of Islam and you have chosen your own version of Javanese Islam.'

Zak laughed. 'Maybe but we do not all read the Koran and believe it is 100% fact. It is a story. A way to have faith and believe. A way to live your life.'

'But a lot of Muslims do read it as 100% fact.'

'Yes, there are radical Muslims who believe in Wahabism.'

'What's that?'

'The belief that we should read the Koran as literal and return to the rules of 8th century Saudi Arabia. This movement is still small but is growing in this country. At the same time, the traditional Javanese Islam that I believe in is less popular. Now girls wear the *jilbab* headscarfs; there is Sharia law in Aceh in Sumatra; the Islam Defenders Front are attacking bars in Jakarta; there has been church burning and genocide in Maluku. Yes, there is hatred growing in this country.'

'And these people are terrorists?'

'To believe in Wahabism is not to be a terrorist.'

'But there are terrorists in Indonesia. My friend Josh read the Foreign Office website before we came. It said there was a high threat. That's why he didn't want to come.'

'There are many *madrassa* schools near here mainly in Solo. They are like Muslim boarding schools. There is rumour that Jemaah Islamiyah, a group who are linked to al Qaeda, are training people in these schools. But the more worrying is they go to the kampung. They tell things to the poor. People who hear only one story in their life and do not know nothing else. It makes me very angry.'

'What do people here think of al Qaeda?'

'I know what I think.'

'What?'

'That those terrorists know nothing of Islam. They only know ignorance and hatred. They die in the name of Islam but they do not understand it. They think Islam is there to defeat something. To beat the West. To beat their own people. But it's not. Islam is there to complete you, not to take something away.'

Leon laughed. It was a strange laugh. Meaningful yet without mirth or cruelty. 'So this is another thing you feel strongly about then?'

'Yes! If you trust only the media or George Bush the world is divided into terrorists and their supporters and western saviours who love freedom. But that is not true. They are two extremes of opinion. Almost everyone else is in the middle. We love religion but not violence. We also love freedom. But freedom of mind, of spirit, of the soul. Not freedom of capitalism, freedom of greed, freedom from morality.'

Zak felt Leon staring at him. His features appeared to soften. For the first time since they left Yogyakarta the intensity dropped.

'You really are incredible,' Leon said.

Zak didn't speak – he was waiting for Leon to say he was joking or to contradict his words. But that moment didn't come that night or ever again.

*

When Josh heard the news that Cinta didn't want to see him again and that she had a boyfriend he felt sad and pitied himself before the anger took over. Then the stage of defiant euphoria took over. He convinced himself that everything was alright and didn't care about Leon or Cinta or his latest rejection.

And as he, Elok and Simon drove over a flyover to the Stadium, he thought about that first taxi ride with Leon, back when he hadn't even met Elok, and how much his life had changed since then.

He gazed at her and experienced the excitement and

admiration he felt when Leon was at his most captivating. He came to the realisation that despite their flaws, he'd always be drawn to people like them and that, in the end, everyone lets you down, even those like Cinta, so why not be let down by people like Elok and Leon and enjoy the ride while they let you share their incredible energy, before they become bored with you and surge past you onto the next person.

'What you look at? Does *bule* want a picture?'

Josh didn't divert his eyes because he knew Elok now and knew that she loved the attention and the drama of every moment of her life. She returned his stare, looking at him and not at the road, but he didn't care because people like Elok didn't crash.

'Why aren't you telling me to look at the road?' she said, her sentence not containing a single error; her pronunciation perfect.

'Because you don't need me to tell you, do you?'

'No, I don't,' she said. Her taut brown skin relaxed. There was a silence, which Elok failed to fill and, for a moment, she was comfortable in that space. He smiled as he watched her fight the return of the mania: fidgeting in her seat; her shoulders twitching energetically.

'Of course you not need to tell me. I brilliant driver,' she said, slamming the door shut upon the tiny glimpse of her soul. 'Simon, we going to have a great night in Stadium, OK?'

'Maybe,' said Simon, from the back seat. He appeared distant - perhaps he was aware of the significance of what had just happened.

*

Leon and Zak nestled together and watched the red of

the rising sun melt into the surrounding dark. In the east, the cone of Merapi glowed orange. The sun burned through the low mist and blue gusted across the scene.

'I think I feel it.'

'What?'

'The spirit you mentioned earlier.' Leon took in the panorama and felt a moment of pure joy - where worry dissipates and nothing whatsoever is wrong. 'It's divine.'

*

The line stretches a hundred metres down the road. But not for Elok. She walks right to the front. The bouncers search the entrants. Everyone except Elok. It costs 100,000 rupiah to enter. For Elok it's free.

Up countless stairs passing through seven floors. We are going to the top level – of course. Elok struts across each scene, friends or enemies with everyone we pass. She half-*bule*. She think she so cute but she ugly. He so stupid. Look at way he dress. Those girls in corner all prostitute. The music so bad on this floor. Who dance like that. If I dance like him maybe I die. He smell. She smell. They smell. You smell.

Reaching the top floor. Drinks and people. So many women. All staring. Like being famous. Like being Elok. Surrounded by men she laughs and throws her head back and reveals her long, slender neck.

The bass overloads and euphoria vibrates through the crowd. Hands in the air. The glitter ball sparkles upon the floor but nothing shines like Elok. She is the most popular. The most sought after. The one.

The light dips. Swallowed by a wave of bodies. But we are alone. I'm lost and can't find my way back. She gazes at me. At me. Her. At me.

She moves closer and I feel her force. Her willpower and beauty draw me in. There is nothing but her and her eyes and lips. She leans in and we kiss.

I don't see Simon. But he sees us. And it is that little inconvenience that pursues me for the rest of my short life.

BOOK 3:
INDEPENDENCE DAY

17 August 2002

The illumination of the curtains. The calmness of the air. The clarity of song. Dawn. The moment to escape had arrived.

Already fully dressed, Cinta placed the sheet to the left and swung her legs to the right. One foot on the floor and then the other. She faced her sisters in the adjacent beds. But the beauty of their untroubled sleep offered her no comfort.

She rose, picked up her already packed bag and crept across the room on the balls of her feet. Counting her steps didn't help her progress or her nerves but she did so nevertheless. She winced as she heard her weight groan through the floorboards. Never had nine steps been taken so deliberately: never had nine steps meant so much. She reached the bedroom door.

The cry of a rooster outside. The clucking of the hens it awoke. The sound faded and all she could hear was the gasp of her breath and the slow thump, thump, thump of her heart.

She gripped the handle and drew the door back towards her. The wood scraped along the floor. Her sister, Nur, rolled over and opened her eyes. She inspected Cinta and appeared confused but perhaps didn't believe what she saw and rolled back over and fell asleep again.

Cinta stepped into the hall and closed the door behind her. She could hear the sheets being disturbed in her parents' room. A stifled moan, rummaging and then calm - another episode in her mother's battle with the terrors of sleep.

She tip-toed to the stairs and descended. One at a time. Each tread jarring through her limbs. She reached the ground level and stepped into the dark living room. The smell of last night's food and male body odour. The finishing line in sight. Her pace quickened. Goodbye caution. Get it over with.

The final obstacle: the front door. She opened it. Daylight burst into the room. It stirred something she hadn't seen. She spun around and froze.

*

Josh opened his eyes, groaned, and closed them again. The light trapped under his lids scalding his vision. He rolled over and drew the sheet up over his head. He collided with another body.

A hand met his chest: drowsy breath his neck.

A thousand thoughts but no ideas. A collection of disparate images refusing to come together. They all featured the same person. Josh opened one eye. They all featured the person lying next to him.

*

He sat upright in his chair, hands gripping the

armrests, and stared right at her. Cinta shut the door and walked back across the room. She lowered herself onto the sofa and faced her father but couldn't meet his eyes.

'I'm going to Elok's house to find Josh. I know you hate him but I have to.'

Her father remained unmoved in his chair.

'I don't care what you say. This is my life. Are you listening?' She got up from the sofa, marched over to him, seized his arm and shook. It wasn't until later, when she replayed the scene in her head, that she realised she'd never spoken to or touched him like that before. 'Are you listening? I'm going now.'

'Do what you please. It is no longer my concern,' Ahmad said, finding the only words that would have made her stay.

*

They lay in bed, their bodies symmetrically aligned, their visions filled with nothing but the other. The fledging wrinkles in the corners of her eyes creased and her smile moulded into a yawn. Elok crawled closer to him and fell back asleep.

Josh cradled her and listened to her loud, rhythmic breathing. His nose filled with her smell: not the smell of her designer perfume, but the taste of her sweat, of her diet, of her.

He held her and listened to the inner workings of her body and gazed at her bedraggled hair and for the first time didn't see the spoiled brat or the drama queen or the Asian goddess, but a person, a woman, a soul, breathing in perfect time with him.

*

'Why do you stay? I told you. Leave,' her father's voice

croaked through the semi-dark.

Cinta cast her eyes on the door. She couldn't explain it to herself, let alone him, but she couldn't leave it like this. She'd rather have been trapped in there forever more. A tremor emanated deep in her gut and rose. At first the tears came out slowly. Then her eyes filled and she became blinded by her own sadness. She sucked in each breath and sobbed it back out and felt overwhelmed by what was happening to her.

'Please stop,' her father said, his tone lacking the earlier emphasis. He always softened when she cried. Cinta contemplated that that was probably why she did it so much and felt all the worse for it. 'Sorry,' she said, dabbing her eyes.

He rose from his seat and stood before her. He cast uncertain eyes on her before jerkily putting his hand on her shoulder. He kept it there for a second, looked like he didn't know what to do next and removed it. His attempt at affection had only increased her sadness and the tears returned.

She stood there and cried and knew all her earlier certainty was leaving her and that each sob was reducing her resolve. She wiped her palm across her face, took a deep breath and went to the front door. She turned to look at him before she left. His sad and tired eyes peered back. She tried to smile but couldn't. It was too late. No words or action could take them back. She couldn't be herself without upsetting him and she couldn't be what he wanted her to be without upsetting herself. When he feigned not to care she felt a deep sadness; when he showed he did, she was consumed by guilt. The only way they could love each other was away from each other. It was that thought, and that thought alone that gave her the strength to walk out the door and away from her father.

*

Elok stirred, releasing Josh's arm, which had been trapped under her body. Recognising the opportunity, Josh threw the sheet to one side, got to his feet and scoured the room for his clothes. They lay in a bundle in a corner next to a desk. He paced over, picked up his jeans, straightened the coiled material of the legs, and attempted to put them on. The denim blurred. No object would remain static. He dropped them to the floor, rested his hands on the desk surface and lowered his head.

'Are you OK?' Elok said, from somewhere behind.

He swallowed, trying to rid his mouth of that deep acidic tang, and said, 'No.'

'Silly.'

Josh glanced back to see her sitting on the edge of the bed smiling at him.

'What is wrong with you?' she said, getting to her feet and walking to him.

'I've got a hangover.'

'You sad because you have hangover?'

'Elok?'

'Yes?'

'Why are you naked?'

Her hands met her hips squeezing her waist inwards. 'You not like?'

Josh wanted not to look but was unable to prise his gaze away. 'Of course. But...'

'But what?' she said, moving closer still.

Josh dodged her advance, hurried over to the bed and sat down.

She followed him and perched on his knee and repeated her earlier kiss - this time on his lips.

*

Cinta walked the short distance through the *kampung* to main road of Jalan Suprapto and caught an *angkot* minibus heading west across the city to the district of Pondok Indah. Although it was too early for the parades, red and white bunting zig-zagged across the streets. Banners displaying the words *Dirgahayu RI* hung from offices, schools and mosques.

The bus was crowded even by Jakarta standards yet no one appeared discomforted. Instead they crammed together and smiled and chatted merrily about their plans for the day.

Cinta viewed their bright faces and thought that they probably looked at her and, in turn, mistook her fidgeting for the same anticipation they felt. She smiled at their ignorance but envied it and thought of their untroubled lives and what she'd just done and what she was about to do.

After over an hour trapped in the inevitable stutter of the Jakarta traffic, she clambered from her seat, paid the driver and squeezed her way out of the door. In front of her was Pondok Indah mall – a short walk from Elok's house.

*

Elok sat on his knee and didn't fidget or divert her focus. Her expression was soft without a mark of tension. It was like she was being someone else that day – perhaps herself.

'What happened last night?' Josh said.

'We go to Stadium and drink and then come home.'

'I mean, what happened between us?'

'You not remember?' Elok said, the smile of her mouth not replicated by any other part of her face. 'You drink too much.'

'Yeah, I think so.'

She got to her feet from his lap. 'Silly *bule*.'

'I remember going to the club... dancing,' Josh lowered his voice, 'The kiss.'

'The ML?'

ML? Where had he heard that phrase before? His mind focused with all its grim reality. The Orchid House. Bogor. With Cinta. His question, *What does ML mean?* Her answer, *Make love*.

He stared at Elok, imploring a change in her demeanour or an admission that what she'd just uttered was a cruel joke - the flurry of fresh images that engulfed his mind's eye telling him otherwise. 'We can't have done?'

She paced over to her wardrobe and rattled through the selection of clothes, dwelling on each item for a fraction of a second before moving on to the next. She reached the end of the rack and flicked back through the already rejected outfits.

'Elok...'

She stopped her search and her energy seemed to drain and she appeared to become aware of her nakedness for the first time and covered herself with her hands. She snatched a pair of jeans and a loose-fitting red top, wrestled them off their hangers and dressed quickly.

'I didn't mean to upset you.'

'If you not remember last night why you hug Elok this morning?'

'Because I liked being close to you even though I

know it's wrong.'

'*Bule* gives Elok the worst night of life and he say I wrong?' She pounded towards him squeezing her hands together in a throttling motion.

Josh sprung from the bed and retreated backwards. 'Listen, I said what we did was wrong not that you are wrong... whatever you think that means.'

'You use Elok to make angry Cinta. I know, Josh,' she said, tapping her index finger on the centre of her forehead. 'I know.'

'I didn't honestly.'

'You wrong bule. You wrong.' She rained blows upon his torso. With each strike, her hits became soft, almost apologetic. She relented and moved close to Josh and rested her head against his chest.

At first Josh did nothing, fearful that any movement would break the impasse. Then he gradually ran his hands across her back and hugged her. This action brought her out her malaise and re-ignited the Elok of old – the forceful, reckless women with whom he'd spend the last day.

She shoved him away, marched over to the desk and gathered up his jeans, shirt and rucksack.

'What are you doing?'

'*Bule* make me look stupid I make him look also stupid.'

Josh followed her out the room and into a hallway. The coldness of the marble on his feet and the low murmur of a gathering below suddenly made him aware of both himself and his surroundings. He crept forward and peered through the gap in the banister rail. At least thirty people were in the hall below. The noise levels from the living room suggested there were more people out of his sight. Salim's house. Independence Day. Cinta's words in Bogor, 'The party of the year.'

He watched more guests streaming through the front door. Through them and out the house strode Elok, clasping a rucksack and a man's trousers and shirt. The newcomers looked at each other, shrugged, appeared to put the behaviour down as another typical episode in the life of Elok, and continued into the house.

This episode was not, however, typical in the life of Josh. He was naked except for his boxer shorts, in the house of a local millionaire (a man who appeared to have all the requisite connections in the right and wrong places) having just had sex with his daughter and, in the process, having cheated on his niece. That daughter who had now left with all his clothes, money and passport.

He ran up the steps back into Elok's room and shut the door behind him.

*

Leon stirred, opened his eyes and squinted across to the driver's seat. Zak focused on the road, his face illuminated by the brilliance of the early light.

'Where are we?' Leon said.

'Back in Yogyakarta.'

'Already?'

'You have slept since we left the Borobudur temple.'

Leon checked to see if Zak was looking and wiped some drool away from the side of his mouth. 'Well, we did get up before dawn.'

Zak eased the car into the side of the road but didn't kill the engine.

'So what's happening now?' Leon said.

'You go in there,' Zak nodded to a two-storey house. 'Meet Aji and go to the protest.'

Leon studied the house. Red slate tiles dangled over the edge of a detached guttering. Two birds nested in gaps between the bricks. 'I'm not going in there.'

'OK, wait outside.'

'What about you?'

'I will go alone.'

'Why can't we go together?'

'I do not want to see Aji. Pak Bok says that I must avoid all conflict before my speech.'

'Well, if you don't want to see Aji then neither do I.'

'Do you want to come to the protest?'

Leon nodded.

'Then go with Aji. I need to be alone.'

Leon looked at the crumbling building and back to Zak. Even after a night sleeping in the van his skin shone, his batik shirt looked fresh, his hair neatly side-parted. 'Why do *you* hang around places like *this*?'

'Maybe, I will not anymore.'

'Why do you go out with Aji?'

'Maybe I won't anymore.'

'I mean no offence but he's not exactly –'

'OK, Leon that is enough.' Zak reached across Leon, opened the passenger door and pushed it open. 'See you later.'

Leon got out and gently closed the door. He watched the van trundle out of sight. He reluctantly turned to the house. A plywood board rested against the entrance, the smell of moss and mould searing out of a small gap on one side. The board shifted to the right. Out of the opening stamped a Doc Martin boot, laced to the knee. Aji contorted out the gap and straightened. 'Hi, Leon. How long have you been here?'

'Not long.'

'Where's Zak?'

'He's gone. I don't think he's friends with you,' Leon said, trying his hardest not to smile.

Aji's pierced nose curled. 'Never mind, we have never really been friends.'

*

Josh descended the curved staircase and stopped on the final step. All the men (dressed in either modern suits or the more traditional attire of turbans and sarongs) and all the women (wearing beautiful embroidered, silk *kebayas*), and all the children (dressed in smaller versions of the costumes adorned by their parents), gawped at him. Josh couldn't blame them. It probably wasn't often a *bule* wearing skin-tight jeans, flip-flops and a woman's t-shirt attended Salim's Independence Day party.

'Does anyone speak English, please?' Josh said. No-one replied - his voice appeared to be inaudible despite the hush. He cleared his throat. 'Does anyone speak English?' This time, his voice rang out from marble floor to chandeliered ceiling. Still no response.

The crowd began to part. A cream chinos and white shirt fastened with golden cuff links. The precise steps of polished tanned shoes. A familiar face wearing a peculiar expression. 'Good morning Josh,' Salim said, placing his hand on Josh's elbow. 'It pleases me you have decided to come to our party.'

'Yes,' Josh said, realising he was being led by Salim's gentle touch through the crowd to a room to the left of the stairs. Inside they went. A computer. A phone. A fax.

The smell of mahogany and polish. Salim closed the door behind them and looked him up and down. His eyes laughed yet his expression was stern, 'Your clothes are very strange.'

'Yes, a little bit.'

'Elok has clothes like the clothes you wear.'

'Yes, well that's because...' Josh had been cast as the humiliated – it was a role he was going to have to accept. 'Because these are Elok's clothes.'

'Where are your clothes?'

Josh didn't know what to say so told the truth. 'Elok took them.'

'A joke?'

'...yes as a joke.'

Sharp laughter filled the tight room. Josh watched Salim, checking for any duplicity and when he saw none, joined in. He stopped the instant Salim did.

'That is Elok. She is very funny.' Salim's eyes shifted across Josh's face. 'OK, but now the joke is finished.'

'Yes, it has.'

'So please, let me take you to my room. I have many clothes for you to wear. All of the items have a very good brand. Boss, Armani, Diesel... they are not fake.'

'It's a kind offer but –'

'A very English reply. Very polite. But I think it is better to wear my clothes than those of a woman.'

'OK, is it possible for me to call Elok first?'

'Why?'

'To try to get my clothes back.'

'Of course,' he said, in a tone of voice that said anything but of course. He gestured Josh to take a seat in the desk chair. From next to his state of the art computer,

Salim picked up a small red book and gave it to Josh. 'You find Elok's number in section E.'

He walked backwards to the door, his eyes boring through Josh. His hand reached behind him, took the handle and opened the door. A group amassed outside, jumped in surprise, dispersed and either started to talk to each other or to gaze innocently in any other direction.

Salim leant against the frame, affording the hall a view inside. His name was called but he ignored it. 'Josh.'

'Yes.'

'The phone.'

'Of course,' Josh said, leaning over the cool, wooden surface and lifting the receiver.

Salim's name was called again – this time louder. Two quick glances over his shoulder. He turned and the party immersed him.

After what felt like a minute, Josh crept across the room and closed the door. He rushed back to the desk and dialled Elok's number. Ten drilled rings and through to an answer phone. He pressed the receiver to his mouth and spoke in a quiet yet firm tone. 'Elok, listen this has gone too far. I'm stuck in your house at this party with nothing to wear and you have all my money and my passport. Come back and we can talk about this. Even if you hate me and never want to see me again, at least bring back my stuff. Don't be stupid. Bye.'

*

Cinta reached the foot of the drive and hesitated next to the front gate. At the top of the garden, she spotted some people gathered in the porch. The door opened. A swell of excited chatter drifted down the lawn. The party had started. Elok would be there, lapping up the attention.

Would Josh still be with her? Would he witness her telling Elok that bringing Josh to her house and telling her father that she'd lost her job was the most deceitful, treacherous thing that anyone had ever done to her? Would he understand and take her side and see Elok for what she was? With her mind racing as to the possibilities of the next few minutes and their consequences, she began the ascent up the drive to the house.

*

Josh dialled Elok's number again. It went straight to answer phone. Maybe she was out of battery or signal. He stared at Elok's name at the top of the list of numbers written out in the section marked 'E' in the red book. Who was he kidding? The crazy bitch had probably heard his message and turned her phone off.

He got up and paced to the door and stood next to it. Outside, he could hear more voices, more laughter, more people. He looked back to the desk and the red book. The red *address* book. Of course.

He walked back to the desk and picked up the book and flicked through to the section marked 'C.' No entry for Cinta. After what he did with Elok the night before did he even want to risk calling her anyway? What would he say?

He flicked through each page, scouring the names for inspiration, without knowing who or what he wanted to find. Towards the end of the book any hope he did have, began to fade. That was when he read the section marked 'S.' A name stood out from the rest. An English name: Simon. No phone number just an email.

Josh's eyes shot to the computer that sat on the desk in front of him. He glanced at the door before grabbing the mouse and wiggled it. The desktop screen lit. He looked at the wallpaper picture of Elok smiling and thought about Salim outside and the rudeness of using his computer without his permission and quickly selected the Internet Explorer icon. He logged onto his email and waited for the server to upload his inbox.

His head shot back to the door. If he could just send this email to Simon before Salim returned. Simon would understand Josh's position and if he wasn't with Elok, he'd surely know how to find her.

Finally, his inbox booted up. He had one new mail from someone called Ryna Anang. He frowned. The name looked Indonesian but he couldn't remember giving it to anyone. He marked it as junk mail and opened a new message. From the red book he copied Simon's email address.

Hi Simon,

It's Josh here. I'm in Elok's house and looked up your address. I hope you're OK and had a good night. I didn't see you at the end. You must have left before I got a chance to say goodbye. I've had a little bit of an incident with Elok. She has taken my money and passport. She was pretty angry and I don't know what she is going to do next. I really need those things. They are my life. Can you get hold of her and talk some sense into her and get her to bring my stuff back to her house? I'll wait here until you get this and reply.

Thanks so much for your help. Josh

*

Cynthia lay on the sofa watching state television's

coverage of the day. The camera followed a float, sponsored by an oil company, which contained tens of school children dancing. On either side of the road, hundreds of people watched the parade and waved plastic flags.

Upstairs, she heard a slow opening of a door. Footsteps trudged around the upper balcony and down the staircase. Simon came into sight. She took a long drag of her cigarette, crushed the butt in the ashtray and exhaled the smoke with a sigh.

She'd met him two years ago when she moved from Melbourne to work in the same language school. She'd liked him immediately. Although he tried to mask his self-consciousness with an overt confidence, she saw through the act and found him endearing. They soon became friends. So when he told her of a vacancy in his shared house at a good rent and near their workplace she took the room.

The change came about a year ago.

Still affable but not quite as endearing, Simon's doubts and insecurities came to the fore. He started to pity himself for weaknesses that he hadn't previously perceived. He became more acquisitive – over possessions, money, even women. He spent hours on his appearance; bought designer clothes; drank in the most expensive bars. Fewer people saw through the act – in fact, Cynthia struggled to think of anyone who spoke well of Simon anymore.

It was a year since Simon had met Elok.

A whiff of stale alcohol preceded his arrival. He dropped onto the sofa next to her with an exaggerated groan. Cynthia reached for the TV remote and eased up the volume. It failed to drown out the sound of his nasal huffing and puffing.

'What's wrong with you?' she said, without taking her eyes from the TV.

'Leave me alone.'

She hit mute and glared at him. 'Leave you alone? You're the one who came crashing down here and sat next to me.'

'Well, I don't want to talk about it.'

'Look, if you've had another argument with Elok...'

He sat up and shouted. 'How do you know it's Elok?'

She drew her legs up to her chest. 'I don't.'

Simon appeared to become aware of his aggressive posture and shuffled along the couch. 'Of course, it was. It's always Elok.'

Cynthia rolled her eyes. She was so bored with talking to Simon about his feelings for Elok... yet, however hard she tried to ignore him or feign indifference, she'd cave in and listen and cajole and counsel him. She found the experience tedious and repetitive and frustrating, but, in truth, she did it because she was worried about him. The most placid of men, he would, like a second before, become agitated at the mere mention of Elok's name. He wasn't sleeping well. Sometimes, if they'd had an argument, he wouldn't dress or go out. 'OK come on... what's wrong this time?'

'I said that I didn't want to talk about it. Can I use your laptop to check my emails?'

'You mean you want to send an email to Elok?'

'No, of course not.'

Cynthia reluctantly handed him the laptop.

She watched him log into his inbox and click on a new

message. Simon leaned closer and seemed transfixed by the screen. A lopsided grin spread across his face smiled. 'Well what do you know?' he said.

'What?' Cynthia said.

'I have just received a very interesting email from a guy called Josh.'

'Who's that? A friend?'

'No, I wouldn't say that,' Simon said.

The doorbell rang. Cynthia stared at Simon who was now typing furiously.

'Are you going to get that?' she said.

'No, I'm writing a reply.

It rang again. And then once more.

'Fine,' Cynthia said, getting up and going towards the front door.

*

As Leon and Aji hurried under the walkway the clamour intensified into a crescendo. They met a ramp that descended down to a concourse. They both stopped.

Leon first squinted and then opened his eyes very wide. Both actions returned the same information. 'Were you expecting this many?'

'I thought five hundred. There are two thousand. Perhaps more.'

'What are they all wearing?' Leon said, taking in the costumes, banners and characters. In his immediate vision, a Chinese Dragon, manned by six men and held aloft by sticks, swooped and dived. A bonfire of conical hats roared a deep orange. Three people held up a giant cardboard *wayang* figure, each with their own wooden control rod. Its red body danced in front of the black smoke.

'In Yogya it's not possible to protest on Independence Day without big trouble. So Zak makes a plan. The official Independence Day Parade goes down Jalan Malioboro. It is a big parade with many colours and costumes and dancing. Once Zak finishes his speech we will go and... how do you say? We will join the parade but quietly.'

'Infiltrate the parade?'

'Yes, with these costumes maybe we have a camouflage. People see our opinion but they don't realise it.'

'Subliminal messages - I like it!'

They walked across the concourse and rounded a group of people who lay on the floor with their eyes shut and a banner draped over their bodies. They paused to watch a role play that involved protestors dressed as farmers on their knees being shot by other protestors dressed in army combat suits.

'Who are all these people?'

'Farmers, students and activists...'

'Why do they all have those things on their faces?' Leon said, noting the prevalence of bandanas pulled up to their noses.

'Because they remember four years ago. Here at Gadjah Mada University. This is where it all started. The revolution that helps to finished President Suharto.'

'It started here?'

'Here and campuses across the country. On this island, there were protests in Yogya, Surakarta, Malang, Cirebon, Jakarta. But it wasn't just Java. They protested in Irian Jaya, Banda Aceh, Sulawesi, Timor, Kalimantan, everywhere. People say Indonesia isn't a real country – only a group of islands. But man that year we...' he shook his head, seemingly unable to express his pride in words.

'Why did you hate Suharto so much?'

Aji laughed. 'I don't have time to tell you, bro. The man was evil. Pure evil. But his leaving was an accident. A nice accident. We didn't think we could achieve that.'

'When was this?'

'It started in March 1998. I returned from Australia and started this university six months before. I was eighteen years old. When I came back I saw this country with new eyes. I thought I would rather die than live here. You think it is fucked up now, man, you should see it then. I was angry. Angry that we couldn't protest, that the press wasn't free, that twenty years after winning our freedom from the Dutch we gave it back to an Indonesian – someone even worse than them. When I started my course here I joined this group called the KPRP. I don't know how you say it in English – the People's Struggle for Change or something. When we heard about the protests in other campuses in Indonesia we joined. But here was special. It wasn't just people like me,' Aji said, gesturing to his tattoos, baggy shorts and ripped vest. 'It was everyone – normal people, rich people, conservative people. Even the Yogyakarta Muslim Student Group organised protests against Suharto. I gave up my studies for that protest.'

'That was brave.'

'No,' said Aji, flicking his hand in dismissal. 'It wasn't brave of people like me to protest – I had nothing, so what could I lose? But people like the professors of the university who came, they had important jobs, children and families. They gave us the strength. I remember thinking if these guys, international experts, think that we are right, maybe we are. There was this one guy, Dr

Loekman Soetrisno. He was bald and wore glasses. Really official looking. He gave this speech. He told us not to ask for only small things. He said that if Martin Luther King could change America, you can change Indonesia. Before, we didn't think it was that big or the same. But it was. This country is as big as America, you know? After his words we started to believe.'

'And Zak?'

'He was, like me, eighteen. Very young. Very innocent. I brought him to the protests. He always stood at the back and left before the trouble started – because of who he was.'

'What trouble?'

'Every day was the same. We met on campus, did a speech, sang a song, marched to the campus gates and met the riot police. At the start, when we saw their bamboo sticks we were nervous and walked away. But they still beat us. After that we didn't care. If they're going to beat us for nothing why not fight? I saw hundreds of people hurt. They hit my head with a stick; I was kicked and punched. Suharto did everything to stay in the power. Then things started to go out of control. The police killed four students from Trisakti University in Jakarta. In 1974 when the killing started, people stopped the protest. But these killings made people angry. Trisakti is a business university in Jakarta. It makes the next people to work for the big companies. Important people send their children to that school. People started to realise that now Suharto wasn't killing "communists,",' Aji said, miming quotation marks with his fingers. 'He was killing his own. Things exploded. Thousands of people came to our march the day after the Trisakti killings. The police did nothing. There were too many of us. Maybe they agreed. In Jakarta people went crazy. A few days later Suharto left. We won... incredible. When we started to protest we were the children of Suharto. It was all we knew. By the end, we were men.'

'Men of what?'

'Our own men. Whatever we wanted to be,' his speech slowed and reduced to a whisper. 'It doesn't seem that way anymore...'

A roar from the crowd brought him out of his contemplation. In the distance, Zak climbed the stairs of the faculty building. He turned to face the crowd and jerkily lifted his arm to acknowledge their support. The sound dulled.

Aji motioned to Leon. They cut through the crowd until they were close enough to see the expression of helpless fright on Zak's face. He raised the megaphone up to his mouth, held it there for ten silent seconds and lowered it again.

*

Each Independence Day the neighbourhood association organised events in the *kampung*. The day would start with a mass *kerja bakti*, which involved residents clearing drains, picking up litter, repainting walls, and burning debris. Once they'd finished, the area would look transformed. Subsequently, the men would play with the children while the woman returned home to prepare for cooking competitions that included who could make the biggest *krupuk* or the most delicious *nasi tumper*. The real point of the competitions was not victory but for the *kampung* to feast upon the food after it had been judged.

As soon as they rose, Ahmad sent Wening and his daughters out to join the celebrations, under strict instructions, to tell anyone that inquired, that Ahmad and Cinta were visiting a sick relative. Ahmad knew that the men, who sat on the side of the road chewing tobacco, and the woman, who hovered next to the drains ringing their washing, would note his absence and talk and exchange words and looks and draw conclusions - conclusions that for once would not be as bad as the reality.

At first Wening refused to leave. When finally persuaded, scowled at him all the way out of the door. But Ahmad cared not for this slight. Today he needed to be alone.

He waited until they left and bolted the door shut. He ran up the stairs to their bedroom and pulled out his father's cardboard box. He opened the flaps. Dust blew up into his face but he did not blink. He plunged his hand inside and rummaged through the contents.

He removed a flag, a bundle of pamphlets, a bamboo spear, a folder of letters, a picture of his father when he joined the civil service. At the very bottom he found what he was looking for. He lifted it out of the trunk, unravelled the cloth and laid it on the floor. A revolver and a case that contained six bullets. He unfastened the case, blew the dust out of the barrel, opened the chamber, twisted it and inserted a single bullet. He paused and then removed another bullet from the case. He'd forgotten he'd need two.

*

Zak wrestled his way through the crowd. People spoke to him but he didn't hear their wishes of luck or feel the slaps on his back or the shakes of their hands. He saw only the steps, which he now jogged up. He reached his mark and pirouetted and shielded his eyes but there was no sun.

The crowd began at the foot of the steps of the university faculty building and stretched over the concourse back to the outer perimeter wall some fifty metres away. The single drone of the drums and chatter and horns lulled and a great cheer rang out. His arm felt heavy as he lifted it in acknowledgement. The audience swayed. People adjusted their stances and all faced him and lifted their banners in the air. A hush spread until there was near silence.

Zak puffed out his cheeks and exhaled. Tension gripped his face. He could taste bile in his mouth.

Pak Bok had told him this would happen. Control your breath: control your thoughts, he'd counselled. You stand alone in the world. All that exists are your words. Other noises or movements or reactions are external. Your world is all that you can control. Your words will be spoken with tranquillity and precision. They can't be altered by your nerves or by the actions of others.

Feeling the strength of the old man invigorating his soul, Zak lifted the megaphone to his mouth. He lowered it again. He couldn't remember a single word.

The near silence had given way to a buzz of low voices. Sweat lingering on his top lip as he surveyed all the people he was about to disappoint. His eyes settled on Aji and Leon, stationed near the front on his right hand side. He'd seen them moving forward as he prepared to speak.

He watched Leon's head rotating as he took in the scene. The familiar, somewhat idiotic, smile spread across his face and he bounced on the spot. Zak thought about what Leon would do if faced with this situation. Leon thought not of what would come before or after but acted only with what he thought correct at the time. He was fearless and instinctive. He loved any form of attention.

Zak smiled to himself. If Leon was Zak right now: he'd just do it. And with that thought, the first line of the speech blurted from his mouth. He took a short breath and rushed out the second line. Fear vibrated through his words and stung the pit of his chest. But as he spoke the words that he'd rehearsed over many months began to flow. His nerves hadn't settled: his body had adapted. The sickly feeling of despair had become his natural state. His reality heightened and he surveyed the audience and noted each display of distraction - slight head movements, a yawn, someone not listening. And the audience laughed and cheered on cue but somehow it never seemed loud or long enough.

Since the speech had started, Aji had spoken throughout into Leon's ear. Leon, at least, had had the decency to look at the stage even though he didn't understand what was being said. Aji on the other hand... his grip tightened on the megaphone. He felt his voice getting louder and speeding up. He glanced at them again. Still Aji spoke. Zak resisted the urge to shout Aji's name; to make him listen; to draw attention to his ignorance in front of all these people. Why was he doing this? Why was he taunting him?

Zak lowered the megaphone and glared at Aji. The protesters thinking the speech had ended started to chant, 'Reformasi! Reformasi!'

*

Cynthia walked into the hall, flicked on the light and opened the front door. Elok stood in front of her holding a magnum of champagne. She wore no make-up; her eyes were swollen and puffy; her hair unwashed and straggly.

'Simon doesn't want to see you.' Cynthia said,

wondering how even in this bedraggled state Elok's beauty made her feel so inadequate.

'Please,' Elok said, using the word as a dismissal rather than a request.

'I can't let you in. You've upset him again.'

'Well, if you not let me in you upset me,' Elok said, walking through the door.

Cynthia's outstretched arm blocked her.

Elok's eyes narrowed. 'Move, jealous bitch.'

'Jealous? Of who?'

'Me and Simon.'

'Why would I be jealous of you and Simon?'

Elok cast her eyes on Cynthia's feet before working her way up her body. She could feel Elok's mind computing the baggy trousers that she wore to hide what Cynthia considered to be her overly-large waist. Cynthia yanked her t-shirt down. Too late. Elok's eyes had found a new target – her hair. It was cropped in a style which, Cynthia thought, brought out her best feature - her eyes; eyes which Elok met with a sneer. Defeated, she removed her arm from the frame, closed the door and followed Elok into the house.

*

Aji watched Zak and noted his growing confidence. His speech was now slow and measured, like they'd talked about during all those hours of practice. His words grew louder as the end of the sentence drew close; the final word the loudest and accompanied by a fist clenched in the air. Occasionally, he'd pause to allow his words to sink in before powering on.

In these breaks, Aji translated for Leon, paraphrasing in order to keep up, 'He says that many people will know him as a puppet master of the Sultan. But now he has left his job and will dedicate his life to changing this country. He gave his own performance the other night and there were many problems. He left the city and thought that maybe he made the wrong decision. Two days ago he was sat in a field with a good friend.'

'Me,' said Leon, thumping his chest. 'Did he really say, "good friend"?'

'Yes. Zak says that you went to a coffee plantation and saw thirty men leaving. They were dirty and very tired. At that moment, he knew he couldn't stop and that he must fight for the poor and disadvantaged...' Aji trailed off and studied Leon. 'What other places did he take you?'

'We went to his uncle's house. You know the one that's all *feng shui* and has a Dragon Head location? We also went to see a *dukun* called Pak Bok to get spiritual protection and watched the sunrise together in Borobudur.'

Zak hadn't ever taken Aji to Borobudur or to see Pak Bok or his uncle's house. He'd told him those places were personal and not to be shared. Clearly not that personal...

'Do you have a problem with that?' Leon said, who had been studying his face like he was trying to measure the effects of his words.

If there was one thing the Javanese specialised in it was hiding their feelings with a smile. Aji did just that. 'Let's listen to the speech,' Aji said, in his most measured tone. 'Zak is talking about the problems of large plantations like the one you saw together.'

Even saying the word, 'together,' had a strange effect on him. He swallowed and told himself that his jealously was irrational and started to translate again. 'Zak says that

Suharto government sold people's land and forests and parks to big companies. Now a small number of people own most of the land in the country. Since Suharto went the government does nothing to change this and continues to sell land to large companies.

'All these protestors have lost their land?'

'Some have. Others have family in Sumatra, Kalimantan and Papua who have lost their land. But these plantations make many different people angry. For example,' Aji said, on his tiptoes and pointing to a group holding up a banner that said, SPI, 'the Indonesian Farmers Union is here. They are angry because their farms are destroyed. Greenpeace are here too. They are angry because the plantations cut down the rainforest trees and kill orang-utans.'

'So what's the solution?'

'Zak explains now. He asks for three changes. One, that the government sells no more protected forest land. Two, that the government cancels the contracts in the areas where wildlife is affected. Finally, and most important he wants the government to return land to small farmers and the poor. Then small farms, as well as the big companies, can make profit from palm oil, coffee, teak wood.'

Zak lowered his megaphone and stared directly at Aji and Leon. The crowd sensing the end of the speech cheered and began to chanting. Leon joined in, stomping his foot and yelling, '*Reformasi, reformasi...*'

Aji dug his elbow into Leon's ribs. 'He's not finished.'

'Yes, he has.'

'I've heard him practice this speech a hundred times.'

'He must have changed it when we were away

together. Come on, let's go and talk to him.'

'It doesn't appear he wants to talk with me.'

'Don't be daft,' said Leon. Something in his tone or expression made Aji think he was being mischievous but before he could gather his thoughts Leon had grabbed his wrist and was leading him through the crowd to the stairs. Ten people already surrounded Zak but Leon barged to the front. He pulled Zak towards him and smothered him with a hug. Leon drew away and grinned at Zak, 'Great speech.'

'How do you know?'

'Aji translated it.'

'Is that why you were not listening?' Zak said, shooting a glance in Aji's direction.

'How could I translate it and not be listening?' Aji replied in a flash. Their eyes met for a fraction of a second before they both looked away.

'We will talk later,' Zak said. 'Take Leon to the protest and make sure you look after him.'

*

Simon glanced over his shoulder to see Elok striding into the room followed by Cynthia. 'Elok,' Simon said, turning the laptop screen away so she couldn't see its contents. 'What are you doing here?'

'I tried to stop her,' Cynthia said.

'Why?'

'I have no idea why Simon. Here, give me my computer I'm going to my room.'

'Ok, wait one second.' Simon re-read the email that he'd composed.

Hi Josh,

Thanks for your email. Let me see? Shall I help you

get your stuff back? Well, let me tell you what I saw last night and you can guess my answer.

I saw you kissing Elok in the club. You knew fine well that me and Elok were on the verge of something. You'd have to be blind not to see it. You aren't blind but you chose to ignore me and my feelings when you decided to steal my girl. Do you have any idea how long it took me to get to this point with her? To make her trust me? To care for me? To find me attractive? Months. And all of that is ruined by you.

So anyway, do you still need me to answer that or can you work it out yourself?

Simon clicked on send, handed the laptop to Cynthia and faced Elok.

*

Josh stared at the computer monitor. Still no reply from Simon. He pressed F5 on the keyboard and pedalled the desk chair to the door, while he waited for the webpage to refresh. He opened the door ajar and peered into the hall. More guests arrived. His eyes rested on the latest female entrant and moved on but moved back to her. It couldn't be. He squinted through the gap. It was. Salim greeted Cinta with a hug. They released each other and Josh saw Cinta's face. She appeared upset or angry perhaps both. Josh closed the door and pressed the chair against it. His heart drummed against his ribcage. He got up and paced to the window and tried to open it but it was locked. Why was she carrying such a large bag? Why was she looking so agitated? Had Elok told her? Is that why she was there? Was Cinta's father there as well? He rattled the window but it wouldn't budge. Had she just told

Salim? Why was this window locked?

He sunk to his knees beneath the sill and crouched in the nook between the desk and the back wall, and tried to breathe and to control his thoughts. Should he run and forget about his passport and wallet? But what would he do for money? His mother could wire some over but then he'd need to tell her about Leon leaving. She'd tell Leon's mother and all hell would break loose. Alternatively, he could order a new passport and report the travellers' cheques and bank card missing but the replacements could take weeks to arrive and the wait would ruin the rest of his trip.

He rested his elbows on his knees and hid his face in his hands. He couldn't risk it. His only option was to get the hell out of there and forget his things.

The door crashed against the computer chair that blocked it. Another push barged the chair out of the way and the door opened. Josh sprung to his feet, just in time, and pretended to be gazing out the window.

'What are you doing?' Salim said.

Josh turned and pretended to look surprised. 'Just looking at the garden.'

Salim inspected the computer chair that had blocked the door with a frown. 'Did you speak to Elok?'

'No, not yet.'

'Cinta has arrived. She asks for Elok as well.'

Josh felt his stomach muscles tighten. 'Why?'

'I thought you can tell me. She asks for you also. She seems very... upset.'

'Where is she now?'

'I told her to go to the garden with my sister, Misbah.'

'OK, I think I better leave now. I don't want to

outstay my welcome.'

Salim pressed his hands together and frowned at Josh. 'You cannot. Cinta waits in the garden. She has come a long way to see you.'

On the spot, all the argument and counter-arguments left Josh's head and he had a few seconds to reply, whilst relying on that which he trusted the least – his instinct. 'OK, before I do please can I take you up on the offer to borrow some clothes.'

Salim's eyes scanned up and down Josh's body and a smirk formed around his lips. 'I see... now Cinta arrives you want to look very elegant.'

'No, it's just that the joke was between me and Elok and as you say it is strange for me to wear a woman's clothes to a party.'

'I remember... a joke. Yes, a joke.' Salim's eyes wandered in direction of the computer screen. If he noticed Josh had switched it on and logged onto his email he didn't let on. 'Come with me.'

Josh stood up and followed him out of the room, failing to log out of his email or to see Simon's reply.

*

Ahmad stepped outside into the barren white of the mid-morning. He shut the front door and set off down the narrow street. Within twenty metres, he reached a group of people surrounding Ali, the head of the *Rukun Tetangga,* neighbourhood association. Ali's duties included the ceremonial change of date on the independence archway that marked the entrance to the *kampung*. In red paint on one pillar it read *17 Agustus 1945*. On the other, Ali had painted over the date *17 Agustus 2001* and was replacing it with *17 Agustus 2002*. As Ahmad passed, Ali finished the final curve with a flourish. He held the paintbrush aloft and the onlookers cheered. Grateful for the distraction, Ahmad stole past.

He took a right along the thoroughfare of Jalan Sumur Batu. He passed girls wearing multicoloured dresses and carrying matching fans; children with their faces painted red and white; women in veils doing their last minute shopping.

Ahmad allowed two men pushing a cart filled with junk to pass. Foraging through the urban rubble, their hunger both driving their speed and causing their slowness. Ahmad watched them trundle away, deep in admiration of the intelligence and persistence needed to live off what other people, with nothing themselves, thought they didn't need. He lingered and watched them struggle on, as invisible to the world as he was himself.

As he walked down that godforsaken road and passed his father's old shop, the previous night flashed through his mind. Black spots and a haze of memories. Sitting on the sofa. Too hot: too cold. The whine of the mosquitoes. Bursts of sleep broken by sharp pangs of panic. Fits of prayer through clenched teeth. Trying to think of anything but his sister's face when she left; of Cinta; of his wife; of Elok. Thinking only about his sister's face when she left; of Cinta; of his wife; of Elok.

Soothed by the calm of dawn, touched by sleep, until he heard a noise on the stairs. Cinta floating across the room like a ghost. Reaching the door, she turned and stopped. If she had left he'd have thought he was dreaming. But she closed the door and sat down and spoke and that was when he knew it was her and she was leaving. He tried to remain dignified and firm. But her tears broke his resistance and his heart. Then she left. That seemed like a long time ago now. Something that couldn't be rectified. No, not now.

Ahmad reached the end of the street and paced on.

*

They crammed into an alley, three abreast, all facing forward, the sounds of the trumpets and drums and songs of the official parade reverberating through their midst.

In the far, upper, distance, Leon spied a splice of grey light and shuffled forwards a couple of feet towards it. Bodies pressed against his. Odour and breath and elbows and more shuffling.

He yanked his arm free and rapped Aji on the back.

Aji craned his neck, wincing at the unusual angle he'd created, 'What?

'What's going on?'

'Those sounds are the official Independence Day Parade passing. When the final people of the official parade pass we join them and follow them to outside the Governor's Residence. We arrive and the Sultan lifts the Indonesian flag and we hear the national anthem. Zak says we must stop and listen in silence like the rest of the crowd. When it has finished we stay outside the Residence and give out posters and flyers. Then we go back to our home in the Art Campus to celebrate the –'

Before Aji had finished, the protestors surged forward. Leon didn't feel his feet move as he was transported along the alley. After fifteen metres, they burst out of the lane and dispersed. Leon gripped his ribs and looked to the other side of the road where protestors spilled out of an adjacent lane and into the street. The two groups, each made up of about fifty people, merged and joined the slip stream of the final float bobbing along the main procession. As they trooped around the corner, Leon noted the ingenuity of Zak's plan. Each time they passed a side street or alley a further twenty to thirty protestors slipped into parade. Without drawing too much attention, their numbers quickly increased. The Chinese dragons, *wayang kulit* puppets, farmers and social activists dressed as orang-utans, soldiers and grim reapers looked like they were all part of the festivities.

While some of the onlookers were confounded by what seemed to be an unusual end to the official parade, the majority kept on vacantly waving their Indonesian flags and flinging the red and white confetti in their path. Further ahead, a group of youths, who had been studying the banners, decided to hurdle the barriers and join them. The whistles and the drum beats increased with each step.

*

Josh fastened the top button of light blue shirt and checked the silver cufflinks were attached. He adjusted the tanned belt and tugged the cream chinos downwards but still couldn't make them cover his ankles.

'Very elegant,' Salim said, stepping into the room without knocking. He'd taken Josh up to what he called his, 'dressing room,' thrown open the doors of the wardrobes and left telling Josh to take his time. For each second that he was in the dressing room, Josh had felt Salim's impatient presence, lingering outside the partially closed door.

'OK,' Salim said. 'I will make some introductions and then we go to find Cinta in the garden.'

Josh trailed him out of the room, Salim's leather shoes digging into his heels as he squeaked across the marble-floored hallway. He reached the stairs and negotiated them, one at a time. When he reached the bottom hallway, he was met with the interest and friendliness that he'd become accustomed to throughout the country.

The guests' initial bemusement had faded and, now that he was sensibly dressed, the consensus seemed to be that his earlier attire had been some exotic joke or an attempt to join in the fun. On a day where the absurd was welcomed in all forms of celebration, and being the only foreigner in attendance, Josh was now quite a hit. Salim, never more than a couple of feet away, was on hand to introduce and translate for any person who wished to speak to him. Josh shook hands and posed for pictures, lifted up little children and answered questions of varying relevance upon each aspect of his life (Why are you here? Are you a Muslim? Do you have a brother and sister? Are you married?). Excusing himself, he entered the living room and went through the same process and then again in the kitchen. By the time they stepped into the garden, he felt like he'd met, greeted and spoken to all the people in the party. All except one.

The garden was quiet save for four children playing football on a patch of lawn. He followed Salim around the outer perimeter fence into the depths of the grounds and met no one on the way. Rounding the path and returning back on himself in the direction of the house, he saw, through a gap in the foliage, a figure perched on the edge of a wall, the tips of her feet brushing the ground. Through the leaves in the soft light she looked almost ethereal. A semi-transparent blouse, fastened in the centre by a brooch, curved with her breasts. An embroidered gold and copper skirt flowed down to her feet. Eyeliner accentuated her big, brown eyes; red lipstick the fullness of her mouth.

He parted the branches, stepped amongst the sweet-smelling leaves and saw Cinta sitting with her aunt Misbah. The last time he'd seen them both was when Cinta's dad was chasing him from the house. His foot crunched down upon a root.

Cinta lifted her head. Her eyes glazed and she seemed unable to focus. Her aunt rose from the wall, bent forward, cupped Cinta's face and whispered something in her ear. She met Salim's eyes and together they set off along the path towards the house. Her aunt's face was very still as she passed Josh; her expression inscrutable. A sharp pain in Josh's chest dropped to the pit of his stomach. She knows, whispered a cold voice in his head. He took a step closer. Then two more. He felt like he was shivering inside. He sat on the wall next to Cinta.

'You are here,' Cinta said quietly. Her eyes passed across his face and she touched his arm and removed it like she couldn't believe it was him or that he was real.

He forced himself to meet her stare but couldn't hold eye contact and looked away and instead followed the course of a silver-winged butterfly that swooped amongst the adjacent flower beds.

'Why are you dressed like Salim?' she said.

Josh glanced down at his clothes and frowned like it was the first time he'd seen them, 'I bought some smart clothes for the party. These were the only ones I could find in the shop.'

Her hand ran down his arm to his fingers, slipped into his palm and clasped.

Josh looked down at their hands and frowned.

'You do not like?'

'Isn't this a family gathering? In Bogor I couldn't even walk with you,' Josh said, his eyes shooting in the direction of the house.

'Now it does not matter.'

'Why?'

She touched his jaw and directed his face to hers. 'I have something to tell you.'

'My father knows about my job, about you, about everything.'

'What did he say?'

'He is sad.'

Josh studied her face closely, 'Did Salim say anything when you arrived?'

'He is happy to see me.'

'And your aunt?'

'She told me to be calm and to follow this,' she said, pressing her hand against her heart.

He nodded to himself but felt no relief in the knowledge he'd gained. At that moment, all news, good and bad, was indistinguishable and he couldn't piece any of it together and felt sure that at any moment something would happen that would out him and cause his ruin.

'I came here to tell you we can be together,' Cinta said.

The dejection dropped from his stomach to his feet and he felt dizzy and exhilarated like he was stood at the edge of a great height peering over.

Cinta gauged his reaction and her smile flickered and left her face. Her voice lowered, 'I also come here to speak to Elok.'

'Elok?'

'I am very angry with her'

He now felt like he was falling.

*

Elok slammed the magnum of champagne down on the coffee table and looked at Simon expectantly.

'What is that for?' Simon said.

'To celebrate.'

'What's there to celebrate?'

'Independence Day.'

Elok tore the golden foil off the neck of the bottle. She pointed it towards his face, gripped and twisted. With a pop, a rush of air whizzed by his ear. The cork thudded against a wall behind him before dropping to the floor.

'What the hell did you do that for?'

She laughed and ducked her head to meet the foaming bottle with her mouth and sipped the overflowing liquid. 'Simon, get glasses.'

'I don't have any champagne glasses.'

'Why?'

'Because I live in Jakarta? Do they even sell champagne here?'

'Yes, of course.'

'Where did you buy it?'

'Buy it? No, I take from my father. He have many bottles. Come on,' she said, gesturing towards the kitchen with her chin.

*

Josh lifted his face to the sky but no wind touched his brow. He adjusted his shirt and in the most measured tone he could manage said to Cinta, 'Why are you angry with Elok?'

Cinta said that Elok had told her father that she'd lost her job chasing Josh out of the shop. She explained that was the reason why her father had reacted so furiously and chased Josh from the house.

Josh said that Elok had told him that Ahmad had guessed about Josh and Cinta. She'd told him that Cinta didn't want Josh to contact her again and that she already had a boyfriend.

'She is a liar,' Cinta said fiercely. 'I come here to tell this to her face but Misbah tells me she is not here. Where does she go?'

'How should I know?' Josh crossed his arms and lifted to his chest. 'She just left.'

'Typical Elok. It is very rude to leave a guest alone in a party.'

Josh nodded and thought about telling Cinta everything but didn't. He his knew his remorse wasn't induced by the revelation that Elok had manipulated and seduced him but by the realisation that he knew she was lying to him the entire time. His error in sleeping with Elok wasn't an isolated mistake or a catastrophic error of judgement but a weakness that had been squeezed out of him. He'd not questioned Elok's story because he wanted it to be true and for Cinta to be unattainable, so he could satisfy his desire for a woman who, although beautiful, he neither liked nor respected. And all the time, the girl he did like, perhaps more than any other he'd met, who had proved to be a bit more of a challenge, he'd discarded because he lacked the moral courage to ignore the encouraging words of Leon and his own insecurities and desires.

Cinta gripped his hand. 'Do not be sad. She will not hurt us again.'

Josh gave a solitary nod.

'What is wrong?'

'Everything,' Josh said, telling the truth for what felt like the first time that day.

'I understand,' Cinta said, moving closer and gripping his hand tighter.

But she didn't. She didn't understand at all.

*

Ahmad walked through the back streets, avoiding the masses and the police and parades. He gripped the revolver in the pocket of his jacket and the whole time, he talked to Cinta, to his brother, to their father. He explained everything but they didn't reply. He passed abandoned shacks, run-down stores and scaffolding that clung to unfinished buildings. He walked down an alley filled with weeds, broken furniture and chain-linked fences, every fifth step accompanied by the crackle of plastic or the crunch of glass.

He reached a bridge that overlooked the banks of the Ciliwung river and stopped. Below, a man paddling in the vicious brown water, fished out plastic bags and bottles and slopped them onto the deck of his makeshift raft. On the bridge beyond, a parade bobbed past; people dressed in red and white; a brass band celebrating their nation's freedom. He gripped the rails and felt a wave of vertigo and stepped back with a grunt.

The sound of footsteps pattered behind him. A young girl in red dungarees. Ahmad blurted out Cinta's name and couldn't explain why she chose to ignore him or why his own daughter looked so young and confused. A car crossed the bridge and he saw Cinta again in the driver's seat, but much older.

He closed his eyes and saw her face in the dark and

wondered what he'd done to deserve this and thought of all of the sins of his life: when he stole as a child; of the petty gambling in the *kampung*; of the times he'd broken fast. And as he closed his eyes tighter words came to him but he didn't know from where. Perhaps chanted as a child in a mosque or in the dusty classroom in the local school. Words from the Holy Koran,

"*Do not destroy yourselves Surely Allah is Most Merciful to you*,";

"*Do not throw yourselves with your own hands into destruction*";

"*Anyone who commits these transgressions, maliciously and deliberately, we will condemn him to Hell.*"

The final word rang through his head over and over. He shouted out the words, '*Do not take life, which Allah made sacred, other than in the course of justice,*' and laughed. Was this not justice? Was this not right? If He was the most merciful, the most perfect, the ever forgiving, the loving, the truth, would He not understand what Ahmad needed to do? Ahmad began to pray, asking for His mercy and begging for His eternal forgiveness and protection, but as he spoke he'd never felt so far away from Him.

Ahmad opened his eyes and a wild, ironic smile spread across his lips. The Allah he believed in, who his father had taught him so much about wouldn't forgive him for what he was about the do. The words were clear. One should never take their life or that of another. And what did it matter - living in sin or dying by the same token. Even in contemplating what He so clearly forbade, Ahmad knew that the eternal judgement was already made.

He glanced down at his watch and saw twelve minutes had passed since he'd stopped. Or was it an hour and twelve minutes? He inspected his watch. Had it been tricking him like the rest of them? He ripped it from his wrist, breaking the strap, and flung it into the water below. He was late already. He started to run but was out of breath within one hundred metres. He placed his hand on his heart and wheezed but hobbled on through the considerable pain.

*

As Josh and Cinta sat next to each other on the wall in Salim's garden the scent of food that drifted from the open kitchen door became stronger.

'Do you know what the smell is?' Cinta said.

'No.'

'Come with me. I show you.'

As they walked up the garden the meringue of flavours separated into different odours. Cooked meats, fried rice, vegetables and sweet tea. His mouth watered but tasted bilious and he swallowed the metallic saliva and trudged on until they reached the kitchen door. Before Cinta could go inside Josh caught her wrist and pulling her back towards him. 'Cinta, I really should go home now. It's very rude of me to come to the party like this.'

'You not need to worry any more. OK?'

'I know but I really have to go.'

'Josh,' Cinta said, fixing him with a look of such intensity that he needed to look away. 'I leave my family for you. I come across the city for two hours and you want to leave?'

Josh forced himself to meet her eyes, 'No, of course not.'

Inside, the buzz of people remained but they hummed a different tune – expectation had replaced polite merriment. He followed Cinta through the kitchen into the living room. Platters of food on tables framed the guests who shuffled around the edges, stopping occasionally to scoop food onto their plates. Those who had already served themselves sat wherever there was space: on the sofa, window ledges, floor. Josh and Cinta joined the queue.

'Are you hungry?'

'Not really...'

'It is not like the food in my house,' Cinta said, tilting her head and giving him a knowing smile. 'There is more than one choice.'

He smiled back – well, as much as the rigidity that clamped his face would allow. How did she know he'd hated the food at her house? Hadn't he hidden it? What else had she guessed from his behaviour that day?

'You do not like Indonesian food?'

'Not really, no.'

'OK, now is the time to change. Trust me. There is something you like.' The queue moved and they reached the first table. 'This is a *selamatan* feast. We have it in Java in special times. Jakarta is a big city but many people who live here are from another part of Java or another island. This feast celebrates the food from each region.' She flattened her blouse with her palm and looked at him, 'I spend a lot of time learning to translate food at school.'

'Well now is your chance.'

She cleared her throat and offering him a quick, furtive smile. 'OK, uncle Salim is very careful in his arrangement. This table has dishes that are very traditional and popular. That is why there is a small Indonesian flag on the table. This is *gado-gado*, steamed vegetables in peanut sauce. This is *sate*, meat kebap. That is *sambal goreng hati*, spicy chicken and potato. For dessert, there is *lontong sayur*, rice cake in coconut milk soup and *pisang goreng*, fried banana cake. If you are thirsty there is a bowl of *halia*, hot ginger tea...'

Cinta took him around the tables and described dishes that included watercress soup from Lombok; *bawang goreng*, fried shallots from Padang, West Sumatra; *rendang* beef from Flores; and *cakalang suwir*, spicy tuna from the Moluccas. As she ran through the descriptions, she looked up to see if he understood and smiled each time her eyes met his. When she looked away Josh didn't look at the food but analysed the certainty of her movements, her full sonorous voice and the radiance of her smile and found her behaviour strange but enchanting.

*

The protestors marched down Jalan Malioboro towards the Governor's Residence. The alternative protest now appeared entirely absorbed into the official parade. Initially quiet and subdued the protestors' confidence grew. At the front, someone with a megaphone had started chanting. Hundreds of people echoed his words.

'Whose voice is that?' Leon said to Aji.

'Zak's.'

Leon got to his tip-toes and searched ahead. 'Cool, let's go and find him.'

'It is safer here,' Aji said, gesturing to the cover provided by all the surrounding bodies.

'I don't want to be safe. I want to get involved.'

'Zak told me to look after you. Remember you are very easy for the authorities to see.'

'I see what this is about... just because you don't

support Zak doesn't mean I don't.'

'I do support Zak but –'

'You've been against this from the start. No wonder he doesn't want to go out with you anymore.'

Aji opened his mouth to reply but before he could Leon walked across the flow of people to the side of the road. He jogged for three or four hundred metres until he felt sure he was beyond all of the protestors.

He waited as the band marched past. Crashing symbols, stomping feet, thumping drums accompanied trombones and trumpets. Behind the band, a jeep towed a gigantic, golden-coloured float. On its stage, school children danced to the music emitted from the speakers on top of the jeep. Every thirty seconds, golden and silver confetti blasted out of a pipe attached to the float, showering the crowd and causing great cheer. Leon peered through the sparkling visage and saw the unofficial parade following – their vibrancy and colour matching that which went before.

Zak powered ahead of the protestors, ten paces to the fore, a megaphone to his mouth, his followers echoing his chants. Leon waited until Zak drew level with him, bounded over and slapped him on the back. Zak lurched forward, his muffled cry of shock reverberating through the megaphone. The chanting he led ceased.

Leon draped his arm around him and sauntered on. 'How's it going?'

'Fine.' Zak motioned to his megaphone. 'Listen, I need to –'

'Amazing protest, man.'

'Thank you,' Zak said, slipping under Leon's arm and freeing himself. He lifted the megaphone to his lips and started to chant again. He strode on, moving so rapidly that Leon had to break into a jog to catch up. When he did, Zak slowed to a near standstill. Leon did likewise.

Zak lowered the megaphone and glowered at him, 'Leon, please. I need to concentrate.'

'Ok, what do you want me to do?'

'Be calm and enjoy.'

'Nothing else?'

'No.'

'So that's it?' Leon said with a frown.

'Yes.' Zak marched ahead with the megaphone back to his mouth.

Leon stood motionless, the crowd buffeting and winding around him.

*

Ahmad pushed through the dense crowds onto Jalan Medan Meredeka Utara. To his left, the single pillar of the Monas monument cast a long slanted shadow across Merdeka Square. In front of the square a line of barriers penned in a crowd who waited from the arrival of the President's car.

Ahmad crossed the street, vacant save for security personnel, and stalked towards a building that looked like a grey stack of concrete blocks. He eyed the top floor. That is where they would be. The army. The murderous scum who taken his father away. His pace quickened. A hand on his chest deflected him backwards. He met the eyes of a young man wearing a beret.

'Back,' the man said. Two more men, both wearing the same berets, flanked the young soldier.

Ahmad studied the men, with their stern-faces and khaki uniforms and rifles slung over their shoulders, and laughed. He side-stepped them and sidled up to the black wall that read, *Tentara Nasional Indonesia Markas Besar Angkatan Darat*, Indonesian National Army Headquarters. He spat on the silver writing, wiped his mouth, turned to the soldiers, laughed again and went on to the building next door. He reached the pronged railings and peered through them at the home of Indonesian justice, the *Mahkamah Agung*, Supreme Court, with its white facade and black windows. He laughed again but this time louder. Justice? What did they know of justice?

Another soldier approached and ushered him back across the road. His hand gripped Ahmad's bicep, his elbow pressing against the object in Ahmad's jacket pocket. He led him to the queue that had formed to enter the viewing area behind the barriers. Ahmad met his eyes. Not a flinch of feeling touched his young face. Silence denoted strength in the Indonesian military. Failing to spot a revolver in your subject's pocket did not.

Ahmad grinned at the young incompetent, turned and walked directly to the front of the queue. As he pushed his way inside the people at the front of the queue exchanged strange looks but didn't say anything. They hurried away from him the moment they entered. He followed them to corner of the street, where he wrestled his way to the front of the barrier. Across the road, stood *Istana Merdeka*, Freedom Palace, the residence of the President of the Republic of Indonesia.

*

Josh and Cinta took their plates to the corner of Salim's living room and sat side by side and ate together for the first time. Cinta had chosen him the beef soup and fried rice and fish. The steam waved from Josh's plate into his face and filled his nose and drenched his mouth with anticipation. He studied the plate and forgot his plight and his sensitive palate and instead felt a twinge of anticipation; that feeling of excitement of the unknown that had made this past few months so special.

First he sipped his soup before sampling the fish. 'Really, really good,' he said, whilst still chewing.

'No, you say to be polite.'

'Why would I? You didn't cook it.'

Cinta laughed, 'Yes, it is true.'

'How do you say thank you in Indonesian?'

'Terima kasih... you do not even know this?'

'No.'

'You should learn some Indonesian if we are going to be toge...' she looked down at her plate. 'Well, *Bahasa* is easy. There are no tenses like in English.'

'Is that why you always speak in the present tense in English?'

'I do?' Her brow furrowed creating a single crease on her forehead, 'Sorry, when I write I am OK but when I speak I forget.'

Josh studied her soft, flushed face and felt something re-awaken within him. He thought of their brief kiss in Elok's car and felt the sudden urge to lean in and kiss her again. 'Cinta, I can't speak another language. Your English is brilliant. I love it.'

'It is true?'

'Yes, really. You are right I need to learn Indonesian.'

'It makes you feel bad not to know anything?'

'Yes.'

'*Kasien de loh*,' she said. 'It means you are so poor.'

'Like, "Aw, poor you"?'

'Yes,' she said. He watched her sit upright, her blouse riding up to reveal her slender waist. 'Josh, if I teach you, you need to look at me... here,' she said, tapping her finger beneath her eye.

'Sorry,' he said, returning her smile.

A blast of music startled them out of their world. Unnoticed by the couple, people had finished their meals, left their dirty plates on a designated side-table and gathered at the front of the room. Cinta got to her feet and tugged at Josh's arm. 'It is time for the flag-raising ceremony at *Istana Merdeka*, the Presidential Palace.'

Josh followed her through the guests until they could see Salim's 40-inch plasma television screen. Cinta leaned back against him. He pressed forward and luxuriated in their unseen contact.

*

Leon trudged along at the rear of the parade, hoping that no one would talk to him. He couldn't believe the way Zak had dismissed him- like he was any old protestor, trooping along and parroting his chants. He needed to show Zak that he wasn't just someone else. That he cared about this protest. That he cared more than Aji.

Leon pushed through the crowd trying to get back into the hub of the action. As he did he stumbled and collided with someone. The man ignored Leon's apology and strode on. Twenty metres down the road, he removed a knife from his belt. With a quick slashing motion, he cut a rope that held together two metal barriers. From the pavement, a group of men hurried through the gap and joined the parade. The newcomers weren't wearing costumes, didn't greet other people, or make eye contact or chant or dance or protest. They merely walked forwards

- trying so hard to fit in that they stood out. Leon drew level and walked next to one of the men. His square jaw. His shaved head. Sunglasses covering his eyes. Recognition? But from where?

Leon trailed him along the street. *The taxi driver when he first arrived...* Twice he looked back. Twice Leon avoided his sight. *The guy who ripped him off for the room...*The man repetitively tapped his ear, his touch lingering for a number of seconds as the crowd noise grew louder. *The guy being hypnotised by Pak Bok...*

The music dulled and then died. Leon stretched to his tiptoes and saw the final float from the main parade bobbing to the right and disappearing around the corner.

With the main parade gone, the protestors funnelled through the narrowing street towards the junction. Leon was pressed against the man. A crackly static noise like the sound of an un-tuned radio. The man plunged his hand into the inner pocket of his padded jacket and half-removed a walkie-talkie. He flicked a switch and the sound ceased. His head flitted from side to side – a movement that allowed Leon a full view of his profile. He lifted his sunglasses. One of his eyes was glazed and still. Leon's heart surged. *Eye Patch* - the nutcase from the squat who had threatened Aji about this very protest.

Leon's eyes darted in each direction searching for Zak. He attempted to fall back but was no longer in control of his movements. As the parade met the right turn, more people piled in from the side. He gripped those in front, trying to control his forward momentum. The man in front half-supported him and the man in front of him did the same. A surge of panic. If he fell, a hundred feet would trample him into the floor.

'*Maju, maju*,' came the cry from a megaphone. A deep voice. Demanding not encouraging. Not Zak. With each command their momentum gathered. They trampled over the security barriers and spilled into a square. Seventy five metres ahead, stood a row of armed soldiers. With nowhere to go the protestors dispersed and waited in the square.

Leon massaged his shoulder and took in his surroundings. Directly in front, he caught glimpses of the green lawn of the Governor's Residence. More armed personnel, two men deep, guarded the black iron gates. A solemn tune filled the air. A red and white flag inched its way up a pole.

He looked back around the square but saw no one he knew. From the direction they'd come lumbered a pack of black wraiths bearing shields with the word 'Polisi' emblazoned in yellow writing. They separated, creating a further ring around the protestors.

The flag rose slowly to the top of the pole.

*

Ahmad leaned against the barrier and watched lines of men with rifles holstered over their shoulders marching in rhythmic unison through the gates of the President's Palace in Jakarta. To the right, a television gantry towered above, the cameras trained upon the inner lawn. In the background, out of sight of the cameras but not the crowd, the riot police gathered behind armoured cars and water cannons. A brass-band trooped past in pristine blue uniforms and white hats. The onlookers responded with a cheer and a round of applause.

Ahmad swivelled and eyeballed those behind him. He saw people taking pictures wanting to be seen in the moment more than wanting to be in the moment; couples forced together who couldn't divorce; innocent faces of young children who lied to their parents every day. He saw imbeciles and traitors and turned back around in disgust and waited for President Megawati: the most imbecilic and treacherous of them all.

The final marchers entered the gates of the palace. The audience settled and waited. Silence descended. Two tanks rolled up the street and stopped in front of the palace. A black limousine glinted in the distance.

Directly in front, two feet away, stood a member of the military police, his face taut and impatient. Someone whispered something to Ahmad's right. It was about him of course and what he had in his pocket and what he was going to do and that he was a communist like his father. The military policeman tapped his shoulder twice. A signal? Perhaps to a sniper across the road. Ahmad stole a glance at the policeman's face and saw no mercy and shuddered and turned to escape but couldn't penetrate the crowd, who were moving in trying to catch a glimpse of the President's limousine. The stench of other peoples' bodies. The repulsion of their discarded breath. Ahmad barged and fought for space. One young man started to protest at Ahmad's physicality but met his eye and stopped abruptly.

Ahmad dug his hand into his pocket and met a cold metal handle. Remain calm and take your opportunity, he told himself as he refocused on the limousine.

*

The room was quiet save for people hushing other people. On the screen, the camera focused upon the lawn of the Presidential Palace. In the centre of the screen, groups of people dressed in full-military regalia performed a series of well-rehearsed marches around a flagpole.

Josh took advantage of his first moment of quiet since Cinta had arrived. Before he assessed his options he needed to check if Simon had replied to his email. With practically the whole party watching the television and Salim nowhere to be seen, he had the ideal opportunity. He said to Cinta, 'I'm expecting an email so I'm just going to check it while you all watch this.'

She frowned at him. 'The flag-raising ceremony is the most important part of the day.'

Josh breathed heavily out his nose, 'Sorry, I didn't realise.'

'Why you look so sad? You can look at your email after.'

Josh focused back on the television and tried not to show his disappointment. The camera cut to a veranda filled with people sitting in rows of chairs watching over the lawn. 'Who are they?'

'Important people. The Vice President, government officials, army generals and old Presidents. Now they wait for the President. She does the ceremony –'

A boom from the TV made Cinta jump. A series of small explosions cackled in the distance. It sounded like gunfire. The camera cut to Merdeka Square outside the President's Palace. Men in khaki uniforms stood to attention behind four cannons, which fired another round of blanks. The action cut back to the veranda in the grounds of the palace. A woman with short, curly hair and glasses stepped ponderously down the red-carpeted stairs and eased herself onto a golden throne.

'Megawati Soekarnoputri,' Cinta said. 'Our president.'

Megawati surveyed her realm, her eyes narrowing and following some movement in the distance. She rose abruptly. A woman dressed in a pristine, white uniform came into shot. She held out a tray covered with a yellow cloth with golden tassels. Megawati placed a red cloth on top.

'*Sang Saka Merah-Putih*,' Cinta said. 'The Indonesian flag.'

The scene cut from Jakarta to another veranda, the caption at the bottom of the screen displaying 'Yogyakarta.' The camera focused on a man rising from his seat. He wore a rimless hat, glasses and a trim black suit.

'The Sultan of Yogyakarta,' Cinta said.

The Sultan, repeating the actions of the President, placed a flag on top of a tray borne by a white uniformed woman.

The programme cut back to the ceremony in Jakarta. The woman bore the flag to two men wearing red jackets. One man attached the flag to a mast; the other noosed the rope. The waiting battalions raised their weapons. A conductor rousted the orchestra of trumpets, trombones and base drums.

'The national anthem,' Cinta said. 'It is called Indonesia Raya. It means great Indonesia. Listen, you can hear the words "*Indonesia kebangsaanku, bangsa dan tanah airku.*" Indonesian my nationality, my nation and my native land. '

The camera followed the red and white flag, hoisted in rhythm to the slow, solemn tune, cutting between the scenes in Jakarta and Yogyakarta. Despite the 270 mile distance, the flags were raised in perfect sync. Josh's skin prickled as he looked around at the proud faces in the room watching the screen. The camera focused on Megawati saluting from her golden throne in Jakarta and then the Sultan doing the same in Yogyakarta. The picture faded back to the flag, now at the top of its mast, flapping indolently in the gentle breeze.

*

Leon lingered with his fellow protestors and waited for something to happen. Those with authority eyed those without. The wind picked up. The Indonesian flag billowed at the top of the mast. The music had long ceased. The cameras of television gantry, erected in the grounds of the Governor's Residence, faced the unrest outside not the ceremony within.

The impasse allowed the authorities to re-group. In front of the Governor's Residence, two officers unravelled a meshing of barbed wire. Behind it the soldiers bristled, their rifles no longer resting on their shoulders.

In front of the wire barricade a wall of iron shields advanced towards the protestors. After ten metres, they stopped and held position.

In the end all it took was one stone: originating from somewhere at the back of crowd and dropping at the feet of the police. The wall of shields responded by clomping forward again; this time into the territory of the protest. Prang, prang, prang: a fusillade of missiles rained down upon their shields in response.

Leon stepped backwards and almost trod on the feet of Eye Patch. He removed what looked like a starter pistol from his waistband and lifted it above his head. A shot cracked into the air. From behind, and apparently on cue, flares and rockets swooshed overhead, landing within the police line. A further shot rang out this time from the police side. Chaos ensued as the crowd collided into one another: people either charging forwards to attack the police or backwards, trying to get out of their range.

From the police line, a grey truck with grilled windows and lowered suspension hulked forth. Riot police grouped around the assurance of its presence. Above its meshed bulldozer blades read the words, 'Pasukan Anti Huru-Hara.' A metallic nozzle on the roof of the vehicle extended and targeted the crowd. A short pulse of water fired. Tens of stones clanged off the vehicle. In response it fired again, a longer pulse with a 45 degree arc, knocking some protestors off their feet. The water slammed into Leon's stomach. He doubled forward, the feeling akin to a well-placed uppercut thudding into the cavity below his ribcage. He groggily moved his head to either side and saw he was adrift from his back-tracking companions. The ground reverberated as the vehicle and the iron wall of officers advanced. As the police neared, two retreating protesters grabbed his arms and dragged him back towards the group.

On the way, they passed one man who remained in the gap between the two sides. Already isolated by more than twenty metres, he strode on through the foaming water, rocks and fizzled out flares and stopped ten metres from the water cannon. He lifted his hands up and blocked its path. It creaked to a halt a couple of feet in front of him. The clump of leather boots receded. The advancing officers stopped.

Zak faced them and raised and lowered his arms - his tranquil movements reminiscent of those of a soaring eagle. He turned from his becalmed foes and paced towards his peers, his hands now spread to their full span.

Without a word, he transposed his feelings to his fellow protestors: *Go home. It's over.* With a resigned yet resentful mumbling, those who remained began to follow the protestors who had already left the battlefield.

As the retreat turned into a rout, with a deathly hiss the water cannon fired a valedictory pulse hitting Zak in the centre of his back. The power of the torrent lifted him off his feet and skittled him twenty feet across the square. He sprawled across the ground and didn't move.

With a roar, Leon broke from the crowd and sprinted forward. He scooped up a boulder and flung it at the water cannon. His one-man assault, created a swell of defiance. Dozens joined him, charging without fear or plan towards the police line. Wooden placard against baton; rock against plastic bullet; bone against Kevlar armour. Yet, for a brief moment the rioters gained the upper hand, their passionate anger making up for their lack of ammunition or numbers.

A whistling above and a clatter of metal on tarmac broke their resistance.

Leon was kicking a Perspex shield. He lifted his foot again when the hissing smoke hit him. Staggering back, he gripped his throat and hyperventilated.

A further rattle. Another canister landed near him. The density of the smoke intensified as did the symptoms. He put his hands over his face and fled.

*

With the national anthem completed and the flag hoisted to the top of its mast, the spectators drifted away from the television. Josh and Cinta remained in the same position, watching the set, their bodies faintly touching. The camera cut back to Yogyakarta, where outside the Governor's Residence, there was a standoff between the police and what looked like a group of protestors. The scene soon developed into a full-scale battle.

Josh brushed his lips against the tip of Cinta's ear and whispered. 'What's happening?'

She shuddered and giggled. 'Sshhh. I try to listen. They say people riot outside the Governor's Residence in Yogyakarta.'

'Is that normal?'

'Riots yes. But today no. Not near the flag-raising ceremony and for the eyes of the Sultan.'

The rioters fell back and the violence seemed to lull. The camera zoomed in on a solitary man who broke from the group and attacked the police line. A camera on the ground provided a close up of the man's face. A white man's face.

Josh's eyes widened, 'It can't be.'

*

On Independence Day in 1949, Ahmad's father had stood on the inner lawn and watched the new national flag being hoisted onto the roof of the Presidential Palace. Later, he spoke of the great roar as the flag was unfurled; of the spirit of the people; of the sense of belonging; of the naivety of the dark days that would follow.

Fifty-three years later, Ahmad gazed up, beyond the army and water cannons and tanks and fences and barbed wire and glimpsed the same flag reaching the top of the mast. He thought of Megawati, invisible from his vantage point, and wondered what she thought of as she sat there on her golden throne. Did she listen to the words of the Indonesian Raya and feel their pain? Did she think of the War of Independence? Of 1967 and what they did to her father and his? When she'd swept into the palace in her limousine, with blacked-out windows, did she see those outside? Did she comprehend the irony of the layers of defence that segregated her from those her father had liberated? Those same people she now claimed to represent?

Or did she see only the cameras? Want only the attention and the power? Feel only pride and achievement in her position?

Or in this vacuous age did she think of nothing at all?

Ahmad looked west, towards the minaret of the great mosque and back to the palace. He thought about his father's black and white picture with President Soekarno in the brown box under his bed. A generation later and he stood tens of barriers and hundreds of armed personnel away from Soekarno's daughter. With a slow, defeated shake of his head, he pushed his way clear of the spectators.

He left without the answers he sought, to do something that he knew, later, he'd need to provide answers for himself.

*

Josh left the living room through the patio doors and walked into the garden in a daze. He sat on the bench and leaned forward and ruffled his hair with his hand and tried to take in what he'd just seen.

Cinta came and sat next to him and placed her hand on his back, 'Why does your friend attack the police?'

'Because he's Leon that's why.'

'It is normal for him?'

'No, he's just an idiot. He was probably showing off or someone had offended one of his principles. Probably both. That's when he really loses it.'

'I don't understand.'

'Neither do I, Cinta. Neither do I...'

She took his hand. 'It is OK. We do not need to talk of him, if you do not want.'

Josh squeezed her hand, 'Thanks.'

They sat in silence watching games unfold in the late afternoon sun. On the lawn, a group of children with spoons in their mouths bearing marbles raced past some men playing football in sarongs. Victory went to a small girl with a gummy grin and heart-shaped face, who beat a tall skinny girl with darker skin and a broader smile still.

'Who are they?'

'My cousins,' Cinta said. 'Not my *real* cousin like Elok but I am related to her... how you say?'

'Distantly?'

'Yes. We should play. It make you forget about your friend.'

'I'm not sure...'

'Yes! Come it is fun. Let's play that.' She gestured to another game that involved items of fruit strung along a rope. 'You have to collect coins with your teeth from inside the fruit. You cannot use your hands.'

Josh watched the two doll-like girls wearing matching pink tops and embroidered sarongs trying to master the swinging melons, their faces covered in pulp and pith.

'They are my *real* cousins,' Cinta said. 'Intan and Kasih. You see my aunt Misbah is very serious about what she and her children wear. At my father's birthday you remember what Misbah wears?'

'I've been trying not to remember too much about your father's birthday.'

'Thanks,' Cinta said, her smile straining.

'No, I didn't mean it like that.'

'How do you mean it?'

'I shouldn't have said anything.' Josh shuffled in his seat. 'Listen, remember I said before I needed to check my email?'

Cinta cleared her throat and mumbled something to herself in Indonesian.

'What was that?'

'Nothing,' she said, in a low-husky tone.

'What?'

'You want to leave before the feast. You not interesting in the flag-raising or the games. You not want to talk about your friend making problems in Yogya. You not interesting in nothing in this party. You only want to look at your email.' She got to her feet and walked towards the house. 'Come. We go together if it so important.'

*

Simon set the water and aspirin pack on the coffee table and glared down at Elok lolloping on the sofa. She'd located his black hooded top and put it on. The black hood expanded and detracted with the rhythm of her sleep. Simon sat next to her and prodded her arm with his index finger. 'Wake up.'

The television blared out the national anthem. Cannon shots boomed. People cheered. Simon leant in, 'Are you listening?'

The whites of two eyes appeared under the shroud of the hood. 'Give me asprin,' she said, gesturing to the blister pack on the table.

'I want to talk to you first.'

'Well, I not want to –'

Simon yanked down the hood. 'What happened last

night?'

'We go to Stadium... why you wake me to ask stupid questions?'

'I saw you and Josh kissing in the club.'

She leant towards the coffee table, picked up the pack, removed a white pill, put it in her mouth, lifted the cup and took a long drink. She replaced the cup on the table with slow deliberation.

'I said, "I saw you",' Simon said.

Her facial expression had returned to the impassive; the tendons of her neck still strained. She nodded to herself and it appeared even she realised that even she wasn't going to get out of this one. Cornered, she responded in the only way she knew how. 'Fuck you, Simon. So what if you saw me? What you my father?'

'It's rude when there's only three people and two of the people kiss.'

'It simple,' Elok said, taking out a cigarette out of the packet that rested on the armrest. She lit it, took a long draw and blew the smoke out the corner of her mouth. 'You jealous.'

'Well, what if I am, Elok?' Simon said, wafting the smoke away from his face. 'WHAT IF I AM?'

A door opening. Footsteps on the upper balcony. Cythnia's face appeared over the banister, her brow knitted in concern. 'Simon, are you OK?'

Simon glanced up at Cynthia and back to Elok but it was too late then to gauge Elok's reaction to his admission of jealousy. Why did Cynthia need to interrupt the moment he'd finally revealed his feelings?

'Cynthia,' he said, spreading his arms in a pleading motion. 'I'm fine. Please leave us.'

'Well, you don't look fine. Why are you shouting? Wait a minute,' Cynthia leant over the banister and studied Elok. 'Is she smoking my cigarettes?'

Elok held the cigarette loosely, took a slow draw, cocked her jaw and puffed rings of smoke in Cynthia's direction.

'Look,' Cynthia said. 'This is my house and if she's going to upset you and steal my things I want her to leave.'

'Cynthia, the only person upsetting me now is you. Please go away and mind your own business.'

'You hear him. Fuck off,' Elok said.

Cythnia's face burned red and she gripped the balcony and appeared on the brink of combustion. She turned and stomped back to her room. The slam of the door rattled around the walls of the house.

'What a baby,' Elok said.

'Well?' Simon said.

'Well, what?'

'About what I just said?'

Elok crushed her cigarette inside her cup and gave Simon a long, sideways glance. 'What was that?'

'You know! The kiss.'

'Pleeeaasse. One small kiss and you angry for nothing.'

'One small kiss?'

'Why you see anything more?'

'No, I left after I saw you together.'

'Exactly... if you stay you see me stop and say it a mistake.'

'Why did Josh send me an email saying you'd taken his his passport and wallet?'

'Because Josh sleep on sofa at my house and I leave

quick to come here to see you and I forget to give Josh things back from the car. It a mistake.'

'Do you think I was born yesterday?' Simon stood up. 'Come on get up. We're going to your house to give him his stuff back.'

Elok dug her hands back into the pockets. 'I do not want to go.'

'The sooner he gets them the sooner he leaves. Then we... I mean, things can go back to the way they were.'

'Fine,' said Elok, getting to her feet, over-balancing and falling back onto the couch. She giggled, clambered to her feet again, lifted the champagne bottle, took an elongated swig and swayed towards the door.

*

Leon hared down the *gangs*, dodging left and right, avoiding people and objects, seeking no destination other than distance from anyone who was pursuing him. After the tear gas, the protestors had dispersed. He'd dodged through the crowds and somehow managed to escape the square.

He ran away from the old city heading east towards the *Taring Padi* compound. After sprinting for three or four minutes, he began to tire. He glanced back. No one followed. He ran a further fifty metres and checked again.

He'd lost them: he was lost.

He slowed to a jog and then a trot before coming to a standstill. His nose ran, his face stung, fluid streamed from his eyes. He shut one eye and tried to take in his surroundings. An alley. Houses on either side. A collapsed wall. A concrete garden. Wild purple flowers sprouting from the crevices in the cement floor.

He looked in the other direction. Heat distortion

blurred the horizon. A dog sniffed a drain. Fireworks, car horns, cheers. A plastic bag flapped towards him.

Suddenly, three policemen appeared at the junction. Before they'd turned their heads, Leon was over the wall and into the garden. He darted to the left and pushed open a splintered door of what looked like an outhouse or shed. He ducked inside, slipped, fell forward into the outer wall and dislodged a brick with his outstretched hand. He drew his shoulders up in anticipation but the structure held firm. He glared down at the greasy, algae-covered floor and the line of grime that marked where his foot had slipped. Next to it, a blocked hole, which some years before had clearly been a toilet, accounted for the stench.

Through the gap provided by the dislodged brick, he spied the arrival of the policemen. They stopped and scoured the area. They were clearly looking for protestors. After a prolonged discussion they trooped on down the lane.

Leon waited as long as he could but overcome by the noxious fumes and dashed out of the open door into the garden. He rested his arm against the wall and threw up. His stomach knotted and he threw up again. He wiped his mouth, staggered to the edge of the garden and scanned the street. People passed further down the road but he saw no police. Well, none in uniforms.

He looked down at his ripped t-shirt covered in the red dye of the water cannon. It was obvious he'd been in the riot. A right turn would take him back towards his guest house. He should go back and lay low. An image of Zak lying prone on the floor after the water cannon hit him flickered into his mind. He couldn't forsake Zak. Not now. No matter what the consequences were.

He strode out of the garden and went left, back towards the crowds and in search of the *Taring Padi* squat.

*

Josh followed Cinta through the patio door and into the living room, which was as busy as during the flag-raising ceremony. The guests gathered around the TV on which they'd watched the flag raising ceremony. The screen displayed song lyrics. Two microphones provided the amplification.

With their passage blocked, Josh and Cinta watched the performances. Despite the lack of alcohol, which Josh associated with most karaoke performances, there was no shortage of volunteers. In fact, there appeared to be a waiting list. The source of the enthusiasm became apparent when he heard them sing. 'Why is every singer incredible?' Josh said to Cinta.

'We Indonesians are born singing. You see all the guitars on the streets. Every party ends in a song,' Cinta said. Perhaps still wound up from their argument, her voice was a shade too loud. It also coincided with the silence that followed the end of a song. Someone near the front called Cinta's name. Heads turned. Encouraging cheers rang around the room. Cinta hid her face with her hands and shook her head. They started to clap. Giving in, she lowered her hands and stuttered forward. She cast a timid look back at Josh, stepped over the people sat on the ground and reached the TV screen. Josh shut his eyes and felt his toes draw back. The poor girl was about to enact his living nightmare. He was sure she'd told him she couldn't sing.

A strong, clear voice accompanied the first line of the song. Josh opened his eyes and blinked. Was that powerful sound really coming from that small frame? As the song continued it was no longer just the beauty of her voice that astounded him but her whole being. She was transformed: her shoulders loose; her chest pushed out; her hips swaying to the music. She sang and although he didn't understand the song, he knew that she directed the words to him. She held the last note, allowing her eyes to meet his, and slowly lowered the mic. The audience applauded and followed her movement back to him. They no longer looked at Cinta.

'They want me to sing, don't they?' Josh said.

'Yes.'

He stared at Cinta and without moving his face tried to transmit his panic whilst not showing the onlookers how panicked he was.

'It is OK,' she said.

He looked into her reassuring eyes and for a moment felt like it was. Then Cinta's Aunt Misbah walked over to him and took his hand and attempted to drag him up. He leaned back and smiled and shook his head firmly. Cinta's cousins, both real and otherwise, joined in, clapping and pointing at the TV. Salim ran his hand through his moustache and smiled knowingly. Cinta's words in the garden in her adorable fragmented English, *you not interesting in nothing in this party.*

She gave him a slight push and with that gentle touch his will was broken. Ghosting to the stage. Someone handing him a booklet. Flicking through. The aircon whirring; the cold breeze chilling the sweat that lined his skin. The rustle of plastic leaves. A cough near the back. A child starting to cry.

Feeling the intensity of the silence, Josh paused on the

first song he recognised, *I Want It That Way* by the Backstreet Boys. He glanced up. They all watched. Everyone knew boybands couldn't sing - how hard could it be?

He placed his finger on the song and held the book up for Misbah to see. She nodded, scrolled through the menu and selected it.

The title lit up Salim's giant TV screen. The audience roared with delight. This was exactly what they wanted to see: a *bule* singing a *bule* song. Misbah handed him the microphone. He took it, tapped the top and mumbled, 'Hello.'

'Hello,' the audience replied in unison.

The doorways to the hall and kitchen were suddenly teeming with people. There was standing room only at the back. The sold out event kicked off as the tune bellowed out from the speakers. The first lyric appearing on the screen.

The audience waited.

Josh opened his mouth and sang.

The audience erupted in laughter, Josh having delivered the punch line right on cue. Cinta passed her hand over her mouth, trying to hide the amusement that spread across her face.

He couldn't remember the words. The song bore no resemblance to his memory of it. Usually he knew he was out of tune by the horror on people's faces. But this was a different type of reaction. No one grimaced or looked away. They just laughed - not the harsh variety but kind of affectionate derision reserved for performances from small children, old people or the infirm.

He thought maybe the familiarity of the chorus would

lead to an improvement but even to his own ear he could hear he was murdering it.

In the second verse, two young boys were sent onto the stage to dance. One boy took the mic and hummed the tune and everyone ah-ed and appeared relieved for the diversion.

At the end of the song, Josh left the stage to a standing ovation from those standing and a sitting ovation from those sitting. A moment passed before the next person got up and, singing beautifully, restored normal service.

Josh reached Cinta and muttered. 'Thanks a lot.'

Cinta wiped a tear of mirth out of her eye, 'It was brilliant.'

'They felt sorry for me because I was so bad. Do you know how much I hate singing? How much I hate being patronised?'

Cinta held her stomach and tried to reply but instead started to laugh again.

Josh scowled at her, swivelled and barged his way out of the room. He ignored the out-stretched hands and pats on the back and marched through the hall into Salim's study. He shut the door behind him and paced to the window. Squinting through the dusty light, he slammed his hands down on the windowsill and shook his head. What are you doing? he said to himself and thumped the sill. Why are you wandering around a house of strangers acting like a clown? Elok isn't going to come back with your things and if she does and opens her big mouth you'll probably get lynched.

He resolved to leave immediately when he heard the floorboards creak. A touch on his lower back. He jumped.

He hadn't heard anyone enter. Breathe in his ear. '*Kasien de lo.*'

He turned and looked at her and knew why he hadn't left the party earlier. He took her waist and drew her closer.

*

For an hour, Ahmad stalked through the city without a paradigm or plan that sprawled and sweltered lawlessly along the swamplands of the north-eastern plain. He cut through a maze of passages, streets without signage or name, navigating potholed pavements, swatting away lingering flies, diverting his eyes from drips of sunlit sewage. He went from *kampung* to *kampung* passing street parties and celebrations until he met a wall of static traffic and beeping horns on a main road.

Ahmad heard the crowd long before he saw them. Hundreds of people sat on the parched grass of the riverbank, in small groups chatting and sharing picnics. On the other side, the scene was replicated - if anything with more people. The crowd faced the river half-watching the entertainment. A twenty foot wooden pole stood in the water. At its pinnacle, televisions, radios, CD players, clothes and cuddly toys filled a platform. At the base, two men gripped each other's shoulders and provided a bridge that allowed another smaller man to clamber up and scale the base of the pole. He wrapped his legs and arms around the shaft and shimmied up ten feet before resting. In his next burst, he scaled a further five feet before losing his grip, slipping, clinging on and dismounting. He crashed into the water, scattering the other contestants. The crowd ceased their chatter and erupted with laughter.

Ahmad watched another wire-like man, who had

ascended higher than the previous competitor, fall to the river with a slap. He felt his fist ball. Did the poor people who climbed the poles have no shame? Did they not see they were striving for things they didn't need anyway? What about the mirthful idiots sitting on the riverbank and laughing at the struggle of those less fortunate than them? Did they not see the irony of their own lives and struggles and all the people who in turn were taking advantage of them? What connection did this idiotic *panjang pinang* game have with their independence as a nation anyway? Is this what his father had fought for? This?

Ahmad crossed the road and left behind the game and entered an area with avenues of introduced trees, gridded streets and cut lawns. After five minutes, he arrived at Salim's street and looked up to the house that he hadn't visited in over ten years. He leaned against a tree and watched people leaving the party. Connections and cronies in big cars peering out at him without recognition or care.

He'd wait until all the witnesses left.

*

Cinta gazed at Josh and felt the skin on her lower back prickle. She ran her hands up his shoulders and she rose to her tiptoes and kissed his cheek.

He turned his face until her lips met his mouth but then withdrew and nodded to the door. 'We can't.'

'Yes, we can.'

He kissed her again before lifting his hands and cupping her cheeks. 'We can't.'

But by then she knew he couldn't resist.

She sat on the desk and wrapped her legs around his waist. Enveloped around him, she threw her head back and let him kiss her neck and closed her eyes and stroked his lower back in slow, absent, circular motions.

On the desk for those few, short minutes, they experienced no senses apart from those of each other: they didn't feel the phone being knocked off its hook; hear the guests filing into the hall outside; flinch at the brilliant sunlight slanting through the window illuminating their conjoined bodies.

She tugged him closer and writhed against him. Her chest moved up and down and she dug her nails into his back. The longing and intensity became unbearable as she sought an unknown release. No longer able to kiss him, she rested her chin on his shoulder and gripped him and released a series of short, quick breaths and stiffened and convulsed in his arms before relaxing and dropping back onto the desk.

She opened her eyes to see Josh stood over her body. She groaned, reached for his hand and tried to pull herself up. Giving in, she collapsed back on the desk.

*

The sun was low when they arrived at Salim's house. Simon killed the engine and faced Elok.

'I finish champagne then we go to the house,' Elok said.

He'd told her to stop drinking. She hadn't listened. She never listened.

Simon watched the dusty light reduce to a single slant glowing orange on the bonnet of his old car and realised another Independence Day had almost passed. He remembered his first: when he'd been in the country but a week. Fresh out of university and thoroughly bitter, he'd despised his course, his fellow students, his father's reaction to his failure. Most of all he despised how fruitless the supposed, 'best years of his life' had been.

He'd flown to Indonesia to escape the questions of what he was going to do next; the mountain of debt; the smugness of his colleagues moving on to graduate schemes or to jobs in the City; all ready for the next stages in their perfect lives. He'd planned on staying in Indonesia for a couple of weeks but soon found he couldn't leave. The crazy country with all its beauty and sadness and hope felt like the answer. That was long ago; before things changed; before Elok.

He ran his sleeve across the sweat gathered on his brow, sighed and wound down the window. Outside, the thick shadowy air hummed with dragonflies. He slapped his arm and killed a mosquito without thought – an action now automatic after four Indonesian summers. Squinting through the amber light, he lowered the visor to shield his face and caught his reflection in the mirror. Acne marks. Two expression lines grating across his forehead. Three grey hairs in his sideburns. Older. In a different country. Still unhappy.

The shadows lengthened. Wherever he looked she remained in his field of vision. He wanted to grab her; to shake her; to be free of her. But he couldn't. Nothing could save him from her nor did he want to be saved. The chance that she may, one day, say yes was better than having someone else say no.

He looked at her but she didn't look back. She'd only looked at him twice since he'd parked. Yes, he counted. Perhaps sensing his attention, she took another gulp of the champagne and finally looked at him, 'What?'

'Why is everyone leaving the party already?'

Elok shut her eyes and slurred, 'They not leave. It the

biggest fucking party in Jakarta.'

'They are leaving.'

She re-opened one eye, to see a group of people exiting the driveway. She sat up and looked at her watch. 'Ah, now 8 o'clock already. Late for families.'

'You think Josh will be there still?' Simon said.

'Who cares?'

'He's the reason we came, remember? To give him his things back.'

'OK, you go. I not want to see his ugly face.'

'Will you be OK here?'

'Of course, I OK. Why you ask?'

'You seem...' Simon lifted his hand to his mouth and gnawed at the loose skin around his knuckle, '... drunk and tired and a bit, you know, upset today.'

'I no drunk. You drunk. I am happy... so fucking happy.'

Simon watched her and smiled wryly. As with most cases when people emphasise their happiness, she appeared entirely miserable in the process of doing so. He knew that none of her so-called friends or boyfriends had noticed how lost she was. It was he alone, who understood the woman who practised encouragement by insult; who never allowed a moment to linger lest it lingered on her; who pretended to use but was used; who had a stoic disregard for other people in case they disregarded her first. Sure, for others, like Cynthia, these traits were examples of someone who was arrogant beyond belief, a complete bitch without a single redeeming quality. But they didn't see the needy and lonely girl that he did, who was so blinkered, so stubborn, that she couldn't sense the derision of others nor his unwavering devotion to her. If only she comprehended that their shared misery could be ended by a happiness that they could find together; that she didn't need to be like this around him; that all the other men wanted one thing but he wanted more.

He unbuckled his seatbelt, reached into the backseat, took Josh's bag and opened the door. 'I'll be two minutes.'

'Be quick,' she said. 'And do not talk to that liar Josh. Only give him things and come back and then we go...'

Simon followed her stare to a man dragging himself into Salim's driveway. Despite the heat he wore a heavy jacket, his hands stuffed in the pockets. 'Is that Cinta's dad? What's wrong with him? Is he drunk?'

'Of course, he not drunk. He a Muslim. Do not speak so bad of him.'

'I thought you said the other day you hated him?'

'Yes, but he my family not yours. So shut up.'

'Why's he going to the house? I thought your fathers did not get on?'

'They do not...' A mischievous smile spread across her face. 'OK, I change the mind. I come with you to house.'

'Elok,' Simon said, but her door was already open. She half-strutted, half staggered around the bonnet towards the house.

*

Cinta gazed at the ceiling and watched it revolve. Her vision blurred and her body tingled and she couldn't feel the surface of the desk on her skin. Josh stepped into her vision and looked down at her but didn't seem real. She could see shadows passing the window and could hear voices in the hall but couldn't move nor contemplate anything other than what had just happened.

As she lay there, barely nineteen years old, Cinta knew

that her lack of knowledge of sex would probably have seemed inconceivable to someone of a similar age in Josh's country. She'd received no education in school or mosque; certainly nothing had been forthcoming from her parents other than an unvoiced and implied contract of abstinence; and she had access to the internet only in public places and cafés. As for her friends, girls like Ryna made Cinta seem worldly. Of the people she knew, only Elok and her work colleagues were sexually active and Cinta wasn't likely to broach her inexperience with them.

Before Josh, she'd kissed two boys. During those fleeting experiences, she felt no intimacy or eroticism and instead worried about whether she was doing it correctly; if the boys were enjoying it; what they'd tell their friends afterwards. Yet, sometimes, when she sat on the bus and positioned herself to feel the vibrations, the sensations absent from her own experiences would come to the fore and wildness would course though her body and all those unthinkable thoughts that she quelled deep in her inner being, would spark into her mind.

Those sensations multiplied whenever she washed at Salim's house under the powerful electric shower. She'd remove the detachable head and position it between her legs and let the warm water gush up and hit her. She'd turn up the power and the heat until her toes curled and pressure inside became overbearing. She'd pull it away at that point; scared to continue; scared of the feeling that made her legs so unsteady and her head so light. Whenever she removed the shower head, she'd feel ashamed and worried she'd sinned and would vow never to do it, whatever it was, again.

Her first encounter with sex had occurred the previous

year, when she went to Ryna's house to watch a film. They pressed play on the video player, thinking it already contained their film, only for two naked people to appear on the screen. They sat transfixed as the camera lowered and revealed a close-up of the man entering the woman. The man moved his body with increased speed, thrusting his penis into the woman, who lay very still beneath him. Each fresh attack was met with moans from the woman, which encouraged the man to push harder. The camera panned upwards to the woman's face. Despite her vocality, she seemed tired and disinterested. Only occasional winces of pain broke through her glazed expression. A noise on the stairs. They looked at each other and stiffened. Ryna hopped to her feet and removed the video – which she later confided must have been left in the player by her father or brother.

The girls didn't speak much that night. Later, as they lay in bed, Cinta could tell from Ryna's breath that she couldn't sleep either. Was she thinking the same? Is that what it was like? Was it as sore as it looked? If it was, would she enjoy it or be able to satisfy her husband? Would she be able to have children or even want them? If she waited until marriage how would she know before it was all too late? As she lay there she just couldn't equate the overpowering and other-worldly feeling of Salim's shower with her experience of kissing those boys or what she'd witnessed on the TV.

But the moment she'd just shared with Josh had connected it all. She'd experienced a complete a loss of control, convulsions of joy overtaking her body, a deep implosion of pleasure – nothing like with those boys, or how it looked on TV and hundred times better than when she was alone in the shower.

In years to come, when she was no longer a virgin and had children of her own, she still thought of that first experience in Salim's study with Josh. And even though not an item of clothing was withdrawn during their tryst, she'd never experience such intimacy again.

She felt his hands gripping her forearms pulling her up into a sitting position. She stared at him and saw the wildness of her passion mirrored in his eyes. She rose from the desk, flung herself on him and hugged him as hard as she could.

A knock on the door. She ignored it and held him tighter – in this cocoon no one else existed or would again.

A sharper knock.

Josh broke their clinch.

'Someone is outside,' he said. His voice was thin and sounded like it came from a great distance.

The door handle lowered.

*

Leon's footsteps filled the corridor. A shard of moonlight that illuminated his path extinguished and he took slow, measured steps in near darkness. At the end of the corridor, a light flashed on and off under the gap at the bottom of a closed door. He reached the door and pressed his ear against the wood. It opened with a jolt and he fell inside. Flurries of movement. Someone grappled him. His back slammed against the wall.

'Hey,' Leon said. 'What are you doing?'

A figure faced Leon. Another appeared at his side.

'Friend,' Leon said, patting his chest.

A third figure approached. He muttered something to the other two, who withdrew into the veil of the semi-darkness.

'Sorry, they didn't know who you were.'

'Aji?'

Aji gave Leon's hand a short, tense shake and guided him into the midst of the room.

The television lit the scene. A shirtless man, his arm pressed against his chest, supported by a temporary sling. Someone slumped in the corner pressing the heel of his hand against his forehead. A woman sat in the corner, thin, young, frightened. Aji's face creased with anxiety, 'Why did you walk away? I worry about you?'

'Sorry, I wanted to get more involved.'

'Did you see want happened?'

Leon stepped back and waited for the TV to illuminate his ripped, red dyed t-shirt. He held out his arm and rotated it to show Aji the grazes that marked his skin.

'You also,' Aji said.

Leon nodded. 'I've been looking for the squat for like two hours shitting myself in case I saw the police and got arrested. What the hell happened out there?'

Aji guided Leon to the back of the room. They leant on a table positioned against the wall.

'We tried to follow the main procession but some enemies joined our protest,' Aji said.

'Yes, I saw that guy with the scar who threatened you in the squat.'

'He was there? It was... how do you say... a plan?'

'A sabotage. A set up.'

'Yes. They pushed us into the square. Then they threw things at the police. The police reacted and attacked everyone. And it looks like we started it.'

'Pretty clever... '

'What I want to know is why were the *Anti-Huru Hara* forces there? Why the riot van? Why all the secret police? All ready for trouble...'

'You think they were all in on it?'

'Who knows in this country,' Aji said, shaking his head. 'Whoever it is did a good job. It looks like we attacked the official ceremony. That we disrespected the Sultan. That we care not for the tradition nor the people. Now they can say that Zak is a traitor –'

The door opened and slammed shut. The room hushed. Zak strode across the floor holding an oil lamp, a trail of light following his wake. He sat down in front of the television, drew his knees up to his chest and rested his chin on his forearms.

'He's very upset,' Aji said.

'If the police did that to me I'd –'

'He's angry with us not the police. He expects this from the authorities. His problem is that after the water hit him many real protestors attacked the police.'

'How does he know that?'

'It is on television. Our faces are shamed across the country.'

Leon leant in closer to Aji's ear and said, 'After Zak got hit... you attacked the police, right?'

'No.'

Leon rubbed his neck. 'No..., me neither.'

A TVRI logo flashed up on the TV screen. 'Well, now we'll see,' said Aji.

The programme opened with the story of Yogyakarta.

'The presenter is saying that there were terrible scenes in Yogykarta,' Aji translated for Leon. 'A group of artists called the *Taring Padi...*' he took a deep breath. '...attacked the police outside the Governor's Residence. The celebrations stopped and the official ceremony was interrupted.'

They watched the highlights: snippets of truth; the shots not in order and edited to detail a different story; the absence of the water cannon attack on Zak; Leon, seemingly without provocation, attacking the police; the swell of rioters following his lead; the juxtaposition of the War Memorial in the background; violent clashes in front of the copper heroes lionised on the pedestal of marble; the Sultan inside the Residence, a deep frown dominating his face; the injured police; a close-up of the fury on Leon's features; throughout, the words *Taring Padi* blaring across the caption at the bottom.

One by one the room turned to Leon.

'I thought you did not attack the police?' Aji said.

'Look that's bullshit. You all know they cut that to make it look like I started it.'

Zak slowly got to his feet. He straightened his clothes and picked up his lamp and walked to Leon. He stopped two feet away and lifted the lamp to illuminate their faces. His eyes reflected the orange flame deep in the centre. 'Are you stupid?'

'I was only sticking up for you,' Leon said.

'You gave them what they want. It was a trap. You fell in it.'

Leon licked his lips and then opened his mouth. No sound came.

'Leave.' Zak's body, contorted in self-denial, failed to mask his quite evident desire to hit Leon. 'Leave now.'

Leon followed the direction of Zak's raised hand to the door. He lowered the handle and eased it open. He began to look back but couldn't face what he knew he'd see. He stepped out into the corridor and closed the door behind him.

*

The door crept open. A hand reached through the gap and groped at the light switch. Booming yellow light. Josh and Cinta stood abreast and watched a stooped, white-haired woman bustle through the doorway. She looked up, emitted a stifled shriek and slapped her hand against her chest bone. Muttering in Indonesian, she wiped her hands furiously upon her apron whilst scrutinising the couple.

Cinta stepped forward and began to talk to her. Following a quick exchange the woman left, walking backwards out the room, flicking the light off on the way out.

Josh paced away from Cinta, tucking his shirt back in his trousers and adjusting his belt. 'Who the hell was that?'

'Dewi, Salim's *pembantu*. She works in the house.'

'What did she say?'

'She tells me everyone is leaving now. That the party is finish and that she needs to come into the room to clean. I tell her to come back later.'

'No, I mean, what did she say about us?'

'She did not see anything.'

'It was pretty obvious!'

'She is a *pembantu*. They see everything and say nothing. It is their job.'

Josh stalked to the window and looked out. 'Shit! People are outside. Anyone could have seen.'

Cinta followed him and took his hand. 'No one saw. People leave in the other direction.'

Josh looked down the driveway to the tall trees of the

avenue and the faint orange that coloured the lower sky. He glanced at Cinta, squeezed her hand and released it. Whether people had seen or hadn't, he knew what he needed to do. 'I've got to go,' he said. 'I should've gone a long time ago. I don't know what I've been doing here all day... in fact, I do. I stayed because of you. Because I like you and I love spending time with you. The day in Jakarta, in Bogor, today, all of it. I loved all of it. But that doesn't make it right.'

'What right?'

'This... what I've done.... any of it.'

Josh watched her absorb his words and the hurt sink into her body and return to the surface - written all over the features of her disconsolate face. It ignited his unreleased passion, his pity, his remorse. He pulled her to him and gripped her arm. 'Look at me. I promise it's not you. I just need to leave.'

'Josh, you are shouting and hurting me.'

Josh let go of her arm and stepped back. 'Sorry, I didn't want to hurt you. I really didn't.'

'You did not. You hold a little hard that is all.'

'No, not just now... all of it... never mind... I have to leave.'

'Will I see you tomorrow.?'

'Where are you going to stay?'

'At Misbah's house.'

'Cinta, listen to me. What would you do for me?'

'Everything... everything.'

'Your father is right. He's right about everything. Go home and say sorry.'

'I have packed my bag and left. I cannot.'

'For me.' Josh kissed her on the cheek and walked to

the door. He opened it and looked back at the silhouette in the bay windows. She didn't move or turn to watch him leave. A final look. And out the door into the hallway.

If he hadn't heard the faint cry of, 'Wait' he'd have left the house and the party and the whole mess behind him. But he did hear her and paused and during that brief moment Salim came out of the living room. 'Josh,' he said, his deep voice full of cheer. 'How are you?'

'Good.'

'The guests have left. My family has tea together. Please join us.'

Josh backtracked towards the front door. 'Sorry, I can't. I have to go.'

'Where is Cinta?'

'I don't kn –'

'Here she is. Cinta, your aunt is in the living room with the children. We have made tea. You and Josh should join us.'

Cinta didn't respond and instead looked to Josh. He broke eye contact and gulped past the lump that seized up his throat and addressed Salim. 'Mr...' he said, realising he didn't know his second name. 'Salim, I have to leave now. So I can't come for tea but thank you for your hospitality.'

'Josh, you cannot leave yet,' Salim said, gesturing at Josh's body with his chin. 'You are wearing my clothes.'

Josh's eyes shot to Cinta to see if she'd noticed the significance of Salim's words. She viewed him, her eyes lifeless and unresponsive like she no longer had the will to listen or care.

'Yes,' Josh said hurriedly. 'First, let's have some tea.'

*

Leon trudged along the corridor. A rectangle of light

slanted diagonally across his path. He stopped and looked into the open door. Through its breach he saw a window, its two frames ajar. He looked back down the corridor. Blackness returned his stare. He stepped into the room, approached the window and pushed the frames outward. They parted to reveal the night outside. He placed his hands on the ledge and looked down. A twenty-foot fall. His skin prickled.

'No,' he murmured and took a step back. The back of his knees met a chair. He drew it closer, lowered his weight onto the seat, slumped forward and pinched the bridge of his nose with his thumb and index finger.

He remained in that position for a long time listening to the respiration of the building; the creak of the wood contracting; the grind of the pipe work.

Eventually, he sat up and looked out the window. The moon had risen. Pale and round. Dark blue clouds crept towards its light.

His dad.

His brother.

Josh.

And now Zak.

*

Ahmad reached the top of the drive. The front door was open. The hallway was deserted. He stepped inside. Ice cold air-conditioning gulped down his dry throat.

He walked to the living room door and pressed his ear against the smooth wood and heard smothered voices. And footsteps. Getting louder. The light under the door reduced. He stepped back. The door pushed outwards. Light spliced onto the stairs behind, bright and expanding. The smell of people and cooked food. Two girls stepped out of the room: Intan and Kasih, Misbah's girls.

'Uncle Ahmad?' Intan said.

He put his finger to his lips. They looked at him with curiosity then fear. They looked at each other, exchanged a wordless consultation and hurried off up the stairs. They reached the half-landing, kneeled down and watched him through the banisters.

Ahmad ignored their attention and instead peeked through the gap in the door to the living room. Chairs strewn in random arrangement; dirty plates piled upon fold-up tables; two people on a sofa pressed against the far wall.

Salim, right ankle resting on left knee, sipped from a tea cup. To his left, Misbah faced him, listening and verifying his words with little touches on his elbow. Her eyes were soft; her cheeks raised; the spitting image of their mother. Salim with his long nose, upright posture, and proud, bony face had matured to resemble their father. Never close as children, Ahmad could see the affection and respect that had grown between his siblings through the years of his absence. He stepped back around the corner and pressed his back against the wall.

Intan and Kasih watched him from the stairs, unwavering and intent. He pushed himself off the wall. Shivers convulsed through his body. Why was he sweating when he was so cold?

He heard movement inside the living room and peered back around the door. Cinta walked across the room carrying a tea cup followed by Josh who held a glass of water. They sat on the sofa opposite his siblings, but rested at opposite ends. Cinta faced away from Josh and blinked rapidly like she was trying to prevent herself from crying.

Ahmad put his hand in his jacket pocket and gripped the handle of the gun. Blood thudded through his temples. If he had hurt her...

A click in the dark. The hall filled with a brilliant light. Elok and a fat, blonde-haired man next to the light switch nearest the door. They were so deep in conversation that they failed to notice him. Ahmad's eyes hardened as he watched Elok swaying around holding a bottle of alcohol. She snarled and jabbed her finger into the centre of the blonde man's chest and then fell into him. He caught her and tried to ease her back out of the door.

Ahmad turned his back on them, rounded the corner and entered the living room.

*

Aji led Zak through dusty corridors, down flights of stairs and out into the dim mist. They walked to the centre of the courtyard and stopped.

'Why have you brought me out here?' Zak said.

'There were things I couldn't say in front of the others.'

'Like what?'

'Like the way you spoke to Leon for a start.'

Zak looked down at the gravelled floor and scuffed it with his foot.

'He didn't ask for this,' Aji said. 'He only ran at those people out of loyalty to you. Of all our enemies he is not one.'

Zak lowered his head further.

'Did you see his face? How upset he was when he left?'

'Ok, stop it. Yes, I agree. I'll talk to him.'

'Did something happen between you and Leon when

you were away?'

Zak's head jerked up. 'What do you mean?'

'The way you just spoke to him.' Aji ran his hand through his hair and looked at Zak, 'You blame the people you love when something goes wrong. You always have.'

'You mean I blame you?'

'Normally...'

A firework went off above. A cascade of colour crackled in the night sky. Aji watched Zak's face reflecting the coloured explosion. 'You can't stay here. You need to leave, tonight.'

Zak threw his head back like he was visualising something - perhaps his future. 'I know.'

Aji stepped closer to Zak and said, 'You can fight the world but you don't need to fight the people who love you.'

Zak's hand met his cheek and stroked it with soft, horizontal motions. 'I'm sorry.'

'I only tried to stop the protest because I care. Not because I don't support you.'

'I know,' said Zak quietly. 'I always knew it.'

Aji took Zak's hand and removed it from his face. 'We don't have time for this. We need to leave now.'

'We?'

'Yes... we.'

Zak drew Aji towards him and hugged him.

*

Ahmad staggered across the room to the coffee table that rested in front of the sofas and stopped. They watched him in silence, as if in a communal trance. Salim looked confounded and turned to Misbah but she looked at Ahmad and, perhaps recalling his recent behaviour, looked petrified. Josh and Cinta whispered together - she appeared to be holding him down and preventing him getting up.

Ahmad looked to Cinta and at Misbah and then lowered his head.

The squeak of leather. Footsteps rounding the coffee table. 'You came.' Salim's shiny brown shoes came into his vision. 'You came at last.'

Ahmad didn't want to look up but curious at his brother's reaction drew his eyes up Salim's pressed trousers and white shirt, up to his face, a metre away from his. His initial impression was that Salim's expression showed relief. He narrowed his eyes and scrutinised his face and then felt certain.

Salim drew in his stomach and then exhaled. 'Every year, I wait for you,' he said, his voice cracking, 'but you never come.'

He offered his hand with such sincerity that Ahmad took it and clasped it and met his brother's glistening eyes.

'You've been away too long,' Salim said.

Ahmad found himself nodding.

'I wondered earlier why Cinta had come here but I didn't ask. Was this a surprise?' He looked down and scrutinised Cinta, 'You knew about this, didn't you?'

Cinta shook her head. Salim looked to Misbah, who also shook her head.

'Where are Wening and the girls?' he said to Ahmad.

'The *kampung*.'

'Shall I send my driver to bring them here too?'

'No...please, no.' Ahmad closed his eyes and re-opened them. Suddenly he felt exhausted.

Salim placed his hand on his back. 'Are you OK?'

Ahmad watched Salim blur into and out of focus. Blackness framed his outer vision. 'Yes... fine.'

'Take off your jacket. You must be boiling.'

'No. I can't do that.'

'OK, sit down, you need to rest... Dewi,' Salim said, drawing the attention of his passing *pembantu*. 'Quick. Get some water for my brother.'

He guided Ahmad onto the spare armchair. Ahmad watched Salim retake his place next to Misbah and realised why he'd stayed away so long: it was much easier to dislike someone from a distance than in person. He hated Salim's past actions: not Salim.

Salim's *pembantu* came back with his glass of water. She handed it to him, breathed in through her nose and appeared disgusted by the result. Ahmad looked away in shame only to meet Cinta's eyes. 'Why are you here?' she asked.

White leather stuck to the back of his thighs as he shifted in his chair. He looked down at his dirty clothes and saw the outline of the revolver in his pocket. He wiped his brow with the back of his hand and took a long drink of water. A warm drop of sweat ran down his face and stung his eyes. The truth was he didn't know what time of day it was nor the time of year nor how he'd got there nor why there was a gun in his pocket nor what his intentions were.

He was about to excuse himself and leave when Elok's blonde friend entered the room clutching a black rucksack.

*

Leon watched two figures walk into the centre of the courtyard. They stopped and stood a few feet apart. Leon dragged his chair closer and peered out the open window.

The clouds that scudded across the night sky cast shadows across the scene, the collage of passing blue shades reminiscent of the ocean bed. Zak and Aji flitted into and out of focus as they spoke. The muffled sounds reached Leon but were incomprehensible.

Pre-empted by a whine and a crack, green and red light burst into the stratosphere. With the eruption of each firework, the courtyard became entirely visible. Leon's eyes fell upon the doorway in the far right corner, opposite where Zak and Aji had initially appeared. His hands gripped the arms of the chair. It couldn't be. A firework whistled upwards and combusted with a loud bang. Four men huddled in the corner. The stars crackled, dispersed and faded. The men faded back to black.

Leon got up and leaned as far out of the window as he dared and squinted at the group of shadows: ill-defined yet present. Zak and Aji's voices were raised. He heard his name. Instinctively, his attention returned to them. Zak appeared to be stroking Aji's face.

In the corner, the mirage of shadows divided. A human form broke from the mass. The others followed. Four shapes inched sideways, against the outer wall, hugging the cover of the deepest shadows.

Leon followed their movement. Pale smoke drifted across the courtyard. Gunpowder hummed in the night air. The men advanced out of the shadows, crept into a circular formation and surrounded the couple.

Aji and Zak now held each other. Still they didn't see the danger. Leon's mouth opened to hail a warning. A brilliant flash of green ignited the scene. Aji and Zak's faces moved closer and then merged. The men froze. Leon's mouth remained open, the words vaporising in his throat.

His head flopped and his whole body numbed. He'd never felt such sickening jealousy before. Still their kiss persisted.

He watched the events like they weren't real, the whole time the firework display crashing and flashing above. The men surrounded their prey. The first blow was delivered to Aji's head. He crumbled to the floor. Next to him fell Zak. A sliver of metal swung into Zak's torso. A boot ruptured his jaw. Plumes of dust wafted up as the kicking intensified. Bamboo sticks hissed in the air.

Leon got up and turned his back on the attack and walked out of the door. His pace quickened as he came to the end of the corridor. He jogged down the steps and exited the building. He scaled a wall and dropped down it into the street. No one pursued him but he ran as fast he could. He ran and ran but still they followed. The feelings that he'd never escape.

*

Simon placed one foot in the living room and turned back to Elok in the hall. 'Elok please go and wait for me in the car.'

'Why?'

'Your whole family is in there and you're drunk.'

She folded her arms. 'I wait here.'

Simon studied her firm, uncompromising features and knew she wasn't going back to the car. 'OK, but stay there.'

He entered the living room and met the musty aftertaste of revelry. Napkins littered the floor. Glasses sat on every flat surface. The group rested in the far corner. Ahmad dwindled in an armchair - alone, mute, peculiar -

clenching a glass of water in his right hand. From the adjacent sofa, Salim and Misbah watched Ahmad with doting eyes. On the other sofa, and not sharing the joy, sat Josh and Cinta, aligned away from each other.

Simon made a noise in his throat and awaited their response.

'Simon!' Josh said, gawping at the rucksack Simon carried. 'You've got it!'

Before Simon could acknowledge the other family members, Josh was on his feet and leading him away from the group.

'Seriously,' Josh said, pounding his fist against his own heart. 'You've saved my life... I don't know how to say thanks... how did you get it back?'

'Never mind.'

'Is Elok here? You know that crazy bitch took –'

'Sorry Josh I don't have time for this.' Simon glanced down at his watch-less wrist. 'I've got to go and... you know.'

'Sure... well thanks again.'

Simon stuffed the rucksack into Josh's hands, waved goodbye to the rest of the room and trudged to the door. Two sets of green-varnished fingers gripped the door frame. Elok's head poked around the side. Her big devilish eyes fixed upon Josh's return to the sofa.

'OK, Elok,' Simon said, sensing what was about to unfold. 'Let's go.'

She released the frame and balled her hands. 'No,' she said. 'Not now.'

She staggered into the room. 'Hello, my family and friends,' she said, hissing the word friends and directing it at Josh.

'Cinta, you are here with Josh, huh?' she said, with a nasty, grimacing smile. 'You forgive very easy.'

Cinta dismissed her words with a smile.

'Why are you here, Josh? What balls you have? Now everyone will know.'

Cinta still smiled but only from the left side of her mouth. 'Know what?'

'About me and Josh.'

Cinta laughed. 'We know about all your lies, Elok.'

'Lies? What lies? That we ML last night?'

Cinta laughed again but with less certainty. Her eyes wandered to Josh, who was lingering next to the sofa gripping the rucksack against his chest.

'Liar,' said Cinta, her voice trembling.

'Lie? OK, ask Simon. He see us in the Stadium kissing. Simon tell her.'

Simon looked at Misbah and Ahmad, who didn't understand their conversation, and then Salim, who did. He looked at Josh and then Cinta and said. 'Yes.'

Elok moved closer to him and cupped her ear. 'What you say?'

'I said that I saw you and Josh kiss.'

'Josh?' Cinta said.

Josh nodded and cast his eyes back down to his rucksack.

Cinta's head collapsed in her hands.

Salim rose, the veins and sinews of his neck bulging. He stalked to Josh, grabbed him and wrestled him towards the door. 'Get out of my home!'

Josh allowed himself to be bundled away until his bag fell to the floor. He dropped his weight and halted their progress, 'My bag,' he said, his voice straining with desperation. 'Please, my bag.'

Salim continued to push him toward the exit. Josh gripped Salim's shirt and fought back. They fell to the floor, where they struggled briefly before Josh overpowered the older man. Josh straddled him and pinned him down. 'Simon,' he craned his neck back. 'Get the bag. Quick!'

Simon's eyes left Josh and wandered around the room. Misbah remained on the sofa, her hands covering her mouth. Cinta sat, knees pressed together, cheeks wet and glistening. Ahmad watched on, his dark eyes trancelike, his hand gripping an object in his jacket pocket.

Elok watched her father being overpowered, a look of horror enveloping her previously gleeful face. Simon looked back to Josh and shook his head.

Josh stared at Simon, his eyes wild and confused. Salim took advantage of Josh's distraction and tried to free himself. A metallic snap. Salim's silver watch skittered across the floor and came to a standstill in front of Ahmad's armchair. Salim twisted his neck, laying his cheek on the floor and first looked at the watch and then up to his brother.

Salim opened his mouth and gasped, 'Ahmad... help me.'

Ahmad clambered out his chair and picked up the watch. He rose to the upright holding the watch, its face sparkling in the light of the chandelier. A twisted smile ruptured Ahmad's glazed expression as he inspected the watch before setting it on the coffee table.

His attention turned to the grappling couple. He approached them and heaved Josh off his brother. He then stamped down a foot on either side of Salim's upper body, his shadow hulking over his prone brother. Salim lay very still and waited.

Ahmad crouched down over Salim and helped him to his feet. Salim straightened his shirt collar and positioned himself slightly behind Ahmad's left shoulder. They faced Josh.

Ahmad went for him first. Salim followed.

Josh walked backwards, inverting his palms and holding them up. 'Please, I'll leave... I just need my bag.'

His retreat took him out of the living room. Ahmad and Salim pursued.

Simon rushed after them into the hall. Elok appeared at his side, mouth covered, a smirk wheezing out from between her fingers.

Ahmad had twisted Josh's wrist and trapped it behind his back. Salim pushed Josh's head down and locked his arm around his neck. Together, they marched Josh to the door and cast him out onto floor of the porch.

Josh lay there panting and looking back into the house.

Salim brushed past Simon back into the living room and returned with Josh's bag. He threw it out into the gloom and slammed the door shut.

BOOK 4:
THE SUN SETS IN THE WEST

Eight weeks later. Friday, 12 October 2002. 3:00am

The bus pulled across a deserted street into a forecourt and drew to a halt. The six remaining passengers brushed past him as they got off. He took a deep breath, picked up his bag, side-stepped down the aisle past the driver and clambered down the stairs onto the concrete floor. He lugged the battered purple backpack onto his back, adjusted the straps and looked around.

The other passengers appeared to have already left. The lights of the bus cut, plunging the station into darkness. A hydraulic hiss. The clamp of the door. The sound of the driver walking away. He stood listening to the cooling vehicle clicking and groaning and looked up to the sky. Above, the moon had long waned but the stars twinkled still. He narrowed his eyes and looked beyond the station to the road and the outlines of the ink-black houses. The wind picked up and groaned through the streets but the forecourt remained still.

He heard the vehicle long before he saw it. The bike

pulled into the station, the headlights bringing the dormant buses and shelters to life. He shielded his eyes and watched the hundreds of flies mingle in the solitary beam. The bike growled towards him and stopped a couple feet away.

The rider lifted the visor of his helmet to reveal the darkened outline of his face. The rider acknowledged him with a jerk of his chin. 'Have you been waiting long?'

'No, I just arrived. Where am I?'

'Denpasar.'

'I know that. Where in Denpasar?'

'Ubung Station.'

'Where are you staying?'

'Kuta.'

'Is that where we're going?'

'If you want.' The rider's features changed but his expression remained undetectable. 'I know you hate bikes.'

'I don't hate bikes.'

'I've only got one helmet.'

'I don't care.'

'Here take mine.'

'No, I'm fine. Stop fussing.'

They glared at each other.

'Are you getting on or not?'

'Yes,' Josh said. He lifted his leg over the seat and perched on the back of Leon's bike.

*

Cinta hurried alongside the train and studied her ticket. The carriages were numbered in descending order. At the rear, she met coach 8 and climbed the stairs.

She made her way to the far end of the carriage before spotting her seat number. In the next seat, a *jilbab*-clad teenager looked up and smiled at her. She squeezed past the girl into her seat next to the window and nestled her small bag under her feet.

Ten minutes later the train departed.

*

They approached Kuta from the north, the quiet of their surroundings accentuating the chaos beyond. In the distance the thud of a thousand basses vibrated through the land. Above, the neon hum overpowered the stars, creating a red halo over the town.

They rode along Sunset Road bypassing the resort before looping back on themselves. They crossed Bemo corner and turned right and met the thudding vibrancy head on.

Josh blinked and his mouth dropped. He hadn't seen such unnatural brightness for a long time. Perhaps since their first night in Jakarta; when they'd met Elok; all that time ago.

They undertook the line of taxis crawling down the main drag honking their horns at potential customers. The wind rushed through Josh's hair and as he looked out from the back of the bike all the bars and drunks and cars collided into one multi-coloured mess.

Leon swung left down an alley so narrow that Josh had failed to notice its existence from the main road. The streets darkened and quietened like someone had thrown a blanket over the earlier madness. Leon released the throttle and they eased into a space at the side of the road. 'Home,' he said, gesturing to a single-storey building. 'Well, for a couple of nights.'

*

As the journey stretched out through the night she slept long but not well. When she was asleep she dreamt that she was awake and couldn't distinguish between reality and illusion. Yet throughout, she only regained consciousness for brief moments when the train stopped or the next round of sellers entered the packed carriage.

With the break of dawn, her head jerked even more and she cried out and drew an imaginary sheet up to her neck. She stiffened and awoke and her head rocketed to her right to check on her sisters but they weren't there.

The girl wearing the *jilbab* smiled at her and she smiled back but sensed the attention of fellow passengers and dared not fall back asleep. She rested her forehead against the window and watched the train's passage east.

Within five minutes her head was bobbing uncontrollably again.

*

When they woke they left the guest house and walked down Poppies Gang II until they reached a shack-like bar. Josh squinted through the morning light at a sign that read Rainbow Café in flaking paint. 'Here?'

'I suppose so,' Leon said.

They climbed a step bowed by the tread of hundreds of feet, over tens of years and made their way to a table deep in the shade of the dried palm roof.

Leon sat down and picked up the laminated menu. He tutted and tossed it across the table to Josh.

'What's wrong?'

'The price.'

Josh scanned the contents with the speed that only a practised traveller could. 'Want to go somewhere else?'

'It's all like this around here.'

A Balinese man with a round face and wide smile arrived at their table. He wore a Hawaiian shirt that missed two buttons and looked so cheerful it appeared he was about to burst into laughter at any point. 'G'day boss. You boys were in here yesterday, weren't cha?'

Leon glared at the waiter. 'No, *boss*.'

'Musta been someone else. Got any brothers?'

'I'll have the porridge,' Leon said.

'... and the cheese jaffle for me, please,' Josh said.

'Alright, coming right up,' the waiter said. With the smile still plastered across his face, he picked up the menu and left.

Leon's eyes followed him to the wooden-flaps of the kitchen. 'You hear that fake Aussie thing. They all do it here. It drives me mental.'

'He's just copying the accents he hears.'

'He's showing off.'

'Showing off to who?'

'Us.'

'Why would we want to show off to us?'

'You're so naive.'

'Oh that didn't take long. We've got one day left so please don't start with this naive shit again...' Josh realized he was gripping his right wrist with such force his hand was throbbing. He released his hold and folded his arms. 'I don't know why I'm even getting involved in this.'

'Me neither.'

'Good, let's change the subject then. What do you want to do today?'

'Nothing,' Leon said.

'You want to do nothing on our last day?'

But Leon's attention was, of course, elsewhere. Josh followed his stare to a woman walking past wearing a long loosely-fitted blouse and a sarong and bearing a tray filled with biscuits, jasmine and palm leaves. She reached the entrance and stopped next to what looked like a bird table. She put the tray on the table and lit the incense sticks. A wisp of smoke tapered upwards and sailed back into the café.

'Those baskets are called *canang*,' Josh said. 'They're offerings. The ones on the ground are to placate the evil spirits. The ones higher up to express gratitude to the good spirits. The Balinese believe the smoke of incense carries the offerings to the Gods.'

A loud cheer rang out. The woman hopped back to avoid a large group of men wearing Aussie Rules football shirts, who stomped past her. They recognised another group of men sitting in the café and streamed inside. After backslapping hugs with the other lads, the newcomers commandeered a nearby table and loudly ordered ten beers.

Josh looked at his watch. Ten o'clock. A roar of laugh and another cheer. Leon's chair scraped as he twisted his body to view the men.

'Leon...'

'What?'

'Stop evil eyeing them.'

'They're annoying me.'

'What by having fun?'

'There's a time and place.'

'If you were with them you'd be having the time of your life.'

Leon studied the men and shook his head. 'Nah... I've changed.'

'What in two months?'

'Yes, in two months.'

'Well, it doesn't seem like this new Leon is any less argumentative.'

'This new Leon is like a mirror. If you're sound with him, he's sound with you. If you don't like him, you don't like what you see in yourself.'

Josh lifted his hands above his head and started clapping. 'Bravo Leon. Bravo. Even for you, that's some seriously brilliant bullshit.'

Behind them the Aussie Rules players passed around a pink cowboy hat; the Hawaiian-shirted waiter served tables with a smile and an Australian accent; outside, the woman closed her eyes and flicked water over her offerings; and Josh and Leon kept on arguing, each one seeking nothing but the final word.

*

She awoke to a soft, grey light, yawned and squinted out of the window. The train's shadow ploughed on through endless brown marsh land. Beyond the miles of flood plains, the Java Sea appeared; a thin, grey line disappearing and re-appearing as the train followed the coast to the city of Semarang.

They set off again and cut across the northern-central Java plains through the low, flat fields. Occasionally, the cloud broke and the great line of volcanoes became visible in all their tall, powerful, might. Names she'd learned at school – Gunung Merapi, Lawu, Arjuna, Bromo – returned to her mind and she tried to guess which pale-blue peak was which.

Twelve hours after leaving Jakarta, the train arrived at the port city of Surabaya. She couldn't hear the name without thinking about her grandfather. Her father had talked many times about her grandfather's role in the War of Independence and was particularly proud of his role in the Battle of Surabaya. Still she hadn't realised the significance of the battle until it was the subject of her history class at school. She remembered sitting at her undersized desk smeared with graffiti and for once listening to every word that Mr Panggabean had said and feeling such depth of pride that her own blood had been there. She could still see Mr Panggabean recounting the story, his entire body animated by the narrative, his enthusiasm undiluted by the disinterest of his teenage audience. After the initial combat between Allied Forces and the Indonesian rebels, thousands of men, including her grandfather, had answered the call to defend Surabaya. When he arrived a cease-fire of sorts had been reached. The rebels broke the truce when they killed a British commander. In response the Allied Forces levelled the city with a barrage of gunfire and bombs. The city fell in a mere three days. Thousands were killed in the process. Yet the battle went down as one of the most celebrated defeats in Indonesian military history and became symbolic of the resistance that was to follow.

As the train entered Surabaya, known to that day as the City of Heroes, she thought of Josh and how strange it was that little more than fifty years before he'd have been her enemy and that his countrymen had tried to kill her grandfather and vice versa, and it all seemed so unimaginable and distant.

*

They left the restaurant and walked towards the beach. On both sides of the alley, market stalls sold fake watches, kitsch Hindu art, rude t-shirts and beer-holders. They passed people offering massages and transport and blow and Viagra and tattoos at a special 'morning price.'

Josh watched Leon stride past all these temptations without bantering or bartering or showing any interest in people or their products and said, 'Are you feeling OK?'

'Why?'

'A market selling tat and a bunch of local people to argue with about the price - this is your dream.'

'How many times have I told you? I'm new Leon. I'm not interested in these superficial things now.'

'What are you interested in?'

'You know, cultural and things...' Leon scanned their surroundings, an expression of disgust forming on his face, 'Things you obviously don't get here.'

'You're in one of the most cultural islands in the world!'

'All I see is the same junk.'

'This is Kuta beach. It's different down here. But there are still signs of Bali. You just need to look a bit harder. Look at those for example.' Josh gestured to a group of bamboo poles. Decorated by coconut leaves and over seven metres tall they drooped over the market stalls like an ancient reminder of what came before the craziness below. 'They're called *penjors*. People put them up in their houses and temples to appease the Gods. They... are you even listening?'

Leon looked back at Josh with a vacant expression. 'Yup.'

'No, you weren't. You were looking at that guy's motorbike.'

'It's a pretty good bike though. Look at the–'

'So in fact you have no interest in the culture... *new* Leon... you never changed.'

'Give it a rest. Let's just get to the beach.'

They walked in silence until they reached the end of Poppies Gang II. They dodged through the swathes of taxis and parked motorbikes and met the beach.

The sun was high and fierce and the sand scorched the rubber soles of their flip-flops. They followed the slope and sat down and looked out. The beach stretched for miles in both directions.

Josh looked to Leon and said, 'Can we just cut the atmosphere?'

'Fine by me,' Leon said. 'Who first?'

'Who first what?'

'To say what they've been doing.'

Above birds glided over the blue and white swells. Salt water sprinkled from the waves and the sun beat upon Josh's back. The last thing he wanted to talk about was what happened in Jakarta and listen to Leon telling him that he'd told him so.

'I've been in Bali,' Josh said.

'I see.'

'You see what?' He glanced over to Leon, who wasn't even trying to conceal his smirk. He clearly knew Josh was trying to avoid talking about Jakarta.

'Oh that's why you were doing all that showing off in the café about that woman and the offerings and those coconut poles and everything. You think you're some sort of expert on Bali now, don't you?'

'Yes...,' Josh said, relieved at the return of the open hostility he shouldn't have broken. 'I am a bit of an expert actually.'

'What makes you think that?'

'Because I've been living in Ubud for the past seven

weeks. I found this room. It overlooked a rice paddy in the middle of town. The people I stayed with were opening a temple in their compound.'

'A temple?'

'I watched them finish it. I got to know the people and even helped a bit. They opened it up on the night of a full moon. It was incredible... I sat on my balcony and listened to the chanting and the frogs croaking in the field for hours.'

*

As they sat on Kuta Beach and watched the tide go out, Josh told Leon that over the weeks that followed his arrival in Ubud, he'd learned that the spirituality of his host family was commonplace amongst the Balinese. On the largely Hindu island people displayed their beliefs through offerings and art. The Balinese believed that the physical world was full of gods, demons, and other mystics that needed to be worshipped or appeased but never ignored. Like his host family, grandiose displays of belief were not reserved for the rich. He learned that many people spent almost all their money on their religion and art. As he walked around Ubud every fence, gate, even bridge seemed to have been touched. Creativity was everywhere: around each corner there seemed to be a Gamelan workshop, an orchestra or a gallery. It was in a gallery that he discovered the weaving, circular, cartoon-like drawings of the Balinese master, I. Nyoman Gusti Lempad. The gallery displayed a picture of the great man in his final year. Josh looked into his deep mystical eyes and saw past the emaciated body to the vibrancy of his sole. The caption said Lempad died in 1978, three weeks after the photo was taken, aged 116.

When he went out at night he passed groups of topless men wearing sarongs walking to and from traditional dance performances and felt the vines that hung over the road brushing his shoulders and found the whole experience unreal – like a dream of what the East once was or should have been.

*

'How long did you stay in Ubud?' Leon said.

'Seven weeks.'

'I could never stay that long in one place. The longest we stayed anywhere was like four days.'

'And?'

'You never wanted to stay somewhere that long before.'

'No, *you* didn't.'

'By the sounds of it you'd have done nothing without me.'

'Except have a better time.'

'Alright don't get nasty.'

'Look Leon, you wanted to do what you wanted to do. I wanted to do what I wanted to. The time passed and it's over now.'

'Stop being so touchy and get on with your story.'

*

At night, around 7pm, the local men, who worked in stalls or drove taxis or ran guesthouses, joined together to form a troupe. Topless and wearing black and white chequered sarongs they gathered in an open-air shrine lit by candles. These eighty or so men formed concentric circles and sat in the lotus position. The passing hum of cars and motorbikes ceased and Jalan Hanuman quietened and the *kecak* dance took over. They began chanting their repetitive and soothing mantra ('kac, 'kac, 'kac) and threw their arms up and back down and swayed to the rhythmic cries. Within the layered circles, Josh recognised members of the family he lived with and their friends and neighbours.

The dance enacted a battle from the Hindu epic Ramayana. Arms at full-stretch, their fingers vibrating in the air, they paid homage to the entrance of Princess Sita. They leant back on their knees and swayed in rhythmic worship. Like an ancient deity she sashayed into the centre of the circle.

*

'She wore a golden crown and a green *kebaya*,' Josh said. 'The way she moved, her poise, her arms... she was so supple and graceful. Like the most beautiful girl I've ever seen. She was in a deep trance. It was like she was shining; like she was perfect.'

'Sounds like you had a bit of a thing for her.'

'No, it wasn't like that. I couldn't have anyway.'

'Why?'

'She looked a bit like...'

'Cinta?'

'No.'

'Elok?'

'Yes.'

*

When Josh tired of Ubud he gathered his remaining money and agreed to a two-day tour with a local guide called Ketut. The first day they drove north, cutting through small villages and settlements on unfinished roads towards the Jatiwih rice terraces. They reached the terraces and got out the car. Josh's breath sharpened as he viewed the sculptured landscape. To his fore, miles and miles of dipping, chiselled, emerald green beauty shimmered in the midday light.

Leaving the rice fields behind, they joined the main highway. They climbed north into the mountainous terrain and Josh felt a slight chill on his skin for the first time in months. A collection of dark clouds swept over the lakes and great plops of rain fell from the sky. Leaving the car, he charged to the cover of a nearby pavilion and caught a glimpse of the temple that sat on the edge of Lake Bratan; its solitary beauty seemingly immune to the descending shrouds of the mist and rain.

Back in the car they followed the upland trail before winding down the northern ridge and stopping at a coffee shop that grew its own beans. They ordered the freshest coffee you could taste and sat on a terrace that overlooked twinkling plains that led to the northern coast. The expanse decreased by the minute and dusk fell and the moon rose. Below, the lights of a solitary vehicle wound through the ink black void.

Ketut asked Josh what he would do next. Josh told him he was going to catch the last bus that night to Kuta to meet Leon. Ketut's smile narrowed and he said that Kuta was a crazy place full of dirty, drunk people. The Balinese called the locals the Sand People but now they were in the minority because most of the people who lived in Kuta came from Java. Kuta wasn't really part of Bali anymore. Now it was all Sand People and *Orang Jawa* and *bules*.

Ketut inched closer to him and lowered his voice and asked if he knew about the people from Java and the problems they caused.

Josh thought of Cinta and didn't break eye contact and told Ketut that he liked people from Java.

Ketut's eyes narrowed and he studied him and then broke out in a smile and nodded and said so did he.

*

As the story continued, Leon's glances at Josh had become more frequent. At first, he shuffled a little closer and began to nod. Then he punctured the monologue with the odd question. Now, his legs were jiggling. 'Man, I wish I'd seen more of Bali. I just never got the time.'

He scooped up handfuls of sand and opened his fingers and let the grains sift back onto the beach. He thumped the ground and got to his feet. 'Let's miss our flights tomorrow and go look around the island. We don't need to go home.'

'We do.'

'It'll be like the good old days, us travelling together again.'

'If we miss our flights tomorrow we'll never get home.'

'Yes, we will.'

'Leon, it's over.'

*

Leon's mouth slanted down and he sank back down on the sand. He was quiet until Josh asked him what he'd done in the past few weeks. And in typical Leon style his mood swung and his disappointment about their trip ending was forgotten the moment he began to tell his story. As he did, his arms swirled and he recounted the tale in what Josh imagined he considered to be some form of epic verse. Throughout he spoke like he'd practised this speech many times in his head during the long hours he must have spent alone during the eight weeks before.

After he left Yogyakarta he continued the restless wander that had characterised their trip. He travelled to Bali and went across the island in a single day. He took the ferry, crossed the Wallace Line, and docked in the neighbouring island of Lombok. From there, he caught a boat from the port town of Bangsal and headed further east along Indonesia's rugged and remote chain of islands. Lombok dropped beneath the horizon and the vessel ploughed on through the rough seas, sailing parallel to the jagged cliffs of the island of Sumbawa and into the depths of the East Nusa Tenggara.

Three days after leaving Lombok, they docked in the port town of Labuan Bajo on the westerly tip of Flores. Leon shuddered at the memory of the trip in some of the roughest seas he'd experienced, sleeping on deck with the water sloshing between his belongings and haunting his dreams. Back on land he fell desperately ill. He retired to his bed for nearly a week. When he'd recovered, he chartered a boat to take him to the neighbouring island of Komodo.

He told of hiking in the wild for two days whilst imagining that every crunch, movement, click or snap was the fabled Komodo dragon. Finally he encountered the power and beauty of the prehistoric beast and stood feet away with only a staff pole for his protection. He watched their evil wraith-like movements and saw their sharp poisonous fangs and thought about the stories he'd heard about the men they'd killed and felt a twisted addiction to his petrified wonder.

When he returned to land, he ventured across the beaten, creviced, landmass of Flores. Thick palms and packed buses. Undulating roads and never ending journeys on the trans-Flores highway. Through the canyons and mountains and remote villages to the small mountain town of Moni.

He rose long before dawn and climbed to the peak of Gunung Kelimutu to see the famous multi-coloured crate lakes. He sat at the top in the dark with only one local man to keep him company. He wore a cap and scarf and shivered and sold tea. Leon bought a couple of cups and over-paid and wondered what time the man arrived and whether it was worth it.

When the sun rose over the eastern rim, a turquoise lake shimmered through the gaps in the low-hanging mist. Within half an hour the haze had risen and another rusted, orange coloured lake appeared. Soon, in brilliant blue skies, he turned 360 degrees and gazed at the jet black lake that lay at the bottom of the scarred cliffs and then at the orange and the turquoise and felt a giddy awe.

After that he had one final goal. He travelled to the east of Flores to the town of Larantuka. He rode on roofs and hung out of doors for tens of hours and couldn't believe how little distance they'd covered. When he arrived, he caught a wooden boat and made the short, yet perilous, crossing to the island of Lembata. From there, he travelled across the desolate terrain to the town of Lamalera.

*

'I remember you talking about that place in Vietnam.'

'Yes.'

'You got there then?'

'Eventually.'

'Was it worth it?'

*

The town, bitten by a strong breeze, shambled down a palm-treed hillside. On the coast stilted houses stood upon the black sands.

He found the whale hunters on the beach fixing a wooden boat with a single mast. They saw him and knew instantly why he'd ventured so far and why he'd chosen their village. He bartered with a man, who introduced himself as the *lamafa* of the boat, whilst his crew repaired their netting and sharpened their bamboo spears. Finally they fixed a price.

The last kill, which had occurred two weeks before, hung from the porches and poles of the town. That night, Leon ate the black meat, fried in oil from the whale's own brain, and loved the soft, fatty taste.

They left early the next morning. Ten men crouched inside the small craft their spears at the ready. The *lamafa* stood at the prow holding a longer, fifteen-foot bamboo spear. Every now and then they'd paddle at full speed only to find nothing. There were numerous false alarms. During those two days they took two dolphins - both killed by the harpoons. They caught no sight of the sperm whale.

On his final day, they caught a whale but not the one they sought. Speared and reeled in, the whale-shark flapped in the ocean. Ropes wrapped around its body. Three quick stabs from the *lamafa*'s spear and it was dead. They dragged it back to shore, a red-trail following their course. Its beautiful white-spotted corpse lay out on the sands. Children ran around its body and cheered and watched as the adults carved up their meagre portions of gain.

*

'Aren't whale sharks endangered?' Josh said.

Leon nodded.

'I thought you loved animals.'

'I do.'

'So why did you go out and do that?'

'Don't look at me like that. I know it's cruel but how the hell do you want these people to eat? I left the next day anyway. '

*

Afterwards he made his way back to Maumere in Flores. Three straight days of buses and boats and punctures and travel sickness. When he arrived he went straight to the ramshackle airport and bought a ticket. He walked past the unmanned X-ray machine, through a metal detector that was switched off, and waited in a shed-like building next to the runway. Four hours later, and three hours late, a small plane landed on the single runway. It taxied around until it faced the direction from which it came. Passengers got off carrying their own luggage. The smattering of people in the terminal exited, passed the disembarking passengers on the tarmac and got onto the plane. No one checked his ticket or bothered where he sat or that he'd put his dirty old backpack in the seat next to him. Two hours later they landed in Bali with a thud. Leon lifted his bag, exited the plane and sauntered into the airport terminal. He saw corporations and branding and adverts and neon lights. It was like entering a different age.

From there he'd taken a taxi to Kuta Beach. He'd been there for four days.

*

When Leon finished they sat together on Kuta Beach and talked about Bali and its beauty and Leon denied it could be better than Hat Rin or Yangshuo or Chiang Mai or Dalat - without having seen any part of the island other than Kuta.

They didn't discuss their final days together in Jakarta or the days that had followed. Josh didn't mention seeing Leon on television or anything about Yogyakarta lest he face questions about his time in Jakarta. Leon thought likewise and knew Josh thought the same. And with that unspoken covenant they relaxed together for the first time since their reunion and talked about the things they'd seen and the immediate things in front of them.

*

Leon took off his hat and angled his face to the sun. He held the pose for all of thirty seconds before succumbing to a bout of restlessness. He got to his feet with an exaggerated groan and dusted the sand off his shorts. 'I can't sit around here all day.'

'I thought you wanted to do nothing today?'

'That was then. Now I want to,' Leon scoured the beach, 'surf.'

'You surf?'

'Yeah... I've been practising,' he said, massaging his chin with this thumb and forefinger and surveying the sea. 'Some guys told me yesterday I was a natural. You want to watch me in action?'

'I can't think of anything I'd rather do, Leon.'

'Good. I'll go and rent a board.'

Leon jogged off up the beach towards the clusters of boards tied to palm trees. A few minutes later, he returned with a boogie board under his arm. He'd attached the board strap to his ankle rather than his wrist. With the cord at full extension, he struggled past. He reached the shoreline, paused, held out the board and looked back up the beach. Josh waved and then signalled to the strap but Leon didn't notice and turned and joined a part of the sea where there were no other surfers. He splashed through the swallow water before diving into the swell.

Josh watched him struggle out, waited until he was sure Leon had forgotten about his promised spectatorship, got to his feet and began to walk. Next to him flapped a red flag. He passed it and headed along the beach.

*

The train rattled past fields of corn and wheat and single-storied houses with red roofs. In the fields, girls, Cinta's age and younger, stooped in the afternoon sun and tended to the crops. She watched them and wondered how different her life would have been if she'd been born in their place. Maybe she'd have been a good girl who stayed at home with her family and married the man of her parents' choice and would have known no difference. Maybe she'd have been happy. She definitely wouldn't have met Josh.

Thoughts such as these circled and spiralled and passed the hours but pained her greatly. Urging herself to think of other things, she took out the map that she'd bought in Gambir Station. Her finger followed the broken lines of the railway tracks south from Probolinggo and then east until the train reached its destination: the frontier town of Banyuwangi; the end of the line; the end of Java.

She got off and walked a few hundred metres to the port. Stalls and groups of men lined the route. They gawped at her, alone with her large bag, and their attention felt knowing. At the end of the road, she reached the docks. People of all ages, lingered, without order or purpose. Some carried bundles of clothes and cardboard boxes. Others had nothing.

After making a number of enquiries and receiving conflicting information, she located the ticket booth. Inside the door-less shack, she spoke with the attendant and noticed how different his accent was to her own. She paid and took her ticket and walked out and sat on the edge of the pier and watched the buses being directed onto the ferry. The breeze picked up and blew through her hair and for a moment the dry salty air overpowered the lingering odour of the ship's fuel.

The rag-tag collection of people in the square now grouped next to the ship's ramp. With the buses fully-boarded, the foot passengers got on. Cinta joined the queue and removed her ticket from her pocket and checked it.

Ketapang, Java to Gilimanuk, Bali
One-way
Departure: 3pm

She looked back to the square and then across the Bali Strait. It had taken her eighteen hours to reach this point. She'd never been this far away from home.

She went down the sloping concrete, gave her ticket to the man, clanged across the metal ramp and climbed the gridded stairs of the ferry into a lounge.

In the far corner, she found a spare seat and sat down and hugged her bag. A deep grinding sound. Through the window, the harbour moved. The horizon slanted and re-adjusted. The gentle bobbing increased. A long blast of the horn. The ship had embarked.

*

Leon paused at the edge of the water and attached the ankle strap. He lifted the boogie board up and the strap extended fully and seemed too short. He looked back to the top of the beach and contemplated exchanging it. In his peripheral vision, he spied Josh waving at him. Pretending not to notice him, and with exaggerated assurance, he strode into the water.

He waded until he was knee deep, whilst struggling to keep his balance. Beneath him the tide pulled out. Rocks and sand strained through his toes and thudded against his calves. It caused him much pain and he wanted to turn back but couldn't – not with Josh watching.

He forged on, the waves battering against his torso and splashing into his face. Before another set could thrash against him, he straddled the board and paddled and managed to manoeuvre the board to face back towards the shore.

A surge of water crashed over his head and everything went grey and sound distorted. He bobbed up and gasped and grabbed his board and found the raw power of the sea dragging him towards the next gathering swell. His toe skimmed the sandbar and he tried to dig his feet in and brake with his heels but found no grip. It felt like the current sucked the very seabed away. The impending wave seethed and hissed and he closed his eyes and waited for the impact. It hit him and the board squirmed from his grasp again and caught the break and followed its course. He flipped over and his head crunched against something hard. A plethora of bubbles circled. He gulped a mouthful of sea water and pushed desperately against the sandbar and managed to propel himself up to the surface.

A moment of orientation. Salt water stinging his eyes.

The coast seemed distant. He couldn't see Josh; he couldn't see anyone.

He took a lungful of air, ducked under the water and kicked to the bottom and swam with all his might. Behind, his board caught the outward current and dragged him further out and inhibited his kicking. He floated to the surface and trod water and grabbed at his ankle and tore the two pieces of Velcro apart to detach the board. It swept away in an instant.

He took a deep breath and dived back under.

*

Josh walked along the soft, wet sand and tried to place his feet inside the imprint of the footsteps of others but didn't find the perfect match. Three hundred metres later, he stopped next to a tall pole with a yellow and red flag at the top. The shallow water teemed with paddlers and swimmers. Out to sea, the waves barrelled in a perfect left to right motion. Balinese and western surfers paddled out and rode them with differing levels of skill and success. Occasionally, a local surfer would catch a wave before pushing themselves up into a handstand position. Backs bowed, legs bent over their heads, they gripped the boards whilst cutting through the water.

Three life guards shaded under a parasol watched the showmanship. They wore red boarding shorts, long-sleeved yellow shirts and the compulsory shades. One lounged on a rescue board. The other two leaned on their buoyancy aids.

The wind picked up and Josh breathed in the salty bliss and luxuriated in the white foam frothing through his bare feet. He wondered when he'd next feel such a sensation and concluded it wouldn't be for a while. He sighed again, wiped his face with the back of his forearm and returned from the direction he'd come.

He cut through the sun-loungers to the shade of the top sand. He walked until he met what looked like a bar. Judging that he was more or less in the same part of the beach where he'd left Leon, he approached the bar and ordered water. The vendor opened a cool box and picked out a bottle from amongst the ice and handed it to him. Josh received it and paid and pulled over an empty Coca Cola crate and sat on it like the other patrons. Parched by the blast of oven-like air, he unscrewed the cap and closed his eyes and drank.

*

For fifteen minutes Leon swam but made no progress. He slapped the surface and growled great barks of frustration and swam harder, whilst around him the sea pulsed and ground and controlled and defeated. He tired and the sensation that he was battling something too strong overcame him.

Then the thought came to him with staggering clarity: the agony would end only in one way. His acceptance was absolute. He felt no fear or anger. Only surprise that it had come to pass at that moment and in that way.

Thoughts. So simple. Usually neither treasured nor considered. Now so limited. So precious. He knew he only had a certain amount left and the only control that remained was that which was in his head.

But it wasn't like they said. His life didn't pass before him and he didn't think about the past or his regrets or what could have been. No, instead he thought about the one thing he didn't have: the future.

He thought about his family. About the small caption

in the local newspaper talking of some daft lad called Leon who went out surfing and drowned all that way away from home. His body just more cargo on a plane. Ripples of sadness in the town. The rain at his funeral. Mourners leaving and their own lives passing until they reached the same point and others came to their funeral and shuffled away at the end to do the same. The few who would never recover. His mum – losing both sons. Josh who would blame himself. His father who wouldn't.

Would Zak ever find out or was Leon already dead to him?

The corners of his vision darkened and he stopped swimming. He trod water but his legs gave up and he went underneath. The ripple of the surface. Light blue shimmers. The breath of the sea. His mouth opened instinctively and he inhaled. Liquid piercing his lungs. Saline; sickening; suffocating. A jolt of pain wrenched through him like a zap of electricity. Kicking with a power summoned from somewhere unknown, he resurfaced.

'Help,' he yelled, waving his arm above his head before being engulfed again.

A plea smothered by the relentless grey.

*

Josh sat on the crate and sipped his water and allowed the scene to lap around him. The drilling from the construction site had ceased and the wind touched the trees and he heard many different voices: chatter between the vendors; new sales techniques; local and international surfers sharing tips whilst rubbishing their counterparts in the water. To a man, they all looked dishevelled: some due to economic imperatives; others due to fashion considerations.

Through the sun-loungers, approached a lithe man with a surfboard tucked under his arm. He stooped forward as he ran, taking short, precise steps like he was running downhill. He slowed as he reached the shade, laid his surfboard against a tree trunk and shook his tightly curled blonde hair. He walked towards Josh and collapsed onto the sand. The man looked around and caught Josh staring. 'Good day,' he said.

'Hi.'

'My name's Steve,' he said, offering his hand. Josh took it and shook it firmly.

'Josh.'

'Surfer?'

'No, travelling.'

'Travelling long?'

'Too long?'

Steve smiled. 'I'm just here for a week to surf.'

'What's the surf like?'

'The boys told me it's a bit tame down here on Kuta but I'm a bit fed up of going south so thought I'd have a paddle here. And you know what? The swell is pretty big today. I mean, look at that set there,' he said, pointing towards the section of beach where Josh had just watched the surfers. 'They're good seven- eight footers.'

'Is that big?'

'For a tourist beach, that's massive, mate...' The skin around his eyes narrowed. He shielded his eyebrows and squinted into the acute light. 'Someone's in trouble out there. Looks like he's lost his board.'

Steve got up and put his thumb and forefinger in his mouth and whistled before lifting his arms above his head and crossing and uncrossing them. People stopped what they were doing and looked towards him. Soon the whistles and cat calls echoed down the beach.

'What are you doing?' Josh said.

'Calling the lifeguards.'

'Where are they?'

'The guys running.'

Josh strained his eyes. 'Them? I saw them earlier. They're miles away. Is there no one closer?'

'Give 'em a break, mate. This beach is huge and they've put the flags up to tell people not to swim.'

'What flags?'

'That red one there.' Steve pointed at the flag Josh had walked past as he left Leon. 'They put them up where the rips are to stop people going in. Looks like that guy is stuck in one.'

'A rip?'

'If you get stuck in one it takes you out.'

'Where?'

He shrugged. 'Depends. Here they call it the Java Express.'

'It takes you to Java?'

'Not literally, mate. But you know about twenty people die on this beach each year. And I tell you what, it's pulling hard today. Five metres a second or something.'

Josh had nothing to relate the figure to but concluded it didn't sound good.

'Look, a lifeguard is in to get him. Jeez, he's brave. He's got no board... he doesn't look the best swimmer either... idiot *kook*'s going to get them both killed.'

'Kook?'

'Beginner.'

'How do you know this guy is a beginner?'

'Those red-flags have skull and cross-bones on them for a reason meaning you'd have to be a complete beginner or fucking idiot to go out between them.'

'And it's only complete beginners who don't know this?'

'Yeah.'

The bar flies rose. People sat up on their sun loungers. Three girls dressed in veils covered their mouths. Two children halted the construction of their sand temple. They all watched.

Josh looked to flapping red flag and felt no doubt that the *idiot kook* in the water was Leon.

*

In his memory later, he couldn't recall anything between the shade and reaching the shore. As his feet hit the water, two arms wrapped around him and held him back. He twisted in those arms and met Steve's face. 'Get off me!'

He kicked himself off his feet as he tried to free himself but Steve held on whilst saying, 'No.'

He wrestled Josh away from the water and back to the sand. He released him but blocked his path towards the sea and Leon.

'My mates's dying out there,' Josh said.

'And what you going to do? Die as well?'

'Yes, if I need to.'

'Are you a swimming champion? Got a board? Know anything about this tide?'

'No, no, no,' Josh said.

'Well, they do,' Steve said, nodding down the beach to three lifeguards pelting towards the incident. Two ferried a rescue board. Another charged ahead, sprinting at full pace, his arms pumping, his left hand clasping his rescue float. He rounded the red flag, galloped into the water and dived in. A flurry of legs and arms beat the surface. Within seconds, he was far away, swept out like he was attached to a conveyor belt. Behind him, the other two guards splashed into the water and launched the board through the waves. They both leapt aboard, riding the initial momentum before kneeling and paddling with both arms.

Josh jumped up and down on the spot but could no longer see Leon.

*

The final five minutes were the worst. Dipping into and out of consciousness. The water black and glassy; returning grey and cold. Longing for the end: unable to hasten it. His innate want of survival prolonging his agony but bringing no solution.

A dream of hands gripping and lifting him up it. Flashes of red cloth and brown skin. Then air. Great gasping, mouthfuls of air. Clutching a float. A man's face next to his, kicking the water and holding him up. Like a newborn child in its mother's arms, Leon succumbed wholly to his support. It didn't matter what happened now. Another person had seen him. He existed. He wouldn't die alone.

Then another red-shorted angel appeared. Hopelessly overpowered by the waves, he clung onto the other two. The trio clasped each other and kicked and spun. The line between the rescuer and rescued blurred. They were losing.

A yellow board glided through the water, drawing up next to them. Hands gripped Leon's arms and yanked him upwards. His upper body was draped over the hardened mass: his legs remained in the water. They clutched the seat of his board shorts and tried to heave him onto the board as the waves kept crashing over him and snorting up his nose.

'Push, push,' he heard between the torrents. But he couldn't.

*

'They've got to him,' Steve said.

'Have they?'

'There are four guards around him. They're trying to get him on the board.'

'It's all my fault. He asked me to watch and I went for a walk down the beach.'

'Listen, there's nothing to blame yourself for. They'll get him in all right and you'll laugh about it over a couple of beers later.'

'We won't.'

'Sure you will.'

'It's not that type of friendship,' Josh said. 'I mean, he's not that type of friend. He doesn't laugh at himself. He doesn't question himself. He blames others... and for this he'll blame me. Fuck, what are they doing out there? What's taking so long?'

Steve rested his hand on the centre of his back. 'Mate, you're not breathing. Look they can't get him on the board in that current, so they're paddling out the rip.'

'Why can't they get him on the board?'

'He's probably too tired to move. It's pretty hard getting someone on one of those things. Look, they're out the rip now and they're trying to jack him onto it now... yeah there you go he's up... fuck.'

'What?'

'That's a pretty big set coming... they're right in the

impact zone.'

A giant wave gathered and soared.

*

Leon lay across the rescue board. He stirred and opened his eyes. In front, two lifeguards straddled the board. Two others were treading water and holding onto the board by the side-handles. They bobbed and braced themselves for the next wave - the biggest yet. They yelled in anticipation as it approached and began to kick and thrash. The wave broke over the group.

*

Sprawled across the cold, rough surface, looking up at the naked sky. The enemy sucking in and heaving out one last time. The wave broke and rolled on and on. Gliding on the crest, beyond the salt and silt and suffocation until they met the crunch of the sand.

Laying there, gulping down great breaths, experiencing a mesmeric elation that almost made the whole ordeal worth it. Rolling off the board and trying to get to his feet. Drooling and spluttering and swinging this way and that. His legs buckling. Descending back toward the sand. Meeting it with a thud. Laying there face down laughing. Laughing so hard he thought he was going to burst. Two lifeguards rolling him over and sitting him up. Seeing their faces and all people horse-shoed around him, all looking utterly confounded by his mirth, making him laugh all the harder.

Someone breaking from the group and approaching. His face stern and less than a foot away.

*

Josh dashed through the crowd to him. 'Leon!'

Leon looked up. 'What?'

'Why the hell are you laughing?'

'Cos I got away with it!'

'What do you mean you got away with it?'

'I'm going to live forever.'

'All that bullshit earlier about new Leon and how you've changed. You never change. You're the same selfish prick you've always been. Why don't you ever think? Think about other people? Think before you act?'

Arms guiding him away. Soft but firm. 'Leave him for now,' Steve said.

Josh pushed him away. 'Get off me. Who the hell are you anyway? It's nothing to do with you.'

His eyes circled the spectators, who'd effectively just watched him shout at a man who had almost drowned and stranger who had helped to save him. Josh noted each look of disapproval that he received. He looked back down at Leon laughing deliriously and hiccupping as the lifeguards wrapped him in towels. Josh's mouth opened then closed.

How could he explain it to the crowd? How could he explain Leon?

*

Four thick concrete pillars elevated the Kuta Surf Rescue tower twelve feet from the ground. Nestled amongst the palms in the southern-section of the beach, a flight of concrete stairs led up to a room measuring ten -feet by ten. The windows on each of the four sides afforded both views out to sea and back into the town. In the centre, lit by an oblique slant of sunlight, Leon lay in what looked like a discarded dentist chair. Wrapped in towels, his breath was quick and over-pronounced. Josh propped against the wall with arms folded. His eyes didn't leave the patient.

'They saved my life, man,' Leon said, slurring like he was drunk. 'I thought that was it. That I was dead.'

'Leon, liste –'

'I never prayed you know that? Maybe I should have done. Maybe this was all a message. Maybe it was a good thing.'

'It wasn't a good thing.'

'It's a good story though.'

'That's it, isn't it?' Josh's back arched. 'It's all just a big story to you.'

'Well, it's quite a good one. I almost died.'

'You almost killed the lifeguards as well. I thought you said you'd been surfing and were quite experienced now?'

'Nah, I just made that up to impress you. I've never been surfing before.'

Josh paused momentarily disarmed by Leon's candour. 'Did you not think I'd notice when you started surfing and you were shit?'

'I wanted to see your reaction. If you said I was shit I would've been like well it's my first go – so no face lost. If you told me I was amazing then I could say it's my first time and you would've been like, "wow you're a natural."'

'What are you talking about?!' Josh could feel the blood thumping through his arteries. He wanted to scream. 'Do you think this is normal?!'

'What?'

'Any of this... I just don't know how you can be such an idiot all the time. I mean you've never surfed before and those waves were massive... you went in past a red flag... attached the boogie board to your ankle... and lied. If you hadn't lied I wouldn't have walked off down the beach.'

Leon sat up very quickly. 'You walked off?'

Josh pushed off the wall and paced the room. 'Well... only a little bit.'

'I wondered where you were. I was shouting for your help.'

'No, you weren't.'

'Yes I was... "Josh save me. Save me," I was shouting... I see what this is all about. You walked away and now you feel guilty because you abandoned me.'

'What, like you did to me in Jakarta?'

'You weren't dying in Jakarta.'

Josh only realised the level of their voices when the door opened. A man entered. His muscles sculpted his tight fitting vest. His hair was wet and slicked back from his face. He held a clip-board. Leon quickly lay back down and resumed his suffered breathing. The lifeguard approached Leon, a trail of water marking his path. Leon fluttered his eyes and said. 'Were you out there?'

The lifeguard nodded.

'You saved my life.'

The lifeguard nodded again. If he felt any joy at those words he concealed it well. He stepped to the side and drew the clipboard up to his chest. The scratch of a pen. A pause. More scratching. The direction of the lifeguard's eyes and the absence of thought told Josh he wrote nothing. The guard finished his pretend writing, lifted the clipboard up and read in slow, deliberate English.

Leon had broken the rules of the beach. He had swum in an area marked by red warning flags. The consequence was severe. He had endangered his life and that of the lifeguards. He would need to pay a $300 fine. This money would help train the lifeguards who had risked their lives to save him. This money would save more lives.

Leon took the lifeguard's hand and cupped it with his other hand. 'Anything for the heroes who saved my life.'

The lifeguard removed his hand stepped back. Leon beamed at him. The lifeguard cleared his throat. Leon's smile widened. He cleared his throat again.

'Leon,' said Josh, opening his eyes very wide and making a circular motion with his hand.

'What?'

'The money...'

The lifeguard gave Leon a quick nod before diverting his eyes back to the clipboard.

'Yes, of course. OK, Josh can you go to the room and get my bank card and take out 300 dollars and come back here.' He turned to the lifeguard. 'OK, my friend he go to our room and he get money –'

'I understand,' the lifeguard said.

Josh studied Leon and tried to gauge his intentions. Leon met his eye. Josh saw no doubt or message or sign. Josh shrugged, walked to the exit and jogged down the steps. At the bottom, he afforded himself a smile. Leon agreeing to pay $300 just like that. He really must have almost died.

Josh snaked through the palm trees and met the road that ran adjacent to the beach. He walked between the parked bikes and waited for a gap in the traffic. He saw one and dodged through it and took the first right onto Poppies Gang II.

Twenty or so metres down the alley, he heard his named called and turned around. Leon struggled towards him.

'Quick... run,' he said to Josh.

'From what?'

'What do you think? That bullshit fine.'

'I thought they were heroes who saved your life?'

'They were,' Leon said, hobbling past. 'Now they're wankers trying to my steal money.'

*

Cinta sat inside the passenger deck as the ferry bobbed towards Bali. She eyed her fellow passengers and checked that no one was watching and pretended to adjust her blouse but instead slipped out a small, lace purse from under her top. She loosened the drawstrings and counted the contents with her eyes. It was all still there. She eased her hand back inside her top and stuffed the purse back into her bra. Her eyes darted to and from each potential thief but no one appeared to have noticed her movements.

Taking it had been the hardest part. She shut her eyes and tried not to think of her father's face. He would have discovered that morning – the afternoon at the latest.

A lot had happened in the eight weeks since Independence Day. That night she'd gone home with her father in a Bluebird Taxi paid for by Salim. By the time they got home the fare neared 100,000 RP or a hundred bus journeys. All they shared during those forty minutes was silence.

She entered their front door and bustled past her mother and the girls, who grabbed at her dress and begged her to tell them where she'd been. Up the stairs, to the room that she'd left that morning and sworn to never set foot in again. Laying on the bed: the same bed she'd slept in since she was a child; the bed she'd probably sleep in forever more.

In the following days, the narrative was fixed without

conference or consultation and understood by all. The ghost of Josh fluttered from their lives and attached all their unwanted memories to it. The *bule* had tricked their daughters and abused their hospitality and trust. The years of silence forgotten, their shared victimhood brought Salim and Ahmad together. Both were fathers wronged, with daughters corrupted; brothers who had dealt with the situation swiftly; united in love and protection.

The narrative said no one in the family was to blame. Still further action was needed. Cinta got a new job working as a secretary for one of Salim's friends. She didn't meet any tourists. Elok was relocated away from Jalan Jaksa and enrolled in a business course at Triskali University. Their collaboration to secure their daughters' well-being afforded Salim the opportunity to offer Ahmad premises in one of his new constructions. The location was ideal: the rent nominal. The arrangement was made as part of the rectification for the damage caused by the *bule* and both the offer and acceptance were justified and validated on that basis with neither man losing any face.

With that, the matter was closed. The incident had happened and like all good families they would deal with it by never mentioning it again. Each person would be left to contemplate their regrets and humiliations in private and in silence.

Her father had handled the situation with dignity and restraint. She knew not mentioning the issue was his brand of forgiveness. He'd seemingly made up with Salim and started going to Mosque again. Of course, he'd been proven correct about Josh and Jusuf and her job on Jalan Jaksa and it was she who was in the wrong. And despite her father's emotional reticence and inscrutability, she noticed, mainly at meal times or when he returned from evening prayers, a changed demeanour, flickers of positivity, maybe even happiness.

All this made resenting him more difficult but resent him she did. She tried to stop herself and knew it was unfair but couldn't help it. Perhaps it was the hypocrisy of it all. Or jealously that he could move on but she couldn't.

The end of September: the start of rainy season. *Hujan* boys roaming the street. Umbrellas. Wet clothes. Wet roads. Wet floors. Bitterness building. Inside and cancerous. Spreading through her thoughts and rationalities. Hatreds hidden behind a benign smile. Seeing no future but the future that had been given, she began to hurt the innocent to get back at those she dared not confront.

It started with a lessening of care for the twins: sending them to school with dirty uniforms; dressing them in odd socks; not brushing their hair. One morning she failed to wake them. Another she didn't make them breakfast.

Her father must have noticed. Yet, still he wouldn't be goaded into the confrontation that she didn't have the courage to initiate. He probably said nothing lest she mention that all of this was the job of their absent mother. It was then that Cinta recognised that it was not her family that she despised but herself. That was when she first emailed Josh.

He didn't respond.

Two weeks later she emailed again.

He didn't respond.

She had one piece of information. The flight that he'd booked from Jaksa Travel. She'd memorized the details:

from Bali to Sydney; the airport and the time. Her last chance before he left for a different world: a world she'd probably never see.

She began to plot the journey including the train and the boat times. She read on the internet that lots of backpackers stayed in the Kuta Beach resort, which was also near the airport. She'd rise early and spend the day searching for him. If she didn't see him by noon, she'd go to the airport and wait at the gate.

She knew what to do but didn't have the means to do it. As part of the arrangement with Salim's friend, her wages were paid directly to her father. She knew where he kept them. But she couldn't.

A couple of weeks passed. Saturday 13th October neared. She found it difficult to comprehend the complexity of her feelings for Josh. He'd betrayed her but what was worse was that she didn't have an explanation why. But when she thought about him, she forgot about Elok and her mother and father and the twins and her job. She forgot because when she thought about him she was too angry, too hurt, too filled with animosity to think of anything else. Mainly, she forgot everything else because she loved him so much it hurt her in the stomach. And even if she met him one more time and told him what he'd done to her then at least she could be rid of him and hate him forever more. But maybe... and that was the problem. Maybe.

Maybe he was sorry. Maybe Elok had tricked him. Maybe...

She stole her father's money and left for that maybe.

The boat reached the harbour. She headed down the stairs to Bali.

Maybe.

*

After a sleep, some food and a lot of water, Leon declared himself fully recovered.
He stalked around their room and alternated between clicking his fingers and cracking his knuckles. Josh watched him and sensed the excitement seething from him and knew he was in one of his wild moods. His near death experience, their reunion, the finality of their last night, the thought of home, all blazing through those uncontrollable eyes.

One last big night. This is it, he kept on repeating.

And why not? He was right.

Cold showers and bars of soap. Roll-on deodorant and shaving foam to style their hair. Matching their attire for the occasion. Nothing but the best: their least ripped T-shirts; faded jeans; odorous, sea-stained trainers atop their hand-washed socks.

Leaving the guest house with that night out walk: pacey, swaggering, hands in pockets, chins up, shoulders touching. That walk you do when you're young; when you're going out, with your mates, to get hammered. When you float because you're invincible; when tomorrow doesn't exist because you'll always be young and it's all going to last forever.

They strode through narrow lanes touched by pale orange light and onto Poppies Gang II. Leon ducked out of the way of a passing taxi, almost collided with a man offering transport before darting to his right and taking a flyer from a pretty masseuse. He grinned at Josh. 'Ever heard of a New York minute?'

'Yeah.'

'Was that a Kuta second?'

They laughed and strolled along Poppies through the two lines of stalls.

'Come here you need this,' shouted one of the stall owners.

Grinning and shaking their heads. Onto the next.

'G'day boss... How are you?'

'*Panas*,' said Leon.

A delighted smile broke across the store owner's face – the reaction you got from almost every Indonesian when you showed a modicum of interest in them or their country or spoke even a single word of their *bahasa*.

They met the main strip, Jalan Legian, and broke not a step as they crossed the street and went into the nearest bar and ordered. They ordered twice more. Warm up completed, they slammed down their empty glasses and left.

Offers and promotions. Flyers and coupons. Chalkboards and banners.

Two-for-one.

Three-for-two.

Shots, shots, shots.

Free for you.

Into the latest place to be, greedy fingers running down the menu. Ordering Jungle Juice. Orange liquid, thick and syrupy, brimming over the edge of a goldfish bowl. Two twisted, multicoloured straws bobbing on the surface. Slurping it down.

Next.

Leon returning with two sports drinks bottles. Arak Attack. Green, luminous, citric. Wincing after each swig. Pounding their bottles onto the bar.

Your round! No yours!

Back with a bucket sloshing with ice. Something red. Family sized. A picture of Josh. All six straws in his mouth. One of Leon tipping the bucket into his mouth. One together holding it aloft. Guzzled down leaving only slush. Leon putting the bucket on his head and wandering around the club. Girls covering their mouths and shrieking. Men drawing back their shoulders and scowling. Leon nearly tripping and falling. Josh's laughter ringing out.

*

Cinta exited the ferry and took the short walk up a hill to a bus station. Inside, a bus circled the concourse. The conductor hung out the window shouting, 'Denpasar.' She flapped her hand at him. The bus slowed and she boarded. The conductor spoke Balinese to her. She replied in Indonesian that she didn't understand him. He smiled. From Java? Yes. Going to Denpasar? Yes.

She took her seat and waited as the bus circled. The conductor's voice boomed out rallying calls to potential passengers. No one joined her and the five other passengers.

*

They went into the next pub and searched for somewhere to sit. They went past tribes of men ogling bikini-topped local women gyrating on the bar towards a table next to the dance floor. Josh picked up the cocktail menu and shut one eye and tried to read it. He cast a glance at his watch. Only ten o'clock.

He looked across to Leon who had planted his elbows on the metallic surface and was supporting his cheekbones with the heels of his hand. His eyes were bloodshot, face sullen. He looked drunker than Josh felt.

'Want another drink?' Josh said.

Leon shrugged.

'Two waters? It was hot today.'

'Yes,' Leon said instantly.

They ordered and a waiter brought across two bottles. Josh undid the top but didn't drink. He held the cap between his thumb and forefinger and rotated it and surveyed the scene. Down three steps and ringed by an outer rail, a group of girls wearing pink cowboy hats and t-shirts that said, "Kuta Girls 2002," in bold pink writing filled the dance floor. A sleaze of men loitered around the fringes.

Josh looked to Leon, who appeared totally disinterested by all that surrounded him. 'What's up with you?'

'Nothing. Why?'

'We're in a club with music and women and guys trying to pick them up...'

'So who cares?'

'You love shit like this. What do you call yourself: a "Student of the Art"?'

'Student of the Game...' Leon cast Josh a weary glance. 'I don't know what's wrong with me. Maybe it's because I've not drunk in ages... Maybe it's the place... I didn't see this many white people the whole time I was in East Nusa Tenggara. The only brown people I can see in here are working. It's just wrong.'

'I think you just like to stand out.'

Leon took his water and glugged it down in one. He crushed the plastic and discarded it onto the table. With an impatient flick of his hand, he signalled to the waiter. 'Two beers.'

Josh studied him and recognised Leon's night was adhering to its usual progression.

Stage 1: excitable, mind-whirring, foot-tapping, brilliance. The optimist, the romantic, the joker.

Stage 2: Introspection. The depressant controlling not controlled.

Stage 3: The return of the instinct. When he became so drunk that he couldn't process enough information to question things anymore - when the wildness returned and overpowered the self-analysis and doubt.

Mired in stage 2, Leon slumped down in his seat. 'I can't believe this is it. There's still so much to do. I mean, are you ready to leave?'

'Yes.'

'Really? Why?'

'Because it's been good. So good. But for something to be good it needs to finish and for something else to start. Well now it has. We'll get on the plane tomorrow and it'll end. And I'll always look back on this and remember what happened and what I learned and kind of regret some stuff but that's the way it should be in life. You do something and you move on.'

'Yeah but move onto what. We aren't children anymore are we?'

Josh smiled. 'You are.'

'You know what I mean. Before we came here we got up, went to school and then went home. We did what we were told. Now we choose. If something goes wrong it's our fault. Not my mum's or my dad's or the teacher's. My fault. Know what I mean?'

'Yeah, I suppose I do.'

'What are you going to do when you get back?' Leon said. 'Go into the plumbing business?'

'Yeah... why you pulling that face?'

'You're clever. You could go to uni.'

'Imagine saying that to my dad, "Hi dad, I'm not going to do my apprenticeship and take over the business because I'm too clever for something that's fed me my whole life."'

'I don't mean like that,' Leon said. 'You're clever with your head not your hands.'

'You need both.'

'Exactly,' Leon said, clapping his hands. 'So do you think he'd take me on?'

'No chance! You really annoy him.'

Leon laughed. 'I do, don't I?' To exist in someone else's thoughts was bliss for him whatever their opinion.

At that moment, three middle-aged Indonesian women entered the bar. They scanned the area. Their experience told them exactly who to approach. 'Massage?'

'Yes: No,' Leon and Josh said in unison.

'Only me,' Leon said, slapping his hand off his chest. 'I need this... I'm stressed out,' he said to Josh.

'Yes, all three,' Leon said, pointing at the women in turn. 'You feet. You back. You head.'

Josh watched Leon assemble the massage troupe and realised that he said no because it made him feel demeaning: Leon said yes because it made him feel special.

Leon kicked off his shoes and adjusted his seat and luxuriated in the three oriental women rubbing his body and was probably imagining himself as some sort of Indonesian sultan or a foreign dignitary. Josh watched him and wondered how Leon would cope back at home.

Young and without qualifications or the ability to compromise. The best footballer at school but not good enough to be professional. The keenest mind but no ability to harness it. Perhaps he'd look back on this trip as his zenith. Something he talked about for the rest of his life. Or maybe it would be the first chapter of his many successes. Who at nineteen knew? Many never asked.

*

When Leon had finished receiving his massage they left the bar and continued down the strip. A bouncer wearing black stood between two giant fake palms and guarded Paddy's Bar. He rubbed his leather gloves together and stared vacantly into the chaos that was his world. They walked past him into the bar but his eyes didn't move.

Inside, they pushed through throngs of people towards the drink. Josh joined the three -deep queue and waved Leon towards a ledge next to the dance floor. Leon couldn't queue. Not in this mood. Josh queued for ten minutes and thought of nothing. He didn't feel impatient or angry or intense.

He bought two beers and located Leon slouched against the ledge. He crossed the dance floor and handed Leon his drink. The first bars of Eminem's, "Without Me," boomed around the club. Anticipation grew. People gravitated to the floor. Leon and Josh watched. The song ended.

Leon licked his lips and fixed his eyes on Josh. 'Look let's stop avoiding the subject. What happened in Jakarta?'

'I wondered when you'd ask.'

*

Realising that he could no longer avoid the subject,

Josh talked about the days after Leon had left; his mistaken belief that Cinta had given him the wrong number; his dejection and loneliness and leaving the guest house without a destination or plan; the moment he found her waiting outside the guest house; how he'd never felt exhilaration like it; excitement that only increased when they arranged to meet in the nearby town of Bogor; palm trees and orchids and rolling lawns; her reticence and fear; sitting on the train on the way back; drenched from the rain; doused in the reality that it would never work.

He then told Leon about the day he'd spent with Elok and the growing allure of her beautiful madness. He spoke about Elok's lies and manipulation and his drunkenness and their night together and waking up the next morning and telling her it had all been a mistake; that in response Elok had stormed out of her father's Independence Party with his wallet and passport; how trapped and confused he felt; that the height of his panic coincided with Cinta's arrival; his reconciliation with Cinta; the reawakening of the feelings for her that he'd tried so hard to suppress.

He spoke of the building passion throughout the day; the little touches, eye contact, petty arguments, all leading to their uncontrollable tryst on the table; the clarity afterwards that he needed to leave this girl and the party before he did any more damage.

Before he could leave Elok arrived and so did Cinta's father. His infidelity was revealed in front of the family. Of all the things he remembered about those crazy few days in Jakarta, Cinta's distraught face as he was wrestled from the house remained the clearest image.

'They threw you outside and that was it?' Leon said. 'You are lucky something else didn't happen'

'This was worse. Like I was a dog that wasn't worth beating.'

'Why did you stay around Elok's house after what you did?'

'Maybe I thought she was going to come back and give me my stuff and I'd just slip off.'

'I think you wanted to get caught,' Leon said.

'I've thought about that too but I don't think it's true. Maybe deep down I knew it'd be the last time I'd ever see Cinta. I couldn't leave her - whatever the risk of staying.'

'Do you think about her now?'

'All the time.' Josh swirled the contents of his bottle and watched the beer froth towards the neck. 'I suppose I'm in love with her.'

'Have you heard from her?'

'A couple of emails.'

'Did you –'

'I couldn't even read them let alone reply.'

'If you really loved her you'd have replied.'

Josh shook his head. 'It's because I love her I didn't reply.'

'How does that work?'

'It's best she thinks I'm the worst person in the world.'

'Even if you're not?'

Josh took a long drink of his beer, wiped his mouth and looked out to the street, 'To her I am.'

*

In turn, Leon told Josh about meeting Zak in Yogyakarta; how mystical and exotic and eloquent he was; his perfect English; the genius of his art; the revolution that ran through his spirit. He spoke about Zak quitting the Kraton to fight an establishment that he was part of;

his *wayang kulit* show; the preceding riot.

Leon recounted his trip around Java with Zak with the same wonder as when he'd experienced it. He spoke about visiting the dragon head location; the three tastes of Java; the hypnotic magic of Pak Bok; the sunrise at Borobudur; their return to Java for the Independence Day protest; Zak's speech; the costumes and banners and colour of the protestors; about the audacity of the way they infiltrated the main parade and marched right down the main street in its wake.

Leon took out a cigarette and lit it. He knew the next part of the tale would be the most difficult to tell. Their enemies infiltrated the protest and attacked the police during the flag raising ceremony. Zak managed to calm the protestors but was knocked off his feet by a water cannon whilst walking away.

'Is that why you attacked the police?' Josh said.

'Yes.'

'I saw you on television.'

Leon didn't show any surprise. 'Most people did...'

'I was in Elok's house when they showed it. People were gathered around the TV watching the flag raising thing. They were proper solemn and emotional. Then the TV cut to this riot taking place in Yogyakarta. When I saw you I almost fell over. It was surreal.'

'It was a trap. They wanted Zak's group to look like rioters not peaceful protestors. And I fell for it. They obviously edited it to make it look worse. Zak was really angry at me...' Leon stopped and checked around them to make sure no-one could hear their conversation.

'You don't have to talk about it if–'

'I do... I went into a classroom and sat there for ages

just thinking. I thought about my dad and my brother and leaving you and Zak being angry at me. You know, when I was sitting there it was like the worst I'd ever felt.' Conscious that his voice sounded dry he took a drink of beer. 'Zak came outside with Aji. They stood in the middle of the courtyard talking. Anyway, I saw some guys gathered in the shadows. There were about four of them all lurking. I was about to shout when I looked back at Aji and Zak. They were kissing... I mean, I already knew he was gay and they were a couple but for some reason I couldn't believe what I was seeing.'

'Why not?'

'I thought they'd broken up. That Zak and I had... I don't know... a connection or something. To be honest, I didn't know what I thought until I saw them together. Just watching them it was like I was paralysed. That's when they attacked them. He fell. They both did. I can see it now. They were kicked, beaten with sticks... I wanted to shout out or to run down and help but I couldn't. I just couldn't.'

'What did you do?'

'I ran away.'

'What happened to them?'

'Zak emailed me to say sorry about getting angry at me. They were badly beaten. He was in hospital for days. They were evicted from their squat. His name was all over the papers. He was arrested and charged with rioting. His family is shamed. They've ruined him.'

'Did you tell him in the emails?'

'How could I tell him I watched him get beaten up and did nothing?'

'Not that. The other thing.'

'What other thing?'

'The way you felt about him.'

Leon wiped the sleeve of his t-shirt across his forehead. 'Is it hot in here or is it just me?'

'It's quite hot...'

Leon met Josh's eye. 'Does it matter?'

'Does it matter to you?'

The dance-floor lights flashed full-beam, illuminating Leon's face. Pale and sweat-drenched. He looked haunted. He winced like something had caught in his throat. 'I don't know what to think anymore.'

'Maybe you need to work out what you do feel,' Josh said. 'When you do, you need to make sure, and this is the most important thing, that it doesn't matter to you.'

'But what about everyone back home?'

'Anyone who is your friend, your real friend, won't care. I promise.'

'How many real friends have I got?'

'How many do you need?'

'I can't talk about this anymore. I've already said too much.' Leon took a long draw of the dregs of his cigarette and flicked it away. It rolled across the trodden down glass and extinguished in a pool of alcohol. 'Come on. Let's go.'

They lingered outside Paddy's. Josh checked his watch. 'Half ten. You still want to go to the Sari Club?'

'Not really.'

'Come on. It's only over there,' Josh said. 'Last drink of the holiday.'

*

Cinta didn't arrive in Bali's capital city Denpasar until nearly ten o'clock at night. She got off at the same station at which Josh had arrived the previous day and walked outside onto the main road. After consulting a number of drivers, she boarded a dark blue *bemo*. She sat with three other passengers and waited for the universal Indonesian departure time: when the bus was full.

Whilst they waited, a tout emerged from the terminus flapping his hand. Behind him trailed three white men lugging huge backpacks. The tout ushered them onto the bus; his eyes wide with sincerity; his head bouncing with encouragement. When they were on onboard the tout rounded the bus, took the 3,000 rupiah that the driver dangled out the window and jogged back to the station to resume his fishing.

They set off. The bus wasn't even half -full.

The traveller with the lightest hair and skin sat next to Cinta on the three-man seat. Although he left a seat's distance between them, she could smell his over-perfumed, under-washed scent. He draped his arm over the seat and faced his friends, who sat in the back row. They spoke in English. They spoke very quickly. Something was debated. Cinta recognised a lot of the words but couldn't put them together.

The man next to her halted the conversation and rotated his body to face her. 'Hello, I'm Ian,' he said, his tone entirely altered. 'Do you speak English?'

She tried to reply but felt her face flush and nodded.

'Does this bus go to Bemo Corner in Kuta Beach?'

'Yes, I think.'

'OK... me and my friends paid that guy in the bus station 10,000 each for this journey. They think he's ripped us off. Is that the real price?'

'Sorry, I do not know.'

The man relayed the news to his friends; his speech

four times quicker; his words merging into one long drawl. After a brief exchange finished, the blonde-man fidgeted and glanced at her. 'Sorry to bother you again but my friends want to know how much do you pay for the bus?'

'This is my first time on the bus,' Cinta said.

The man's features, already closely packed into the centre of his face, scrunched together into a single mass of confusion. 'Where are you from?'

'Jakarta.'

The man silenced. He shifted on his seat and glanced at Cinta three or four times. Twice his mouth opened with a smack but he aborted the action. Finally, he spoke, 'Sorry, I thought you were from Bali. I've never been to Jakarta. I don't know if you look different or the same... what I mean is... I didn't mean anything bad by it.'

Cinta met his blue eyes and smiled, 'Are you English?'

'How did you know?'

'You remind me of my English friend. '

'In what way?'

'He is polite and worries and says sorry many times also.' Even in the dim light he could see his blush. 'I joke only. This is one reason why I like him.'

Ian smiled. 'He's a lucky man. Is he in Kuta?'

'Yes, I think.'

'You don't sound very sure.'

'I am,' she said, her voice reduced to little more than a whisper. 'Yes, I am.'

The bus pulled to a halt next to a line of other minibuses near an intersection.

'Bemo corner,' the driver hailed.

Ian allowed his friends to drag their backpacks out the bus and onto the street before he made to get up.

'Wait,' Cinta said. 'Now I have a question for you. If you are my English friend, where do you go in Kuta tonight?'

He smiled shyly, 'I have just arrived. I'm probably not the best person to ask.'

'You are from his country. You all have the same book. You go to same places. Where do foreign people go in Bali?'

'There are probably hundreds of places –'

'The most popular.'

'Well, there is this one club that everyone goes to. We were thinking of going later. It's quite famous. It's called the Sari Club. It's on the main street.'

'Thank you.'

'No problem. Good luck.' He lifted his bag off the bus and he and his friends disappeared into the Kuta night.

Cinta picked up her own bag and rose. The conductor held out his hand. She gave him 10,000 rupiah. He took it and pressed some change into her hand. She stepped off and stood on the street and opened her palm. Nine thousand rupiah. An old woman followed, handing the conductor a 1,000 note and getting off without a backward glance.

*

They cascaded from both directions towards the neon magnet in the centre of the strip; where Poppies II met Jalan Legian; where Paddy's bar stood thirty metres from the Sari Club. The sweaty masses dripped out of taxis and staggered from nearby bars, guiding themselves and each other towards that big, white, SC circle in the sky. Below it, Josh and Leon joined an ill-formed queue mobbed around six bouncers blocking the narrow gateway. In front, a group of Indonesian men who had been refused entry argued with the security.

'Why do they even bother? It's like the referees in football. They never change their mind,' Leon said to Josh whilst inching forward.

Like Leon, those desperate to enter pushed towards the door. On the other side, those desperate to exit did the same. As the Indonesian group stepped back in defeat, drunken foreigners seeped into their space, trying to force their way into or out of the rickety structure. But no one moved as fast as Leon. He grabbed Josh's arm and surged forward. The bouncers gave them not a sideways glance as they battled through the narrow channel. Sea salt and fags. Booze and body odour. Bikinis and board shorts. More skin than cloth.

They squeezed inside the club and re-grouped next to a wooden beam that supported the meshed -bamboo ceiling. Leon looked back towards the entrance and said, 'Jeez, doesn't look like they care how many people they let in.'

'It's that door. It's too small.'

Leon cupped his ear. 'What?'

'Nothing,' Josh shouted. 'Want to do a circuit?'

The beat pulsated through the scorching brick floor as they walked through the bar. They climbed a couple of steps to meet the first dance floor. The group of guys they'd seen in the Rainbow Café that morning dominated the floor. Still wearing their Aussie Rules tops, they'd formed a ring and were taking it in turns to hop into the centre and perform an outrageous dance. They laughed and joshed and competed and mocked. Further back, another dance floor stretched out to the back wall. Upon it danced groups of women and more serious -looking men. Behind them, in a makeshift booth, a DJ scrabbled amongst his CDs whilst pressing earphones against the side of his head.

Sweat prickled their sunburnt brows. The stale air smelt of cigarette smoke and sugary alcohol. The music grew louder. Three topless men barged past Leon. He grimaced and caught Josh's eye and thumbed in the direction they'd come.

They crunched through fragments of broken glass back to the front of the club. They noticed a free table behind a pillar and settled under the mock shade of a dried palm umbrella. Fairy lights drooped from the thatched cover. Most of the bulbs blinked or were knocked out.

Leon looked to Josh.

Josh shrugged.

'Fucking, shit hole,' Leon muttered.

*

Down the Kuta Strip. Girls with golden and raven hair pile into open air bars. Others stagger out. Inside, the lights dull and the strobe flickers and their silhouettes bob to the electrifying blue. Gangs of men whoop past with gigantic grins. Bottles drop but not a crackle is heard. Different beats pulse out of each bar: techno, rap, reggae, rock. Two lines of liquid wheedle across her path. Two men with their shorts lowered facing a wall. Stepping onto the road away from them, the tarmac beneath her feet warm and new.

The traffic slows and stops. Waves of diesel dry Cinta's mouth. Revellers dodge between cars. Motorbikes mount the pavements. All people seem to be heading in the same direction. To the Sari Club. Where *everyone* goes.

*

Leon looked at his nearly-empty bottle and then his watch. It read 10.55. 'I suppose this is it.'

'Yes... eight months away.'

'Still got tomorrow I suppose.'

'Tomorrow you know you need to go back to the life guards. I mean they –'

'Saved my life. Yes, I know.'

'And the guy whose board you lost.'

'Yes, him too.'

Josh slapped his hand off his head. 'Shit... Steve!'

'Who?'

'The guy who saw you in the water and called the guards. I didn't even thank him. In fact, I was quite rude to him. He probably saved your life. You know, doing what I should have...'

'What was that?'

'Looking out for you.'

'Don't say that.'

'He probably saved me as well.'

'Why?'

'I was going in. He had to hold me back.'

'You can't swim.'

'Yeah, but you don't think that at the time do you.'

They broke eye contact and both took a swig and put the bottles back on the table.

'One more?'

'OK, one more.'

'You got any fags?'

'No.'

'Shall I get some?'

'I'll go.'

'It's fine. You like *kretek* don't you?'

'Yes.'

He pushed back his stool and got to his feet.

'What do you think was the best part of the trip?'

'Probably the first day in Jakarta.'

'You mean the last day before I left.'

Their eyes met and they smiled and then laughed.

'I think you needed a break.'

'I think we both did.'

'You know if I could take it back –'

'Stop it. You don't need to say anything like that.'

He finished his drink and walked towards the door. On the way, he pushed past groups of people, who still poured into and out of the club. As he left, he saw across the road that Mama's German restaurant and the Sport's Bar were also full. Outside the entrance, a stationary white minivan blocked the road. Behind, a line of vehicles stretched as far as the eye could see. Car horns wailed. The van remained.

As he passed the van, a bulky man wearing a black jacket and carrying a backpack got out of the front seat and lumbered down the street. The horns grew louder overpowering the music. A figure in the driver's side wriggled down in his seat like he was trying to hide and still the vehicle didn't move.

He followed the man with the backpack down Jalan Legian passing the Aloha Surf Shop. The man crossed the road, walked towards Paddy's, passed the bouncer, who was talking to a group of people and went inside. He watched the man disappear amongst revellers, reached the corner and headed in the opposite direction onto Poppies Gang II. He approached a seller stood next to a cart ten metres down the street. 'A packet of Sam Soe.'

The man patted his upper body and fished out a scrunched up pack from the top pocket of his checked shirt. 'I give you two for ten.'

'Ten thousand for two cigarettes?'

'Sorry mister. They my cigarettes. I not sell Sam Soe. The tourist not like. You want Marlboro Light?'

'I'll keep looking,' he said, beginning to walk away.

A pop. A flash of light. The shatter of glass.

He spun and frowned and walked backwards whilst looking back to Jalan Legian. The lights in Paddy's had gone out. People appeared amongst the traffic. Faint whiffs of smoke curled in the car headlights. A blown fuse box probably. He looked away and scoured the street. Not another vendor in sight. Only a Circle K convenience store and they wouldn't sell *kretek* cigarettes. In Java there would be hundreds of –

It took less than a fifth of a second for the shock wave to reach him. White light. Noise. A thermal wave searing past in an instant. A moment of profound darkness. Thud. Thud. Thud. A hard rain falling.

He lay in deafening silence amongst the rubble and glass watching glowing embers sprinkling down from above. First, vibrations. Then, the impact. Blackened shapes trampling over him. Treating him like the detritus amongst which he lay.

To his knees and then his haunches and then his feet. He stood there surrounded by the chaos and looked down at his body and couldn't believe the information his eyes returned: he was perfectly intact. He went back up the street colliding with objects tearing in the opposite direction. He wanted to do the same but couldn't. Not until he'd found him. Tripping and stumbling and fighting to the corner of Poppies II, where he stopped and gawped at what passed before him.

The flames bit into the sky. Cruel and orange and barbarous. Burned out shells of cars. Power cables sparking and swinging from above. Feverous dreams of people, trance-like and haunted, stumbling away. A man unconscious on the floor with a leg missing. People naked in the rubble, their clothes vaporised into their skin, their mouths open, their necks stretched in exquisite agony.

Fighting back towards the Sari Club, he went with one thing in mind. His best friend inside. He reached a crater, smouldering in the road, metres wide and deep, steaming with noxious fumes. He shielded his eyes and faced the remnants of the club. Cries from deep inside the burning cavern; final howls of anguish. He ran inside.

The flames roared him back.

Out of the rubble came a man dragging a limp body. He lowered it, spread his arms, shook his head and pointed to his face, glowing in the light of the fire. Blackened and covered in the flesh of others. The man shoved him back and mouthed, 'No.' He looked down at his chest where the man's hand had touched him and strode past him into the club.

Inside, he met the cracking lick of flames. Wooden beams crunching to the floor. Each breath agonising and tearing through his ribs. A pillar to his fore. Like the one behind which they'd sat. He waded towards it. A body on the floor. No time to check. With all his strength, he hoisted it onto his shoulder and turned towards the exit. Sulphurous waves of burnt hair. The shape of burning bodies, disfigured and dismantled, the fire engulfing their flesh, stripping them to the bone. The corners of his eyes blurred and he swayed and almost dropped the body. He looked to the outside. Just a few more steps.

He reached the street but didn't stop. The mound on his back was hot but still. So very still. He carried him as far away as he could. Sporadic fires burned amongst the debris. Sirens blared. Bodies strewn across the back of bikes. Makeshift stretchers. Death all around. He expended the last ounce of his energy trying to get away. But the scene wouldn't end.

On the verge of collapse, he laid the body on the pavement but was too scared to look at it. The headlights of a stationary bike illuminated them and he couldn't resist any longer. He looked down at his face and saw that it was him. Untouched by the flames, his features were calm and untroubled. His body uninjured. His eyes open and looking up towards the stars. A surge of hope. He got down on his knees and placed his hand on his chest. No movement. A dark pool was forming around his head. He took the body's arms and rolled it over into the recovery position. The body's head fell forward. That was when he saw the large hole in the back of his neck.

He glared back towards the club. The red glow of the fire reflected in his eyes. A groan emanated deep inside but didn't surface, trapped in his throat for then and forever more.

Saturday, 13 October 2002

Soot grimed the meagre lines of his face. His sweat beaded and coloured his forehead grey. His cut hands bore no bandages. He stood on the beach and watched the sea slipping over the horizon. Overhead, the sun was sinking in the westerly sky.

He spotted her thirty feet away but felt no surprise. She approached and stopped in front of him. A shard of light hit them and their faces glowed in the famous Kuta Beach sunset. He studied their long shadows creeping up the beach before looking back out to sea.

'Is the light only hitting us?'

'I do not know.'

'Maybe, it's like Mona Lisa's eyes. Wherever you stand you think it's only looking at you.'

'I do not know what you mean.'

'Neither do I,' he muttered.

He watched a plane depart from the runway that curved around the edge of the beach. It silhouetted the sun and broke the beam in the water and flew on and was gone. The sun lowered further, bleeding into the water. Her face shimmered in the scarlet light.

'Why are you here?' he said.

'You know why.'

'How did you find me?'

'I looked all day.'

'I think a lot of people have come to the beach, to, you know –'

She stepped closer and gripped his arm, 'Tell me.'

Birds wheeled and screeched above the crimson swells. Salt water sprinkled from the waves. He shuffled his feet in the sand.

'Tell me.'

'Let's sit down first.'

They sat side by side on the sand. The light dimmed. The sky coloured chocolate. Along the beach, fires and circles of candles took over from the natural light.

'I don't know what to say...' He sucked in a breath of salty air and talked forwards into the impending dark. 'I mean, it didn't seem real. People were carrying people away on doors, surfboards, stretchers, mattresses... But I couldn't move. I couldn't help even though he'd... gone. I sat there with him for ages. A Balinese guy came past and took off his shirt and put it over him. That small thing... I don't... It was like the nicest thing I've ever seen anyone do.'

She sobbed and seemed to choke on her own tears. He placed his hand on her back and felt the sadness tremble through her body. 'What do they do with him?'

'They wrapped him up in a sheet and put him in a van with all the other bodies. They just shut the doors and drove off. Like they were shipping some drinks or something. They took him to the morgue. It was just a big room in the hospital. I went down to identify him today. It was like hell in there. You'd see families going from body to body and then you'd hear this terrible scream when they recognised one.'

'Is he still there?'

'Yes. But he didn't belong there. Some people, I mean, they weren't people. Like all the skin was peeled off their face and their hair was burnt off. Some of them could only be identified from the jewellery they wore... like a necklace or a ring. Some of it was cheap stuff bought here for a few thousand rupiah... strange that it's stronger than our flesh...'

'Please stop.'

'Sorry, it's just he wasn't like that. I think the pillar we sat behind protected him. Something small but heavy must have hit his head. No, he wasn't like them. He was perfect. No burns. His face... his nose... his body... everything the same. The only thing was he didn't move. And now he's dead. Just like them. I don't see how they are all called dead. He wasn't like them. It's not the same.'

'It is.'

'I know.'

The sky was black now. The sea a sound.

'Did you hear they think it was a car bomb?' he said.

'Yes.'

'I saw the van stop outside the Sari club. I saw the suicide bomber get out the van with his backpack. Do you know what I thought when I saw them?'

'No.'

'Nothing. All I was thinking about was getting cigarettes like that was the most important thing in the world. If I'd been thinking... if I wasn't so drunk... I could have stopped them.'

'You could not. It was too big. Too strong.'

'Did you see it?' he said.

'Yes... fire... smoke... noise... people... I run. I cry. I worry about you both. Now I feel... I... sorry my English...'

Leon felt for her hand in the dark and took its cold grip. 'You know he talked about you last night.'

'He did not... you only say that.'

'He did. He loved you.'

'Do not tell me. Not now.'

'Sorry, I didn't want to make it worse.'

'What do you do now? Will you go home?'

'I need to wait here for Josh's family to fly out. Sort things out.'

'Then you go home?'

'No, then I'll go back to Yogyakarta.'

'I think you need to go home. Some people have no home. No family. They leave and they cannot return...' She trailed off as if she had forgotten what she was talking about. 'What I say is if you have a home and family you should go to them. You need them now.'

'You should take your own advice.'

'What do you mean?'

'You need to go home to your family. Josh is... he's... gone.'

Cinta sat up and composed herself with a series of short sniffs. 'I cannot. I left. I stole money.'

'They'll forgive you.' Leon squeezed her hand. 'You can come with me to Yogyakarta if you want. It'll give you some time to think about things.'

'Yes, I would like that. Why do you go to Yogya?'

'Someone is there. I cannot lose him as well.'

The End

52516560R00284

Made in the USA
Charleston, SC
20 February 2016